Praise for …

SOLITARY

"A YA novel for the hip, the savvy, the thinker-outside-the-box—and anybody else who wants a great read. And don't even try to predict this one. Just hang on and let it take you straight into the real world of the newest generation."

Nancy Rue, best-selling author of
tween and young adult fiction

"*Solitary* is a cautionary tale, startling and suspenseful. The characters are unforgettable, the prose stark, and the dialogue masterful. Travis Thrasher is a versatile storyteller who walks his readers through life's uncertainties while leading them toward glimmers of hope."

Eric Wilson, *New York Times* best-
selling author of Valley of Bones

"Though pegged as suitable for teens and tweens, this one's no more 'young adult' than The Hunger Games, the Harry Potter books, or the Twilight series. But instead of hype and hoopla, Thrasher generates authentic suspense and the feeling that something wicked this way comes. Superior entry in the genre of Christian horror and teenage angst."

views, Solitary

GRAVESTONE

"The saga of young Chris Buckley continues in the second volume of the Solitary Tales series. As in the first book, Thrasher adroitly mixes elements of horror and high school in equally terrifying measures. And thanks to Internet access, Chris can now receive super creepy emails. A solid, suspenseful follow-up to the mesmerizing debut."

Kirkus Reviews, *Gravestone*

"If you enjoyed Lost, you'll enjoy *Gravestone* and all that is Travis Thrasher's *Solitary Tales* series. If you weren't a fan of meandering through endless mazes of questions without answers, it might not be the ride for you. But still, packed full of endless plot twists, fascinating characters, and engaging dialogue, it's easy to see how this book will enthrall audiences and keep them coming back to see what Thrasher has to throw at them next."

Lori Twichell, *FictionAddict.com*

TEMPTATION

"In the third volume of the Solitary Tales, the face of evil shows itself. At the book's core is Chris's escalating moral crisis (the titular 'temptation'), well illustrated by a pricey, enticing gift from the very man he most deeply distrusts. So far, the three volumes have sustained an impressive level of suspense and artfulness; the last chapter should be no different. An engrossing, well-plotted third volume that whets the appetite for the series' finale."

Kirkus Reviews, *Temptation*

"*Temptation* is about a kid who reaches the end of himself—and rightfully so, given what we know of his story—and finds that it's only then can he make the decision of who he is going to be. Thrasher writes in such a way that Chris's journey becomes our own and we find ourselves sucked into the story and unable to escape … I wouldn't want to actually be in Chris Buckley's shoes, but being able to step into them through Thrasher's art of story has been an entertaining and thought-provoking experience I won't soon forget."

Josh Olds, LifeIsStory.com

ALSO BY TRAVIS THRASHER

THE FOURTH BOOK OF
THE SOLITARY TALES

A NOVEL

TRAVIS THRASHER

David C Cook
transforming lives together

HURT
Published by David C Cook
4050 Lee Vance View
Colorado Springs, CO 80918 U.S.A.

David C Cook Distribution Canada
55 Woodslee Avenue, Paris, Ontario, Canada N3L 3E5

David C Cook U.K., Kingsway Communications
Eastbourne, East Sussex BN23 6NT, England

The graphic circle C logo is a registered trademark of David C Cook.

The website addresses recommended throughout this book are offered as a
resource to you. These websites are not intended in any way to be or imply an
endorsement on the part of David C Cook, nor do we vouch for their content.]

This story is a work of fiction. All characters and events are the product of the author's
imagination. Any resemblance to any person, living or dead, is coincidental.

All Scripture quotations, unless otherwise noted, are taken from the *Holy
Bible*, New Living Translation, copyright © 1996, 2007 by Tyndale House
Foundation. Used by permission of Tyndale House Publishers, Inc., Carol
Stream, Illinois 60188. All rights reserved. Psalm 34:7–10 in chapter 4 and
Psalm 27:1 in chapter 5 are taken from the Holy Bible, New International
Version®, NIV®. Copyright © 1973, 2011 by Biblica, Inc.™ Used by permission
of Zondervan. All rights reserved worldwide. www.zondervan.com.
Ezekiel 20:45–48 in chapter 40 are from the New Living Translation 1996.

LCCN 2012951903
ISBN 978-1-4347-6416-4
eISBN 978-1-4347-0551-8

© 2013 Travis Thrasher

The Team: Don Pape, LB Norton, Caitlyn Carlson, Karen Athen
Cover Design: Amy Konyndyk
Cover Photo: Veer

Printed in the United States of America
First Edition 2013

1 2 3 4 5 6 7 8 9 10

103012

For Timothy

REACH OUT AND TOUCH FAITH.

—*"Personal Jesus" by Depeche Mode*

PREFACE

That's no ordinary dog.

It looks more like a sickly and bloated leopard. It doesn't quite have thick fur but does have something shaggy hanging off it, like dried leaves or clumps of mud. It's snarling and growling.

That's the same dog that attacked me on the Staunch property that one time.

I stop, unsure what to do. Keep walking and just ignore it? Put Kelsey down and try to fight it with … with a Zippo lighter? I'm all out of supernatural stuff in my pockets.

Why couldn't I have found a magical dagger or something?

There's a howling from behind me that sounds like a dying wolf.

No. No, don't let there be more.

The demon dog starts walking toward me. Its open mouth is dripping gray spit. Its eyes are glowing, a disturbing kind of glow, not a majestic kind. I smell a rotten odor.

I back up. One step. Two.

I have to get to those woods.

The dog is coming faster, and I know I have only seconds.

Suddenly I hear the wild wolf sound again, but this time it's ahead of me.

Then I see something coming out of the woods, rushing toward the demon dog.

It's a wolf.

No, it's not a wolf. It's *the* wolf, the one I've seen before. The gray wolf that I saw at the creek and also near the barn after Jocelyn died.

I hear its teeth ripping something apart and then hear the high-pitched wailing of the dog. It's awful and makes me close my eyes.

Another wolf comes out of the woods and attacks from the other side. And I realize—not all animals around here are possessed or evil.

Especially not these wolves.

I hear gnawing and biting and growling and wailing, and then it seems like the air around us gets sucked in and the lights go out for the moment and I feel a chilling breeze

death

blow past Kelsey and me and then it's done.

The dog and the smell are gone.

The wolves are sniffing the ground where it was standing and seem as puzzled as I am about the disappearance.

They turn and face me, and I look at them. I want to say thanks or toss them a hamburger or something. I'm not sure what to do.

The gray wolf bolts into the trees and is followed by the darker one. The path ahead is empty now. Empty and safe.

I just hope that it's not too late for Kelsey.

1. Joyful and Lovely

The first thing I see when I unlock the front door to the cabin and turn on the light is Lily.

I freeze and clutch Midnight a bit too tight.

Lily is dead. I saw her die with my own eyes. I can still close them and picture her body in the woods after the car she was driving took a sharp turn over a mountainside and ejected her. I still feel fortunate I was wearing a seat belt, but when I think of Lily, that word doesn't come to mind.

Regret is more like it.

I shut my eyes as I hear Mr. Page's truck backing out of the driveway and heading back home. I know I'm just seeing things. It's just the stress of having flown back from Chicago with Kelsey and somehow managing to keep the truth from both her and my father. It's knowing they've taken Mom, of knowing she's not here, of knowing that I'll open my eyes and Lily won't be anywhere—

The golden-haired goddess gives me a flirty smile as she stands.

No.

This is not happening. Not now.

It's too soon.

I just got back to Solitary. We need a little warm-up, folks.

We can't get the dead girl waving in the opening scene, can we?

"Welcome home, Chris."

Something about the way she says my name isn't quite right.

I stop breathing.

Midnight jumps out of my hands and scampers into my mom's bedroom. She's probably going under the bed.

I wonder if she can see what I'm seeing.

Lily flips her long curly hair over her shoulder and grins. "I won't bite. At least not today."

I have a weird case of déjà vu as I swallow and then shut the door, knowing this is one of those things. I'm still not sure what to call them. Episodes. Visions. Occurrences.

Somehow I'm the chosen one to see faces of the dead like this.

I've already been seeing weird things since leaving Chicago. Perhaps these are all signs that tell me I should've stayed there. But I had no choice. I had to come back or Mom would be hurt. Or worse.

"Do you want to play a game, Chris?"

There it is again. The thing with the name.

Did she say Chris or Chrisssssss?

I start to back up.

"You still want me, don't you, my dear little boy?"

She starts to laugh in a weird way I don't remember ever hearing.

This is just a dream just a bad spooky thing to start my stay back in Scary I mean Solitary, North Carolina.

As she smiles, I see her face suddenly become hard, as if the makeup has dried up and is starting to crack and flake and fall off.

"It's time to see behind the mask, Chrissie-pooo," Lily says.

But of course it's not Lily and I know this and I'm about to open the front door when the lights go off.

I expect a cold, dead hand to touch me, grab me. But instead I hear the shuffling of footsteps upstairs.

My body is shivering. I can't tell if it's from the cold January night or from this cold greeting inside.

Suddenly my stereo is blasting upstairs. No, strike that. Uncle Robert's stereo is blasting. I recognize the song but can't really think of the title or the group because I'm about to pass out.

I've got to get out of here but I know this is just a dream or a vision and it can't hurt me. Right?

The droning singer upstairs calls out, and I know this is a message. Perhaps this is something I need to know for the battle ahead. Or for the ongoing war.

The song grows louder with each step I take. The light is on, and I know it wasn't on when I first stepped into the cabin. When I reach the bedroom, I don't see Lily or the Lily-thing anywhere. I just see the familiar record player turning and a record sleeve on the bed.

I pick it up and see the image of a stone angel lying on her back with one arm outstretched and her other hand covering her face. Above the image is the song title.

"Love Will Tear Us Apart."

I know the Joy Division song. There's nothing joyful or lovely about it or the image.

So I wonder why the ghost of Lily wanted to share this joyous song with me as I scan the room and see the outline underneath the blanket on my bed.

Just get out of here do what Midnight did and scramble for the closest dark corner and hide do it Chris come on!

But as the song continues on, I move toward the head of my narrow bed and then pull back the comforter, squinting because I'm unsure what I'll see.

I jerk back, and the blanket pulls back with me.

The lifeless figure on the bed is not … it's not human.

For a minute I just stare, wondering if it's going to move. I'm shaking. The song ends, but I hear the record continuing to turn and the crackling through the speakers.

I'm standing in my room, staring at a mannequin. But this isn't just any mannequin.

It's wearing the same thing that *thing* was just wearing. A shirt and a black jacket and jeans.

And the face and the hair actually resemble Lily.

I take a deep breath and walk over and touch it. It's hard and cold.

My heart is racing.

I shiver as I take in the blank look staring back at me.

I'm back in good old Solitary, and this is how it begins.

Wonderful.

2. DARK OUTSIDE

When the phone rings, I gladly answer it.

"How's your mom doing?" Kelsey asks.

It's only been an hour since I walked into the cabin and found that thing. After freaking out and then regaining my senses, I finally managed to bring the mannequin downstairs and put it in the laundry room. But it's very real. And I swear—if I hear the washing machine going tonight, I'm seriously going to move out.

"Everything's cool," I say.

This is technically not a lie, because I'm playing it cool to keep things cool. I don't know where Mom is and don't have any idea when I'll find out. All I know is I can't say anything to anybody or she will die.

"Tell her thanks again for the plane ticket," Kelsey says.

"Sure."

I know I don't sound like myself and after the time we just spent in Chicago with my father, Kelsey is surely picking up the bad vibes.

"I didn't mean to call so soon—"

"No, it's fine."

"Look, I don't mean to pressure you or anything."

"Kelsey, it's fine. Seriously. I'm glad you called."

Because there's this mannequin in my cabin that resembles that hot chick I got to know over the summer.

"Thanks," she says after a pause. "For everything."

"Thank you for coming."

For a moment I remember why I asked Kelsey to come away with me. It wasn't to temporarily escape this crazy place. It was so she would live past midnight on New Year's Eve.

I'm really glad to hear her voice.

"School seems far off," she says.

"So does graduation."

"We'll make it. It'll be here before we know it."

"And then what?"

"And then … I don't know. Drive off into the sunset."

"Can we do that now?" I ask.

"It's pretty dark outside."

"Yeah."

I know that. And I have a bad feeling it's going to stay dark outside for a really long time.

3. Five Months

Blink and it will pass you by. This place, a town always in the shadows, an address no one pays any attention to.

It's close to midnight, and I sit on my motorcycle, looking at the sleeping buildings and feeling the stillness. I've been back for just over twenty-four hours and everything feels the same. Bleak and cold and lifeless. Not just this town, but me.

I rub my chilled hands together. The only sign of life I got today was a text from an unknown number. It said to be downtown at midnight.

Lots of people could have sent me that text. I'm hoping that my mom sent it, but I'm afraid that it belongs to the people who have her.

If she's even still alive.

I try to silence that voice, but it keeps popping up inside my head. It's been wondering the same thing ever since I discovered that the rugged mountain man happened to be Uncle Robert in costume and that Mom had been kidnapped. The same thing the next day when we discovered the plane tickets from "Mom" for flights from Chicago to Asheville. The same question that greeted me as I opened the door to the cabin and felt the cold inside.

Is Mom still alive, or did they kill her?

The good news is that Mom spoke to Dad before emailing the tickets, explaining that she was too busy and too tired to make the drive up to Chicago. I think she said a few other things, perhaps some relationship stuff that Dad didn't feel like mentioning. He never questioned the tickets or the call or anything.

I have enough questions for both of us.

It's strange how I feel. The chilly, empty feeling is there, but the fear isn't. Looking at the darkened buildings and the black windows doesn't frighten me. Waiting out here doesn't frighten me. The thought of dying doesn't even frighten me.

All I hope is that it's not too late to save Mom.

I see the bright lights and the big SUV, and I know who it is without even needing to hear the voice inside. I get off the bike and walk over to the street where the massive Hummer waits. I open the door and see Staunch behind the wheel, just like the first time I ever saw him.

"Get in."

"Where's my mother?"

He jerks his head and then grits his teeth. This guy doesn't get many people refusing to do what he's asking.

Especially teenagers.

"Boy, I'm gonna tell you this once: get in the vehicle now."

But he doesn't frighten me. He can't hurt me, not anymore. He's no longer going to bully people around like his son does at school.

"I'm not going to go anywhere unless you tell me—"

He curses and opens his door and then I hear the big rushing footsteps coming around the front of the car. My stomach drops, and I see him coming on like some wild animal. He pounds the side of my face with something hard and flat.

I slam against the side of the SUV, then crumple to the hard asphalt.

I feel something grab my shirt and jacket like a crane and lift me up, then launch me backward against the car again. I'm out of breath and half the side of my face is paralyzed and I can't even shout out. I'm back on the street, then lifted up again and propped against the side of the car.

Staunch curses at me. I can only really look out one eye, but I see something thin and black in his hand.

"Your time has run out, boy, and I mean it. No more. I don't care who you are, do you hear me? Just 'cause I can't kill you doesn't mean I can't hurt you."

And with that he takes the black thing he's holding and whacks it against my forehead. Then my eye. Then my cheek. It feels like some kind of heavy weight or piece of metal or steel.

I cry out in pain, but he pounds my mouth, cutting my lips against my teeth. I start to sink away, but he lifts me up again and swats me on my ear. Then he curses in my face and shakes me over and over and over again until I start to black out.

"Don't go just yet, don't you—"

But I'm losing it all.

"Open your eyes and look at me. Hear me out, boy."

I squint out of my one working eye. I taste blood, and my entire head and face throb and I cough and begin to choke.

Then I start to scream until he puts the black thing in my mouth, almost making me gag.

I suddenly realize that I'm biting down on his cell phone.

"From here on out, you do what we say. What I say. You got that? Do you?"

He shoves the phone in my mouth further, ripping the sides of my mouth.

"You got five months to shape up and start playing by the rules. Five months. You got that?"

I try and say some variation of "Uh huh."

"Marsh is an idealist and others have patience and that's fine, but I'm not here 'cause of my patience. I will kill your momma, and if that doesn't work I'll kill that pretty little blonde thing, and I'll keep killing until I finally make you choke on your own blood. I don't care whose blood it is and what kind of special boy you are, I will do that 'cause that's what I do."

He yanks his phone out of my mouth and then releases me. I drop to the ground like a bag of heavy garbage. I'm moaning and coughing, and I've never felt so much pain in my life.

Staunch is cursing now, saying something about his busted phone and about what I made him do. My head feels ripped open and suddenly I realize I'm going to die here, just like this, after being beaten to death by a cell phone.

Can you hear me now?

I'm not sure if Staunch said that or I imagined it.

I hear the door shut and hear the engine throttle and then …

4. THE ONLY BATTLE

The sound of a bird chirping wakes me up.

I can see sunlight coming through a window—actually like a wall consisting of one giant window—and landing at the foot of the bed I'm in. I'm under heavy covers, and my eyes are having a hard time opening.

When they're finally opened for good, I brace myself for the pain I know will be there.

But nothing comes.

My eyes look out what appears to be a bay window at the front of the room. All I can see are trees and bushes and flowers. A door to my left at the base of the bed seems to be open. Wait—no, it's a screen door.

For a second I try to get up, but then feel light-headed and know I'm going to fade away again.

"Chris?"

For some reason I think of Frodo waking up and seeing Bilbo. He's in that faraway place where the elves live. He's alive and everybody's happy to see him and everything looks warm and glowing.

Wait—am I wearing a white nightgown?

"You might want to drink a little of this," the voice says.

I open my eyes, and there sitting on the side of the bed is Iris. Those wide eyes bursting with sweetness. For a second she looks about twenty years old, but then my eyes adjust and I see the wrinkles all around her face.

"Try and sit up for a few minutes."

I do as I'm told, and she gently brings a glass cup up to my lips. It's a warm tea of some sort. I take a little, then keep taking it until I finish it.

"This will help you heal."

"Where am I?"

She smiles. "In a safe place."

"A dream?"

Iris shakes her head. "No. You are alive and conscious, Chris. And at a very important juncture in your life."

I sigh and can only say, "Huh?"

"I'm not going anywhere. Just take it easy for the moment."

"Are you a ghost?"

She raises her eyes and appears a bit offended. "I might be old, but I'm not dead, thank you very much."

Iris takes the cup and then walks into another room. I sit propped up, trying to keep my eyes open, wondering what I'm doing in this small room with the bay window surrounded by a garden outside.

I wonder if Jocelyn is going to come out next and serve me some cookies and milk. Or maybe Lily will come and offer me a drink of something I couldn't buy in the store.

The chirping bird seems to have brought a crowd with him. They're all outside singing away like some choir. It's pretty.

I believe Iris when she said this was a safe place. I'm not sure why, since most everybody I've come to know has lied to me.

Maybe they don't lie to you in dreams.

But this doesn't seem like a dream. I feel my face and can tell that it's partially swollen. My lips have cuts on them, and one eye is a bit harder to see out of.

All of that, yet I don't feel pain. Maybe Iris gave me some kind of weird drug.

I'll have to ask for more before I leave.

It's weird, because it's January, yet the screen door is letting in the sounds of springtime or summer.

I hear steps and see the thin figure in black come back into the room.

"Where am I?"

"In Solitary, not far from where you were beaten up."

"But it's—the door—it doesn't feel cold."

She nods, glancing down at me with curious eyes.

"What?"

"You took a nasty beating," she says. "You're not very pretty to look at."

"Guess my modeling days will have to be put on hold."

She smiles, and it's good to see something so—so pure. Like the morning sun coming in.

"All of the events surrounding you, Chris … is it impossible to take them all in?"

"I don't know. I guess, when I think of everything."

Iris takes a chair and then sits next to my bed. "Remember when I told you about those unseen places? About the spaces in between?"

I nod.

"This is one of those. The Crag's Inn—that was another."

"What happened to you? I didn't mean—Jared lied to me—if

he's even called Jared. He told me he was my cousin and then he came with me and I didn't know—"

"I know. It's okay."

"The place burned down to the ground. I can't believe he actually did that."

"He wasn't the one who did that," Iris says.

"Then who?"

She doesn't answer but only looks out the window. "That place was only temporary anyway."

I don't understand how she can say that. "But the history—I swear I didn't mean to bring him there."

"It served its purpose. And perhaps—maybe that was just one step in your journey toward God."

I'm still waiting for this to be a dream. Or for Iris to be a ghost. Or an angel. Because how could she know something like that?

Nobody knows, not my father and not Kelsey and not anybody.

She smiles, either reading my mind or being able to hear the thought.

"I'm like you, Chris. I can see things that aren't obvious to others. And I see it in you."

"See what? Do I have some halo around me now or something?"

"I see you've kept that wonderful wit about you."

"What do you see? You actually see something in me?"

"Call it a glow, a hue, perhaps a color, and the look in your eyes."

I glance at my arms, but I don't see anything.

"Chris—you were able to come into this place. I could not have brought you here if you didn't believe."

"Like the inn?"

She nods. "You were allowed to come to the inn because your heart was opening up. And you were starting to see. But then—you ran the opposite direction. You tried to do it yourself."

I can't believe she knows this. "Have you been spying on me?"

"I don't need to spy to know. You've been missing. I've been unable to reach you. And that was your own choice, Chris. You were almost lost for good."

"Missing? Lost? What—I've been here the whole time."

She stands for a moment and goes to look out the door. Then she comes back by the bed.

"There has been a great war going on. Over you, Chris. Not just with those you've been able to see. But with those whom you've just started to see."

"I don't know if I really wanna see anymore, you know?"

"A gift like you have—like we have—it's not to be taken lightly. It is very serious. It's very powerful."

"To see the boogeyman?"

She looks at me the way Mom might. "You're seventeen years old, and I know you feel like that's old, Chris, but you are still just a child."

"Thanks."

"I'm wanting to encourage you. I understand all the questions and the grief and the anger and the confusion. I had the same thing. God works in all of us in different ways."

"I just want this to go away."

"No. I don't believe that. I think that deep down you want to know what to do now. You tried on your own, and you failed."

"So tell me—all these things I see—every time I trust someone they lie—everything I do seems to backfire."

"Pray."

I just look and wait for something more.

"That's what you need to do now. Pray. In earnest. Seek God's will."

I think of that train ride in Chicago where I finally said enough and gave it all over to God.

And just a day later I end up getting beaten almost to death by a cell phone.

"'The angel of the Lord encamps around those who fear him, and he delivers them. Taste and see that the Lord is good; blessed are those who take refuge in him. Fear the Lord, you his holy people, for those who fear him lack nothing.'"

I look at the woman sitting across from me. "Are you my guardian angel?"

Iris shakes her head and laughs. "I've done many, many things that I regret. That is the curse of so-called wisdom, to learn how much you've failed and see how far you still have to go. You wouldn't want me as your guardian angel."

"Yes, I would."

"See—right there," Iris says. "That fire deep inside. You are stronger than you think, Chris. And you are young enough not to know any better. Which is good. Because you're going to need that for the road ahead."

"For what? What's going to happen?"

"I don't know. I can't see the future. I just know that one battle was won. A very big battle. Perhaps the only battle that you really needed to win."

"What's that?" I ask.

"The one over your soul."

5. CONCRETE

Iris is right. My face looks like a piece of fruit that's started to go bad. It's black and blue and swollen and soft. I look at it in the mirror of the small bathroom at the back of the room.

Turns out, this is another inn that Iris is staying in. She tells me it's in the middle of Solitary, but I refuse to believe her because I've been in the middle of Solitary and have never seen this place. There's the bed-and-breakfast that Lily was staying in, but Iris says this is different. This is just behind the sheriff's office and Brennan's Grill and Tavern, but I say it can't be.

She uses the words *haven* and *refuge* a lot when she talks about this little room and this inn. It's only for those who need a safe place to come and heal.

There are so many things I want to ask her, but she tells me I need to leave. She says I can come back, but I can only bring myself, and I have to be careful who sees me come this way.

We open the door to the garden outside, and I'm surprised to find that the temperature feels like a warm spring day. The birds are still chirping away. I see some squirrels running around playing. A cocker spaniel is lounging by a weathered bench under a tree. The garden surrounds us like a circling wall.

"It doesn't feel like January," I say.

She nods, smiles, then leads me over stone steps in the ground until she seems to walk right through a wall of shrubs higher than me. It's only when I get closer that I see it's somewhat of an optical illusion. The path takes a sharp left turn, then veers right through the shrubs until reaching a gate that comes up to my chest. Iris opens it and leads me out to the street.

Suddenly I feel the cold. The sun that was streaking through has disappeared, and I see thick gray clouds above us. I look back and see the same wall of shrubs behind us.

The gate's nowhere to be seen.

"How did we just—"

Iris turns around, then puts a hand into the shrubs. She pulls open the gate.

"Just find the old church and make a left and head straight to here," she says.

I'm about to ask what old church, but then I see it. A building that was once white and once opened its doors to guests. Now the windows and doors are bolted up, the paint is faded, and the landscaping looks like it's been ignored for a decade. I've seen it before because I've noticed the old battered cross at the top of the steeple.

"What am I supposed to do now?" I ask.

"What I told you to do."

"Pray?"

She nods. She's still standing next to the opened gate. "Your bruises and cuts are already starting to heal. They will probably be gone by the time you get back home."

"Is my mother still alive?"

"I don't know," she says. "But Chris, listen. 'The Lord is my light and my salvation; whom shall I fear? The Lord is the stronghold of my life; of whom shall I be afraid?'"

I want to ask why she's suddenly spouting off Bible verses to me.

I mean—yeah, great, fine. I'll try to see if they help, but right now I need some concrete answers.

Maybe those are the concrete answers you need, Chris.

I see her slip behind the gate and then watch it turn back into an unmovable wall of shrubs.

I look at the church, then stare at the street heading downhill toward downtown Solitary.

Whom shall I fear? Well, the list is long—where should I start?

I make sure the motorcycle key is in my pocket, then start walking downhill to do battle with those I shouldn't be afraid of.

6. FIGURING IT OUT

I can hear the music blasting from the cabin even before I head up the steps to the front door.

Maybe I should be afraid, but this doesn't scare me. For some reason I think it might be Newt, or someone else I haven't seen for a while. Maybe Poe. Or maybe—well, maybe ghosts like to hear some tunes as well. So do mannequins.

The music is seriously loud by the time I reach the top of the stairs and look inside my bedroom. Sitting slumped on my bed is Uncle Robert, an orange album resting on his chest. He doesn't look surprised or even mildly interested in talking as I stand before the door.

The singer is talking about a sweet and tender hooligan. Robert eventually nods and then waves as if he wants to finish this song, which we do. He hands me the album, and I see that it's *Louder Than Bombs* by The Smiths. It makes me think of the first day I attended Harrington High and the trio of girls that came up to me because of my T-shirt.

That seems like ten years ago.

Robert turns down the volume but doesn't shut the music off. For a moment I think he's going to remark about how bad my face looks, but he doesn't say a word about it.

"This makes me think of my high school days," Robert says, looking at the record cover. "These guys spoke the things I felt. It was like they somehow were singing for me."

I don't say anything.

Guess Iris was right about my face and the magical mystery potion.

"So have you enjoyed listening to my records? And wearing my clothes?"

"Why have you been watching us? Why have you been hiding?"

He rolls his eyes and sits up.

Morrissey says "That's the story of my life" as another song fades away. Uncle Robert just nods and ignores my question.

"I just talked to Staunch downtown," I tell him.

And, oh yeah, his phone has bits of my cheek lodged into its keys.

"What did he say about Tara?"

"He said he'd kill her."

Robert rubs his dark stubble. "Well, that's good."

"That's *good*?"

"Yeah. It means she's not dead."

"Spoken with such emotion."

My uncle curses. "Don't give me that. I didn't have to drive back down here, you know. I've saved your life twice now. I'm not cut out to be anybody's guardian angel, especially yours."

"I didn't ask you to be."

He laughs at me. "What a sad look." Again with a curse. "You're just like your mother."

Robert stands and turns off the stereo. He glances around the room. "There was a time I thought I'd never see any of this again."

"Why?"

He pats me on the shoulder as he passes. "Come on—let's go downstairs. You hungry for some lunch?"

"No."

But actually I am pretty hungry.

"Well, I'm thirsty, and if we're going to talk, I'm going to need a drink."

Robert has that unhealthy look that Mom was starting to have when she drank too much—pale and thin and messy. He holds a can of beer in his hand, and I wonder where he got it from.

"You sure you're not hungry?" he asks as he sits on the couch across from me.

"Are you staying here now?"

He shrugs. His eyes look at me, but they don't really connect. They seem distant and busy.

"I don't know what's happening. I tried, Chris. I really tried."

"Tried what?"

"To keep you guys okay. To look out for you." He sips his beer, and then somehow the can seems to be empty. "I've been looking out for people ever since I came to this place."

Those same eyes are now glassy, and I can't tell if it's from sadness or from the booze.

"You want to know something? I was the one who put that gun in your locker."

For a second I forget that it ever happened. But then I remember being called into the principal's office and getting kicked out of school.

"Why'd you do that?"

"Because—the very thing you needed was to draw attention to yourself. To not fit in. I knew they'd find out it wasn't yours. It was like I was sending them a message."

"What? That I was going to shoot someone?"

Robert laughs. "No. That I'm just as serious as they are. Plus—I needed you and your mom to bond."

"So you got me kicked out, huh?"

"It worked, right?"

I recall Mom taking my side and threatening the principal and teachers.

"Yeah, I guess so. In a weird way."

"The thing they wanted from the very start was for you to fit in. To make friends and have a good ole time and feel nice and comfortable and then begin to learn the truth. But ..."

"But what?" I ask.

"Well, you chose to fall for pretty much the worst person you could have fallen for."

I get a small fire going in the fireplace and then sit on the hearth. Uncle Robert grabs another beer from the fridge.

"Do you know everything that's happening?" I ask.

"I thought that moving here would give me the answers I needed." He leans back on the couch and sighs. "Boy, was I wrong."

"Why did you move back here?"

"Because I wanted to know what happened to my parents. Why my mom died when I was just a kid. I wanted to find out what happened to her, because I've never bought the whole car crash thing. Just like I never believed Dad was shot by some random thug when I was in college."

"Did it have something to do with this place?"

"Ya think?" He takes a long draw of his beer, then wipes his mouth and curses. "It all comes back to this place. And back to our family. Really majorly sucks, doesn't it?"

"But why did you disappear?"

"If you could vanish now, would you? Knowing that nobody would get hurt? Knowing that everybody would be okay? Would you?"

I think about it and nod.

"But I—it's been confusing. I came back here and didn't have anybody else. I wanted answers, and I wanted to fix things. But instead I got shackled down. In the end, it all went away."

I'm not following him. "Are you talking about Mrs. Marsh?"

Robert groans and crinkles up the beer can, then tosses it into the fire. "Please. Don't call her that. I mean, like *ever* again."

"Okay, then—Heidi."

"I tried to rescue her. I just didn't know how hard it would be.

I was doing something good, but it killed me inside because I also knew I was doing something wrong. But I loved her."

"She's still around."

"I know," Robert says. "But she made it clear. She chose to stay. We were going to leave, but she just couldn't. That monster has some kind of hold on her."

"Staunch?"

"Marsh. The little leper-healer. That's what I call him. The whack-job with the glasses. That guy—I'm telling you, you stay away from him."

"Did they tell you about everything? About our—your grandfather?"

"They wanted me to become like them, and I said no way. But then—they really thought they'd gotten rid of me. But I wasn't going to leave Heidi. I can't." He pauses, looking into the fire and watching the crackling wood. "Then you guys show up and ruin everything."

"How?"

"They destroyed my family. *Our* family. This sickness—this evil. And they wanted to do the same with you two. All because what? Because your mom had to get some answers. Just like her big brother."

"Why didn't you tell us?"

He stands and then leans over the couch. "Do you really want to know? I spend every hour of every day wondering if I've lost my mind. I drink to keep the nightmares away. You know that, right? That's why your mother came down here and started drinking like a fish. She couldn't help herself. And you ..." He examines me for a moment. "You don't drink, huh?"

"Not really," I say.

"I want to say don't start, but—but look. I have no suggestions for you."

"You have to help me."

"How can I help someone else when I can't even help myself?" Uncle Robert curses, then goes to the fridge again. "The things I've seen—you don't want to see them."

I sit there, watching this man I barely know, wondering what I'm supposed to say or do to help him.

I'm seventeen and unsure how to help myself.

Another voice tells me to shut up, that I'm different.

You're stronger, Chris. You've always been strong.

"What's going to happen?" I ask Robert when he sits down again.

"I don't know. But it's something big. And I don't want to be around here to find out."

"I have to do what they tell me."

He only nods.

This guy is the nodding man. And it's really making me angry.

"Aren't you supposed to, like, help out a little?" I ask.

"Don't get annoyed at me. Listen, I was here sorting all of this out by myself. Okay?"

"So I'm supposed to just do what I'm told by those guys?"

"For now."

"Until what?" I ask. "Until you finish enough beer not to care anymore?"

Uncle Robert yells at me and tells me what I can do with my frustration, then he sighs and apologizes.

"Listen, Chris. I thought if they didn't know I was around … I didn't realize that they'd given up on me. I'm a lost cause to them. But you—you're their last hope. You're like their Luke Skywalker."

"Why?"

"Because—I think they know how strong you are."

I shake my head.

"It's true, Chris. Look at all this you've been dealing with. By yourself. Just a kid. I would've freaked out if this all happened to me at sixteen. But you managed. And you're still managing. And that's why—you keep it up. Okay? Until we know Tara is okay."

"And then?"

"We'll figure it out then," he says.

"And what happens if she's not?"

"We'll figure it out then."

7. Like a Disney Movie

I don't need to ask if Uncle Robert is going to spend the night. He's passed out on the couch where he was watching television all day and I was watching him drink beer. He's as lifeless as that mannequin still in the laundry room with nowhere to go. I leave one light on as well as the fire fully stoked to make it through the night. If it somehow spills over to the rest of the cabin, well, I might get out, but Robert is a goner.

In the bathroom I examine my face, which doesn't look bruised or touched in any way. I wonder if Iris was using the magical mystery water from Marsh Falls. This makes me think of a dozen other questions, all of which give me a headache and force me to avoid answering any of them.

My room is extra cold tonight. Normally Mom would make sure I had an extra blanket on nights like this. Even after she'd been drinking so much. Now I'm forced to look for another blanket, and then I just give up and go to bed.

I wonder what sort of dreams my uncle has. Or maybe he doesn't dream anymore. Maybe the booze completely coats over the dreams and drowns them out.

Maybe he used to dream of Heidi Marsh.

I want to ask him more about her. I know they were living here for a while. What were their plans? Why didn't they just run away together?

Then I think of Jocelyn and know that life isn't always so simple.

The wind blows outside. It's January.

I wish I could close my eyes and wake up in July. To know I've made it past The Big Whatever that is going to happen. To know that I've graduated Harrington and I'll finally be able to leave this place. Hopefully with Mom. And maybe even Uncle Robert.

I think of school. Then of Kelsey.

Sweet, adorable, likable Kelsey.

The girl that I definitely should not be with.

What will these next few months look like?

My eyes close then open then close again.

I awake hearing something.

Birds. Lots of them.

And something else.

I must have slept in, since the sun is already coming up. I glance out my window and just see the drab emptiness of the surrounding woods. Sometimes it seems smothering, this wilderness that never seems to want to go away.

The sounds keep coming from downstairs, not from in our cabin, but outside.

The deck.

It sounds like people shuffling. Or like animals. I get up and sprint down the steps.

The couch is empty.

I check Mom's bedroom, but the bed is untouched.

"Uncle Robert?"

No response.

I hear tapping on the window. More birds.

I go to the window and look out.

No way.

The bird that was pecking at the window flies off, but on the railing of the deck are maybe fifty or a hundred others. All different kinds. Just sitting there, some moving and making noises, some just sitting there.

Like that Alfred Hitchcock movie *The Birds*.

But that's not all.

I see more animals shuffling on the deck itself. There's a groundhog—no, there are several—and a dog. Several cats. Other animals that I have to study to see what they are. A woodchuck maybe? I see a possum. A skunk.

These animals are having a party on our deck.

"Uncle Robert?" I shout out.

Nothing.

I look out the bedroom window down on the driveway to see if his car is there. Then I remember I never saw one yesterday.

Like a ghost, he's disappeared.

I go back and look out to the deck again. That's when I see it. Right dead in the center of the action, as if guiding them all in this craziness.

Iris's bluebird.

It's like she told them where to come.

But why? What's with the animals?

I bang on the window, and the bluebird flies off the railing and heads toward me, then swoops up and away.

Suddenly all the birds follow.

They're gone.

I hear the stampede of animals shuffling away down the steps and around the deck to the other side of the house like they might in a Disney movie.

I wait for a second, then open the door. There's not an animal in sight.

The wind is freezing and makes me quickly go back inside. I check my cell phone to see if there are any messages, then look around the back of the house for my uncle. Maybe he had more to drink last night and fell off the deck, like I always used to worry about Mom doing. But he's nowhere to be found.

Uncle Robert is gone.

8. RAY OF LIGHT

I FINALLY FOUND THE ANSWER TO YOUR LIFE'S BIGGEST PROBLEM.

The text is somewhat shocking because it comes only an hour later from Kelsey.

How does she know?

Then, like I usually do and will probably continue to do until the day I die, I wonder if she's with *them*.

That blonde hair is really just dyed and that whole cute shy girl thing is an act and maybe she's secretly an international spy.

WHAT'S THAT? I quickly ask her.

CHECK THIS OUT.

She sends me a link. Guys with my luck should never, ever open links.

But of course I do so anyway.

And after a few minutes of checking out the site on my phone, I laugh.

SECRET TO MY BIGGEST PROBLEM, HUH? I ask her.

YOU STILL NEED YOUR LICENSE, RIGHT?

She does have a point.

YES. AMONG OTHER THINGS.

THERE YOU GO. NO MORE SAYING YOU DON'T KNOW HOW TO GET IT.

THAT'S NICE. THANKS VERY MUCH.

I'M JUST BEING SELFISH, she writes.

WHY?

WELL, SOMEONE HAS TO DRIVE ME AROUND ON DATES.

Even on cold, dark mornings, there's a ray of light not too far across town that never hesitates to shine on me.

When the phone rings and I see that it's Dad, I know I'm going to tell him about Mom. I have to. There's no way I can keep this from him.

"I just wanted to give you an update on what's going on the next few months," he tells me after greeting me.

Yeah, me too.

"I'm going to be taking a couple of courses at Covenant College."

Of all the things I imagined him saying, this isn't one of them. "Okay."

"I'm still looking for a job. Trying to make connections. But my sole focus is on my spiritual walk, Chris. There's a lot I need to know."

Do you know anything about the spaces in between and great-grandfathers who lurk in tunnels?

"The classes go till May," he continues. "They'll give me some knowledge of the Bible."

"Great."

I guess my answer comes out a bit too strong, because Dad asks me what's wrong.

This is my chance to tell him everything.

Yet I'm suddenly reminded where I'm at. The eyes and ears and fingertips of the wicked and whacked are all over me.

"Everything's fine."

"Can I talk to your mom?" he asks.

"She's not here."

"Okay." He pauses for a minute.

Tell him, Chris, do it. Now.

"You know if there's anything you need, just let me know," Dad says.

I want to cry. Like a serious mushy cry a middle-school girl might do after her favorite vampire couple has a baby or something.

"Sure," I say.

I know they'll kill Mom. I think back to Staunch nearly killing me in town.

I can't take that chance.

"I'll keep in touch," Dad says. "Remember, call me for anything you need."

I tell Dad good-bye and stare at the phone. I'm tired of holding back and not saying everything and not asking for help when I desperately need it.

I'm tried of being forced to keep quiet in order to keep someone I love alive.

9. M & M S

I awake in the middle of the night in pitch black in an empty cabin that has suddenly been invaded by a silent monster.

His name is fear, and he steals through the locked door without a further thought.

He casually climbs the stairs and slips under the crack of my doorway and then sits cross-legged on a chair across from my bed. Then he begins to whisper slow and steady thoughts to me.

"Your mother is going to die in Solitary, Chris."

The voice is strong, low, fearless. And very, very real.

"Your father will die alone and miserable knowing he abandoned all of you."

I close my eyes because I want to go back to sleep, then I wonder if I'm still dreaming.

"You will never amount to anything, and this silly, stupid faith of yours will never mean anything."

I grip my hands and force them into fists. I can feel the sweat on my forehead and face.

What's happening to me now?

"This is your life, and I will be here by your side for the rest of it, Chris."

The voice is as real as the burning heat filling my body. I tear off the cover and just rest there, eyes opened but not seeing anything.

"It's only going to get worse. And you're only going to be more frightened and freaked out until *everything* splinters away into ashes."

I get out of bed then and kneel on the cold carpet.

"It will do you no good," the voice says right beside me.

I start to pray, folding my hands and bowing my head.

I pray, and I don't stop.

I don't know how this works—I really don't. But I know that I have to do something and I have to do it now.

And eventually all I can hear is my own voice, praying. The other voice is gone.

I'm rinsing out my cereal bowl and glance at the half-opened laundry door. I wonder for a moment if I left it that way, then I sigh and walk toward it.

If I could bet, I'd put good money on the mannequin being gone. But the creepy thing is still there, lying facedown on the floor. The curly long hair looks just like Lily's.

Oh man.

That's not the best way to start a day after the last day and a half I've had. I stare at the lifelike figure and see the back of its shirt pulled up, revealing the cream-colored "skin." I wonder what these mannequins are made of—certainly not plastic. As I'm wondering this, I see some writing on the dummy.

Up close, I see it's a business name and an address.

GRAFFIC NATURE

1947 Zebulon Lane

Solitary, North Carolina

It's wonderful to see that whoever bought this mannequin and brought it to my cabin is supporting local business. Or artists. Or freaks.

Before leaving for school, I drag the Lily look-alike out the back door and leave her there. I hope she finally gets the hint and runs away.

On the way to school I think about my midnight prayers and know that I need help. Not just help with finding Mom and trying to keep Staunch satisfied, but help in trying to figure out what to do next with this whole faith thing. Maybe I'll go to church, but the nearest church … oh, right.

There are those around who have real faith.

I remember what Jocelyn showed me so long ago, the group of people who used to have church under Marsh Falls. If I could find someone there and try to reach out—maybe it would be someone I could trust. Someone I could get a little help from.

Someone who can help me figure out a few things.

I think back to the beginning of last summer when I decided to avoid everything, including people like Poe who had recently moved. I never did reply to any of her emails. She eventually stopped sending them, which was what I had hoped.

What did she say that one time?

Before heading into school, I find the letter Poe left in my locker. I've kept it tucked away in a desk drawer.

I SENT THIS TO THE ONLY PERSON I COULD THINK OF WHO I KNOW HAS YOUR BACK AND USED TO HAVE MINE. HINT, IT'S NOT A SHE. AND BOY DOES HE LOVE HIS M&Ms.

I never did try to find out who this person was because—well, frankly, I didn't really care. That was when I had decided to do things on my own.

And when I was going gaga over Lily.

Looking back on that, I can see why they did what they did. It was a perfect setup. I had decided I'd had enough and had told God and the rest of the world to go take a hike. Then into my wrecked life walks this goddess that any guy would be crazy for.

Thinking of Lily hurts. But it's different from thinking of Jocelyn.

Both died. But only one died with hope in her heart.

I walk up those stairs to the entrance to Harrington, wondering what this final semester will bring. My mind is going over Poe's words.

Has your back ... Not a she ... love his M&Ms.

The last bit is a clue, of course.

I haven't even reached my locker when I finally realize how not-so-subtle that clue is.

I figure this out when my history teacher passes me by with a smile and a "Welcome back, Chris."

I just say hi to Mr. Meiners like always and keep heading to my locker.

M&Ms.

Then I stop.

Mr. Meiners.

I wonder if it's that easy.

Suddenly things fall into place.

The time I saw Mr. Meiners holding a crying Jocelyn in his arms. A crying yet laughing Jocelyn.

Was this because she had gone to him for answers? Was this because she'd started finding some?

Then I think of him grabbing me in the hallway after a run-in with Gus. His telling me to see the bigger picture, saying that I'm not some stupid kid, that I'm different.

But how does he know?

I know that I have to contact Poe, first to apologize for not responding to any of her emails.

Then to ask for her help.

10. WHEN YOU SMILE

These students who don't have a clue move through hallways that are long bored with them, and in the middle of them I see Kelsey. Walking toward me, smiling.

And like that, I know.

This is my reason here, my meaning and my motive.

I have to do the one thing I haven't been able to do so far.

I have to be her hero.

I have to save her.

For Jocelyn, it was too late.

For Lily, it was too late.

For my mother, the verdict is still out.

But Kelsey is still there, still smiling, still hopeful.

Don't you dare let that hope die, Kelsey.

I want to box it up with her and mail it to a place with no forwarding address.

"Hi, Chris."

I want to save that hi and be able to hear it many mornings from now when I can do something with it.

"Hi," I say back.

I'm not letting you go or giving up or being stupid or being nonchalant.

Kelsey is not going to get away.

No way.

Not this time.

11. IN THE END

I don't go home after school. Instead, I ride my motorcycle to Jeremiah Marsh's house.

It's a Monday afternoon. If he's not home, then I'll wait for him. Maybe Heidi will be there and will let me in. Maybe she'll serve me poisoned lemonade or drugged cider.

Maybe you should pass on a beverage.

The house looks more ominous somehow in the disappearing sunlight. My face and hands are numb from riding on the bike in the January chill. I need to get some gloves, maybe a ski mask. Then I can start robbing banks and have a nice quick getaway.

I knock on the door, not expecting it to open. But it does, quickly, and standing at the doorway as if he could read my mind is Pastor Marsh.

For a moment he looks at me as if confused.

"Are you, uh, busy?" I ask.

I still feel the need to be polite. I mean, he's still an adult and I still have manners and maybe I'm interrupting something like a goat sacrifice or a moose-head stuffing.

"You look well," he says. "A bit too well."

I'm not really following what he's saying. My heart is beating hard, and I'm feeling like I might turn around and sprint back to my motorcycle any second.

"Staunch told me what happened. He said he left you in a mess."

"I heal quickly."

Marsh raises his eyes. "So you do. Please, come on in."

The place is the same. Spotless and looking like a model house that nobody lives in.

Marsh looks a lot like the house. He's wearing dark pants and a sweater with a shirt underneath. All matching and new like a mannequin in the window of a clothing store.

Or like the one in the storage room in the church basement.

"Can I get you anything to drink? Hungry?"

"Where's my mom?"

"She's fine," he says.

No surprise at my question. No hesitation at his answer.

"She's fine where?"

"Why don't you have a seat?" Marsh asks.

"I'll do what you want, but I want my mother back."

He looks serious as he takes off his glasses, wipes them, and slips them back on. He looks at me.

"She's at another rehabilitation center."

"Don't lie," I say.

"I'm not lying. I have no reason to lie to you, Chris. This is not my doing. It's out of my hands. But I do know she's in rehab, thinking she needs to be there. Trapped. Going out of her mind. All on purpose, of course."

"What do you want me to do?"

"I want you to relax. Please. Nothing is going to happen to your mother."

"That's not what Staunch said."

"Of course not. And that's why—listen to me, okay?—just listen. But sit. You're making me nervous standing there."

I sit down on a couch, and he sits across from me. For a second he seems to look at me as if he's trying to figure out what I'm thinking. Or what brand my shirt is. Or whether I'm wearing cologne (and no, I'm not).

"I told you when we first met that I'm only here to help, Chris. To help you find your way."

"I just want my mom back."

"She'll be back around soon."

"You take orders from Staunch. Who takes orders from that ..."

I can't say what I'm thinking and feeling. There's really no word to describe my great-grandfather.

That old man who turned into a monster before my eyes.

"Do what I say, and you'll end up very happy. They don't want your mother. They don't want anything other than you, Chris. You."

"But why?"

"Because it's time. It's been time for a while, but soon he won't be here."

"You mean Walter Kinner?"

I'm tired of saying *great-grandfather*. I don't want to claim him.

"Yes."

"So is there a crown and a ceremony? Do we have to kill a cow?"

Marsh laughs. "That's funny."

"I wasn't trying to be."

"I can't answer that, Chris. I don't know."

"But I'm supposed to just—take his place? What place is there to take? What does he do?"

Marsh's eyes shift downward, as if thinking about something. Maybe whether to tell me the truth. Or what lie he needs to tell next.

He rubs his hands together, then leans over with his elbows on his legs.

"This gift of sight that you have is useful to them. That's—that's all I know."

"Oh, okay," I say. "That explains everything."

"Which way do you want it then? Tell me."

He curses, then stands up and heads back over to the kitchen. I stay on the couch while he grabs a couple of waters out of the fridge. He tosses one over to me.

"I can make up lies that sound nice and easy to you. Or I can do what you're wanting—what you've been asking for ever since you came here. To get answers. To know the truth. But listen—the truth isn't nice and isn't easy, and I don't think you're going to want to hear it."

"The truth about what?"

"About everything. We tell you things bit by bit, and I can just see your mind reeling. You don't understand. That's why I feel it's better to show than tell. Like Marsh Falls. I could have told you that, but you would have never believed. Even now I bet there's a part of you that doesn't believe. It's too surreal. Too crazy. Right?"

I sigh and nod. Marsh opens his bottled water and takes a short sip.

"There are those who come to Solitary, those who do business here. They do business with Kinner and always have. He takes care of them."

"How? Who are they?"

"You will meet them soon enough."

"And do what?"

"That—that I do not know. It's being a—a guardian of sorts. A caretaker. At least that's what I think. But I might be wrong."

I'm sitting there wondering how a scrawny seventeen-year-old is going to be anybody's guardian.

"So how—" I start to ask.

"You do what you're supposed to do. You go to school. You study. You pass your classes. You be an ordinary student and just get through."

"Until what?"

"When the time comes, you will find out. All I know is that it will be Memorial Day. That's at the end of May."

"What's the significance of Memorial Day?"

"There are a lot fewer families around to be suspicious."

"Suspicious of what?"

"Chris, listen, and listen well. The people you care for will only end up hurting you in the end. So the less you care, the less painful it will be. Because in the end, everybody dies. Do you understand? Everybody."

12. THE JOKER

I hold the Zippo lighter in my hand, an old relic that supposedly belonged to dear old great-grandpa, who my mom thinks died in World War I.

Who turns to a rotting corpse before your very eyes if you wait around long enough.

I went into a store in Asheville to fill it with fluid, but it still doesn't work. The guy told me it was too old to ignite. Yet I keep flicking it, trying. Flicking it to see if anything comes, even the slightest spark.

As I do I can't stop thinking of something.

I never had a chance to tell Lily good-bye.

With Jocelyn, it was different. She knew how I felt, and she also knew what was coming. But Lily's death was somehow, in a strange way, more shocking. Not the how but the why. The suddenness of it. One minute I'm sitting right next to her, and the next she's gone.

Because in the end, everybody dies. Everybody.

Marsh might not be right about many things, but he's certainly right about that.

I'm in my cabin thinking of everything but mostly thinking of Lily. I recall what she said about heaven.

If heaven is real, I don't want to go. Because it's probably bright and sunny, and I won't belong there.

In this cabin, stuck in this dark town that's terrorized by evil people and hidden secrets, I want to believe in that bright and sunny place. A place of hope. A place of second chances.

I tried. I tried to do it on my own and I failed. Badly.

I want to tell Lily that. I want to tell her how sorry I am that after everything that happened, it had to end so fast.

Boom.

For some reason, I think of the Joker. It's stupid, but it's just me and my thoughts so I can let them be as lame as I want. So I think of the Joker from *The Dark Knight.* No, I take that back. I think of Heath Ledger, who played him in an insane role that could never be duplicated.

Then …

Boom.

Just like that, he's gone. And he's immortalized and will forever live on.

He was so young, with so much potential and promise. But like all of us, he wasn't guaranteed tomorrow.

I wish I had that Bible that Dad gave me. I'm thinking that maybe somewhere inside I could find some wisdom or encouragement. Anything.

Maybe that's too simplistic a notion. That this rule book of sorts will give me some answers. But I need something. And watching *The Dark Knight* for the millionth time probably won't help me much.

Heath Ledger didn't get a chance for another act. But I'm still here, and still in the story and ready for another act. Perhaps a final act for Solitary.

If that's the case, I need to do everything I can to be the hero I'm able to be.

That maybe I've always been destined to be.

13. VESSEL

The maps app on my iPhone doesn't work that well around these spiraling roads and rolling hills. Still, I finally am able to find Zebulon Lane not because of my GPS but because I'm stopping at every road off this side street of a side street of Sable Road. And because I see the sign.

The road reminds me a bit of the one leading up to the Crag's Inn, yet this one looks even worse with deep ruts in the road and even a few dead tree limbs stretched out over it. It doesn't look like anybody's driven here for a while.

Maybe the address on the mannequin is an old one. Maybe there won't be anything or anybody at 1947 Zebulon Lane.

I slow down at a driveway dropping from the road. I look down and see a modern-looking house on the side of the mountain. Half of the house is propped up by beams, and a long deck circles that part. This isn't a cabin at all, but looks like some kind of funky house designed by a famous architect.

Like those Frank Lloyd Wright houses my mom would point out back in Chicagoland.

I coast down the driveway and then get off the bike, wondering if anybody lives here. There are abandoned houses all around these parts. Like Jocelyn's old house. Empty and silent.

Perhaps this is one of those.

When the door opens without my knocking on it, I jolt and almost tear back to my bike. Yet the man at the door doesn't appear threatening.

Then again, appearances don't mean a thing. Not around Solitary.

"Hello, Chris," he says without any hint of surprise at seeing me.

"You know me?"

"Of course. Would you like to come in?"

The windows in his modern-styled house looked dark and hidden.

"How do you know me?"

He smiles, and several lines of wrinkles form on his forehead. He looks sixty- or seventysomething, with white hair that's slicked back, at least what hair he has on his half-bald head. He wears wide glasses that hide more wrinkles underneath them.

"I can explain. I won't hurt you. Promise."

"Do you know my mom?"

The man is quite tall, a couple of inches taller than I am, and he just stands there next to the opened door, waiting for me to come in. I nod and walk inside.

I almost bump into a woman with long blonde hair standing in the hallway. I step back and blurt out an "excuse me" before noticing that her eyes look a little dead.

"That's Fiona," the man says as he closes the door behind me. "Lovely, isn't she?"

She's wearing a short black dress with a low-cut top that reveals a golden necklace. In her heels Fiona is taller than I am. She's not quite smiling. It's more like she's … posing. Posing and waiting.

And, oh yeah, she's a mannequin.

"Fiona is five years old and still as beautiful as the day she was born," the man says as he puts a hand on my shoulder and guides me down the hall.

Suddenly Marsh doesn't seem that creepy to me anymore. I really am regretting that I came here.

"You drove all this way out here to find me, yet you've hardly said a word since you arrived."

Maybe that's because I haven't been this freaked out since, well, since the last time I was in a family room looking at a mannequin. In this case, there are probably about half a dozen of them surrounding me. All ladies … the guy's own wonderful set of wives.

"My name is Alfred Graff. And, as you can see, I make these beautiful creatures."

That's what he said. Not mannequins or dummies or figures. He said creatures.

"What brings you to my home, Chris?"

My heart is slowing down a bit, and I notice the old man isn't holding a gun or a knife or anything like that. He just holds a small container the size of his thumb that he keeps dipping his finger into and then spreads the contents over his lips. Which, once again, is sorta creepy.

"Did one of your, uh, 'creatures' recently escape?"

He laughs and glances at a figure right behind him. "A man seventy-seven years old no longer takes offense at comments like that. I've heard them all. I've been making these for a long time, Chris."

"How do you know my name?" I ask again.

"There are quite a few people around here who know your name, Chris Buckley. Who know of your importance."

"So you, uh—are you with Marsh? And Staunch?"

"With?" He says the word as if it's a bad curse word. "This isn't grade school, my boy. This isn't the Cub Scouts. I am paid very well to do what I do and have been for quite a while."

"Make mannequins?"

"Yes."

The room is barely lit, so the figures that are all standing around us seem threatening, waiting to suddenly pop to life and attack me.

That's just my luck. I'm finally in a room surrounded by beautiful and exotic women staring my way. Unfortunately, they're fiberglass models that don't breathe or speak or blink.

At least I hope they don't.

"Who do you—"

"Why are you here?" Alfred interrupts in a deliberate and loud tone.

"A mannequin showed up in my cabin, and it was made by you."

He nods, then dabs his finger in his little jar and rubs it over his lips. "Doesn't surprise me in the least. Was it a lady? Curly blond hair?"

I nod, and suddenly the back of my neck feels sweaty.

"That was one of the last ones I made."

"Who was it for?"

"Is that what you're really wanting to know? Who asked me to make that mannequin? Is that your main question?"

"It's one of them."

Alfred stands and then walks over to a dark-haired dummy with bold eyes that seem to be bearing down on me.

"Do you believe that animals go to heaven, Chris?"

I shake my head, not sure what to say.

"I believe that animals are born without souls. They're wonderful, don't get me wrong. But they don't have *souls*. Yet they are God's creatures, and they can sense the spiritual world. Especially when that world is full of unrest. Am I not right?"

I think about Midnight, then about Iris's bluebird, then about the random kinds of animals I've encountered around here.

"These creatures are the same," he says as he puts his finger on the lips of the lady he's standing next to and does the same sort of weird motion. "They are born without souls. They are harmless. They are merely ... vessels."

My skin crawls. Alfred seemed lost in his weird sort of act with the mannequin until saying that last word and looking at me.

Vessels.

"In most places in the world, these vessels would be merely that." He takes his hand and knocks on the hard face. "Just hollow, empty figures. Beautiful, true, but empty. Yet Solitary, as you already know, Chris, is not like most places in the world. Trust me, I know. I've seen what's out there. This is truly a special place. And you, my dear boy, are truly a special person."

We jumped from creepy to blood-curdling the moment this guy said vessels.

Because in a way, it clicked. Not in a rational, oh-okay, two-plus-two-equals-four sort of way.

I just suddenly get what he's talking about, and there's nothing about it that I like.

"Do you believe in magic, Chris?"

I stare at this ordinary-looking guy who I'd never pay any attention to on the street. Yet now I study his every move and action and word.

"I'm coming to believe in a lot of things these days."

Alfred walks to the back of the room and starts to slowly stroke the red hair of a mannequin that appears to be laughing. "There is a dark magic in the world, a magic I've witnessed with my own eyes, a kind that I used to try and tell Iris about, though she never wanted to hear it or believe it."

Did he just say …

"I told her, but she didn't want any part of it."

I think my mouth must be hanging open, because he looks my way and laughs. "Yes, Chris. Iris. Your lovely Iris."

"You know Iris?"

He walks over to another figure that I haven't noticed before. This one is sitting in a chair in the corner of the room. As if watching from afar, not enjoying herself.

She looks like Iris. A young Iris that I once saw in the pictures.

This is so incredibly wrong. All of it.

"I'm still waiting. Still hoping. Still wanting."

He doesn't say anything more.

For a moment I look back at the hallway and the front door.

"You can leave anytime you want," Alfred says. "There won't be any magic show tonight. If that's what you're wanting."

"How long have you known Iris?"

"Ever since she moved here. And before she lost her son. That poor sick child. I offered to help. I offered to do anything possible. *Anything.* But she refused. She refused to believe. But people always have to learn the hard way. Don't they, Chris?"

14. HELP

Back home I get an email from my father. It's strange because he normally doesn't send a lot of emails, and the timing of this is a bit suspicious. Yet I believe it's him because of what he says.

Hey, Chris. Hope you and Mom are doing well. I began reading Ephesians and thought of you when I read these verses:

"God decided in advance to adopt us into his own family by bringing us to himself through Jesus Christ. This is what he wanted to do, and it gave him great pleasure. So we praise God for the glorious grace he has poured out on us who belong to his dear Son."

This applies to me as well as you, Chris. And please know this: even though I'm up here in Chicago and will be here for a while, I'm praying for your mother and you. I still pray that we will be a family again, and that the work God is doing will continue on in Mom.

Stay strong and let me know if there's anything you need.

Dad

It's strange to hear Dad saying this stuff to me.

I think about that guy in the driveway of our old home as I left Illinois and vowed to never look back. I hated that man and assumed I was going to hate him all my life. I didn't know that he was as confused and struggling as I am right now.

Stay strong.

The words encourage me. I certainly need as much help as I can get.

I don't have any classes with Mr. Meiners, so I have to make a special trip to see him right after morning break. I make it to his homeroom where he teaches history all day long. He's sitting at his desk, grading papers.

"Sorry to interrupt," I say as I enter the room.

Mr. Meiners has a thick beard and thick dark hair. Sometimes I wonder if he used to be a hippie when they had those—back in the sixties or seventies, I think. I'm not as good with history as he is.

"How can I help you?"

"Well, I'm just, uh—"

I'm not sure how to ask him. I'm not even sure *what* to ask him.

"Someone told me that you might be able to help me. To really help me."

His look changes. Is it concern? Frustration that I'm bothering him?

Whatever it is, it looks serious.

"Do you need help in one of your classes?"

I shake my head.

I don't know if I'm being watched. Or if this room is bugged. Or if Mr. Meiners is with them.

"It's not school related?" he asks me in a direct, quick manner.

This was a bad idea.

"Well, not really."

"Then sorry. Why don't you ask your guidance counselor? Or homeroom teacher?"

This doesn't seem like Mr. Meiners. I've always seen him to be a caring, thoughtful teacher. The least he could do is ask me how I need help.

"You better get to your next class, Chris," he says, going back to grading papers.

I nod and want to say something else, but I don't.

I exit the room and hear the door shut behind me. Students are heading this way for next period.

Well, that was a major fail.

I head to my next class, wondering why Mr. Meiners was so rude and uncaring.

Maybe M&Ms stands for something more mysterious.

"The weekend is coming up," Kelsey tells me.

"It's only Thursday," I say.

"That's what I mean. It's approaching."

"Oh."

I love doing this. Playing games with her and teasing. It's cute because it's so easy. And because she always acts shy and unsure of herself.

I know why she's asking about the weekend. This is one area—maybe the only area—where I can be quiet and mysterious.

It's obvious to me that I'm going to see her at some point. But it's certainly not obvious to her.

"I'm hoping someone has a big party I can go to," I tell her.

"You are?"

"You know me. The party guy."

"Since when?"

"Since that one time I showed up and saw you all glammed up."

She turns red, and I figure I should be nice.

"Or maybe I can skip the parties and just hang out," I say. "With you."

"Sure."

It's after lunch, and we're near the entrance to the school. Normally we might be outside, but considering it's freezing out there, we're hanging inside around the corner from the cafeteria. It's a good place to talk because it's away from everybody.

"Kelsey?"

"Yeah."

"Listen—I'm just kidding around with you."

"You like doing that."

"I know. I'm sorry. I'm not trying to be mean. You're just so cute when you're being shy."

"Sorry."

"See—like that. Don't. Don't apologize. Don't be shy. You don't have to anymore. This isn't art class, and I'm not the new kid. Okay?"

She nods, brushing her blonde hair back over her shoulder.

"Look—you know this, but maybe I'll remind you. I like you. A lot. Okay?"

Kelsey looks up with innocent, sweet eyes that you could never paint if you tried a thousand times.

"I didn't forget about Chicago just because we're not there anymore," I tell her.

"I didn't either," she says.

Her comment makes me smile. It's almost as if—as if she's been waiting somehow to tell me that.

I start to tell her more, about how worried I am about this semester, about how things might suddenly get tough and dangerous. I want to tell her to be careful and don't talk to strangers and stay away from the dark woods and all that, but I don't say anything.

I don't want to ruin this moment. This quiet, simple moment.

"I want to see you this weekend. As much as I can. Okay?"

She nods.

A part of me knows that this is dangerous. For her. She's not just playing with fire. It's an inferno she's dealing with. And she doesn't even know it.

At the end of the day I find a note in my locker. It's a printout of a Word document in simple type.

The only way to get help is to do so without another soul knowing or seeing.

There are ways.

You'll hear from me soon.

I fold up the letter and look around. Of course nobody is there watching me. Maybe someone's hiding in a locker, glancing out the tiny slits at the top.

Or maybe, seriously, this is from someone who overheard my conversation and is playing another mind game with me.

Something tells me that's not the case.

I have a feeling this is from Mr. Meiners.

What about Mr. Marsh? Huh? He could be M&M.

I go to find Kelsey to tell her good-bye for the day. I try not to dwell on that last thought, the one about Marsh, but it stays around.

15. A LITTLE GUIDANCE

"Okay, so Chris Buckwheat."

"Buckley," I tell Mr. Taggart quickly.

It reminds me of something my skinheaded friend Brick from summer school might say, but that's just to joke around. Mr. Taggart doesn't joke. He's the butt of jokes.

He nods and looks through the files on his desk. This office is more like a closet where people just toss in random folders and garbage. When I first heard I was supposed to meet with him today, I thought there was a mistake.

"I had Ms. Tooney last year."

"Yeah, well, things change. Here it is."

I haven't seen Mr. Taggart since summer school, where I met Lily and the rest of the gang. I miss those carefree days, when this guy across from me would stroll in with his shirt half untucked and his hair (what little he has) half combed and make a halfhearted effort at teaching.

Staring at his unshaven face and glassy eyes, I see nothing much has changed.

"So have you taken your ACT or SAT tests?"

I shake my head.

"Applied to any schools?"

Once again, I shake my head.

Mr. Taggart looks at the few things in my folder. It's probably as pitiful as this blank vanilla office.

"So are you planning on going to college?" he asks me.

"Yeah. I guess."

"Kinda late to be guessing. You better get on it. And I'll tell you this—just 'cause they got me being a guidance counselor this year doesn't mean I'll be riding your butt. I don't care. Really. Kids these days are graduating with honors from amazing universities, and they still end up going back home to live with Mommy and Daddy. It's a different world out there. Nobody is looking out for you."

"That's truly inspiring," I say with a totally straight face.

Mr. Taggart looks at me for a second, a scowl on his face. Then he realizes I'm joking and starts to chuckle.

"That's a good one."

"I try," I say.

"You were in summer school, right? The session with the hottie?"

"I think her name was Lily, not hottie."

He already looks bored and ready to go back to doing the nothing he was doing when I came in.

"Look, Buck*ley*—you better get on this college thing."

"I always figured I'd go somewhere in Illinois."

"You gotta apply to those too."

"Yeah, okay."

"What's your grand plan for life?"

I want to live past graduation day and Memorial Day and then get far away from here.

"I don't know. Maybe be in a band."

"Play any instruments? Sing?"

I shake my head.

"Maybe you want to start there," he tells me in a deadpan way.

I kinda got other things going on.

"Get on one of those tests, and pick out some schools. Hey— junior colleges aren't bad. I went to one."

I feign a smile and nod.

I leave his office feeling inspired to take on the world.

16. FRIDAY NIGHT

My date with Kelsey is going to have to wait until tomorrow since she's doing something with her parents at their church. I'm not sure what kind of thing people do at church on a Friday night, but I didn't ask. Asking might mean she'd invite me, and I just—I'm not ready for that.

Not just yet.

I feel tired and restless and bored and anxious in this empty cabin.

For some reason, I'm thinking about my age.

Seventeen is not thirteen, but it sure isn't twenty-seven. It is almost. It is not quite there. It is about time and anxious to move on and does anyone care?

It's big and tall but not enough to be legal or official.

Seventeen is so close but not just yet.

Not just yet.

I listen to music on my headphones and scan the Internet, trying not to think of my age. Trying not to think of my fate. Trying not to think, but letting others think for me. To talk for me. To show for me. To act out for me.

I've got a million choices at my fingertips, and it feels good.

My room feels cold, but I turn up the volume on my headset, and the cold seems to stay away.

My room feels lonely, but I scan YouTube and find something to make me feel surrounded and funny.

Maybe others watch, but I don't care. I don't feel special, and I don't feel like trying. Not tonight.

The empty downstairs doesn't echo when I'm listening to stuff I've downloaded for free. I'm watching strangers doing strange things. The world is strange, and I'm only seventeen, wondering if it's going to get stranger. How could it? How could it ever?

The beats bounce, and I try to keep up because if I do I won't think of everything else.

They'll be distant memories if the volume gets turned up loud enough.

They'll be forgotten until tomorrow morning when the cold rips the blanket off of me and laughs.

I can't see God being happy with all of us. Not just me and not just this town, but everything and everyone. Doing their own thing in their own way.

The news talks about all the messes in our country and everywhere else, and it makes me think that God finally said, "Do it your own way."

I tried and I failed. Miserably.

But I don't feel like reading the Bible. I feel like listening to music.

I don't feel like praying. I feel like posting something online.

Could it really be that strong, the wind blowing against this cabin, rattling the walls and the floor?

Is it trying to tell me something?

I look at the sleeping figure of my dog and wish I could trade places. Sometimes.

The peaceful sleep she seems to have.

I'd love a little of that.

I'd love a little peace.

But the beats go on, and I close my eyes and I see Jocelyn avoiding me and Lily teasing me and Poe angry at me and Kelsey blushing around me.

Will the songs always remind me, and if so, will I ever be able to change the tracks?

Maybe I need a new genre, a new playlist.

I don't need the synths anymore. I need an … an accordion. Yes, an accordion. An accordion won't remind me.

But I listen to the drum machines and the synthesizers, and I remember.

The night washes the house with black and forgets to dry it off, leaving it shivering and cold and needing a nice warm blanket.

Seventeen-year-olds shouldn't be thinking this way, but yeah, I guess Staunch and Marsh were right. I've never been a typical kid.

Then again, does any kid ever feel typical?

Really?

17. SOMEONE ELSE'S STORY

"So have you decided what you're going to do about college?"

We're halfway through our meal at one of those sandwich and soup places in the Asheville mall. I'm glad that Kelsey suggested coming here—not that there were many options. There's nothing much to do in Solitary, unless we stayed at her house and rented a movie. Instead, we're going to see the latest picture starring Ryan Gosling.

"It seems like everybody is asking that lately," I tell her.

"It is January, you know."

"Maybe I won't go to college. Maybe I'll just get on my bike and drive across the country."

"And who's going to pay for your gas? And food?"

"Yeah, yeah. Life would be a lot better if we didn't have to think about money."

"You don't want to wait until it's too late."

Kelsey is a rule-keeper. Someone gives a rule, and Kelsey keeps it. I, on the other hand, don't like rules. Or deadlines. Or stuff that others tell me I should do.

That's called stubborn.

"You sound like Mr. Taggart."

"Why?"

I tell her about getting him as a guidance counselor, and Kelsey can only laugh.

"I'm surprised he's still at school. I heard he got kicked out of coaching football for getting in a fight with a kid from another school. Not another coach, but a kid."

"Glad I'm getting 'guidance' from him."

I talk a little about summer school, then realize where that's heading. I stop because I don't want Lily to come up.

"I might follow you back to Chicago," I tell her, switching subjects.

"You're going to go to Covenant?"

"I don't think I have the grades to get in there. And it's probably too expensive."

"Then where?"

"Mr. Taggart is suggesting a junior college. Guess he's dreaming big for me. I don't know. At this point I don't really care, you know? I just want to get away from Solitary."

As I take my last bite of my sandwich I see a tall guy, in his thirties maybe, by himself sipping a drink and reading a magazine. He's sitting at a table nearby, facing me. Kelsey can't see him.

I didn't see him sit down, but I notice him now.

He glances up and looks at me. Then he smiles.

And I know.

He's not just some random guy sitting there.

This guy is spying on me. Or not even "spying," because it's too obvious and he doesn't care.

He's keeping tabs on me.

That's just your imagination.

When I look back at him, he's reading his magazine.

"Chris?"

"Yeah."

"What's wrong?"

I look at Kelsey and shake my head. "Nothing."

"You look—-different."

"I do?"

"You sure you're okay?"

I look at her, and then it comes back to me. I can't help the memories.

Rushing to Jocelyn, only to find her dead with her throat slit and her blood dripping out ...

I close my eyes and wipe them, but I can't wipe the pain away.

Seeing Lily's body not far from mine in the woods at the bottom of the hill through the cracked windshield as I slowly fade in and out and bleed to death myself ...

"Chris?"

"Yeah, sorry. I just have a headache."

"I'm sorry."

I look at her, confused. "What? You're sorry?"

"For bringing up college and the future."

I shake my head. "That's not why I have the headache."

My eyes go back to the table where the guy is sitting. He looks like he's content to stay as long as necessary.

"We don't have to see a movie."

"No," I tell her. "I want to go."

I want a break. A little relief. To sit in a dark room and see someone else's story and know that someone is next to me in the dark, watching the same story.

I'm tired of being alone. I know Mom and Dad had their issues and they couldn't work things out, but I know that two will always be better than one. Especially around here.

Eventually we stand and leave the table. As we do, I look at the man.

He grins at me as if sizing me up.

I don't look away.

I don't smile a polite smile. Instead, I grit my teeth and toughen up my eyes and know that this is what's ahead.

I'm standing in between this stranger and Kelsey, and that's what I'm going to continue to do.

They don't frighten me anymore.

Even if they should.

18. RYAN GOSLING

Kelsey lets me drive her car back to my house just to let me feel a little more manly. I mean—we just spent two hours watching Ryan Gosling be a macho man and woo the ladies and be tough but tender, so I need a little help.

Driving back to my cabin, I imagine for the moment that I'm Gosling and this is my woman. Not my girl but my lady. That we're older and that we can do anything we want and that I'm her lover and protector.

It's nice making up things.

I pull the car around in my driveway and think about the empty house in front of us. But then I ditch that thought. Because it's too soon and because it's Kelsey and because of what happened when I last had those empty-cabin-all-to-myself thoughts.

The engine is running and the car is in neutral and I can see those big blue eyes looking at me in the semi-darkness.

"This was fun," I say.

But that's Buckley talking, not Gosling. He would never say something so lame.

"You can, uh, come in for a while if you want, you know?" I say.

Still far to go to be Gosling, buddy.

"I better go."

She doesn't know your cabin is empty anyway, remember? She thinks your mom is here.

I nod and start to say something very Buckley-esque, and then Kelsey moves over and kisses me.

It's a very non-Kelsey-like kiss.

But as we embrace for I don't know and don't care how long, I think another thought.

Maybe this is a Kelsey kiss that nobody else except me knows about.

And I don't have to be Ryan Gosling to get a kiss like that.

She finally moves and smiles and then waits.

I guess there's nothing left to say because she just said this.

I have a lot more I want to say and a lot more I want to do, but I climb out of the car and head back up to the empty cabin.

Knowing I'll dream of her.

I turn and watch her car pull away in the darkness. Then something in me tears away.

I think of the tossed car off the side of the road like a scrap of garbage that ended up killing Lily.

I stop breathing for a moment.

Who knows who's watching me now? Or following Kelsey back home?

I can't be with her every moment. I can't fully protect her.

"God protect her," I say out loud.

That's all I can do. Even if I still don't really know if that's doing anything.

19. THE WIZARD OF OZ

I'm here because of Kelsey.

And, I guess, because this is the first step to the final page. The big thing that's supposed to be on the horizon. The thing that's supposed to happen that I'm a part of—that I'm needed for—that all this fuss has been about.

So I'm starting at the doorway to New Beginnings Church. I walk inside, hoping that Pastor Marsh sees me. I want him to think that I'm going along with the plan. And that as long as I do what they tell me to do, they'll leave my mom and Kelsey and anybody else I care for alone.

That's the plan.

I remember that storage room downstairs and still want to know what's up with that coffin. And the mannequin I saw.

This makes me think of chapstick guy from the other afternoon. The man who claimed to be into "dark arts," Mr. Mannequin himself.

Maybe I don't need to know any more about those things.

"Christopher."

Anytime someone calls me that, I want to run and hide. My father used to say that when he had to discipline me. Every teacher who announced that I was new called me that.

Pastor Marsh stands there by the doorway to the sanctuary as if he wants to give me a hug.

"Good to see you."

I nod as I walk by and shake his hand.

Even his hand feels weak and dirty.

"Stick around so I can talk with you after the service," he says. Then he smiles and adds, "Please."

Well, fine, now that you said please and happen to be keeping my mom in some loony bin.

I nod again and find a seat.

I don't want to be here.

My slogan for the last sixteen months.

There is nothing strange that Pastor Marsh says during his nice little sermon. At no point does he raise up his hands and say "Slay the beast!" or something weird like that.

No.

But I've been to churches before so I know. This message really isn't much of a sermon. It's more like some self-help session about feeling good and believing in yourself.

Newsflash, Marsh: I tried to do that, and it doesn't work.

He'd tell me that I don't know a thing because I'm only a teenager.

But deep down inside I feel like I do know a few things. And here, in this seat, I realize that this is just a building with people in it. It's no more of a church than our high school or my cabin or that place with the creepy stones where Jocelyn died.

Pastor Marsh never reads a Bible verse. He refers to a verse here and there—a psalm or something like that—but he never talks about the Bible. And he never, ever mentions Jesus Christ.

I think a bomb would go off if he did.

Even the prayers are strange, because he prays them with his eyes open. I guess mine are open too, since I spot him looking out. But it's like the president's speech on national television that's annoying because it's interrupting *Survivor*. It's well spoken, but I wonder if there's any kind of meaning behind it.

"I remember your uncle riding that motorcycle around town," Marsh says to me in a way that looks as if he just swallowed a worm.

We're sitting in Brennan's with drinks in front of us waiting for our lunch. I did as he asked and waited for him after the service. Then I did as he asked and followed him into town, and he led me in here.

I get the idea that he's trying to remind me of Mom. That he's rubbing it in my face. I haven't brought her up, but then again I don't need to. She's one of those elephants in the room. Like Jocelyn. Like Marsh Falls. Like everything.

"You haven't seen Robert lately, have you?"

I shake my head and try my best to act casual. I don't think Marsh can read minds, but I know he's smart enough to be able to detect teens who haven't mastered lying yet.

"He really thought he was something, in the beginning. When he came back and started snooping around, not having a clue. I have to admit—you both share the same DNA. Getting involved with the wrong lady at the wrong time. Only for your uncle it was a bit more serious, since that particular lady was married."

I don't want to say anything like *I know* or ask him how he found out. I can feel myself blushing for some reason.

"I really wanted to make him pay," Marsh says in a distant sort of way that seems like someone telling a story around a campfire. "But I couldn't. They wouldn't let me. In the end it didn't matter. You both share the same DNA, except for one thing, Chris. You are a brave soul. Your uncle is a coward. A wife-stealer and a coward."

I sip my Coke. Is this what he wanted to talk to me about?

Did they hear Uncle Robert at the cabin? Do they care that he's back?

"Those two deserve each other, if you want to be honest. You've seen *The Wizard of Oz*, haven't you? Your uncle is the lion looking for courage. Heidi—well, she's the tin man looking for a heart."

He smiles, then reaches over and grabs my wrist and holds it firmly.

Too bad Mom's not around to come here and see this and take a spatula to his face.

"So, Chris, listen to me. Okay? You listening good?"

I nod as he lets my hand go.

"Are you going to be the scarecrow who's looking for a brain? I really hope not, because I know you're smart. So you listen. It doesn't really matter whether you're falling for another pretty little girl who doesn't belong in your life. You have to learn the hard way. Maybe it will be easy because she'll move off and leave you, and it will be for the better. It doesn't matter if your uncle is around or not. What matters is that you do exactly as you're told from here on out."

"I know. Staunch made that clear."

"I'm just here to help," Marsh tells me for the one hundredth time.

"Yeah, that really felt like helping."

"Here's the picture, Chris. Let me paint it to you crystal clear."

I nod as his eyes narrow behind those glasses. He scans the room, then reaches over and takes a white napkin that my drink was supposed to be sitting on. He opens it up and then puts his palm on it.

"This is what I used to put my faith in. This was my God. White, wholesome, pure. Like the sun and the stars. That's what I believed, or thought I believed. Did I believe in the Devil and evil and hell? No. Others around me did, but I didn't. I studied the Bible, but many of those stories were simply fairy tales to me. I could believe in a God, but I couldn't believe in the other stuff. Then I realized one day that it was the other way around. That from the very beginning of my miserable life all I'd ever—ever—been able to see were the darkness and the evil. I realized that the Devil was very real and that hell didn't start when you died, but it started when you were here on earth. For some, like me, it started during the teen years."

This is the most passionate he's sounded all day long.

It scares me. A lot.

"I grew to realize that maybe God was there, that maybe He was all those things I once thought, but I also realized that He was long gone. If He ever was there, He's not anymore."

Marsh picks up the napkin and slowly rips it in half. Then rips it in half again. Then keeps doing that until he takes it and crunches it in his fist.

"And I realized what Staunch has said and what this place has proven and what history has really taught us: that evil has a power, and that power is a wonderful thing. I no longer questioned evil and its place. Nor did I have any problems believing in the supernatural. But I finally realized my place. Because I wasn't the lion, Chris—I had the guts to admit it to myself and the rest of my world. I wasn't the tin man, because I've always had a beating heart more than most. And I sure wasn't the scarecrow. I knew exactly what I was thinking and feeling. I was smart enough to finally embrace the path before me. It's the only path, really. That's what you have to realize. Because as I said, you, Chris, are different. You're special. I'm just crumbs."

He lets go of the wadded-up ball of paper scraps.

"You can have anything you want. There are things that you're too young to even know that you want. You will have a long life before you. And you won't fear anything, not the sunset or the sunrise or your last breath. Because you'll know that in the end it doesn't really matter."

Marsh pauses, his eyes narrowing, his face growing dim. "Nobody's on the other line, Chris. He left a long time ago."

The server comes with our plates of food, and I see my hamburger and suddenly feel a bit nauseous. It takes everything in me to eat, but I do it quickly because I have no idea what to say.

Marsh grins, takes one of my fries since he is having a salad, eats it, and then laughs.

"Okay, fine, I take it back. You can't have everything. When you get to my age, you'll have to cut back, unless you want to be packing on the pounds. But there again, you're taller than I am. It's just unfair, everything you've been given. Just completely unfair."

He takes another fry.

I want to dump the whole plate over his head and leave.

"There will be official things coming up, Chris," Marsh says after a long and awkward silence. "Rituals. Things that I can't say I care for, but that have been handed down for generations. All I did was have the sense to bring them back. Not because I believe in them, not really. They're all for show. Like a royal wedding. You saw that, right? Did you?"

"Uh, yeah," I say.

"For a second I was wondering if you'd lost your voice. Do you know someone said that the royal wedding cost around sixty million? When people are dying from not having food and water in this world. When the economy is taking a dive and people are looking for work. But they had to do it. Why? 'Cause it was symbolic. It was all for show. And I thought—when I finally came back here after getting my education and getting some experience—I thought I'd come back here to try and make a name for myself. But I wasn't a Kinner. I was no Chris Buckley. But I could read and discover the history of this place. So that's what I brought."

"The rituals?"

Marsh nods.

"Staunch, of course, does whatever Kinner wants, but I was able to convince the old man to start these again. And somehow it worked."

He looks at me as the realization dawns on me.

This is the man who killed Jocelyn.

"All I wanted to do was follow the yellow brick road. I discovered that the old man behind the mask—well, he's the real deal, and you don't mess with him. But his time is short, and there needs to be someone new. Someone in the lineage. The wonderful, glorious family line."

Marsh curses, then takes another bite of his salad.

"But when the wizard is gone, Chris, that will just leave us. Staunch, too, but—well, that story is for another day. But there'll just be the two of us. And I can help you out. I can worry about things you won't have to worry about. All we have to do is play their game and go through the rituals and say what we believe, and that will be all. Got it?"

I look at Jeremiah Marsh's face, which I've grown to hate.

"Got it?" he asks again.

"Yeah. Got it."

I wonder if he can read my mind now.

I'm going to kill you, buddy. This time I'm going to wound you and make sure that you die.

If he wants to know who I am, I'll call myself Dorothy.

And I'll call him the Wicked Witch. Either of the East or the West.

Whichever one Dorothy ends up killing.

20. SAP

You THERE?

It's easy to read Kelsey's late-night text in the dark.

No, I joke.

ARE YOU SLEEPING?

YES. NOW I'M SLEEP-TEXTING.

FUNNY.

WHAT'S UP? I type.

NOTHING.

WHY AREN'T YOU SLEEPING?

For a moment—a brief anxious moment—I worry that something has happened to her, all because of me, the special chosen boy ...

JUST CAN'T, is all she says.

EVERYTHING OKAY?

I MISS YOU.

The three words surprise me.

I can't sleep either. That's becoming somewhat of the norm. I'm worried about what nightmares I'm going to have, what's going to happen tonight and tomorrow. I'm worried about my mom and about others like Kelsey.

But Kelsey—

She misses me.

SORRY, she writes after I find myself at a loss for words.

DON'T BE SORRY. THAT WAS VERY SWEET TO SAY.

YOU SEEM TO LIKE THE NOT-SO-SWEET GIRLS.

I think of Jocelyn and Lily. Yeah, she's got a point.

Sweet and sexy aren't always the same thing.

But what I'd love to tell Kelsey is that she's both.

Of course, I don't and I won't. I don't want her to take it the wrong way.

I LIKE YOU, is what I tell her.

BUT FOR HOW LONG?

WHY ARE YOU WORRIED ABOUT THAT?

BECAUSE SUMMER ISN'T VERY FAR AWAY, she writes.

It sure is to me.

YOU MIGHT REGRET WANTING ME TO STICK AROUND.

No I won't, Kelsey texts.

You better get to sleep.

You too. Pleasant dreams.

Those only come when you're around, I write and send.

I feel stupid seconds after, but Kelsey wishes me a good night and I guess it wasn't *that* stupid. I don't know.

Sometimes guys at school will show me dirty texts to some girl and it feels just silly and strange to me. I get it, sure, but I'd rather find someone like Kelsey to tell my real thoughts and feelings to. Sure, there are feelings there that I'd love to one day tell her, or even more, show her. Guy-girl stuff. I'd love for her to know that she really is something special.

But I guess the way to show that is to be a gentleman.

Now I'm sounding like Dad.

I remember him once telling me that. Maybe it's his voice in my head. I don't know.

Deep down I really think I'm a sap. It's easy to hide it. But with Kelsey, for some reason I don't want to hide it.

Which may or may not be a good thing.

21. RIDICULOUS TIMING

You know how sometimes you'll be walking toward someone in a crowd and they're looking your way, but you know for a fact that they're not really looking at you? Right? This happens after school on Wednesday as I'm walking out the glass doors, talking with Kelsey. We see a woman at the base of the stairs staring up at us. She's wearing dress pants and a fancy leather jacket and is probably thirty-something. She looks tough but attractive. She stands out, since very few African Americans work at Harrington.

Her dark eyes don't seem to leave me, and I actually start to feel a bit nervous walking down to the parking lot.

"Chris Buckley?" she calls out.

I nod.

She comes up to us. "My name is Diane Banks. Do you have a few minutes?"

"I'll call you later," Kelsey tells me.

I nod at her and then glance at the woman. I know what she's about to say.

It's something to do with my mom. She relapsed. Or maybe she killed herself.

"I'm with the FBI," Diane tells me.

I almost want to laugh as I wait for more.

"Can we go back into the school for a few minutes?"

"What's this about?" I ask.

"I will explain inside."

She's no-nonsense, and she appears like a well-put-together business lady. Someone who fits downtown Chicago, not any place around Solitary.

We go back inside out of the cold, and for a minute I wonder if she's going to lead me into Principal Harking's office. Instead, she walks into the first unoccupied classroom and turns on the light.

"I just want a little privacy," she says.

I slowly walk into the room, and she shuts the door.

"Chris, please, have a seat."

"I can stand."

She nods, then scans the room before taking out a card and giving it to me.

"That's my card," Diane says.

"Do you have a badge?"

"Do you need to see it?"

I think about it for a moment, then shrug. She reaches into her jacket and pulls out a wallet, then shows me a badge inside.

"Anybody can reproduce one of these," she says. "Or can come up with a card. That's my information on there—my cell phone where you can reach me."

Her skin is flawless, like a model or something. I want to tell her she's too good-looking to be an FBI agent.

Of course, I don't.

"What's this about?"

"I'm investigating the disappearance of Jocelyn Evans."

It's been just over a year since Jocelyn died.

Now someone shows up looking for her?

No way. I don't buy this for a second.

"Do you know anything about her disappearance?"

I shake my head.

For a moment I think of Jared.

Liar.

Then I think of Lily.

Actress.

This lady is no more an FBI agent than some rising starlet in Hollywood working on a new ABC show.

"Chris, I have been in touch with someone who knows you. She's the one who first alerted us to this case. Your friend Poe. Moved with her family to Charlotte."

Her eyes are unflinching, and she doesn't appear to be lying.

You have no idea who's lying and who's not.

"I don't know."

"You don't know Ms. Graham?" a slightly irritated voice asks.

"No. I know Poe. Sure."

"Have you been in touch with her recently?"

"No."

"What about Jocelyn Evans? When was the last time you saw her?"

"Right after Christmas last year."

"What happened?"

"She moved away with her aunt."

"And when was the last time you spoke to her aunt?"

I shake my head. "When they came over to our cabin. Right before they left."

Don't say "disappeared" don't you dare say that.

I'm not about to start talking to this lady, who is no FBI agent. She might be from the same place they got Lily.

I see the empty chairs surrounding the one I'm leaning on. Even now, so long after coming to this school, this place has a cold, lifeless feel to it. This school belongs in a horror movie, not some kid's life.

"Your friend said you might not be cooperative."

"What else did she tell you?"

"Enough," Diane Banks says. "Enough to get me here."

Is that even your real name? Couldn't you be a little more creative with your alias?

For the next ten minutes, she asks me questions that I barely answer. She soon realizes that she's not going to get anything. Not from me.

"Chris, I am here to help."

"Jocelyn moved a *year* ago," I say. "And now you show up?"

I say this because whoever she is, I'm wanting her to know the timing sucks.

You're too late.

"It took your friend a while to reach out to us. There are reasons why. And you know them."

I have my arms folded and I'm just staring at her, not biting and not flinching.

"I'm going to be around for a while," the woman tells me. "I'm staying at the Blackberry B and B."

I laugh out loud. "Is that the one close to the downtown of Solitary?"

"Yes."

"For real. You're staying there."

"And what's wrong with that?" she asks.

Couldn't you at least pick a better spot? Maybe somewhere different from where Lily stayed?

"It's really the only place in the area," Ms. "Diane Banks" says.

"Okay then," I say.

"Chris, listen—if there are bad things going on in this town, you need to tell me. You need to let me help you."

"I'm fine."

She looks at me, but I'm not going to break.

You don't know how strong this place is making me.

"Keep my card. You might need it."

"Will do," I say.

22. ABOUT TIME

This week I start something monumental.

Driver's ed.

And it reminds me of how much of a loser I really am. Because I'm surrounded by freshmen and sophomores. You can start taking that class when you're fourteen and a half.

Nice.

I'll be taking a two-hour after-school class twice a week for seven and a half weeks.

After those thirty hours of classroom time, which will bring me to the end of March, I'll need six hours behind the wheel.

And then and only then will I be able to drive.

I do the math in my mind as I speed home on my motorcycle from the first class.

23. THE MOVIE I'M IN

That second week in January comes and goes with a strange nothing-ness. Nobody shows up at the cabin. Nobody calls me to tell me they're coming home or being abducted. Nothing weird or sinister happens at the cabin, or school, or on the way from my cabin to school.

Nothing much happens, period.

Kelsey invites me over to her house on Friday night to watch a movie. I tell her great and request that it not be another Ryan Gosling flick. I can only take so much hunk per month. She laughs and tells me I can choose whatever movie I'd like. I'm not really that interested in watching a movie. I'm just glad to be hanging out with her.

And glad that I'm not alone in my cabin, listening to the wind outside.

I get to Kelsey's around six. It's already dark out, and I ring the doorbell, wondering who will answer the door. Kelsey greets me and welcomes me inside a house that smells like tomato sauce and pepperoni.

"We already got the pizza," she says in a bashful way. "I hope that's okay."

"Yeah. It's great. Thanks."

I'm reminded of past Friday nights back home. Usually I'd be at someone else's house, hanging out, playing video games, or watching TV, and their parents would order pizza. We never did this much at our house because my dad was usually working and Mom usually had other things going on.

I suddenly realize that I don't remember much of Mom and Dad at home in Illinois. Except, of course, after they'd made the decision to get a divorce.

Sometimes it feels like they divorced me.

Kelsey's mom gives me a big smile and a bigger hug as I enter the kitchen behind Kelsey. I don't think I've ever felt this welcomed or so warm at that cabin fifteen minutes away from here.

Too bad there's not a direct tunnel connecting the two.

She asks me about school and my mom, and I talk as if I'm an ordinary kid talking about ordinary stuff. Of course I can't tell her the truth.

Mom's locked up in rehab so that I'll do what I'm told and become the next leader of the Ghoulie Tribe of Solitary.

At first I think that tonight is going to be difficult, with a sit-down dinner and more conversation with her parents, but it truly is casual. Kelsey's father is coming home late, so dinner is grabbing a plate and some pizza and sitting in the family room watching television.

After an hour of this, I feel quite comfortable here.

Maybe I can spend the night. And the rest of the semester.

"You're kinda quiet tonight," Kelsey says as we're watching a sitcom.

"So I'm usually really loud?"

"No. Everything okay?"

"Sure. Just—just don't have anything big to say."

"Okay."

She's leaning into me on the couch, and I don't want her to move. I might move closer to her if we were alone, but I don't want to get too close with her mom nearby and her dad coming home any minute.

"So what movie do you want to watch?" she eventually asks, as she grabs the remote and scans the options on their Dish network.

"Anything but horror," I say, trying to be funny but not really joking.

I think my days of watching horror films are done.

Who needs to watch one when you're living one?

"Comedy? Action? Hmm."

She *hmms* the romance that she scrolls by.

"Let's watch some epic love story," I say.

"You call *that* epic?"

"Okay, not that, no."

"What's your definition of epic love story?"

"Oh, you know," I say. "Big. Huge. Like, uh—"

"Epic?"

I poke her side, and she jumps. I've discovered that she's very ticklish, and it's cute to see her bounce like that.

"I don't mean what's your definition of the word," Kelsey says. "What do you mean by an 'epic' love story?"

"You know, against the odds, real tragic. Involving faraway places and lots of violence."

She laughs. "Lots of violence, huh?"

"Absolutely. An abusive parent. Lots of running."

"What?"

I keep going, making it up as I talk. "One of the leads falling to their knees and saying 'No' real loud. Like 'Noooooooooooooooo.'"

"You should be a screenwriter," Kelsey says.

"You think?"

"No."

"It has to have big sweeping movie music. You know. Like *Gone with the Wind*."

"That has sweeping movie music?"

I shrug. "I haven't seen it. But I'm sure it must."

"You should also be a movie critic."

"Seriously?"

"No."

This is far better than watching an epic love story. We keep this up for half an hour before we realize we haven't even started to choose a movie. We soon get on the topic of what genre we'd pick if we were to be inserted into a film.

"If I had to pick, I'd be in a nice, simple romance," Kelsey says.

"What about a romantic comedy?"

"No. Those are usually too crass to be funny. No, I'd be in something set in the South. A nice love story like *The Notebook*."

"They separate for years, and then at the end the woman has Alzheimer's."

Kelsey glances at me and thinks for a minute. "Yeah, maybe I'd pick a different one than that."

"I'd be in a comedy," I say. "Definitely a comedy."

"You are funny."

"Not really," I say. "I'd pick something with a bunch of funny people around me. Something crazy and hilarious."

"It would probably have bathroom humor. At least."

"There are worse things," I say.

She waits for me to share more, but I don't want to share anything.

I don't want to tell her that I've been in a movie for quite some time, and it's a horror flick shown around Halloween. It's the kind of movie that makes you dart up the dark stairs by two at night and pull the cover of your blanket up by your nose.

That's the movie I'm in, until Kelsey walks by and changes the channel.

24. THE BRIDGE

I leave before Kelsey's father gets home. I don't want him coming home wondering what I'm doing there so late. Not that I think he'd mind, and Kelsey assures me it's fine, but regardless I tell her that it's time. She's comfortable on the couch with her legs over my lap, and I think she'd be content to fall asleep like that. I would be too.

Maybe it's because I know Mr. Page is coming home any minute. Or maybe it's because I don't want to rush things. Because deep down, I'm afraid to.

Since every girl I like ends up dead or gone.

Maybe it's all of those things. Maybe that's why I don't spend much time kissing Kelsey before I leave. I know that she wants to—I can tell by the way she looks at me. And I do kiss her once before leaving. Not a good-bye, brotherly, friendly kiss, but a real good one. A kind that might be perfect simply because it leaves you wanting more.

What do you know about kissing, you dork?

I'm driving through the night thinking of kissing Kelsey and about epic love stories. It's cold, but I'm smart enough to be wearing a cap and gloves and Uncle Robert's leather jacket. Well, maybe not *that* smart, because I'm not wearing a helmet, but at least I'm warm.

The winding roads tend to look the same, but as I make the usual turns that lead to my house, I find myself on a dirt lane nobody else is going to be driving on this time of night. Then I see a road I've never noticed before jutting to the left up a hill.

The Crag's Inn.

That's what I first think, because even though I've managed to see Iris again, I still haven't ever been able to find the road leading up to the former lodge on top of the mountain.

No, this isn't the same road. But it looks similar.

I slow down and then decide to see where it leads. It's after midnight, and nobody's waiting up for me at the cabin. At least I hope nobody's waiting up for me. If there is, I'd better stay out here for a long time.

The road is narrower than the main roads around Solitary, the trees closer to the sides. Perhaps I've always missed this road because the overgrowth has been so dense. Now the trees are barren and look like skinny kids huddling together on a cold night.

I drive for ten or fifteen minutes until there is a turn in the road so abrupt that I'm glad to notice it before driving off into the woods. I slow down, and then I see another path descending into the woods.

I steer my bike toward the path so I can see.

The light shows a narrow path flattening with a stone edge on either side, then continuing on into the woods. For a second I can't make it out, then I hear the sound of a creek and realize that what I'm looking at is an old bridge.

I turn off my bike but leave the light on.

This might be the moment the couple in the audience or the critic in the seat goes, *Come on Chris get a clue what's wrong with you and why haven't you learned?* But this is far less frightening than the abandoned cabin I found in the woods. And definitely less freaky than the dark underground tunnel that I can only go forward or backward in. Yeah, sure, I've learned there are some nasty things in these woods, like demon dogs and lisping old men, but I've also come to understand there are other things.

I still never know when a bridge in the middle of the woods might lead me back to Iris. Or Lily. Or Jocelyn.

It feels unusually cold right here. I look around but can't make out anything in the pitch black.

I hear the sound of a cracking branch. Then something shuffling on dead leaves in the woods. The crinkle of stone underneath someone's feet.

Then I see it.

No. Not it, but them.

Figures standing on the edge of the bridge. Dark figures—a group of them—all standing there waiting for something.

Maybe waiting for me.

I can feel my heart racing as I squint to try and make out faces or features. But all I see are these shadows in the shapes of men.

For some reason, I recall the boxcar in the middle of nowhere, which I opened and discovered death inside.

Get out of here Chris now.

I've been scared so many times before around this place, but I'm not scared now, not totally. A part of me wonders who these people are and if I can in any way—

Then one figure emerges out of the pack—maybe six or eight total—and starts walking across the bridge toward me.

I want to see a face.

But as the seconds scratch by, I don't see any face. The figure is cloaked in black and seems to be carrying something large and heavy in one hand.

The light is now directly on his face, but I still don't see anything. I don't see skin or hair or features or anything.

Just a shadow.

Okay bright guy now's the time to bolt before things get really bad.

I start up my bike and am thankful that it kicks in right away, and I head back toward the main street where I came in.

I'll check this place out in the daytime. When I can see faces and figures more clearly and the night's not playing tricks.

I shiver and drive as fast as I can.

But I keep expecting a cold hand to touch my neck at any moment and jerk me off the bike and take me back to the hole the figures came from.

25. SOME KIND OF HERO

I'm sitting on the couch about ten in the morning, watching ESPN and eating a bowl of cereal, when I hear a key unlock the front door and look up to see Uncle Robert walk inside. As if this place belongs to him (and yeah, it still sorta does). As if I haven't been on my own since coming back to this place (and yeah, I have).

"Finished with breakfast?" he asks as he looks at the bowl on my lap.

"Where've you been?"

"I'll show you right now," Robert tells me.

He's wearing a denim jacket that seems to be too thin for the cold weather outside. His leather jacket that I borrowed last night is on the couch beside me. He makes a *huh* sound as he picks it up.

"I hope you don't mind me borrowing it."

Robert shakes his head. "Nope. Never wearing that again. And never riding that bike again."

"Really?"

"Yeah. Nearly got killed riding that thing."

"Don't tell me," I say as I stand up.

"What?"

"I don't want to hear that the bike is possessed or something like that."

"It wasn't the bike," Robert says. "It was the driver. Especially when he likes to drink."

I glance at Robert, and I understand what he's saying.

"Why did you stop working for Iris?" I ask.

"It wasn't for me."

"Being at the Crag's Inn?"

"No. Being around *them*."

The way he says *them* shuts me up.

Because I know what he's talking about.

Of course, I can't say it out loud because I'll sound stupid. But I think back to the people I saw at the Crag's Inn. And the people I saw last night by the bridge.

"Come on, let's get going," Robert says.

"Mind if I wear your jacket?"

"It's already yours."

The outside of the silver Nissan Xterra looks worse than the inside. Somehow, the interior isn't just clean but feels new, with leather seats and a souped-up stereo.

"The rusted and dented look is for show," Uncle Robert says. "This thing looks like it's going to break down, but it actually has a brand-new engine in it. With new tires."

"For your getaway."

Tired eyes and a messy beard turn my way. "I wouldn't joke about it if I were you."

He drives down the road away from the cabin and, after taking a few turns, away from the town of Solitary.

"Where are we headed?"

"To a safe place where nobody will be listening to us."

"Were they listening to us at the cabin?"

"They might be. I don't know. I'm just taking precautions. Just 'cause they have no more use for me doesn't mean they're done with me. They like to dispose of loose ends. Like your friend Wade Sims. Remember him?"

"You know about that?"

Robert nods. "I saw him chained up on Staunch's property. And then I heard the news that he 'crashed' his car."

I think about Wade, the lowlife who lived with Jocelyn's aunt, the man I shot to protect Jocelyn. He left Solitary for a while, but he made the mistake of coming back.

"Everybody seems to know more about everything than I do."

"They think they know. But they can't see. I can see like you, Chris. Trust me—it only gets more intense."

"What do you mean, more intense?"

"I mean worse."

He turns up the rock music blaring from the stereo till it's shaking my seat. I guess he doesn't want to talk anymore about that.

The winding, rocky road (is there any other kind around here?) eventually stops at a dead end near what looks like an old barn on a hill. When we get out and walk toward it, Uncle Robert tells me that this used to be an old mill running beside a creek that's almost dried up now. As we walk over the crest of the hill, I notice the big, rusted-out waterwheel down the hill right next to a shed. A wooden drain with a top that looks like a ladder connects the waterwheel to the barnlike structure.

We head to the small house right next to it.

"Is this where you've been staying?"

Robert nods and then stops by the door, examining something at the bottom.

"I put tape there every time I leave to see if the door's been opened," he says as he pulls the creaking door and then heads inside.

There's really not much to see. It's just one big, empty room with a floor of old wooden planks that appear to be rotting. There are some empty beer cans tossed around, some used cigarettes, but that's about it.

"Home sweet home," he says as he goes to the back of the room and gets a folding chair. He opens it and then puts it in front of me. I feel forced to sit.

"You really sleep here?"

"When I have to," he says. "When it was warmer I spent a lot of nights outside. I have a hole in the floor where I store things. A sleeping bag. A kerosene heater. I don't stay here. It's just for hiding out."

"But why?"

"Why do I stay here? You think anybody's coming up here to check for missing persons?"

"No, I mean why did you start hiding out in the first place?"

Robert is leaning against the side of the shelter. He takes a pack of cigarettes out of his coat pocket and lights one.

For a moment, my uncle looks across the room at the bare wall, trying to think of what he wants to say. I sit on the wobbly, uncomfortable chair wondering if someone's going to break down the door any second.

"When I finally realized the truth about me and about our family, I just went a little postal." He chuckles in a grim sort of way.

"I mean—here I was in my thirties and the prime of my life, and suddenly I discover all this."

He curses and takes a drag of his cigarette.

"Do you know why my father was gunned down in cold blood on a Chicago street in the middle of winter? Why you were never able to meet your grandfather? I was twenty-one, and I thought it was just another bad thing to happen to Tara and me. But no. It was part of this decaying, rotten hellhole of a town. My father tried to get us out. But there's no escaping. Not for me or for you or for anybody with blood ties. That's when I realized that there was no going back."

"No going back to where?"

"To the life I once knew. That carefree life of doing whatever I wanted to do. I don't like seeing visions in the middle of the day or at night. I don't like seeing ghosts. And I didn't want any part of what that evil man is doing with his followers."

"You mean Walter Kinner?"

"Yeah. So I refused. But I—I made a mistake. I tried to help Heidi Marsh out. And instead of helping her out, I just made things worse."

"How?"

Robert laughs and flicks the cigarette across the floor. "I fell in love."

He walks across the floor like some restless animal. "I don't know if it's just that we're stupid males or if it's our DNA or what. But falling for the wrong girl is what we do, I guess. I mean—you come down here, and what do you do? The same stupid thing."

He laughs and curses at the same time.

"I tried to help Heidi out. I really did. Marsh has her drugged up most of the time, and when she's not doped up she's scared for her life. He's ruined her. And he wanted to ruin me, too. I had to make a choice. I was going to try and escape with Heidi, but she just couldn't. She was too afraid. So I had to let her go. But I couldn't leave."

"Why not?"

"Because love doesn't just go away overnight. It's different when you're older, Chris. You'll understand that one day. I just—I'm no hero."

I look at him, and I realize that he's right. He's no hero. A hero would have fought for his love. A hero would have warned his family. A hero would have risked death.

"Oh, don't give me that look." He curses again. "I swear you're your mother. She used to give me these looks that made me feel so freaking guilty. It was all I got. Guilt, guilt, guilt. I didn't kill our parents. I wasn't supposed to take over when they died. But sometimes I think Tara wanted me to. Once the baby, always the baby."

"They're threatening her life. And others."

"Really?" he says in a vicious way, shutting me up. He lights another cigarette and then apologizes. "Listen, this isn't your fault, okay? But I can't help you here, Chris."

"Did I ask for your help?"

Uncle Robert shakes his head. "No."

"You can keep doing what you've been doing."

"What?" he yells out. "Saving your little behind? If you want to say I've been doing nothing, you're mistaken."

I'm not sure what to say or why he's even brought me here.

"All I know is that there's something big planned. They've constructed this memorial for the town's founder in the middle of nowhere. It's like they're planning on rebuilding the old town for some stupid reason. I don't know why."

"I've been there," I say. "I've seen it."

"Yeah? Good for you." He's not impressed.

"Marsh told me the old man wants me to take his place."

"He needs one of us to take his place, and I told them what I thought of that. They think I'm too old, too much of a loose cannon." He kicks a beer can. "Too much of a drunk."

"That's why they want me," I say.

"Exactly."

"I'm not going to let them hurt Mom."

He leans over and puts a hand on the table and looks straight at me. "The closer you get to them, the messier it's going to become. The evil inside them … I never realized that evil like that existed. But that's who they are, especially that old man. Marsh and Staunch and the rest of them don't scare me. But that old man does. Because he's not—he's not a *he* anymore. It's a thing. He's possessed by something horrible."

I think of the face of the old man I saw in the tunnel and again at Staunch's house.

I can only nod because I don't want to admit that I've seen it too.

"When they were after me—when they wanted me for their purposes—I started to change, Chris. And that's why—that's why I'm warning you. You've got it inside of you to be some kind of hero, and that's fine I guess, but you don't understand. I started to become like them."

"I'll never be like them."

"Do you believe in God, Chris? In Jesus?"

"I do now," I say.

Uncle Robert nods. "Good. Good for you."

"Do you?"

"No. No way."

"You're like Mom."

"God took away everything from me and never once bothered to tell me why. And instead I've got this mocking evil monster laughing at me. I don't want a part of any religion or spiritual battle."

"Even if you—"

"Nothing," he shouts. "I'm not here trying to protect you. I'm trying to warn you."

"Thanks."

"I'm staying around to make sure my sister makes it back home in one piece, and then I'm going to tell her everything I can before leaving. That's all I'm going to do. All I can do."

"A real hero."

He curses again. "If you think that's gonna make me feel guilty, you're mistaken. I've felt a lot worse these last few years. And I'm just trying to prepare you. The worst is yet to come."

Suddenly I realize that all the anger I've felt toward my father in the past year has been wrong.

This man in front of me is the one I don't want to become.

I'll be lucky if I can be the kind of man my father is. To have a faith like his.

'Cause I'm beginning to realize without that faith, this is where you end up.

26. A Sliver of Sunlight

The sun has disappeared, and I'm back at the silent cabin, feeling empty. These pep talks with Uncle Robert really leave me feeling so very encouraged.

I think back to the first time I saw him in Chicago. Then I think of that ride back to my father's apartment on an empty L-train late at night.

Were those prayers real?

I know they were. The words I said and thought were absolutely real.

But what if Marsh and Uncle Robert are right? What if God has no more interest or use for any of us?

That's why it's called faith.

I remember the Bible Dad gave me—which I threw over the falls. Great decision there. No wonder God might not want to hear me out. I wish I could have it back just to try and see whether it's true what they say, whether there really are answers inside.

I don't have anywhere else to go or anyone else to ask.

What about Kelsey?

I think about it for a while, and it makes sense. Kelsey and her whole family are believers. Not that I've gone into depth with her about God and Jesus and angels and demons, but I know that her family goes to church and that they seem different.

Marsh seems "different" too, but well, you know …

I said I'd call her sometime today, so I pick up my phone to see what she's up to.

"Just sitting watching television," she says.

"Am I interrupting anything big?"

"I have DVR."

"Wouldn't it be nice to have DVR on your life? You could just fast forward an hour or a day. Or maybe six months?"

"Or you could go back. Like twenty-four hours."

For a second I don't get what she's saying, but then I think I do. "So is that what you'd do?" I ask her.

"Beats watching television by myself."

"Glad to be a seat filler."

"Is that what you call it?" Kelsey asks.

"Hey, I think I came up with a title for an epic love story."

"What's that?"

"*Bloodline.* That way it sounds like something to do with family and with blood."

"Sounds like a vampire saga."

"Well, of course," I joke. "Have to have vampires."

"Is the guy a vampire or the girl?"

I spot Midnight on the couch next to me. "The dog. The dog's a vampire, and she infects the couple."

"Does one of them die at the end?"

"Uh uh," I say quickly. "We can't reveal that just yet. We have to take time to create this story. It's going to be huge."

"Or epic?" Kelsey jokes.

"What about both?"

When I realize that we've been talking for an hour, I say the obvious.

"You know, it's kinda stupid that I'm on the phone with you when I could be talking to you in person."

"I didn't say you couldn't come over," she says.

"Two nights in a row? Your parents might wonder something."

"They think you're a nice guy."

"I've always wanted to be nice."

"You were born a nice guy. There aren't many like you around here."

I think of what Uncle Robert would say to Kelsey's comment.

Good thing.

"Can I ask you a serious question?" I say.

"Sure."

I'm not sure how to bring it up, but with Kelsey I don't have to watch my words. That's the nice thing about being around her. It's always been easy, from the very beginning. So I just ask.

"Is church for you a real thing? Like—is it more than something you go to every Sunday?"

"We actually go on Wednesdays sometimes. And on Saturdays."

"Well, no, I mean, not just church."

"What I believe?" Kelsey asks.

"Yeah."

"Our pastor says that church is not the building, but the believers. It's about the relationships."

"Do you believe everything he says?"

"Sure."

"That easily?"

"Yeah, I guess."

I don't say anything, even though I have a hundred questions in my mind. Kelsey ends up with a question of her own.

"Why do you ask?"

"Do you think God hears prayers?" I ask.

"Yes."

"Do you think He answers them?"

"Yes."

"Well, okay then," I say with a bit of sarcasm.

"I'm just telling you what I think."

"Is it that easy?"

"Yeah. At least, I think it can be. But I don't know. That's just what I believe."

I wish I could see her as she says this. Those blue eyes cheerful and bashful and excited at the same time. Her cute little face and cute little lips.

"I'd kiss you if I was sitting next to you," I tell her.

"Why?"

"Just—just because."

Just because you're a sliver of sunlight in this sad, scary place.

"I told you you're welcome to come over."

"By the time we get off the phone it will be Sunday," I say.

"You can see me tomorrow if you want."

"Okay."

"Do you want to go to church with us?"

And no, I really don't want to because of Marsh and her parents and the whole faith thing, but in my typical way I say, "Okay."

Because it feels right to say it.

It will feel right being next to her while I'm dealing with my fears and doubts.

It'll be nice to sit next to someone I care for who doesn't have the same fears and doubts.

27. WHOLE

I hear the scream in the shadows of the woods and feel myself running toward it.

I'm out of breath running toward the sound, toward the girl who's screaming.

I hit a branch and feel blood coming out of my side and I get this weird sense of déjà vu.

You've done this before, haven't you?

Then I reach a small clearing and see it.

The bridge.

The bridge with an opening beneath it. An oval opening like a mouth screaming or gasping for life.

I see Kelsey standing at the base of the hole.

She's screaming as she's being held by two figures. Dark figures, faceless, nameless, soulless figures.

"Chris, help me!"

I keep running, but I suddenly realize this is a dream.

Doesn't matter 'cause dreams are real too and you know this.

I run down the hill and slip and fall on my back.

By the time I get up, the opening to the bridge is empty.

Kelsey's nowhere to be found.

I hear another cry, but this one sounds worse. Like someone being hurt and tortured.

Like someone being killed.

I race down and look into the oval opening, but suddenly it's pitch black.

Then I remember the lighter. The one that belonged to Walter Kinner. I flick it with my thumb, and I see them.

Hundreds of them.

Hideous dark figures blending into each other, standing guard, looking out and waiting.

Waiting for me to take a few more steps in.

Waiting for me to come to them so they can swallow me whole.

And that's when I wake up.

As I'm getting ready, wondering if I should use some of Uncle Robert's cologne that I found earlier, I notice the picture on the desk.

There I am, smiling and looking carefree on what appears to be a summer day.

The picture that once faded has come back into focus again. No reason why, not that I can see. But the picture is full and colorful and perfect.

I'd really like to be that guy smiling there.

Somehow even though it's me, I don't believe that the picture is real. It feels made up. I pick it up and shake it as if the image is going to go back to being fuzzy. But it doesn't.

It remains.

For some weird reason.

An hour later I realize I really need to get a haircut, because when I get to Kelsey's house my hair looks like I got struck by lightning. I don't have dress pants, so I hope it's okay that I'm wearing jeans. They're nice, dark jeans, but they also have mud on them from riding my bike.

Kelsey doesn't seem to notice any of that when she opens the door.

And when I see her I forget about what I look like.

She is a yellow rose sprouting in January in a dark, muddy field.

I want to pick this flower and put it in a vase and hide it forever. Yet all I can do is stand there and look like some stupid boy who doesn't have a clue what to say.

"Good morning," Kelsey says.

"I feel like I should probably go home and change."

"Why?"

"'Cause next to you I look like a bum."

"Oh stop. Come on in. We're almost ready. You don't mind riding with us?"

Kelsey really does look amazing in her long yellow dress and matching sweater. Everything about her is opposite of how my life has felt since coming to Solitary.

I wish I could tell her that and explain what that means.

Instead, I only manage to make small talk and then hit the bathroom to wet down the volcano of hair on my head.

Before heading out, Kelsey thanks me for coming.

"Yeah, sure," I say.

Such an understatement.

Such a cool, casual comment.

I follow Kelsey and her parents out to their car to head to church,
the way any family might get in their car on a Sunday morning. I
long for a time when I don't have to be understated with Kelsey.
When I don't have to be cool or casual. When I can simply tell her
that she is and always has been a breath of fresh air.

A breath of fresh air in a life that occasionally feels the need to
stop breathing.

28. FAITH

The cold slaps me awake, and I get out of bed, remembering that I'm
the only one in this cabin.

"Sorry, Midnight," I say as I shiver and head down the stairs.

It's five o'clock, and outside it's black and silent. I turn on a light
and shiver as I stand in my boxers and T-shirt. I check the thermostat
and see that it's fortysomething degrees in here. I forgot to turn on
the heat last night.

Mom always controls the thermostat.

When I flip it on, I know it's going to take a while for the cabin to become even remotely warm. I get busy with the sleeping fireplace. It takes me a few minutes to get the kindling and newspaper in place. Then it gets going, and I put some heavy logs on it. It dies down, and I go through the whole thing again.

I'm still not an expert on this whole making-fire-in-the-morning thing.

I'm still not an expert on living by myself, either.

I grab a blanket and wrap up in it and watch the fire slowly build.

I'm wired now and know I won't be able to go back to sleep.

I sit in a strange kind of daze, thinking back to the first time Mom and I were here trying to start a fire. The first few times I attempted cutting wood with an ax. Our first few meals here in this remote, isolated, lonely place.

I could almost hear Mom's thoughts out loud.

What are we doing here?

Yet Mom remained determined to make it.

Despite dealing with all the craziness going on inside of her.

And around her.

I count up how many months we've been here. Or scratch that—how many months *I've* been here.

Sixteen.

It feels like so much longer.

Sixteen feels like twenty-six, the same way seventeen years old feels like twenty-seven.

The crackling of the wood is a pleasant sound. Anything other than a howling scream or a booing ghost is a pleasant sound.

I think of Jocelyn again, and I wish that whatever it was that happened after she died—the dreams or visions or whatever I was experiencing—could happen again. Even if it was a silly dream where I was running around school naked and she suddenly popped up, I'd not let her go. I'd tell her the things I wished I could have said.

But you told her to go away, didn't you?

I tried to do things myself. In some ways, I'm still trying to do things myself.

Playing along with Staunch and Marsh.

I think back to sitting in the pew with Kelsey and her parents. The thing that stood out the most was when Kelsey reached over and held my hand.

It was such a natural, simple thing.

But it made me want to break down because it felt so good.

I didn't let go of her until we stood up for a final song.

I didn't really pay attention to the preacher, but I remember one thing.

He said we live each day by faith. What does that even mean?

I stare at the fire, which is burning well now, and I try to make sense of the words.

Live by faith.

The praying thing—I'm figuring that out. But the other stuff he talked about, like reading the Bible and spending time with other Christians—well, that's kind of a problem.

I tossed my Bible, and I don't exactly have tons of shining examples of believers to be around, huh?

There's a voice that tells me that is all foolish, that I got scared and needed help but that this isn't really what I'm needing or wanting. This isn't real and definitely isn't cool.

Just get over this faith thing and figure out what to do.

But that voice sounds stupid to me. I've tried that out, and it's gotten me nowhere.

The pastor said to stick it out, like running a long marathon and not giving up. I've only just started to run, and I'm already sucking in air and wondering whether to stop.

"Just stick with it and survive," the pastor said.

I guess that's what living by faith means. And I think I can start to figure out how to do that.

But the reality is that while I'm figuring that out, I also have to look out for my mom. And for Kelsey. And for others around me. So I can't be stupid.

Eventually something's going to break.

I just hope and pray it's not me.

29. THE TICKING CLOCK

"Can I talk to you?"

I'm still not completely used to Newt's mouselike voice or the way he can just slip up on me at the locker. He'd make a perfect spy except for his fear of pretty much everything. And spies are supposed to get the girls, right? Well, strike two against Double-Oh-Newt.

"What's up?" I ask him.

He looks around and then talks in a voice barely above a whisper. "Did an FBI lady come around to talk to you?"

"A black woman. Pretty hot, pretty tough? Yep."

"What'd you tell her?"

"Nothing," I say. "She's not FBI. Come on."

"She said that Poe gave her information on Jocelyn."

"Yeah, what—like a year later? No way. She's just another person trying to get information. What'd you tell her?"

"Nothing. There's nothing I could tell her."

"Sure there is," I say to Newt.

"What if she's real?"

"Then she's real. And she'll find out that there are lots of bad people around here."

"Things happen to people who ask questions."

One glance at the scar that's always a bit extra shiny underneath the cold lights of the hallway reminds me that Newt's right.

"They wouldn't do anything to someone like that. A real FBI agent. Or a real cop. They just have people like Sheriff Wells who doesn't do anything."

"I'm afraid."

I can see the fear on his face.

I try to do something I haven't done much of in the past.

"It's going to be fine, okay?" I tell him in my best impression of a leading hero voice. "You don't have anything to worry about."

"But you do," Newt says.

Gee, thanks. I didn't know that.

"Look—there are things—big things—to talk about. But not here. Not now."

Newt nods and looks around the hallway through his big spectacles. "Okay. Keep me posted."

I half expect him to say "Over and out," but he just leaves.

Newt is a spy in training. A wannabe spy. It would be funny watching him if I didn't know the horrible truth behind all of this.

The kid is going to have to know more of the story sooner or later. Because he's one of the few people around here I trust.

And because I need as much help as I can possibly get.

Before lunch, I decide that I actually need Newt's help with something right away. I know I'll be sitting with Kelsey and her friends at lunch as usual, so on the way to the cafeteria I ask Newt a question that's been on my mind all morning.

"Do you know anything about a haunted bridge around Solitary?"

He just looks at me and goes a bit pale. "What do you mean?"

I thought my question was pretty obvious, but I ask again. "Do you know of any kind of bridge around here that's supposed to be haunted?"

"The Indian Bridge."

"The what?" I ask.

"Indian Bridge. That's the name."

"Seriously?"

He nods. "Yeah. That's just the nickname. It's got a real Indian name that I forget."

"And it's around Solitary? Kind of in the woods?"

"Have you been there?" Newt asks.

"I think so."

Newt's eyes grow wide. "They say if you go there around midnight you can see ghosts of the Indians who were killed building the bridge. And there are animals that guard the bottom—it's impossible to walk through the bottom part of the bridge."

"So it's like an urban legend, right?"

Newt shrugs. "If you're wanting me to go check it out with you, you're crazy."

"No, it's fine. I need you for the haunted house."

"The what?" He suddenly looks even paler, if that's possible.

I pat him on the back. "I'm just kidding."

"It's not funny."

He has a point. Around Solitary, joking about ghosts is not a good idea.

When I get home that afternoon, there's a package in the mailbox addressed to me. It's square and white and feels light. I open it and find bubble wrap around something. I undo it and find another white envelope marked *Chris*.

Part of me doesn't want to open this.

Things have a way of just showing up around here.

I think of the cell phone that just appeared one day on our kitchen table.

As I open the envelope, I can see my hands shaking.

Stop it, Chris.

I pull out a note and a wad of money that looks like the kind you see on cop shows after they bust a drug deal. It's a stack of twenties.

For a long time, I just stare at the money that's bound together with a rubber band.

Something tells me it isn't an early graduation gift from Dad. Finally I open the note.

CHRIS:

THIS MONEY IS FOR YOU TO USE WHILE YOUR MOTHER IS AT REHAB. IF EVERYTHING GOES THE WAY IT SHOULD, SHE SHOULD BE COMING HOME ANY DAY.

THE BILLS THAT HAVE BEEN PREVIOUSLY PAID FOR BY YOUR MOTHER ARE BEING TAKEN CARE OF AS WELL.

MR. KINNER WANTS TO SEE YOU THIS FRIDAY EVENING AT SIX. SHOW UP PROMPTLY AT MY HOUSE.

MAKE SURE YOU'RE THERE, CHRIS.

STAUNCH

I let go of the note and feel a dread inside of me.

No matter how often I see Kelsey and how much time I spend around her, I still have this to deal with.

No matter how I try to live my day "by faith," I still have this filling my soul.

I shudder and look at the money.

It only makes me angry.

I wonder how many people Staunch has bought off in the past.

People like Lily …

Friday is four days from now.

And Memorial Day is four months from now.

The clock is ticking.

What will happen when the alarm goes off? Where will you be, Chris?

I really don't want to know.

30. A Gift Returned

The snow is light and doesn't really stick to the ground but rather seems to float upward and around as I walk. I'm heading toward the empty church that's next to the place where I saw Iris.

I want to believe that my seeing her was real and not a vision. But I'm not exactly sure.

My hands are bundled in my coat, and I'm freezing because of the whipping wind. I make sure nobody is following me—part of the reason I chose to come here after school on Wednesday. Tuesdays and Thursdays are my pointless-but-necessary driver's ed classes. By the time I'm old enough to buy beer, I might be driving legally.

I pass along the tall shrubs, looking for any kind of break that might be an entrance. But I can't find anything. I walk alongside it twice.

For a while as the snow starts to stick and the daylight fades away, I just stay by the street in between the hedges and the church. I shiver and wonder again if seeing Iris was only a dream.

A wild burst of wind seems to shake something loose behind me. I turn around and see the door opening.

I don't hesitate, but go inside, shutting the metal gate behind me.

It's almost as if I'm already inside once I walk into this garden. There's no wind and no snow, and I wonder if it's a greenhouse or something like that. I walk up the stone steps to the house.

A chipmunk stands by the door as if to welcome me. He doesn't zip away, but just watches as I walk up and stand right in front of him.

Then he casually strolls over to the side of the house.

I shake my head.

Since when does a chipmunk casually stroll?

Oh, come to Solitary and you'll see it all!

I knock on the door, and as I do, it slowly inches open.

An image of Iris dead and bloody lying on the bed suddenly comes into my mind, and I shake it off like it's a bug that landed in my hair.

I see the same room as before. I smell something too. Something sweet, like cinnamon.

Iris comes out of the back, carrying a tray with tea on it.

"I had just enough time to make this," she says to me.

She looks younger again. This has happened before, but this time she looks almost like she's Mom's age.

No way.

Perhaps it's the light in here. Maybe it's extra makeup and more sleep or my lack of really, truly looking at her.

No, Chris, you know she looks a lot younger.

"Iris?"

"I know," she says as if reading my mind. "Just sit and have some tea."

"Is that you?"

"Please tell me I do not look that different."

"No, it's just—you look—"

"Younger, right?" She only smiles.

The usual lines around her lips and eyes are no longer there.

She had plastic surgery while she's been gone!

"Please, Chris," she says again. "Indulge me."

So I sit and for a while I watch her go through the ritual with cups and hot water. I play along as if I'm really, deeply wanting a cup of tea.

What I really want to know is why she keeps looking younger.

Maybe she's bathing in Marsh Falls on a daily basis.

"How is your tea?" she asks.

"Fine."

I sip it, and then I suddenly get an idea. I look at the cup. "Is this—"

"White tea," she answers. "And no, it's not a magic potion. It's just plain, ordinary white tea."

"How did you know I was coming?"

"I saw you wandering outside."

"You can see out onto the streets?"

"That's the beauty of security cameras."

I nod, a bit disappointed.

"What brings you here on a snowy day?"

"I have a lot of questions."

"I'm sure you do," she says in a manner that sounds like she might actually answer them.

"Do you know a man named Alfred Graff?" I ask.

For a moment Iris looks away from me, her face serious and her body language suddenly changing. "I didn't expect to hear that name."

"So you know him."

"Of course."

I tell her about the mannequin I found in my cabin and how I went to find the man who made it.

"Alfred is a giving man, just completely misguided," Iris says. "I knew him years ago. It was during the most critical crossroad of my life, the moment where I abandoned all hope and faith. But that's precisely what drew me closer to my heavenly Father."

"Is Alfred part of ... them?"

"Alfred believes half the story. He's been mesmerized by the allure of sin and evil. For Alfred, it's a fascination with dark spirits."

"Like demons?"

Iris nods and looks at me. "He is misguided, like so many. And around here, that can turn twisted and ugly very fast."

"I don't know what to do. About Jeremiah Marsh. And Staunch. And Walter Kinner."

She nods, and as she does I notice something that I didn't initially see. Call it being a clueless guy. Iris's hair is not pulled back like it usually is. It's cut short with bangs in the front.

"I cannot do anything about them."

"But why? I mean—do you know what's happening? What they're going to do? And what they want with me?"

"I do not know any more than you."

"But you said you could see things, like me."

"Yes," Iris says. "Some things, yes. But I can't see the future, Chris. I can't read minds."

"What am I supposed to do? They want me to take his place. This creepy old guy who is possessed or something. I don't even know what that means."

Iris sips her tea and nods as if I'm telling her about a new kind of pancake I just tasted. She waits for a moment without speaking.

I hate when people wait to talk, because I want to talk for them.

"Solitary is a gateway," she finally says.

For a moment I think of the term *gateway drug*. I want to tell her no, that Solitary isn't a gateway drug. Nope, Solitary is crack and heroin and every other drug blended together and served as an ice cream cone.

"I do not understand why, or even how, but I do understand that it is true," she continues. "The original settler discovered that, the one the town is named after. The wicked man who already knew and believed in evil. It was as if this town called for him. But that was why the Crag's Inn existed. To combat the darkness."

"And leave it to Chris Buckley to get the place burned down," I say.

"There is a season for everything, Chris. And for some reason, the Crag's Inn had its life. That door is shut."

"What do you mean, 'door'?"

"The gateway. It served as a door, so to speak, to those willing to do spiritual battle."

Those willing to do spiritual battle.

"You mean angels?"

She nods and smiles.

"So what—were those people I saw there—who were they?"

"Do you know that the very mention of the word *angel* conjures up many images for people?" Iris says. "A portrait on the wall attached to a Bible verse. A nice feeling for someone dealing with suffering and grief. A story told in Sunday school or to a child at bedtime. The idea of a white, glowing figure with wings and a pale but beautiful face."

"Angels aren't supposed to look like that?"

"The only ones I've seen look like me and you."

"The ones you've seen."

She nods. "You've seen them too. That was how I knew, Chris. How I knew that you could see. Just like your uncle."

"Uncle Robert is still alive," I say.

"I know."

"Those angels looked just like anybody else I've seen."

"They sometimes can. Not always, but sometimes."

"So the Crag's Inn was like some spa for angels or something?"

Iris laughs. "You have a way of saying things, Chris."

"I do?"

"This entire place—Solitary—is a very special place. I don't know why. I do know that there has been a battle going on here for a long time. When the inn burned down, I thought that the battle was over. But as I said, Chris—I think you might have been the reason why. To allow your heart to shift and you to be broken. The same way I was after losing my son."

"But I don't get why," I say.

"Just because I can see doesn't mean I know all the answers. And it certainly doesn't mean I'm bound for greatness."

I laugh.

If she thinks that's where I'm headed …

"The Bible says that suffering produces perseverance, and perseverance will make you mature and complete."

"Really?" I ask. "Wow, then I'm sure I'm going to be mature and complete any day now."

Iris knows I'm being sarcastic, but she doesn't reply. Instead, she stands and goes in the back.

What's back there? A black hole to heaven? Or to a middle ground that has lots and lots of tea?

She comes back holding something that looks familiar.

The Bible my father gave me.

She hands it to me. "This is yours."

"Where did you get this?"

"Chris—do you need everything explained to you in black-and-white?"

"No, but I—but this—I threw it away."

She sits back down and looks at me. She looks so young, and it feels strange because she also looks so beautiful.

They're all beautiful, all these women coming into your life, but watch out, Chris.

"Not everything can be explained. I sometimes wonder if some things will ever be explained. The story of Noah's ark, for instance. God creates this world only to wipe it out with a flood. The story told in Sunday school is nice and sweet because it involves animals and a rainbow, but the heart of that story is terrifying. The heart of that story is death."

"Noah and his family got out."

"Yes. But the why and the how? I have never understood that."

"I'm just asking about a Bible I thought was lost."

"Some things can be found again, Chris. Without an explanation or even a hint of a reason. All I can say is that whatever questions you might have, they've been asked before, and the answers are in that Book."

I sigh, and I don't realize how loud that sigh is.

"Why the hesitation?" she asks.

"The answers are in that book," I repeat. "That sounds a lot like the Sunday school story of Noah. A bit too simplistic."

"Read this all the way through and then say that to me."

"Is this another assignment?"

She laughs. "No. I won't be paying you to read that. You are on your own. But you came here looking for answers. Looking for help. This is all I can do for you. There won't be anyone else to help you out, Chris. They've left to do battles with others."

I try to understand what she's saying.

"But why. Why did they leave?"

"I don't know."

This is the first thing she's said that isn't told in a positive manner. She says it in an *I have no earthly idea* sort of way.

"Can I keep coming here?"

She shakes her head. "No."

"Why not?"

"This has always been temporary."

"But where are you going to go?"

Iris only smiles. I wait for an answer and even ask her again, but she doesn't reply.

I hold the leather Bible in my hand. "Thanks."

"I didn't give you that Bible. I just returned it to you."

I nod and think of my father.

Then I think of what I'm holding and wonder if it really does have all the answers I'm looking for. Or even a few of them.

I finish my cup of tea, which is now cold, and stay a few more minutes.

Something tells me this is the last time I'll ever see Iris.

Or maybe just down here in Solitary.

31. TOTALLY AND COMPLETELY

Sometimes the conversations I have with Kelsey are totally and completely pointless.

"Our main character has to be dark and mysterious," I tell Kelsey. "You know, for our epic love story."

"But not too dark and mysterious."

"Why not?"

"Because people need someone to relate to. He has to be nice."

"Maybe he owns a puppy," I say.

"That would help."

"Then the puppy gets tragically killed."

"No, no, no. You can't have a puppy killed."

"But then you'll care even *more* for the hero."

"Or you'll think he's dumb enough to get his puppy killed."

I think about it and agree. "Yeah, you're right. Okay. No dead dog."

"He has to have a good sense of humor."

"Really?"

"Women like that," Kelsey tells me.

"Okay. But he can't be like Will Ferrell or somebody like that. We've got to take him seriously."

"Okay."

"And the heroine has to be innocent."

"I thought you'd say dark and wounded but gorgeous."

"Oh, well, that all works fine," I say. "At least the gorgeous part."

"Great. She's gorgeous."

"Yes, totally. But she doesn't know it."

"Does our hero tell her she's beautiful?"

"Oh, yes," I say. "All the time."

"But he likes to joke, so she thinks he's joking."

"Yeah. Amidst all his dark, brooding moments."

"Brooding," Kelsey repeats, laughing. "Do you ever brood?"

I try and make a serious look, but she just laughs at me.

"What?" I ask.

"You looked like you're constipated or something."

"Not funny."

"I'm just being honest."

"Our heroine should be honest. Too honest for her own good, if you ask me."

"Okay," Kelsey says. "And our hero can be too witty for his own good."

"This is sounding epic."

"Really?"

"Sure. Because they're in a spaceship heading to the moon."

"No, no. No science fiction. No spaceships."

"How about a boat?" I ask.

"Let's keep them on land."

"Okay. But they're in the big city."

"Sure."

"And the whole world is falling apart."

"No," Kelsey says.

"Why not?"

"No disaster stories."

"You're a tough editor," I say.

"Cowriter. I'm the cowriter."

"Then you're a tough cowriter."

"We've got to make it last."

"The story?" I ask.

"No. The couple."

Like I said, sometimes the conversations I have with Kelsey are totally and completely priceless.

32. THE GREAT BELOW

It's almost easy to forget about Staunch and his wad of money and his request for me to come over on Friday evening.

Almost.

But the week comes to an end, and no amount of lighthearted conversation with Kelsey changes anything.

Six o'clock hovers over me like the barrel of a loaded gun.

I'm not afraid for my life. No, not yet.

But I'm afraid of what might be asked of me.

And, oh yeah, maybe also of the man who's going to be asking me.

I have to make up an excuse for Kelsey about why I can't see her tonight. I tell her it's a family thing, and I'm not lying because it really is a family thing.

It's just a messed-up sort of family.

I ride up to the Staunch house and find the gate open. Maybe it's magical like Marsh Falls. It senses people coming and opens and shuts on its own.

Coming back here, I think of Wade. I remember when Staunch showed me Wade chained up to the bottom of the small waterfall in the back of the Staunch property and gave me the choice of what to do with him.

I let him go … and Staunch killed him.

The way he—or they—killed Jocelyn.

The way they killed Lily.

The way they might kill Mom or Kelsey.

Or both.

That's why I'm here at 5:55 p.m.

That's why I knock on the door at 5:57 p.m.

That's why I enter the house at exactly the time Staunch asked me to come.

For now, I'm going to be a nice little puppy and do what I'm told. For now.

Until I can find another key and unlock the shackles around my arms and feet and soul.

"Would you like something to drink?" Staunch asks as I stand at the entrance to the large room with all the creepy animal heads stuck on the walls staring down at me.

I wonder what he'd do if I said something like "A gin and tonic, please."

Or maybe "Martini. Shaken, not stirred."

"I'm fine," I say.

He leaves me for a moment in silence in the dimly lit room and then comes back with a bottled water.

"Here. Go ahead. It's unopened."

I take it and nod, but I don't open it. He tells me to follow him so I do, down a wide staircase with carpeted stairs. The basement is finished with another large room much like the one above with animal heads and hunting rifles proudly displayed. There are no windows that I can see, and there's one lamp emitting just a tiny bit of light.

"I doubt you'll be down here very long, but he wants to talk to you by yourself. When you're done just come on back down this hallway and head upstairs. Okay?"

I say a quiet *sure* that must not agree with Staunch. He turns and then leans his big set of shoulders and face down toward me.

"Do you need another wake-up call?" he asks in his gruff Southern voice.

"No."

"Good. Don't make me get mean again. I don't like when I have to get mean. Do you understand?"

"Yes sir."

He leads me down a hallway to the last door, takes out a key, and unlocks the door. I'm not sure why it's locked. He opens the door, and it squeaks.

The room inside is pitch black.

Oh come on. I'm not going in there.

"Go on. Watch yourself. The bed is in the center of the room. You'll find a chair on the right-hand side."

If he wanted to kill me he could have done it by now.

Maybe he wanted to save the mess for a room in his basement.

I slowly walk into the black room that feels about ten or twenty degrees cooler than the hallway. I can't see anything, so I just barely inch along, holding out a hand in front of me.

I half expect to feel Walter Kinner hanging from the ceiling.

Then I hear breathing. Heavy breathing like snoring.

No, like someone hooked up to a breathing machine.

My foot touches the edge of the bed. It feels solid, like metal. Maybe it's one of those big hospital beds.

"Chris?" a hoarse voice asks in the dark.

Good, no hiss. For now.

"Yes."

I edge to my right to try and find something other than the bed to hold on to. Eventually I feel a wooden chair and sit down.

Even though my eyes are adjusting to the darkness, I can't make out anything.

"Move closer," he says in barely a whisper.

The room smells like old people. That musty, stinky kind of smell that reminds me of visiting my grandma Buckley at the nursing home before she died. I move a bit closer but still keep far enough away from the bed that he can't reach out and grab me.

The sound of the breathing machine continues to slowly go in and out.

"I'm not well," the man says, and I wonder why he's in bed when he's been going through tunnels and waiting in the woods.

I hear him let out either a heavy breath or a deep sigh.

"I'm going to die soon."

I don't know what to say. I'm in the dark with this man in a bed smelling bad and the sound of something pumping back and forth.

"I can see you, Chris Buckley."

I look around the room as if he might be really standing in the corner or something.

Don't even think that don't go there Chris.

"I'm right here. Right on the bed in front of you. Dying before your very eyes."

"Where's my mother?" I blurt out.

"She's fine," the weak voice says in a tired way. "She'll be home before you know it."

"I want her now."

"And I want to be twenty-seven again. But life is vicious and cruel and then you die. That is the one thing everybody can agree on. That in the end you and I will die."

He sounds like Pastor Marsh.

Or maybe Marsh sounds like him.

"On May 28 I'm going to leave this place and go down to the great below. And that's when I plan on giving it to you."

I think maybe it's this bed of his that he's talking about.

No, thank you very much, I have my own bed with its own sheets.

"Giving me what?" I have to ask.

"Do you remember the nonsense with that country bumpkin that Staunch dealt with? How he chained him to the rock and gave you the key?"

I nod but don't say anything.

"I can see your nod. I can see better in the dark for some reason. Always been able to. Don't quite know why. But don't quite know many things about my condition. Just know it is what it is."

His condition?

The ability to suddenly turn into a monster before your very eyes.

"That whole thing was all to see what you'd do with Wade. Oh, we were curious. Staunch especially. He wanted to see if you would do it, if you would leave Wade there to die. And you just couldn't. But that's neither here nor there. It doesn't matter. What matters is that on May 28 you'll be receiving another key."

"To what?"

"A key that belonged to Louis Solitaire. It's a special key, Chris. Do you want to hear about it? Do you like ghost stories?"

"Sure," I say, wanting to know what this key was supposed to do.

"Louis Solitaire was part of a family that ran a town in the French Alps. The townspeople claimed that they were vampires because at night they would come and steal people away and leave them dead and drained of blood. They weren't real vampires, of course. But they acted the part. They really were just monsters. They would slip inside people's homes and rape the women and kill the men. Selectively of course. To make sure they ruled with fear. But eventually the townspeople revolted and burned them at the stake. Louis Solitaire was the last of the family alive. The people saved him for last since he was the most vile. They wanted to do something really special to him. But instead he made a deal with the Devil. That's where this key came in to play. It's a key that has a power to look in on the other side. A key that allows the other side to cross through to this side."

By now my head is spinning.

I think I was lost when he said "drained of blood."

"Of course, this is a lot to take in. Too much, in fact. But the truth is that you will be the new caretaker of the key."

"And do what with it?"

"You will know when you take the key. That is where the ceremony will take place."

I just sit there, waiting for more, waiting for anything.

I'm not sure what to say.

"There is one thing that the others don't know, and that you are forbidden to say, even though they wouldn't believe you anyway. Once the ceremony takes place, you must leave Solitary forever. Once I die, the town will die with me."

That's the first thing the hoarse voice has said that I like hearing. At least for a minute.

"The key will go with you back home. Back where you came from. Back to the big city near the big lake where it's flat and cold. You will take the key for this one purpose. The world needs to see a message of despair. We need to send a message that will instill dread in everyone who sees it. Solitary's time has passed. It is time for something bigger and better. It is time to shut this door and to unlock another. That will forever be our legacy, Chris. Forever *your* legacy."

33. NOT SO GOOD

Hey Dad, I'm home!

I'll be staying for another ten decades or so. Do you have a cold, dark room with a big bed in it?

Don't mind this key. It's going to unlock something or other, and there'll be some weirdos coming to dine with us. But it's all good.

Oh, and by the way, I'm now a missionary for evil. I have my black robe ordered and coming soon.

I just need enough money to buy a sword or a spear or something medieval.

But otherwise, what's up with Da Bears?

34. RESTLESSNESS

If I could, I'd lose myself.

I'd be like that iPod that suddenly goes missing for a week. I'd eventually be found under some cushion in the house or in a bag or a drawer.

For a while, I'd be missing.

And I'd love it.

But it's January in the last semester of my senior year, and a lot of people are paying attention to me. A lot.

I feel the same as I always have. I have a nice pimple on my forehead. I feel a little out of shape from all the fast food I've been eating (but I know that track practice starts soon and Mr. Brinks will whip me into shape). My hair needs a trim like it sorta has its whole life. I feel this tired restlessness that won't go away.

Jocelyn made it go away. So did Lily.

Yeah.

And so does Kelsey.

Is that the case with every guy, or is it just me?

I don't know. I used to be able to speak for other guys, but that's before all of this happened.

I feel the same, but I also feel I'm hovering over myself at times, waiting for the next crazy, scary thing to happen.

It's Saturday, and I'm feeling restless and watched and bored.

I asked Kelsey if she wanted to hang out and do something, and I finally hear back.

SURE.

If there was only her to think about, I'd escape right this instant with her. I'd take my wad of cash and go somewhere west and warm. Or maybe somewhere south and sunny. Somewhere away from Solitary.

But there are others to think about. First and foremost, there's Mom.

I didn't want to touch that wad of cash, but I've already spent a little buying some groceries. It made me angry and got me seriously thinking about a job. It's one thing for Mom to nag me about a job. It's another when I'm taking money from a monster.

But I can blow it all in one night, right?

I don't know how I'm going to, or even how much money is there, but I'm going to take Kelsey out tonight and spend every single cent of it.

And maybe that restless weight around my shoulders will disappear again. At least for a night.

35. FREEDOM

My grand plan for getting rid of my fat wad of cash is destroyed moments after arriving at Kelsey's house. It's five in the afternoon and it's freezing outside, so I quickly enter her house and find that she's the only one there.

"I have bad news," she says right away.

"You can't go out?"

"We don't have a car."

"What do you mean?"

"My dad's truck is in the shop, and my parents took the other car out. And my father told me no riding on the motorcycle."

"Really?"

I keep hoping that for once Kelsey will get on the back of my motorcycle and ride with me the same way Lily once did.

"He hasn't changed his mind. He doesn't want me on that thing."

I nod and feel the bills in my front pocket.

What a shame.

Not that I really had any idea what we were going to do. We're not eighteen yet, so that limits a lot. I didn't find any concerts or sports events happening. And she probably has a curfew.

Kelsey shrugs. "Sorry. You don't have to stay."

She looks pretty in a dark sweater and jeans. Then again, Kelsey always looks pretty.

"Yeah, I'm going to leave," I joke.

"I feel bad."

"I'm the one without a license."

"How's driver's ed?"

"I just pray that I don't get stuck having to take my driver's test with someone like Mr. Taggart."

She laughs. We head into the family room, and I can tell she feels a bit awkward.

"I really don't mind," I tell her.

"Okay."

She doesn't sound convinced. Before she can sit on the couch, I take her hand and gently turn her to face me.

"So your parents are gone, huh?"

She smiles, and her cheeks seem to glow. "Yeah."

"That's good news to me."

I kiss her while I wrap my arms around her. We stay like that for a while, slow dancing without the music or the motion. When I finally come up for air and move to see her face again, she looks lost in a daze.

"Do you believe me now?" I ask.

She nods, still in my arms and still right beneath me.

Kelsey doesn't want to talk, so I kiss her again.

It turns out that we have the best thing in the world that teenagers can have.

Freedom.

At least I'm able to pay for the pizza we order. There's no local place, so the driver has to make a long trip to the Pages' house from Hendersonville. I give him a forty-dollar tip. He looks about thirty and in need of the cash. We eat some of the pizza, but neither of us is particularly hungry.

Before watching a movie, I decide to try and tell Kelsey about some of the things going on. The house is empty and we're alone and it's time. She doesn't need to know everything. She can't know everything. But she needs to know a few things just to stay clear of trouble.

"Hey, can I bring up something kinda weird?" I ask.

The box of pizza, still half full, is on the table between us. Kelsey nods and looks at me, curious.

"You remember when I first came over here to have lunch with your parents? I met your brother and everything?"

She nods.

That seems like forever ago.

"I was worried then about—about stuff. I still am. I told you I didn't want to come into your life and mess it up."

I don't expect her to remember, but she nods. "I remember that really well."

"You do?"

"I thought it was just an excuse or something for not wanting to be with me."

"It wasn't. And you just need to know—there are some bad people that I've gotten to know. People around here. People who have it out for me."

"Who would have it out for you?"

She's sitting across the table where I can clearly see her. It's quiet and comfortable here. In a weird way, I could imagine this as our house. We're sitting here and this is our house and we've been married for some time ...

Stop that craziness.

I try and focus.

"Mr. Staunch."

"Why? 'Cause of Gus?"

"No," I say. "Gus is just a dumb bully. I'd probably be like him if I had that man for a father."

"But why then?"

"It has to do with my family. My mom's side of the family. Who we're related to."

I look at her and want to tell her more, but I just can't. I don't want to freak her out.

I don't want her to be afraid of me.

She asks a few more questions, but I'm vague with my answers.

"Listen, Kelsey, you have to just trust me. I can't say more. Not because I don't want to. I do. I'd tell you anything. I really would. It's just—I don't want you involved. I don't want you in the middle. Of anything."

"Okay."

"That might be hard. Especially as the end of the school year comes."

Kelsey nods and just like that, she trusts me.

Just like that, she doesn't need anything more.

If this was some other girl—most other girls—they would need more.

"Thanks," I tell her.

"The school year is almost done. Then—freedom."

I smile.

I don't tell her that I don't believe that.

That I don't know what the word means anymore. I'm not a free man.

I haven't been free for some time.

What I need to do is figure out how to get my freedom. And how to do that without Kelsey or my mom or anybody else getting hurt in the process.

36. NOTHING TO FEAR

Maybe some teens would take advantage of an empty house in a different way from Kelsey and me. A couple into each other might end
up doing something with those feelings. Something more than just
watching another flick on the flat-screen television in a family room.

These are my thoughts as we finish watching the movie, with
Kelsey tucked in between my arms and legs as if I'm a gigantic bean-
bag. I can't help but think them, just because … I can't help it.

But this is Kelsey, and I know she's not that kind of a girl. It
sounds like a cliché but I can't say it any other way.

And all of this proves to be a good thing, because her parents
come home a lot earlier than Kelsey expects. Since the family room
opens up to the kitchen, we see them walk in and greet us. Both of
them are dressed up and look like they're coming from some fancy
adult function.

"How are you doing, Chris?" Mr. Page asks.

I stand and shake his hand. For a while we make small talk. We
tell them what movie we saw, what pizza we ate, just typical chitchat
with parents.

"I'm not used to wearing a tie," Mr. Page says, taking it off and
folding it in his hands. "I'd hate to have to wear one of these every
day."

"Yeah, me too," I say.

Before he leaves the room, I have a random thought that has
occasionally popped into my head at weird times. I don't want

to ignore Kelsey, but I don't think she'll mind if I ask her father something.

The first time I was here, he showed me a map of the original Solitary in his office.

"Mr. Page, can I ask you a question?"

For a second he looks very surprised, a bit too surprised. I quickly add that it's about the history of Solitary. This makes his look calm down.

I wasn't going to ask you if I could marry Kelsey.

"Do you know the history of Indian Bridge?"

Mr. Page unbuttons the top two buttons on his dress shirt as he smiles. "Did you go up there recently?"

"I've seen it."

"We used to go there when I was a kid. They say you can see the ghost of a dead Indian crossing the bridge at midnight. It's silly, but I remember being totally freaked out. You ever go there, Kel?"

"No way," Kelsey says.

"She's like her mother," Mr. Page says. "Hates anything to do with scary stories. So don't ever take her to see a horror movie."

I laugh.

Ha ha.

That's great. Thanks, Mr. Page.

Little does your daughter know she's in a horror story.

"Why is the bridge supposed to be haunted?"

"Everything is supposedly haunted around here," Mr. Page says. "I think it's part of living in the mountains and the woods. People like making up ways to creep each other out and have some fun. That bridge was the first one of its kind built years ago. It helped people get from Asheville to Greenville when there was only a tiny road going through the mountains. They say there were Indians who helped build it, and some of them died during the construction. They say the men building the bridge just tossed the dead bodies of the Indians off the bridge."

"Dad!"

"What?"

Mr. Page looks at Kelsey with an innocent *What did I do?* look.

"I'm going to have nightmares now."

Join the club, Kelsey.

"Sorry. Just telling Chris what they say. I'm sure it's not true."

"Did you ever see anything?" Kelsey asks.

"No. Except one time Bruce, an old buddy of mine, dressed up as an Indian and scared the lights out of two girls we brought up there. One of those happened to be your mom."

"I remember that story," Kelsey says.

I've got some more stories for you. How about faceless shadowy men who live underneath the bridge and hide out, waiting …

"It's actually a really beautiful bridge in the daylight. It's amazing that they built it years ago and that it's now in the middle of the woods. We should go there sometime."

"Uh, no thanks," Kelsey says.

She's beginning to look a bit impatient at this conversation. Either because it's talking about something scary or because it's with her father.

Mr. Page seems to get the message and tells us good night. We're left alone again, but not really.

It's totally different now.

Well, not *completely* different.

Kelsey and I are on the couch with the television on, but we're just watching each other. A blanket covers us, and I have her wrapped up in one arm. It's amazing because she's so delicate but also surprisingly tall when she's standing next to me.

"They're not coming in here," she says.

I nod, but I'm not convinced.

But Kelsey—Little Ms. Shy Kelsey—kisses me.

And once again I'm lost.

Once again I'm free.

I don't want to leave here. I don't want this feeling I have to end.

Before I go, I tell her what I'm feeling.

I tell her what I'm afraid of.

"I don't want anything to happen to you," I say.

She doesn't understand what that means.

How could she?

She doesn't know the truth about Jocelyn or Lily.

You're being stupid, Chris.

"Nothing's going to happen to me," she says.

I want to say more, but she kisses me again and shuts me up.

I could really grow used to that.

It's a pretty awesome thing.

37. THE TERRIBLE BEAUTY
OF BEING A TEEN

It's something like this:

"How's it going?"

"Okay."

"How's Mom?"

"Fine."

"Yeah?"

"Yeah."

"And how's school?"

"Okay."

"Are you in track?"

"Just started."

"What about driver's ed?"

"Been going for three weeks. A few more to go."

"That's not bad."

"No."

"Staying out of trouble?"

"No way."

"Tell Mom to give me a call. When she can. Okay?"

"Sure."

"Take care, okay? I'll see you soon."

"Okay."

"And Chris? Be on the lookout for something I'm sending in the mail. Just a little something. Okay?"

"Yeah, okay."

I hang up the phone and then wipe tears off my cheeks. Not that anybody's going to see me crying. I don't even feel bad for crying. It just sorta happened the moment I started lying to Dad.

But I have no choice.

In something like sixteen months, the man who I couldn't stand is now the very person I wish would come and rescue me. But when I was in Chicago, look what happened. Uncle Robert had to come find me and tell me to come back or else. Or else something would happen to Mom.

I can't mess up this time.

So once again I just act like a typical teenager with little to say and little to feel. Dad hasn't been around me much my whole life so he doesn't know me. Kelsey knows me better than he does. Maybe even someone like Pastor Marsh knows me better.

So as I lied on the phone and deliberately made it a short and simple conversation, my mind and heart and soul all screamed to be heard.

To be found. To be taken away.

Dad has no clue.

Just because a kid doesn't say much doesn't mean there's not much going on inside.

That's the awful truth about being a seventeen-year-old boy.

One more year and I become a man, right?

But it happened a long time ago.

I'm just awfully good at faking the whole not-much-going-on thing.

There's too much going on, Dad. Can't you read my mind?

I force myself to stop crying, not because I'm a seventeen-year-old man. But because it's not going to get me anywhere.

I need to devise a plan. Starting now.

February is almost here, and that means that May 28 will be here soon.

I need to figure out what to do.

And who can help.

38. MOUNDS

It's a Monday afternoon, and I'm sitting on a bench on the sidewalk of the main strip of Solitary. A strip about as big as those nasal strips that professional athletes wear over their noses during games. There's really not any kind of strip, but at least I'll know when the guy I'm supposed to meet shows up.

So as for grand plans ... well, this isn't part of it. I don't think this is part of any kind of plan, to be honest.

It's just completely random. But it's a job. A job that I discovered on the busy bulletin board just inside Harrington High. I took the little note written in regular handwriting.

I glance at it again now.

INTERESTED IN PART-TIME WORK? WEIRD HOURS, GREAT PAY. CALL MOUNDS.

I still have the paper in case Mounds doesn't show up. Or in case he gets lost on the way to Solitary.

This job wasn't given to my mom like the job with Iris was. Iris wanted me to work with her. I was always meant to work with her.

Mounds? Probably not.

Probably the last thing I should be doing is hanging out with Mounds.

The ad sounded like a joke, but I took the notice and called the number over the weekend.

"I'm right here," a laid-back, low voice answered.

"Yeah, I'm calling about a job."

"Really?"

I waited.

"Yeah. At the high school. Said 'interested in part-time work. Weird hours, great pay.' Said to call Mounds."

"Yeah, I'm Mounds."

"Well, then—I'm interested in the job."

"Okay."

More silence.

"So what exactly is the job?"

"You ever hear of a ghost hunter?"

"Is this for real?" I asked.

First the strange ad and the stranger name. Now this.

"Ghosts are for real, sure."

The guy talking doesn't have a Southern accent. He's got the whole laid-back thing down, but he sounds more like he's from the West Coast.

"So the job is for ghost hunting?"

"Nah, that's what I do," he said.

"Then what's the job?"

"Pays great, man."

"Doing what?"

It was like talking to a five-year-old.

"Helping."

That was all he said.

"Helping with what?" I eventually asked.

"Ghost hunting."

I didn't think this was for real, but I was kind of amused. Which lately is a rare thing. Mounds eventually told me to meet him in downtown Solitary at 5:00 p.m.

It's 5:20 when a dirty and rusted-out minivan pulls up and uses two parking spaces, not that anybody will really care. I can't see the guy driving but figure if it's Mounds, he'll get out.

I wait about five minutes and then I go up to his door. He rolls down the window.

"You Richard?"

The guy has wild hair and an even wilder beard.

Of course he does.

I shake my head. "Are you Mounds?"

"Yeah. Who are you?"

"I'm Chris. The guy who called you about the job."

"Oh, yeah. Chris. Rich. Yeah, sure. Come on. What you waiting for?"

How about you?

"Are we …?"

"Hunting," Mounds says, raising his eyebrows as high as he can get them. "For ghosts."

"So I'm hired?"

"Yeah, sure."

"Oh."

"What? You want a job interview? Want me to check references?"

I smell Italian food coming from inside the minivan.

"Come on. The night is calling us."

I guess there are worse things I could be doing than getting into a falling-apart minivan with a ghost hunter named Mounds.

Really? Like what?

This is the moment that I could just bolt and he probably wouldn't care.

He might not even notice.

"Dude, look," Mounds says. "I'm not gonna kidnap you, if that's what you're worried about."

Yeah, that's pretty much exactly what I'm worried about.

"I mean, if I was going to, don't you think I'd be a little more cleaned up? The whole van, too. Come on. That's like just screaming *Silence of the Lambs*, right? Maybe subtlety isn't my thing. But people like me aren't the ones you're supposed to be afraid of. It's those guys looking like ordinary accountants who just sorta fit in and meanwhile they're chewing on someone's foot late at night."

I don't know whether to laugh or be completely grossed out.

He does have a good point.

Staunch and Marsh hired Lily to get to me.

"Man, I don't have all night."

I sigh and shake off my fears. If I keep thinking like this, I'm never going to open another door my entire freaking life. I climb inside.

"So, Rick," he says as he turns up the stereo.

"Chris."

"Uh huh."

Led Zeppelin jams in the minivan. It definitely smells like an Italian restaurant in here. I look in the back and see what appears to be a red plastic briefcase sitting on the seat.

"Oh, yeah, the smell," Mounds says. "I deliver pizza when things are slow."

Taking one look at the very large figure of Mounds, I get the impression that he also tends to sample some of the pizza. Maybe lots of the pizza.

Suddenly the "great pay" seems a bit of an exaggeration.

But Mounds quickly answers what I'm thinking. At least one question I'm thinking.

"I do it so I can meet people. Scope out homes. I've been doing this long enough to just know. You just get that vibe from people. You know?"

"Yeah."

"You do? You really know?"

I shake my head. I was just trying to be polite.

"Some people really do know, you know?"

He starts driving out of Solitary, and I ask where he's going.

"Want some work?"

"It might be good to talk about hours. Pay."

"Yeah, yeah. What, are you an accounting major or something?"

"I'm in high school."

"Oh, yeah."

There's a particularly loud and long guitar jam, and he cranks it up as if I'm not even here.

He's a big guy. His beard and hair make him look like a hippie. He doesn't look like a bum or anything. He's actually wearing long shorts and flip-flops and an oversized tropical shirt as if we're in Miami or something.

He turns down the stereo so we can talk.

"The hours I can't tell you. They'll always be different. I'll give you a hundred bucks every time we head out. Another hundred if we find something."

"How do I know what we're looking for?"

"That's what I do. You just hang with me. Carry equipment. Bring me food and water. That sort of thing." He looks at me, then laughs. "Come on, man. I'm just kidding about the food and water. Unless I need it, of course."

I stare ahead at the winding road. This is the way to Kelsey's house.

How about we stop by and maybe grab something to eat while we're there?

"Where are we heading?"

Mounds looks at me, and for a second I picture a California Santa Claus.

"Into the belly of the beast, man."

He squints his eyes and looks at me. And as he does, the minivan drives off the road and heads toward the ditch next to the woods.

Mounds jerks the steering wheel and gets us back onto the road. Then he gives me a soft punch on my arm.

"Man, I'm just messin' with you. We're heading to an abandoned church a little ways from here. Nothing big. Never been there myself, but heard some stuff. But then again, I always hear stuff."

I nod. Then I ask the obvious question. "Is Mounds your real name?"

"Yeah, like my parents deliberately named me after a candy bar," he says.

"So it's a nickname."

"No. My parents deliberately named me after a candy bar."

I can't tell if he's joking. "Really."

"Yes." He shakes his head. "They smoked a lot of dope on the beach. I guess they really loved their Mounds bars, you know?"

He just laughs, and I laugh with him.

Then a crazy thought comes to my mind.

This guy has got to meet Aunt Alice.

Being a ghost hunter now, maybe I'll eventually end up back at her place. Maybe Mounds will finally be able to tell me what's up with these mannequins that keep popping up everywhere.

39. A Sign

It takes me half a second to realize where we are when we pull up.

I almost grab the guy's keys and jam them back into the minivan and force him to take me back to Solitary.

What at first felt like a joke now feels like a mean prank.

Maybe that's what this is, and this is Marsh showing me he's still in control.

"Getting out?" Mounds asks.

The Chris Buckley who came here with Jocelyn ages ago was a different guy. The field is still the same, wild and overgrown with the abandoned skeleton of the church right next to it. It seems like the church has managed to fall apart even more, with more chunks of the wall missing than last time I was here.

Mounds opens the back door and hands me a suitcase. "Carry that, okay?" He grabs something that looks like a metal detector, and then we head to the church.

The church I remember Jocelyn telling me she was baptized in.

I remember her words to me.

I was only six years old when they died.

But now, knowing everything I know, I realize that her parents' death wasn't accidental.

But why her parents? And why Jocelyn?

I stand there next to the burnt-down church, holding the suitcase. The wind gusts and chills me.

"Come over here."

I do as I'm told. I open the suitcase and take out a boxlike thing that I'm supposed to hold up in the air. It's light and resembles a big speaker. I'm not even going to ask Mounds what all this stuff does.

I think back to something else Jocelyn said.

It's amazing how memories work like this.

Sometimes I think the darkness has swallowed up the light.

If only she knew the entire truth.

You were an answer to prayer. That I know.

An answer to a prayer that never finished the job he came to do.

I did not guard her the way an angel might.

"Come 'ere, Rick!"

This goes on with Mounds for about half an hour, with him checking the grounds of the church and the walls.

After a while, he just shakes his head.

"Nothing."

He's still waving his long ghost-detector stick over the ground as I put the box back in the suitcase, then head out to find the gravestones for Jocelyn's parents. I want to make sure the stone I brought is still there.

It takes me a few minutes to find the gravestones.

I find the stone I made with the marked-in J on it. I'm probably the only one who would know that was a J. That's okay.

Then I notice something beside it.

No.

I don't want to pick it up, but I have to.

It can't be. I got rid of that.

I know that when I touch it, it will disappear.

But the brown leather wristband is real.

It's the one Jocelyn gave me as a Christmas present a year ago. The one her mother had given to her father.

The same one I put in the backpack along with the Bible from my father and the color printout of a picture of Jocelyn and me. The backpack I tossed over Marsh Falls.

My hand is shaking as I hold the leather band.

Then I glance up to the cloudy gray sky.

Are you watching over me now? Are you there, Jocelyn?

I really hope so. Even if I did send her away in my dreams. Maybe, possibly, she's still out there.

Maybe this is a sign.

I touch the gravestone I made for her and then stand up. When I do, I hear Mounds shout something.

I start to rush back to the church, thinking he needs something, but then I hear him tell me to stay put.

"What is it?" I ask, not listening very well.

I make it inside the remains of the church, and then I see Mounds looking in terror at something outside.

A wolf is standing near the doorway as if on watch.

Then I spot another wolf, this one lighter-colored and really long.

Then another. And another.

"There's a pack of them," Mounds says. "Gotta be like a dozen of 'em."

I see them and then look back to the field I was just in. I see another one coming.

It's the dark one I remember seeing when I was last here. Not very tall but almost black.

It watches us but doesn't seem to be dangerous.

"I've seen it here before," I tell Mounds.

"You've been here before?"

"Yeah."

He curses and laughs at the same time. Then I hear a gurgling sound. He's looking at the instrument in his hands.

"This thing is going haywire, man!"

The wolves watch us for a while, then the dark wolf goes over to the rest of the pack. It's as if they were waiting on him.

Or her. You know it sure might be a her.

Mounds is blabbering about his meter picking up all these readings.

I just watch the wolves head into the nearby woods.

I look back at the leather band in my hand.

Nothing is accidental. Nothing is random.

I used to think things were, but not anymore.

I think that Jocelyn was waiting for me to come back here. To give me a gift.

And to give me a sign.

I'm not alone.

40. MY PRAYER

Mounds is driving like a lunatic, telling me he's never in forty-two years of life seen that much activity show up in a concentrated place. He's talking about how the instrument he built from scratch is able to detect spiritual entities and he's explaining this and that but I'm a little overwhelmed myself.

He doesn't have to convince me that what we saw was something supernatural.

The wolves would have been enough. But of course I have the leather band.

When we arrive back in Solitary it's dark out, and Mounds asks if I need a ride home. I tell him thanks but I have my bike. Then he finds his coat in the back and grabs his wallet.

"Here's six twenties, and there's more when I get it," he says. "Man, you're like my lucky charm or something."

I hold the money that's not blood money but something I earned.

Even if I did it in a weird way.

"I'll call you when I'm going out again. I gotta get these findings down in my journals and then blog about them."

He hands me a card that gives me his blog address and other information.

I just want to go back home.

Who knows what's waiting for me there.

Nothing supernatural or extraordinary.

But before I go to bed, I do try and see whether I can get another message from the other side.

Or maybe from one of those spaces in between.

I grab the Bible that my father once gave me and that Iris recently regifted to me.

As the wood in the fireplace is crackling to life, I close my eyes and open the Bible randomly.

I look down at a chapter from Ezekiel.

I start reading and then I glaze over, not really getting what I'm reading.

> *Then this message came to me from the LORD: "Son of man, turn and face the south and speak out against it; prophesy against the brushlands of the Negev."*

Well, this is helpful if I know any Negev, but you know ...

> *"Tell the southern wilderness, 'This is what the Sovereign LORD says: Hear the word of the LORD! I will set you on fire, and every tree, both green and dry, will be burned. The terrible flames will not be quenched and will scorch everything from south to north. And everyone in the world will see that I, the LORD, have set this fire. It will not be put out."*

I shut the Bible and then wait until the fire is fully going. As I do I fasten the leather band on my left wrist.

Maybe not everything has to have a message or a point. Maybe you don't magically get a message every time you open the Bible.

Maybe the whole point is to open the Bible. And to keep opening it.

And to pray.

In this room with Midnight on my lap, sleeping in a contented way I can only dream about, I pray that God will show me the way.

I've heard people say that before, but it's okay.

I need to be shown the way. It's not just a cliché. It's my prayer. It's my need.

Not long after that, I fall asleep just like that.

And I actually do sleep as soundly as the Shih Tzu next to me.

41. Hurley's Numbers

February arrives, and with it comes the first big party of the year. At least the first one I actually hear about.

When Kelsey says that she wants to go (since her friend Georgia is going), it makes me think of the time over the summer when I went to a party with my summer-school friends. Of course Lily is gone and so is Roger, though only one is by choice. I still see Harris and Brick at school. At the time of that party I was still running around after Lily like a dog wagging its tail.

Then Kelsey strolled across my path, knowing she'd get my attention.

I haven't seen her in anything as wow! as that outfit since, though she really has changed from the mouselike girl I met in art class.

Wonder if I've changed, and whether it's been for the good or the bad?

Kelsey agrees to pick me up, which is a good thing because that also means she can bring me home.

Home to an empty house where parents won't be around.

Maybe the timing police will have it out for me again, and my mom will finally come back home.

I'd be glad if she did, of course, because I miss her and want her back around. I don't *need* her—I'm doing okay. But just knowing she's there and safe would make my mornings and nights a whole lot better.

Before heading out, I dash on some of Uncle Robert's cologne, then check out the new shirt and jeans I bought with my ghost-hunter money.

The mirror seems to give me a bored glance back.

Yeah, I know.

Thank goodness there's someone on this earth who might think that a new outfit and cologne mean something.

I hear that someone knocking, and I answer the door and greet Kelsey with a kiss.

I'm not sure where this is heading, this Chris-Kelsey thing, but I don't want to worry about that tonight.

For some reason, this party is a chance to take a break from the blues and actually try to have a little fun.

As long as *they* leave me alone.

The visions and nightmares and people without faces under the haunted bridge.

"You look great," I tell Kelsey after we get into her car.

She thanks me, but something tells me I should thank her. Kelsey doesn't wear many skirts to school, but she's wearing one tonight. I don't want to stare at her legs like some creepy old man, but I have to admit she's nice to watch as she drives the car.

"Stop," she says.

"What?"

"Stop looking at me."

"I'm admiring you."

"Don't," she says in a shy way that makes me want to watch her even more. "I hate people staring at me."

"That time at the party in the summer. You wanted me to stare, didn't you?"

She looks at me without saying anything and only smiles.

"Girls. You're all the same."

"No, we're not."

"I think so."

"Sometimes you just have to get someone's attention," Kelsey says.

"Well, it worked."

Again she only smiles, the way only girls can smile.

Guys just aren't that smart. And they almost never get the things they really want.

Roger from my summer class drapes an arm around me and greets both Kelsey and me. He does it more to talk to her, which I find amusing since he probably could have talked to her anytime he wanted when he was actually going to Harrington.

"Shouldn't you be at college?" I ask.

"Oh, yeah. That didn't work out too well."

He's still got the short, short beard going with the faux-hawk hair, but somehow he looks a little different.

Heavier. He looks heavier.

"Were you going to USC?" I ask.

That's what he told everybody, but I never believed it and I still don't. Especially since you don't just come home for the weekend (especially in February) if you're living in California.

"Universities are a drag," he says, then looks Kelsey up and down. "So who are you?"

Kelsey smiles and then darts away to find someone else. Or maybe just to find the nearest bathroom to hide in.

We're at a large house that's close to downtown but tucked away behind woods on a hill. The kid who lives there is a sophomore. It's the typical weekend party. Loud music and lots of kids standing around looking at other kids standing around.

"You're always hanging out with a hottie, aren't you?" Roger asks.

"Her name is Kelsey."

And she would probably choke to hear she was called a hottie.

"You ever hear from Lily?"

I'm not sure if he's joking or not.

Oli dying made news; Lily dying was different. Everybody knew Oli. He'd been part of Gus's gang for a long time. Nobody really knew Lily.

And because of the way she died, it was easy to cover up.

I just tell Roger I've lost contact with Lily.

"So you getting any from Ms. Long Legs?"

Somehow I think this name is actually worse than hottie.

I look at him to see if he's being serious, and he really is.

"You know—maybe girls would hang around you if you weren't so ..." I pause as if I'm thinking of the exact word to describe him. "You."

Roger doesn't seem to get it, but that's okay. I go to find Kelsey. Ms. Long Legs Hottie herself.

I'll just keep the names to myself.

I'd rather not be slapped tonight.

It's around ten, and I'm bored and in the mood to go home. Kelsey is talking with Georgia, and I leave them to talk since I still get the vibe that Georgia isn't my biggest fan. I guess after the whole Lily thing, I can understand that. Georgia doesn't know me, and really that's fine.

I have to use the bathroom, hoping that it's the last thing I do before we leave. When the two bathrooms on the main floor are locked, I go down the stairs to the finished basement.

What I find is a large group—maybe about a dozen people—sitting on the wood floor in shadows, playing cards.

Playing that card game. The one I've seen before at parties in Solitary.

I think of the time Lily and I played this game. And Lily began to wonder what was going on in this town.

I ask where the bathroom is and someone points to a door a ways down. I'm heading back to the stairs when someone calls to me.

"Come on, Chris. Join us."

It's as if they were told to let me play.

"Nah, thanks anyway. Really."

A tall kid who looks like a basketball player stares at me and says, "I think it's probably good if you play."

"And why's that?"

The faces look at me, and I scan them to see if I recognize anybody. I don't, but it sure seems like they recognize me.

"Go ahead, Chris," the tall guy says again.

Talk about peer pressure.

I walk over to the game and reach down to pick up a card. The last time I did this, I picked up a card that matched Lily's.

But that was fixed, right?

Lily sure didn't know about the card game. And so far Marsh or Staunch have never said that they rigged that game on my account.

But of course they did. They had to.

Maybe this will prove that the game is ridiculous.

I put my card over the lit candle and hold it until an image appears.

It's a number. Or maybe a year.

"1820."

I hold the number and show it to everybody.

"I was personally hoping I'd get 4, 8, 15, 16, 23, and 42."

They all continue to stare at me like characters in a zombie movie.

"You know—Hurley's numbers," I say with a laugh.

Nobody laughs with me.

I nod and then leave as fast as I can.

I recall being told that a number means that there's a task you'll have to do.

But who's going to tell me what to do? Marsh? Kinner? Maybe Mounds?

The very thought of Kinner makes me want to torch the card. I slip it into my pocket so that Kelsey doesn't see it. When I find her, she asks where I was.

"Just getting a tour of the house," I say. "You want to stay much longer?"

She shakes her head and gives me a serious look.

Are you thinking the same thing I'm thinking?

But I have enough thoughts going on inside my head for the both of us. I glance at Georgia, who still mostly ignores me.

"Good night, Georgia," I say just to make sure I get her attention.

"Good night," she says in a mocking way that proves she totally hates me.

I leave the party finally doing what I've wanted to do since Kelsey showed up at my door.

Being alone. With her.

42. LOST FOR THE MOMENT

"Stop it, Chris."

The three words slap me over the face and yank me off Kelsey.

I suddenly feel awful and wonder what's wrong.

I sit next to her feeling like a complete jerk.

She takes my hand and holds it.

"Listen—I'm sorry—it's just ..." Kelsey's eyes are big and bright and sad. "This just doesn't feel right."

"I didn't mean to do anything—"

"You didn't. It's fine. This is fine. I just—I'm afraid."

"Afraid of what?"

"Afraid of where this is headed."

Obviously she knows that the cabin is empty. I told her that my mom wasn't coming home tonight, and Kelsey accepted my lame reason why. Visiting some relatives down south. Oh, okay.

"It's not that I—Chris, you know how I feel."

I nod. But I already know what she's going to say, and I realize that I've been pushing it.

"I'm sorry," I say.

"I'm just—this—I don't feel comfortable."

I hate hearing this.

"If there's anybody—anybody—I want to feel comfortable around me, it's you," I tell her.

"I'm not talking about being around you." Kelsey seems to be closing up like a folding table. "It's here—now. I just—I can't."

I shake my head. "No—I know. I wasn't asking. Or wanting. I'm sorry—I just for a minute—I'm sorry."

She sighs.

"What?" I ask.

She's wondering what she's doing with a jerk like me.

"Nothing."

"No, what?"

Her hands cover her knees as if she's trying to hide the fact that she's wearing a skirt.

Oh I'm such a moron. A typical guy jerk.

"You're going to think I'm such a prude," she says with tears in her eyes.

"What?"

She looks down but doesn't say anything.

Kelsey is crying.

I take her hands. "Kelsey—please—I am so sorry."

"You didn't do anything."

"I shouldn't have—I should have thought a little more."

"It's me."

"No, it's not," I tell her, forcing her to look at me.

"Yes, it is."

"No. No, look—I'm not going to make you do anything and I knew that I probably shouldn't but I swear you showed up at my door looking like this and all night long that's all I've been thinking and I'm sorry. I shouldn't have. I'm really sorry."

Her eyes meet mine, and she gives off a beautiful little shy smile. "Nobody has ever made me feel like that."

"Like what?"

"Pretty."

"Kelsey, you're more than pretty."

"Stop."

"I mean it."

"Jocelyn was more than pretty."

To hear the name now hurts all of the sudden.

It seems to slap me again on the face.

"I just—I just don't think it's right."

"I know," I blurt out. "And that's fine. I wasn't going to—I just—I was just kinda lost. For the moment. I'm sorry."

"I like being lost," she says. "With you."

I still feel like a complete jerk.

"Look, Kelsey—I don't want you thinking that I'm just another guy."

"You're probably not going to talk to me tomorrow."

"What? Why?"

"I just—the whole thing about saving myself. I don't even want to bring up the M-word. It sounds just so ..."

"Okay?" I add.

"I was going to say Amish."

We both laugh, and it's a nice break.

"I think you'd look pretty hot in a bonnet," I tell her.

"Stop it."

"No, I'm serious. Forget wearing a skirt. You put on a bonnet and watch out."

She laughs. I put my arm around her and hold her close for a minute.

I admire this girl.

I know the reasons why she feels the way she does. She doesn't tell me them. Instead, she apologizes to me. And I know—I could feel it—how she feels toward me. It's there in her eyes and her face and in everything she says and does.

She believes that going too far is wrong.

Yet she's not trying to prove her point; she's just living it out.

"I wish I could stay here," Kelsey tells me with her head leaning on my chest.

"Yeah."

Pretty soon after that, I walk her out to her car. The pitch black doesn't seem as dreadfully lonely, not with Kelsey here.

I hug her before she gets in the car.

"Are you angry?"

"No," I tell her.

"Promise me."

"I'm not. I swear."

She gives me a look that says she doesn't believe me.

"I had a great time tonight," I tell her.

She still doesn't believe me.

I kiss her and hope to try to convince her.

But as she gets in her car and closes the door, I wonder if that kiss was the wrong kind of way to convince her.

I don't know.

When it comes to stuff like this, I really don't know much of anything.

43. DRUM SONG

I hear the drums beating and banging. Restless and impatient beats rolling over in my head.

It's like they're sped-up minutes, except the minutes are passing so slowly.

All I can do around here is wait, and I don't want to wait. I hate waiting. Waiting to grow up. Waiting to get a girl. Waiting to have a girl, a woman. Waiting to get out of here. Waiting for whatever's going to happen next. Waiting to hear from my mom again.

Waiting.

It's a Sunday where I've done nothing, and I finally remember to check the mail. There's a postcard from my father.

The image on the front is of a bicycle stuck in a snowdrift. The back says *Don't worry, spring is almost here.*

Then underneath is my father's handwriting.

"If we look forward to something we don't yet have, we must wait patiently and confidently." (Romans 8:25)

I'm still waiting, Chris. Waiting to start over and be a family again.

Love you.
Dad

I look at the card again and wonder if this is a message for how I feel about Kelsey. Or how I feel about life in general.

It makes me think. A lot. But I can't say it necessarily helps.

44. Head Over Heels

It's obvious how I feel.

I put it out there, and Kelsey knows.

But Monday morning arrives and I don't see her and don't end up seeing her until lunchtime where she's with Georgia and doesn't say much.

As we eat lunch, not really saying anything, I wonder if she told Georgia anything.

Next time I see her, she's with Georgia again.

Next time she's with another girl.

Then she's heading home, and I tell her to call me tonight.

But she doesn't.

And despite everything going on I suddenly start thinking about her and second-guessing myself and wondering if she's angry or if she now thinks I'm a jerk, and the questions keep coming.

Another day doesn't change anything.

Neither does another.

I text her asking if everything is okay and she texts back saying everything is fine, but something's wrong.

Near the end of the week I know that something is very wrong, so I finally manage to get her alone by her locker.

"Are you still angry at me?" I ask.

She looks embarrassed to talk about this. Her face is red, and her eyes don't meet mine.

"Kelsey—I'm sorry—I really—I messed up big time. Okay?"

"No. It's not you."

"Then what?"

"I don't know."

She looks around, and I move my head to try and get her attention.

"Kelsey, what's wrong?"

She still won't look me in the eye.

"Please—just say something."

But then Georgia shows up and I realize that this isn't just accidental. It's a girl conspiracy.

"Can we get a minute?" I ask Georgia.

"It's fine," Kelsey tells me.

I look at her.

This time she looks at me, as if having Georgia around gives her a little more strength and courage.

I'm sorry and I've told you half a dozen times and you wanted it as much as I did so what did I do wrong?

I nod and walk away.

45. BROKEN

I want to punch out and break something.

It's Friday afternoon, and I know that last conversation I had with Kelsey means I'm going to have wait another few days before seeing her again. She no longer answers my texts or wants to talk on the phone.

She's making it pretty clear how she feels. She just doesn't have the guts to tell me to leave her alone.

I get on my bike and start it up and drive off.

I've got a full tank of gas, so instead of heading to an empty cabin I decide to stay on the roads. I just ride around thinking and wondering but mostly just riding.

When I get older I want to take this bike across the country. I want to see the Grand Canyon and drive through the desert and through the Rocky Mountains. I want to feel dirt and dust and heat and cold and feel something I'm not able or allowed to feel around Solitary.

I want to ride alone because that's what I do. That's what I'm destined to do, for some reason.

What did I do wrong?

I went too far, and I knew it even when it was happening.

No, I didn't. I wasn't thinking about anything except Kelsey.

Maybe I wasn't thinking about her at all.

Maybe it was something that had been building for a while. Ever since Jocelyn and Lily and everything else that happened.

And maybe I'm just a regular guy doing what regular guys do.

I take a corner a little too fast and feel the bike buckling underneath me as I grip the handlebars.

But I kind of like the out-of-control feeling.

I wish I could be just a regular teenager. Just a normal guy dating a normal girl doing normal guy-girl things without thinking too hard.

I don't want to see any more freaking spaces in between.

I don't want to drive up to the inn or find the hidden bed-and-breakfast or go down to see the creatures by the bridge.

Maybe you don't have a choice.

The chilling wind wakes me up, and I keep driving.

I know that later tonight I'll be on my own. This guy who's bruised and broken and not sure what's going to happen next.

I can't let Kelsey leave me. Not now.

Yet I also know that maybe it's the best thing that could happen.

At least to her.

46. 1820

Pastor Marsh is waiting in his car in my driveway as I get off my bike. He gets out of the car and bundles up his jacket against the cold.

"Have a nice little ride?"

I can barely make him out, and part of me wants to beat him up the same way Staunch laid into me.

"What do you want?"

"Let's go inside," Marsh says. "I'm cold."

My Friday night just went from bad to miserable in a matter of seconds.

After I drop my backpack onto the floor and turn some lights on, I hear Marsh close the door behind us.

"Do you ever get lonely being here by yourself?" he asks.

I turn and look at him to see if he's joking. He doesn't seem to be, but I'm not exactly sure. I don't answer him.

"So I've come to give you an assignment," he says.

"I already have enough schoolwork. But thanks."

"Funny. This isn't exactly a school assignment. Remember the card you picked at the party?"

I nod. I still have it. The number 1820.

"You're going to do something for me."

I don't want to hear this. Really.

I knew I shouldn't have picked that card.

"Tell me, Chris. Do you believe numbers have significance?"

"I'm sure you're going to tell me they do."

Marsh laughs. He picks up the heavy poker for the fireplace and then jabs at the remaining chunks of wood in the fire that didn't burn.

"You know—I remember being the jaded teen. The cynical teen. Do you know that I had quite a few problems as a teenager?"

I don't say anything. Nothing about this guy surprises me.

"I had some episodes. My parents died. Tragic deaths, too. But those are the only kind, at least around here, right? I was bitter. And angry. But as I've shared, I've been able to take that anger to do something with it."

Whoop-de-do. Good for you.

"You can do the same thing. Even the hate that I know you have for me. You can do something with it. Just remember that."

He puts the poker down, and that makes me feel a little better.

"So this is what you're going to do. You had the number 1820, right? I could tell you what it means and why, but I have a feeling you'll just be bored. But since I don't want you to be alone on a Friday night, you're going to do something. Tonight. At midnight."

"What?"

"You're going to visit the Adahy Bridge tonight. You probably know it as Indian Bridge. One of the many haunted places in Solitary."

Why couldn't I have gotten another number? Or does the number really matter?

"And do what?"

Marsh just smiles. "I want you take a walk on the bridge. Then go down below."

"Are you going to be there?"

"Uh, no," he says quickly.

"Will anybody?"

"If you're wondering how I will know whether you're there, I will. There's something that I want you to bring me."

"What?"

"Whatever you find at the bottom of the bridge."

"What am I looking for?"

Again the sick, slick smile comes over his face. "It's different for every person."

"What do I do with it?"

"Bring it to me tomorrow. But make sure you go tonight at midnight."

I don't say anything.

I just stare at him. Or make that glare at him.

"And Chris, remember. You do what I say when I say it. That way your mother will make it home sooner. And safer. Do you understand?"

"Yes."

"I'm not Staunch or Kinner. Soon you'll learn that. Okay?"

He leaves me in the empty cabin. I stare at the poker that he held in his hands. Maybe I'll bring it with me for protection.

Not that I think it will do any good.

47. A LIGHT BLUE NIGHTMARE

It's raining. A cold rain that should be snow but that feels colder somehow. I'm wearing a coat and hat and gloves, but pretty much everything that could be soaked is completely drenched. I get off my bike and then look at my watch. It's a little before midnight.

The area is the same as it was last time I was here. Really dark. Like underground dark, or deep in a cave dark, the kind where every step makes you a bit worried.

I wait for a couple of minutes, hearing the sound of the rain hitting the trees and dripping onto the forest floor. The wind blows the rain sideways and rustles around leaves just to make sure it's really truly creepy out here.

Why can't I just be playing a video game like any other guy my age?

I take out my flashlight and find the trail leading toward the bridge. It's muddy, and I'm careful not to slip.

It takes me a few minutes to make it across the bridge. I walk slowly, so as not to make any noise and to make sure I hear anything or anyone. But there's nothing.

Heavy stones line the sides of the bridge. The beam of my flashlight moves across their wet surface.

When I get to the middle of the bridge, which isn't that far away, I just stand. I can feel my heart beating like it's in the back of my throat. I wait and listen, wondering if someone's going to come out of the trees or rush across the bridge to attack.

But through the howling wind I hear something faint.

Faint but terrifying.

Okay, that's it. Get back on the bike and get out of here.

The sound starts to intensify, but I refuse to believe what I'm hearing.

Yet the desperate screaming sounds just like a baby's cry.

I feel a terrible burning feeling crawl over my skin.

The baby's cries get louder. And they're coming from below.

Underneath the bridge.

So that's what I'm looking for? The thing that's different for everybody?

I scan both edges of the bridge, and then I look over one of the stone walls to see down. I see a small stream but nothing else.

The baby sounds real and terrified and wailing.

I don't think about it any longer. I rush to one end of the bridge and then head down the sloping hill next to it. I make sure I don't slip and slide the rest of the way. It's not far to the bottom. It's not a huge bridge. Just big enough to do its job back when it had one to do.

The half-oval opening underneath is black, and raindrops are dripping from it. The baby must be nearby, but I can't find it. I jerk my flashlight back and forth and can't see anything.

Then I spy something underneath the bridge.

Along one of the dark walls.

Something light blue.

A blanket.

This is not happening. Maybe I'll wake up any minute.

I rush to the blue blanket and pick it up, and the first thing I think is how light this baby feels. It wiggles and moves and continues to scream.

"Shhhh—it's okay. It's okay, I'm right here."

I don't know what to say to a screaming baby found underneath a dark, desolate bridge at night. The few times I've held a baby in my life, I haven't known quite what to do.

For a minute I gently rock the baby as I look into the darkness underneath the stone structure.

There are at least half a dozen figures standing on the opposite side of the bridge, near the opening.

At first I just see their legs, then their bodies. Some are wearing overcoats, others are in heavy gray or black coats. All of them look wet with rain. Some wear hats while others have long hair, like a pack of bikers or hunters or something.

Yet even as I shine the flashlight on their faces, I can't make out any expressions.

All I see are eyes.

Not shining or red, but just holes that are darker than this night.

They all face me, just standing there, maybe twenty yards away.

Then I see something behind them, something flickering, kind of like the way a fire gives off floating embers that drift off into the night. These floating orange and red things hover behind them.

I feel not only cold but sick, like I might pass out or throw up or throw up while passing out. All the while the baby continues to wail.

Do I sprint back up the hill, or do I stay here until the figures leave?

I think this for about two seconds. Then I rush out of there, being careful because now I have a life in my hands.

My body is shivering, but I'm not worried about me.

How'd this baby get down there?

I start up the hill, then slip and regain my footing, then carefully walk up the bank.

I hear breathing sounds behind me. Somehow amidst these screams that could wake the dead, I hear breathing, sucking sounds behind me.

Maybe the screams did actually wake the dead.

Then I hear something else. A moaning sound. Like the sickly breathing is turning to a bunch of moans.

I wipe my doused face with a wet arm, since my other arm has the baby. The rain is coming down harder, the baby's screams getting louder.

When I get up by the road, I see another figure. No, several.

Across the street.

They're everywhere.

If I'm supposed to die, then I die. If they want the baby, they'll have to take it from me. If I'm not meant to leave, then that's that. Shaking and shivering and soaked, I climb up on my bike and try to start it with this baby in one arm.

I get the bike started, then slowly begin to ride away from the side of the road.

A figure in a leather overcoat is walking toward me.

I see holes for eyes and that's it. Somehow the face is missing everything else.

Of course that could just be an illusion. A mask or a bandana or something.

It holds out a hand, and I look to see what it's holding. A weapon? Some weird occult thing?

But no.

It's a baby's rattle.

And I swear—it's just—

Red and covered with blood, and did I ever look to see what baby I'm holding?

With one arm locked as tight as possible around the screaming baby, the other arm locked on the handle of the bike, I get away from this hellhole.

The sound of the motorcycle engine isn't enough to cover up the wailing on the ride home.

48. BABYSITTER

The only thing worse than finding a crying baby at the bottom of a deserted bridge in the woods is getting off the motorcycle and not hearing a sound from it.

There's no way it fell asleep.

I carefully walk up the steps to my cabin and unlock the door. I'm finally inside where it's warm and dry. I turn on a light and look at the wet blanket, wrapped like a burrito.

I breathe in and then touch the outside of the blanket. My hands are shaking. No, make that my entire body is shaking.

Part of me doesn't know if I can open it up.

I kneel on the carpet next to the fireplace and gently put the baby on the floor. Then I peel off the first layer of the blanket. Then another.

And then I see its eyes. They're black and lifeless.

Then I see the hole in the cheek, and I jerk up and away and plow into the lamp on the side table.

On the floor is not a baby but some really old doll that looks like it's been rotting in the woods.

A doll.

I'm losing my mind.

My heart is racing and my mind is doing cartwheels and I'm looking at a doll on the floor as if it's going to sit up and ask what's for breakfast.

This is insane insane crazy insane.

I curse out loud just so I can hear something, anything.

Outside, the rain keeps falling.

I heard that thing crying. I know I did.

It takes me like five minutes to finally go back over and get rid of the wet blanket covering it.

It's a doll with eyes open, and it looks very, very freaky. Half of its dark hair is gone, and other parts besides its cheek have been chewed away.

It seems like there should be a note on the doll, like a prank note from Pastor Marsh.

Of course, around here there are no pranks. Everything is real. Every nightmare is true. Every horror story is something coming to life.

Part of me wants to burn the thing right here and now.

I take off my wet hat and then wipe my wet hair and face. Then I take the wet blanket and wrap the baby back up. I leave it there on the floor.

Maybe it will be crawling up my stairs later. Which will be fine.

There's no way I'm getting any sleep tonight.

No way.

49. SOLITARY FOR STARTERS

So let's see here.

Let's say you just picked up the saga right here with the scream-ing baby turned to a decaying doll.

What have you missed?

Oh, where can I begin?

It's three in the morning, and so far baby dearest hasn't managed to crawl up the stairs with a steak knife.

There's still time, Chris. There's still time.

Let's see—I move to Solitary and fall in love with the girl that the evil people have decided to sacrifice on New Year's Eve.

Yeah, that's right. That's what I thought too. *Come on, for real, there's no way!*

But it was real, and there was a way.

Before this sacrifice happened I met my mother's creepy aunt Alice with her selection of mannequins. Perhaps this doll escaped from her house.

I saw a weird mountain man with a big German shepherd who ended up being my uncle in costume. The man, that is. Not the dog.

There were the nightmares my mother had.

There were the tunnels underneath our cabin.

Oh yeah, don't forget the cabin in the woods. Or the mannequin maker.

There's the creepy pastor and the ignorant bully. But both answer to a twisted man name Staunch who answers to my great-grandfather.

And they all say I'm special and that somewhere down the road I'm going to get a special key that does something special for a special reason.

I don't want to be special. I want to be normal.

Will a key unlock a land full of wild dogs and smiling mannequins and screaming babies?

Thanks, I'll pass.

I could go on, but this makes my head hurt. I would love to sleep, but I don't want to wake up cuddling the baby doll downstairs.

What exactly were those men out there on the bridge?

I'm assuming men, because they were all big. Ghosts maybe? Possibly the dead Indians that haunt the bridge? Or maybe demons guard it?

Or maybe there's another answer I haven't thought about. Something that makes even less sense.

They're magical elves guarding the road to Frodo and Bilbo.

Yeah.

They're Jedi Knights with double-edged light sabers that are just waiting for a chance to get back at George Lucas for creating Jar Jar.

Yeah.

They're shadows of all the things you fear the most made into physical form.

Wait a minute—I was on a roll, but that's not funny.

I don't feel funny at all.

I feel alone.

For a long time I toss and turn and can't tell whether my eyelids are opened or closed.

Sometimes it just doesn't matter.

50. A Smell, a Taste, a Touch

Before I head to see Pastor Marsh to give him the sweet little decomposing baby I found by the bridge last night, I decide to check the mail.

Real stories, true stories, don't follow a rhyme or a reason. Bad things happen. Life moves on. People leave. Others come.

Sometimes you find yourself wet and cold battling something that may or may not be alive.

Then you find yourself opening a letter that has a $25,000 check inside.

CHRIS:

YOU DO NOT KNOW ME, BUT I KNOW YOU.

I'M NOT A PART OF YOUR LIFE IN SOLITARY BUT HOPEFULLY AM A PART OF YOUR FUTURE.

THIS CHECK IS FOR YOUR FIRST YEAR AT COLLEGE. MORE WILL BE COMING.

WILLIAM FAULKNER SAID THIS: "ALWAYS DREAM
AND SHOOT HIGHER THAN YOU KNOW YOU CAN DO.
DON'T BOTHER JUST TO BE BETTER THAN YOUR
CONTEMPORARIES OR PREDECESSORS. TRY TO BE
BETTER THAN YOURSELF."

THIS IS JUST A LITTLE HELP AT MAKING THAT
HAPPEN.

A FRIEND AND DISTANT RELATIVE

MG

I just laugh.

I laugh because I don't even think I'm going to make it to graduation. If I do, I'm not sure what's going to happen next.

I think of the famous clip from an NFL coach during a press
conference: "Playoffs? Playoffs? I just hope we win another game!"

That's how I feel about college.

*College? Don't talk about … college? Are you kidding me? I might
be the High Priest of Puppy Chow by then, so don't talk about college!*

I laugh in a sad, cynical sort of way.

I love cracking myself up.

It's either that or I'll be crying.

At least I have a baby to console me now.

That's just so wrong.

I decide to take the wrong baby to Pastor Make-It-Right.

I'll think about the check from the anonymous friend and "distant relative" later.

Much later.

Jeremiah Marsh's office at church looks like any ordinary office some bigwig at a company might occupy. There's a desk for his secretary or assistant right when you enter, but I guess they don't work on Saturdays. A sliver of light shows beneath the closed door next to the empty desk.

I know Pastor Marsh is in there, because I called him on his cell phone.

I don't knock but open the door and see him at his desk with his laptop on. He looks up just as I toss the doll onto his desk, and it slides onto the floor by his side.

"There's my special present I got last night."

He leans over and picks the doll up, then studies it. "I didn't expect this."

"What *did* you expect?"

Marsh puts the doll down next to a stack of books on his desk. "I try not to expect anything around here. Expectations can be a bad thing when you're constantly being surprised."

"What's that doll supposed to mean?"

"I don't know."

"Yes, you do."

"No, I don't," he says, imitating my voice.

"That bridge is haunted, right?"

Marsh smiles his deviant, snotty little smile. "It's not a favorite place to visit at night."

"But have you ever seen things there?"

"Be more specific."

"People. Beings. Ghosts."

He shakes his head. "No."

"That's the second time I've seen them."

"And as I've told you—you have a gift, Chris."

"That's not a gift. Seeing monsters in the middle of the night is not a gift."

"It is when you learn how to control them."

"I don't think there's a way to control them."

"No?"

He leans back in a leather chair that looks expensive. Everything looks expensive, from the dark wood desk to the plaques on the wall and the portraits of his family.

Portraits that include children.

"I think Kinner might disagree with you on that," Marsh continues.

"I heard a baby crying. I picked it up."

"Has anybody ever told you about the suicides in Solitary? There've been quite a few of them. Young kids, too, not just older people. And it all comes from people who see something that disturbs them, that completely freaks them out. Some people just can't handle it."

"What's finding a baby supposed to mean?"

"I do not know. I have ideas."

"Like what?" I ask.

"It could have something to do with your mom. You don't have a sibling. But maybe your parents tried to have a child, and your mother miscarried. Or maybe you're a father and don't know it."

"I'm no father."

"You sure? Something didn't happen with the skinny little blonde you've been running around with?"

"No."

"Sometimes you see a part of the past, Chris. Sometimes you see the future. Sometimes you see something that is ailing you. Sometimes you see something that will save you."

"The baby was real."

"Terror is real," Marsh says. "Hopelessness is real. It has a smell, a taste, a touch. Despair and horror. They're very real."

"But you've never seen those men around the bridge?"

Marsh shakes his head.

"But if I can see them—who are they?"

"They're the ones who go out to deliver the terror and despair. They're loaded down with it, like Santa Claus coming on Christmas Eve. The difference is they don't slide down your chimney. They sink into your soul."

"What was the number for? Why 1820?"

"That's when the bridge was built," Marsh says. "If you go there during the day, you can see a marking with a date."

"What if the card said 1945?"

"I don't believe there's a card that says that."

I let out a sigh. "So why did you want whatever it was that I got last night?"

"I wanted to make sure you went through with it. And to learn what sort of strange things you might have seen. As always, Chris— you never disappoint me."

51. HUNDRED-YEAR-OLD GRANDMOTHER

I waste the rest of the weekend away.

After going to see Marsh, I come back home and don't leave again until Monday morning. I shut off my phone and don't go online. I just curl up on the couch with Midnight at my side and watch television and eat junk food and drink soda.

When Monday arrives, I am surprised to see that Kelsey never tried contacting me. No texts or emails or phone calls. Nothing.

I just go through the motions of school.

I'm exhausted.

Thinking hurts. Feeling hurts. Being anxious and scared hurts.

Maybe things are finally starting to catch up to me. I've slowed down enough to realize what is happening and why.

It's all just very, very tiring.

I don't see Kelsey at all on Monday. Not that I was looking for her. The day tick tocks away, and I expect nothing remotely interesting to happen.

Nothing interesting except coming back home and finding Mom there.

Her car is in the driveway, and she's standing in the kitchen when I open the door.

I rush over to her and give her a hug.

Yet a weird thing happens.

She doesn't hug me back.

"I can't believe you're back," I tell her.

But I spoke too fast.

The lifeless, expressionless face that stares at me isn't Mom. Physically she's here, but she looks different.

"Mom? Are you okay?"

She nods slowly. "Yes." Her voice is a whisper.

"You don't look okay," I say.

You look a bit like you've been having shock therapy.

"I'm just tired."

I want to ask how she got out and what happened at the place she was staying, but I can tell she won't be able to answer.

"What are you doing?" I ask her, looking around the kitchen.

"I was just straightening up some things."

"There's nothing that—Mom, let's just sit down, okay?"

It's crazy. Mom has come back a feeble old woman. I'm surprised her hair isn't white. She doesn't walk back to the couch with me. It's more like a slow hobble.

"Mom—what'd they do to you?"

"Nothing."

"But what—what's wrong?"

She looks up at me and forces a smile. "I'm just really tired."

Her eyes look puffy, the way they might after crying a lot. They're also red with dark lines under them.

"Do you want anything? Want me to get you anything?"

But she only shakes her head. Very s-l-o-w-l-y.

"Mom, are you okay?"

"I've been on medication for a while."

"Are you still?"

"I don't think so."

I can feel my heart knocking on my chest. I'm angry and elated at the same time. Angry about what they did to her and elated that she's finally back home.

"Mom, who brought you back here?"

"A man."

"Who? What's his name?"

"J—," she starts to say.

"Jared?"

"Yes."

Ah, the dear long-lost cousin who turned out to be a lying snake.

I've wondered what happened to him.

I've been waiting to pay you back for what you did to Iris and the Crag's Inn.

"Are you in pain anywhere? Physically?"

She only shakes her head.

Everything about her seems …

Gone.

She looks thinner than she was, and she had already been looking a little too thin.

Dad needs to know about this. Somehow. Some way.

For a few minutes I sit there beside her, not saying anything. I can see her eyelids closing.

"Do you want to take a nap?" I ask her.

"Yeah," she says, about ready to do it sitting up.

"Here," I say as I help her up and guide her to her bed.

When I tuck her in, I feel like this is my hundred-year-old grandmother lying before me.

She's out, and I just study her.

In a strange way, she looks peaceful now that she's sleeping.

I glance out the window and see the overcast sky.

God, please help her to be okay. Help her to be okay, and help us get out of here one day.

Mom is home. That's good.

But the evil that infected her is right outside our door. Down the street, up the mountain, through the woods ...

I think back to Marsh telling me about how I could control those creatures in the woods.

What if I could control the terror and fear going on around here?

What if I could make it all go away?

My destiny and fate and legacy and all those big-time words are suddenly starting to seem clear.

I know who I need to stop and why I need to stop them.

The only question is how.

52. STRONG

Later that night, after staying up late to see if Mom is going to wake up and need anything, I check on her and see her still sleeping like a rock. I double-check to make sure the doors are locked, turn off the lights, then head upstairs.

It's weird to feel this alone even though Mom is downstairs.

I brush my teeth and wash my face, and then I think of Uncle Robert living here by himself.

Fighting the demons all by himself.

Then just giving up and going into hiding.

Not telling anybody, just closing himself off and shutting down.

I don't want to do that. I can't do that.

I'm the kid and they're the grown-ups, but I guess I have to do what brother and sister cannot do.

Be strong. And stay strong.

Then I think of someone else I need to stay strong for.

Someone I haven't heard from in a while.

I forget about everything else, and I get my iPhone to send a text.

I type it as quickly as I can.

I JUST WANT YOU TO KNOW THAT I'M THINKING ABOUT YOU. AND THAT I'M NOT ABOUT TO LOSE YOU. ESPECIALLY FOR SOME STUPID THING THAT I DID OR TRIED TO DO. YOU'RE NOT GOING TO GET AWAY SO EASILY.

I turn off the lights and am climbing into bed when my phone buzzes.

I'M THE ONE SORRY FOR DOING SOMETHING STUPID. FOR BEING SO LAME.

I read and reread her text and then I think I get it.

She's been avoiding me because she feels stupid and silly.

I laugh out loud and start typing again.

YOU'RE LIKE THE ONLY PERSON AROUND HERE WHO STANDS FOR SOMETHING AND REMAINS STRONG. YOU KNOW THAT? GOOD FOR YOU. THAT MAKES ME ONLY REALIZE EVEN MORE THAT I'M SUPPOSED TO BE WITH YOU.

She doesn't text me back so I ask if she's still there.

Wow, she writes.

WHAT?

DO YOU REALLY MEAN THAT?

OF COURSE I DO.

EVEN WITH IT BEING SENIOR YEAR—WITH COLLEGE AND ALL THAT DOWN THE ROAD?

I'M STAYING BY YOUR SIDE, I write to her. AS LONG AS YOU'LL LET ME.

IT'S A DEAL.

GOOD NIGHT. HOPE TO SEE YOU IN MY DREAMS.

ME TOO.

53. SOON, MY FRIEND

February seems to be a forgotten month, like a stepchild who nobody really talks to. Its cold and snow come in bits and pieces, but nothing big enough to get excited about. Everything is just cold and gray and endless.

It dawns on me soon after Mom's arrival that the timing was no accident. Marsh wanted me to do something, and I did it. I went down underneath the dreary bridge and got the baby/doll and brought it to him. Without hesitation. Without telling anybody else.

Maybe he thinks that means I'll do more for him and Staunch.

And yeah, I'll play along. I'll go for the ride until we reach the end and I open my door and jump out.

Mom's mood doesn't really change. She seems shell-shocked, like someone who just got back from something terrifying.

Every night is the same—leading her to bed and tucking her in like a child. One night it gets me really down, and I go upstairs and cry like a big baby. I get it out of my system. That's what I tell myself. *Just get rid of the tears once and for all.* And as I'm crying, I open my Bible up and find some psalms.

They really do the trick.

So the next night I ask Mom if I can read to her.

A year or even six months ago, my mom would have said "Yeah, right" and laughed. But she's different now.

So am I.

I read one psalm to her at night. I guess if they made me feel better, they might make Mom feel better too.

This is sorta like being in the middle of the woods in the middle of the night stuck in the middle of a tent with only one little flashlight.

A light in the darkness.

This doesn't feel normal to me. What feels normal is sitting in a room by myself listening to music and trying to forget about life outside that door. But that particular kind of thing isn't working.

Not anymore.

And the guy who sat on that train in Chicago did something. Or maybe it's more like God did something to that boy sitting on the train, the one asking for help and forgiveness and hope.

Hope.

These parts of the Bible I'm reading are the only kind of hope I know.

Kelsey remains the bright spot in my day.

I try and figure out where her happiness comes from. Are her parents mixing it in with her cereal in the morning? Is it because she knows she's getting out of here in a few months?

Or maybe it's you, Chris.

But it's not me. It's something deeper, something more meaningful.

Even in the drab month of February, the promise of springtime is there every time I see her.

Things are back to normal, but the normal that was when Kelsey and I were just friends.

For some reason, it's suddenly become less, well, intense.

Less hot and heavy.

Which is good. And safe.

I don't want to blow things with her again.

Not with everything that's coming up in my near future.

A future that doesn't look as shiny and sweet as hers.

An outcome that will be here sooner than I think.

54. MORE TO SAY

One Saturday morning near the end of February, Sheriff Wells pays Mom and me a visit. Perhaps he'll manage to get a little more out of her than I have. Any attempt of mine to ask how she's doing or feeling or what exactly happened when she was gone goes nowhere.

I'm just thankful she's alive. Maybe, hopefully, being able to move away from Solitary after school is over will finally make her be her old self again.

I've gone out on a couple more ghost hunts with Mounds. He's paid me, and a little extra money is all I need.

I still have the wad of money Staunch gave me. Part of me wants to use it to buy Mom something, but I can't get myself to do that.

I'm not taking anything from that guy. Never again.

The sheriff looks older, even though it's only been a few months since I've seen him.

Maybe that's what this town does to you. It turns you into an old person before your time.

He's lost weight, and his goatee looks grayer and his hair looks thinner. He doesn't have the swagger that he had when I first met him.

Maybe that's what guilt does to you. Guilt over letting an innocent girl like Jocelyn die on his watch, then refusing to believe it until it's way too late.

"You folks have a few minutes?" he asks before Mom invites him inside.

She asks if he'd like anything to drink and gets him to have a cup of tea. It takes a couple of minutes before he has his cup and he's sitting on the couch across from us, holding it.

"I want to formally apologize to you folks," Wells says as the wrinkles on his face seem to tighten up.

Mom still has her tired, slow-mo thing going, but it also seems like having a visitor has made her wake up a little.

"I don't understand," she says in a polite way.

"I've been, uh, relieved of my duties. Not that I've been doing even half of them. But it's, well—it's time to go."

"You got fired?" I can't help but ask.

"Not quite," Wells says. "Doesn't work that way. Officially I resigned. Unofficially, I got canned."

"I'm sorry to hear that," Mom says.

"No … Ms. Buckley, I'm the one who's sorry. I have not done right by you and especially not by Chris. When you were attacked in town and someone knocked you out, I should've done more. I just— I couldn't. After the things that happened with Wade and Jocelyn, again, I could've done more. But I didn't until it was too late."

Mom doesn't react, and I suddenly hope and pray that Wells doesn't say more about Jocelyn. I never told Mom. And while I might sometime in the future, I don't think she's in much of a mood to hear about Jocelyn's death.

"The stuff going on—stuff Chris came to me about—I didn't do my part. I didn't step up. And I'm sorry. Chris—I let you down. As a sheriff. And as a man."

Mom glances at me and then looks back at Wells. "Thank you for saying that. But are we—is Chris in danger?"

"Yes, ma'am," he slowly but surely says. "And he has been for some time."

"I'm fine, Mom."

"I'm not leaving yet," Wells says. "And whatever I can do, I will do. It's just—there's been a development that recently came to a head. It's one of the reasons I'm stepping down."

I have no idea what he's going to mention. Perhaps Wade's death? Or Lily's?

"An FBI agent has been around here asking questions. You met her, didn't you?"

So she was legit?

I nod at Wells.

"That started the avalanche. And there are those who just don't like any snow whatsoever, if you know what I mean."

Mom doesn't seem to get it, but she sips her tea and keeps listening.

"That's still an area of concern," Wells says.

"For us? For Chris?" Mom is the most alert she's been since coming back, even though that alertness is more like worry.

"The concern is about secrets coming out, ma'am. And when that happens—if that happens—then the people who are keeping them will be very unhappy. And that means you two will be in danger."

"I didn't say anything to the FBI agent," I say. "I didn't think she was even real."

"Of course not," Wells says, rubbing his goatee. "How could you? I'm surprised you thought I was real. Really, I've just been a grown-up man dressed in this costume. It's been Halloween for the last ten years around here."

Wells is talking more to himself than to us. He refocuses and stares at me.

"I came here to tell you I'm sorry, and I've done that. You listen to me, Chris. You be careful. About everyone and everything. But know this—there's some good around these parts. You wouldn't know it if it suddenly showed up and slapped you across the face, but there are some good folks. I know that. I know that 'cause I've seen them. They have hope, and they believe in the power of good, Chris. They're not going away. And neither am I. At least not for a while."

He tells me this in a way that seems to say *I've got your back*.

I nod and then watch as Wells goes to the door.

He looks as if he could say more, but then again so could everyone else around this place.

There's always more to say.

Always.

55. MESSED UP

I'm walking in the freezing woods over dead leaves and past bare trees. It's night, and I can barely see anything and the wind feels like it's blowing right through me. I glance down to look at my feet, but I don't see anything. Then I reach to touch my arms and don't feel anything either.

I'm a ghost.

No, you're not. You're dreaming.

But this doesn't feel like a dream.

This feels different somehow.

I see the outline of a small house. Some kind of glow flickering in the window. I check the door and it's locked, but that doesn't matter because doors don't hold back wandering, dreaming visitors.

I see that it's a cabin much like the one behind our house. Except this one isn't abandoned with a gaping hole in the middle.

This one has a set of candles in a couple of places that eerily light up the room. The small, rustic kitchen looks like it's been in use. There's a table with bowls and plates on it. An old rocking chair. A bed in the corner.

With someone lying on it shaking and screaming and jerking to get out.

It's a woman.

No, it's a girl.

And one of her arms and legs are shackled to the wall.

You remember seeing those shackles, don't you, Chris?

I want to close my eyes, but I can't.

I want to get away from here, but I don't.

The screams are suddenly louder and her jerking is suddenly more crazy.

Then I see why.

There's a round hole in the center of the room.

Sticking out of the hole is someone's head.

A smiling, sick man who slips up out of the hole and moves toward the girl.

I try to scream. I try to do something. I try to do anything.

Please don't please let her be please let me get out of here.

I tighten up every muscle I have in my body, and I force this picture and nightmare to go away.

I awaken in my own bed with my heart pounding and my face and neck sweaty as if I've been running.

I think about the scene that just unfolded in my mind.

That really happened.

I don't know why, or when, or who that girl was. She was young, a lot younger than me.

The underground passages. The old mansion that belonged to the Solitaire family.

And what about that nightmarish boxcar full of dead people?

I feel sick to my stomach. I sit up and then put a hand on the window. It's so cold outside. The room is chilled, but nothing like outside.

The more I seem to discover about this town, whether it's from being told or from being shown or from whatever these visions seem to be, the more I realize the evil that's been going on for some time around here.

And Kinner wants that evil to move on into other places.

It makes me sick to think I come from this.

It makes me want—no, it makes me *vow* to put an end to this messed-up bloodline.

Either I'll do something about it or I'll die trying.

56. Help

It's a Tuesday after the last period of the day, and I'm about ready to head to driver's ed when Mr. Meiners comes up to my locker.

"Hey Chris. Ready to go for a drive?"

"I thought Mr. Mason would be doing that," I say.

"Sometimes I help out with the actual driving. I taught driver's ed for ten years, so I know a little something about it."

"Okay."

I follow him outside to the parking lot, where we get into a Honda Civic that's seen better days. I go through the motions of listening to his instructions.

We head down the main drag of Solitary, and then Mr. Meiners tells me to take a country road out of town. I'm driving more slowly than I normally would, nervous about doing something stupid, when we pass a deserted gas station and Mr. Meiners tells me to pull into the empty lot.

"Want me to parallel park?"

It's getting dark outside, and the headlights are on. Mr. Meiners shakes his head and just tells me to pull up beside the building.

For a few moments, there's only silence in the car. Mr. Meiners studies the outside, then clears his throat and looks over at me.

"I don't know what to do about you, Chris."

For a second I'm wondering what I did wrong. "Did I miss a stop sign or something?"

I can see the amused look behind his beard and glasses. "No. I'm talking about you. The situation you're in."

I don't answer.

I'm in several different situations, to be honest. None of them is any good.

"Chris, I know about your family. Your mother and your uncle. About Staunch and Marsh looking after you."

"Looking after?"

"Sheltering you."

I let out a grim laugh, because that's crazy. "I'm not sure I'd say that."

"I would. For now. They've had tabs on you ever since you and your mom came driving in to town. Anybody who's gotten close— well, they've either been forced to go away or they've had situations."

"How do you know this?"

"I know."

His eyes and tone of voice say he's being serious.

"How?"

"Chris, you have to trust me."

"I'm not trusting anybody anymore. I've had a bad habit of seeing it not work out so well."

"Why do you think I've never managed to get close to you? They have eyes and ears everywhere."

"What about now?"

"This car was just donated, and I just told Mason I'd help out. There's no way anybody can hear this conversation."

"So you know? Like everything?" I ask.

"I know enough. Enough to know that any slight slip-up means

I might die. Or someone in my family might die. I've tried to reach out. I've sent notes to you before."

"That was you?"

"Yes. But Chris—the thing you have to know is that there is something very powerful and very, very real going on here."

"I know that."

"Do you?" Mr. Meiners asks quickly. "Do you really understand?"

"Well, no, not everything. But I know there are—bad things going on."

Bad things going on?

That's all I can manage to say. Because anything else is going to sound ludicrous.

"It's a spiritual war, Chris. A battle over your soul. And the souls of the many who are here."

I nod and shake my head. "I think—yeah. I'm kinda getting that."

Mr. Meiners shifts in his seat and sighs. Once again he looks out around us. I stare at him and wonder if I can trust him.

"I'm not one of them," he says. "I promise you. I only became a believer five years ago. I spent most of my life not believing much of anything. But around here, you're forced to pick a side."

"I know."

"Do you, Chris?"

I nod.

I want to tell him that I tried to do it on my own but couldn't. I want to say that in the only way possible I tried to give my life over to God.

But I still don't know.

I still don't know anything.

"Chris, you came to me wanting help. What were you asking for?"

"This—all of this, I guess. Stuff about God and Jesus and the Devil. I don't quite know what's what. You know?"

Mr. Meiners tells me he understands.

"My father became a Christian—had a real life conversion and all that. Mom didn't accept it—was actually furious about it. I guess now I see the sort of baggage she might have toward religion and God."

"What did you think of your father's decision?"

"I thought he was crazy. But—I get it now. I think I do anyway. I just—I open the Bible, and it seems like another language. But I don't know what questions to ask or who to ask."

"This is good to hear, Chris."

"What?"

"All of this. That you're wanting to learn."

"It's probably because I'm freaked out by everything."

"That's okay. Many people come to faith through extenuating circumstances. Jocelyn was one of them, you know?"

I swallow and think carefully about Jocelyn's last few weeks.

"Did you help her?" I ask Mr. Meiners.

"Yes. I was there when she'd given up and didn't know what to do. I was there when she prayed to God for help. It was amazing."

"They killed her."

"I know."

"Why can't we—why can't *you* do something?"

"Chris, I have tried. I've tried moving. I've tried reaching out and talking to others. But I don't know who all is involved with Marsh and Staunch. I have my ideas. But getting help—I can't."

"Why not?"

"I have a family. Everything changed when you got here. That was right when I began to suspect the worst. Jocelyn confided in me. I've heard from Poe. But Chris—they cannot know that I'm a believer. They cannot know that I believe in the power of Christ. To them, that is the ultimate sacrilege."

"Marsh says I need to reject the name of Jesus. That there's going to be some ceremony on Memorial Day. Something to do with my great-grandfather."

A car passes, and Mr. Meiners looks at it carefully while it drives off down the road.

"We need to keep going."

"Does that mean I pass my driver's test?"

"You'll have to drive a few more times with me."

"Okay."

I start driving down the road back to the high school.

"I want you to come to our meeting this Sunday," Mr. Meiners says.

"The one that used to meet at the falls?"

"Yes."

"I always wondered who was a part of that."

"It's just a handful. They end up finding you out and getting rid of you. That's what happened to Oli."

I slow down, and the car veers off the road toward the ditch. Mr. Meiners grabs the wheel and corrects our path.

"Pay attention."

"Are you saying Oli was going to your meetings? The secret meetings under the falls?"

"Yes."

"But what—how? I mean, what happened with him?"

"I'll tell you Oli's story. It's like Jocelyn's. Beautiful and amazing in its own way. They are both martyrs, Chris. In a world that seems to believe that there are no more of them. But this place is farther removed from the rest of the world than you might even realize."

"How?"

"I don't know how. Nor do I know why. I just know—I know that God has put me on this earth to help out people like Oli and Jocelyn. And now you."

Perhaps this should be comforting. Perhaps I should find some peace knowing Oli and Jocelyn both found faith.

But both of them died.

I'm not so sure I really want Mr. Meiner's help if that's the outcome.

57. ARMOR

"Sorry buddy. I brought it to a guy I know who fixes everything, and he couldn't fix it. Even though it has lighter fluid and everything."

Mounds hands me the Zippo I had let him take to a friend to fix. I flick it a few times, but it does nothing.

"That thing's too rusted," Mounds adds. "Your mom gave it to you?"

"Yeah. Family thing."

"I have a good feeling about today," Mounds says. "Once we find the place, of course."

Mounds is looking at his phone to try and see what the GPS is telling him, but he doesn't seem to be having any luck. The winding roads that curve around these hills don't always make cell service easy. It's easy to get disconnected around here.

In more ways than one.

"What's your good feeling?" I ask.

"You. You're like my good-luck charm."

I can't help but laugh. I'm a bit nervous. Seems I wake up and go to bed nervous these days.

"Man, I've never had so much action happen in all my time of doing this. I think—I really think some people are just wired differently. It's like they have some kind of magnetic ability about them, something that draws in spirits."

"Must be my cologne."

Mounds looks at my deadpan delivery and then howls in laughter. "You're funny, too."

"Yeah," I say. "Hilarious."

At least someone is laughing.

"So what are we looking for today?"

It's the middle of a murky Saturday. Snow fell last night and then melted this morning, and now everything looks slightly mushy, like something taken out of a fridge that's defrosted but looks kind of gross.

"It's a place called the Grounds."

Oh no.

"What?" Mounds asks, seeing the look on my face.

"Nothing."

"You been there, huh? Heard about it?"

I nod.

"What'd you see? Tell me—what'd you find there?"

How about a beautiful dark-haired sixteen-year-old girl in a white dress, tied to a rock with her throat slashed?

I shake my head and look ahead. I'm not sure where we are. If I knew, I'd be able to point him in the direction of the opening at the top of the mountain that has massive stones circling it like Stonehenge.

"A lot of kids go up there for a little uh-uh-uh," Mounds says. "I bet you did too."

I give him a polite smile. But suddenly I don't want to earn any money. I don't want to see what spirits or ghosts or animals will come out to play today.

I'm scared.

What if she's there?

It's crazy to think something like this. Out of all the things I've seen—and I've seen a lot—I think the absolute last thing I want to see is Jocelyn.

I don't want to be reminded.

"Ah, there it is, Lookout Drive." Mounds laughs. "Kinda fitting, huh. *Lookout for the zombie coming your way!*"

He starts talking about the newest zombie show on cable. When I say I haven't seen it, he proceeds to give me all the highlights. Like every single one.

The road turns to gravel as we bounce along in his minivan. Eventually it turns into flattened grass that cars have driven over.

A grassy hill like the top of a bald man's head inches upward from where we're parked.

In the center of the top of that hill are boulders and stones and a fire pit.

I remember a doubting Sheriff Wells talking about the Grounds and telling me that I was making all of that up about Jocelyn and the men in the hooded robes.

So much has happened in the last year.

We get out of the minivan and feel the cold cloud that seems to be hovering around this place. It just makes it all the more ominous and spooky.

"Can't barely see the stones, but I know they're there," Mounds says.

I grab the equipment box and follow him.

I remember in another life this girl I was crazy about showing me this place from the opposite side in the woods.

Jocelyn mentioned the guy named Stuart Algiers who had gone missing, the one dating Poe. She said he had confided in her about seeing a flat stone suddenly show up as a warning sign—the same type of stone Jocelyn had found in her bed.

She knew what had happened to Stuart. He had been sacrificed in this very place.

She knew and yet—

Time ticked away.

The numbers on the clock fell down on the floor … then went up in flames.

"Come on, pick up the pace!" Mounds says.

When a guy this heavy and out of shape tells you to pick up the pace, it means you're really moving slow.

I'm not even moving at all.

We reach the crest of the hill, and I see the odd-shaped rocks. Everything here looks different in the daytime, even in the fog.

Everything looked bigger.

The boulders are all different sizes and shapes. There are about seven of them, and they're not necessarily in a circle. If you were to connect-the-rocks, you'd get something resembling more of a star. A strange-shaped star.

There are smaller stones within the star.

The place that Jocelyn called the fire pit in the center doesn't seem to be there.

Mounds has something new he bought that looks like a wand with a cord on it attached to a box. He tells me to take out the item I call the ghost detector with the long arm you wave over the ground. I still think these tools are completely useless, and maybe just for show, but Mounds certainly believes in them.

"Scan the immediate ground right inside the stones," he says.

He's already wandering off toward one of the largest boulders as I'm unpacking the piece. The fog is so thick that he seems to fade away. I get the tool and quickly head toward him.

The farther I walk, the thicker the fog seems to get.

"Hey, Mounds."

Nothing.

"Mounds! Hey, where you'd go?"

I reach one of the boulders and am waving the ghost detector on the ground.

I feel a breeze, and it looks as if the fog is being blown away. At least from the center of the hilltop.

As I turn my head toward the center, I no longer feel so cold. The wind is still blowing, but somehow it seems like there's a rush of warm air coming through.

Then I see her.

Jocelyn is standing in the center of these rocks. The ground isn't hard and scarred underneath her, but rather green and grassy.

I drop the junk in my hands.

"Jocelyn?"

I know it's just a dream or a vision, but I don't want it to go. I don't want whatever it is about her to leave, like when you know you're dreaming but you like the dream you're in and you're seconds away from waking up.

I take a few more steps.

The fog continues to disappear, and suddenly I see blue sky.

The cloud has opened up in a circle to reveal the clear sky above and the clear image of Jocelyn below.

I've missed you so much.

Each step I take gets slower, more careful. I know she's going to be like a gigantic bubble that's hovering right in front of you until it suddenly pops and spills soap all over you.

"Jocelyn, don't leave, please," I say.

She smiles, looking the way she did when I last saw her. A grown-up and more beautiful (if that's possible) Jocelyn. She's wearing a dark overcoat that matches her hair.

Her eyes don't look away for a second.

"I'm sorry, I'm so sorry," I tell her as I stand several feet away from her.

"It's okay now."

I start to reach out to her, but she gently shakes her head, then gives me a reassuring smile. "You're doing the right things."

"I don't know what I'm doing," I say. "Or where I am or who I'm supposed to be."

"Be yourself."

"I tried that, and it didn't work so much."

"That's the beauty of grace, Chris. That's the amazing gift we're given. Time and time again."

"Is this a dream?"

"No. You're really here."

"And Mounds?"

"He can't see us."

"I'm going crazy, you know," I say.

"I'm sure it can't be easy dealing with this."

"Yeah, especially when you're trying to figure out trigonometry at the same time."

I'm nervous, and out of my mouth comes sarcasm. I'm glad to see it makes Jocelyn grin.

"What am I supposed to do? How can I get help?"

"You're the one who must help others."

"But how?" I ask. "Like with what?"

"With the things you already have. Faith. Love. Hope. And humility."

I sure don't feel like I have any of those things, but I'm not about to tell her she's wrong.

"I didn't mean to send you away."

"You didn't understand," she says. "It's okay."

"I've messed up."

"You probably will again."

I sigh. "Yeah."

"Take the tools you've been given, and use them."

"What—tools?"

"The things you know. The things you already have. 'Put on all of God's armor so that you will be able to stand firm against all strategies of the devil.'"

"Is that armor like one-size-fits-all?"

Again, the nervous nonsense coming out of my mouth. And once again, the sweet smile to follow.

"Ephesians six, Chris. Ten through twenty. Those are important words for you. They will help you. Especially when you are on your own."

"I've been on my own."

"But you're never fully on your own. It might seem like it. But this world and this life are but a flicker. This world is darkness, Chris. But His light never fades away."

"Jocelyn—can I—are you going—"

"Chris, you have to be strong. They need you."

"Who?'

"Too many to name."

I look around but can only see the haze surrounding us.

"Too many?" I ask. "That feels like pressure."

"You are going to be tested, and you are going to fail."

"Well, that's good to know. Any other advice?"

"Just remember where your strength should come from. Remember what you've been given. The amazing gift you've been given."

I'm not following. As usual. "You mean the ability to see you—
to see the other side?"

"The gift of God's own Son. The gift of eternal life. The gift you
received when you prayed on that train."

Part of me feels like that was just a rehearsal, that maybe I need
to be in some church setting talking to some preacher in order to
make it right.

"You can't make it right," Jocelyn says. "He made it right a long
time ago. Remember that, if and when you fall down. Remember
when you need to get back up for the others. Remember."

I can't take it anymore.

I just want to hug her.

I reach out to touch her, but of course I don't touch a thing.

I'm still standing there in the center of the rocks but suddenly also
in the cloud. The fog has swooped back around and smothered me.

I know she's gone when I hear Mounds calling out my name.

"I'm here," I say.

"Where've you been?" he asks.

"Sorry, I just—I wandered off for a while."

Yeah, that's it.

Wandering off.

"Come on over here," Mounds tells me. "I picked up some really
weird activity."

Yeah, I know.

I've had that same thing happen from the moment I stepped
foot in Solitary.

And it's going to continue until I finally leave. Like Poe did.

Or like Jocelyn.

58. THE CONVERSATION

When I get home that afternoon, red eyes await me.

But instead of belonging to the undead or demon dogs, they belong to my mom and Uncle Robert.

Seeing him just sitting on the couch is strange. But seeing him in the same room as Mom is even stranger.

It seems as if I've interrupted something serious and heavy.

Mom looks like she's been crying. Uncle Robert—I can't tell if he's been crying or drinking.

"Hi Chris," he says.

My mom comes over and gives me a hug.

"What's going on?"

"Everything's fine," she tells me.

I look at Robert.

"It's all good. Your mother and I were just having a talk."

"About what?"

"About life," Robert answers.

"Did something happen?"

Did someone die?

"No. Everything's fine."

Uncle Robert stands and grabs his coat.

"You don't need to leave," Mom tells him.

"I should go."

He looks at her, gives me a nod, and leaves.

"What was that all about?" I ask.

"Family stuff. Sibling stuff."

"Did you know—had you seen him?"

"He visited me a couple of times in rehab. The second time I went in."

"Seriously?"

Mom nods. I wonder if Uncle Robert did that in secret, or if Pastor Marsh and Staunch knew about it.

"What sort of sibling stuff?"

"The past," Mom says.

"That's pretty vague."

"Chris, please."

Here we go again. It's the same old thing.

Aren't we past the stage of not revealing stuff?

"It was a hard conversation to have," Mom continues, brushing back her faded blonde hair. "About our parents."

"Uh, okay."

"About how they died," she says.

I nod.

I'm curious, but I'm also not mean. At least, not now. Not with Mom. Not with everything's she's had to deal with.

"Robert just doesn't want to hear certain things," Mom adds. "But sometimes you have to get things out in the open in order to move on. And this—I believe—is one of those things."

Mom doesn't say anything more about the conversation. It makes me think of Jocelyn again, how she told me her parents were killed.

She believed they were murdered.

I wonder if my mom has started thinking the same way. Maybe Uncle Robert doesn't want to accept that or hear that.

But he doesn't leave. Mom is back, and yet he doesn't leave.

It makes me wonder if he's truly given up, or if there's still some tiny bit of hope deep down inside of him.

Glancing at Mom, and the way she seems to be more *there* these days, gives me more hope as well.

59. SURPRISES

It's a nice dream, and I manage to let myself fall into it with Kelsey at my side.

This normal, average suburban house. Let's say it's far away from Solitary and these surrounding mountains.

This soft and comfortable couch that snugly fits two, especially when they're curled around each other.

The quiet February night, with the chill kept outside and the warmth bundled up underneath a blanket in the family room.

The glow of the television and the hum of the program.

The privacy and the tranquility and the fantasy that finds the two of us next to each other, holding one another, then kissing each other.

I'm wide awake in Kelsey's family room, but I'm in a dream. I'm in another life, and I'm finally not running for mine. I'm warm and relaxed, and all I can think about is this wonderful girl next to me.

The longer time ticks by and the later it gets, the more I lose myself.

Until Kelsey seems to wake me up.

"You better go," she says in her gentle, sweet voice.

I haven't overstepped any boundaries. But I've made it clear that I don't want to go, that I don't want to move.

"Okay," I say, then kiss her again.

"I don't like you driving this late at night."

"Soon I'll have my license."

"I still don't like you riding that motorcycle without a helmet."

"I know. I'll get one. I promise."

I kiss her again.

The dream is being here by ourselves, owning this house and this life. Worrying about the kids upstairs and the bills to pay instead of the demons at the front door.

I'd like to say I can imagine it, but I really can't.

I can't imagine Kelsey being there, or anybody really. I can't imagine anyone having the patience and the courage to stand by me and actually marry me with all my wonderful problems circling in around me.

Better not tell her that.

I know. I'm seventeen and a senior and shouldn't be thinking stuff like that. But I'm no ordinary seventeen-year-old senior, so give me a break.

Someone give me a break.

"Chris?"

"Yeah?"

We're so close, talking so soft.

I don't want this moment to end.

"I meant to ask you—did you put that thing in my room?"

I brush a strand of hair back from her face. "What thing?"

It's hard to pay attention.

"It's like some flat stone. The size of my hand."

Suddenly cold water douses me. The blanket is torn off us and lights blare in our eyes and sirens sound and my heart isn't just racing but exploding.

No.

Of course that doesn't really happen except in my stiffening body. I stare at her.

"When'd you find it?"

"Earlier this evening after we had pizza. Did you put it there?"

No I didn't the boogeyman did and do you know what this means now do you?

"Yeah," I lie.

"Where'd you find something so smooth?"

"Just up the road by the creek. Thought you might like it."

I'm trying not to overreact or overthink or overdo anything. I smile and kiss her again, but it's different. Kelsey can tell.

"What's wrong?"

"Nothing. Just—probably should go."

I gently move my arm from underneath her and then sit up. She's so cute in her pink sweatshirt and matching sweatpants. I had told her to get more comfortable, and she said she didn't want to be a bum around me. But seeing her like that made me find her even more adorable, if that was possible.

But that mood has evaporated. As warm and cozy as it might be in here, it's still cold and dark outside.

I don't want to say anything more about that rock.

At least not to Kelsey.

When we get to the door, I give her a long hug that brings about another long kiss.

This time, I'm the one who moves away.

"I had a great time tonight."

"Chris," Kelsey says, that dreamy look in her eyes that says it all, "I just want you to know—"

But I move my hand and softly put it on her lips before she can complete her sentence.

"Don't."

"What?" Kelsey asks.

"Not now. Not tonight."

I don't want something big happening when something awful has already occurred.

"But what—"

"I want you to save those thoughts."

"For when?"

"For—for another night. For a special night."

"Tonight was special."

I nod. "I've got something planned."

"Like what?"

"It's a surprise."

She smiles.

I kiss her on the cheek and then tell her good night.

Outside in the cold, as I start the motorcycle and look around to see if anybody is nearby, I think about that rock.

Surprises around here are usually terrifying.

But I'm going to break that trend.

And I'm going to make sure that the people who gave Kelsey that rock know that it doesn't belong to her.

It belongs to me. And if they want to do anything with it, they'll have to do it through me.

60. STRENGTH

Sleep is impossible.

All I keep thinking about is what I'm going to do. What I need to say to Marsh when I go see him tomorrow. What I should tell Kelsey. If I should say anything to anybody.

Round and around it goes.

I toss and turn, then toss and turn a little more.

Then it finally dawns on me. I mean—I keep forgetting.

Just pray.

So I do that.

But as the words come out, they don't make sense.

How could God let stuff like this happen? How could He allow someone like Kelsey to be in danger?

What about Jocelyn and Lily and all the others?

I know that bad things happen to good people, even people who believe.

Then I remember Jocelyn's words.

Ephesians six. Ten through twenty.

I climb out of bed and turn on the light.

I'd forgotten about that. I didn't forget about seeing Jocelyn, but I had forgotten about this.

I read the verses. They're not just a nice little story about Moses or Peter or Jesus. I look back at the beginning of Ephesians and see that it's a letter written by the apostle Paul—from prison.

He talks about getting ready for battle. About fighting a war.

About putting on God's armor to stand against the Devil.

One verse that reminds me of Iris.

"For we are not fighting against flesh-and-blood enemies, but against evil rulers and authorities of the unseen world, against mighty powers in this dark world, and against evil spirits in the heavenly places."

The unseen world, the dark world, the evil spirits.

But I can see into that world and see those spirits.

I don't quite get things like the belt of truth and the body armor of God's righteousness. It sounds nice, but I just don't get it.

But then I read this.

"Pray in the Spirit at all times and on every occasion. Stay alert and be persistent in your prayers for all believers everywhere."

I think about it.

At all times.

On every occasion.

And the apostle Paul can talk—he's in chains and still preaching as "God's ambassador."

"So pray that I will keep on speaking boldly for him, as I should."

Shouldn't he be praying for release?

I guess that's faith. That's the real deal.

What I have is kindergarten-level belief.

It'd be cool to have that kind of strength.

So that's what I ask God for. Not to be released from this prison. But for strength like the writer of those words.

Strength to know what to do.

Strength to one day speak boldly and to know what I need to say.

61. SERIOUS

I'm here at New Beginnings Church because Mr. Meiners told me it would be too soon to come to their Sunday service. He said he'll be in touch.

That's what everybody says these days.

I'll be in touch.

Cue the menacing "Muahaha!"

I'm here sitting in a chair and listening to music in order to see Pastor Marsh afterward.

That means I have to stomach another one of his twenty-minute talks.

Today he's talking about taking control of your life. A nice self-help pep talk that he probably copied from Dr. Phil.

Yeah, I watch television too.

But as Marsh talks and sounds so sickeningly sincere, I figure something out.

This guy wants one thing and one thing only.

Control.

And the fact that he grew up around here and then came back means that he figured out he could have a little control in a little place for a little man. He couldn't find it out in the big bad world so he decided to come back to this little bad town.

And he wants me because he thinks he can control me.

Marsh can't control Kinner. He probably doesn't even have a clue who and what Kinner really is. But little old Chris Buckley—there's someone he can control. Just like his little old wife.

So make him believe he can control me. That will be the trade-off.

His control—the idea that he is in control—versus making sure that Kelsey is okay.

Making sure that Kelsey stays okay.

When the music starts playing to signal the end of the service, I already know exactly what I'm going to say to the good old pastor.

"I'll do whatever you want me to do."

He's got his smug politician's smirk on his face and doesn't seem to blink at my comment. "It's good to see you, Chris. As always."

"I'm serious."

"You always are."

"I just want to make sure that one thing happens."

He glances around and keeps smiling. Marsh definitely has a better way of being a fake around other people than someone like Staunch does.

Then again, everybody is scared of Staunch. People aren't supposed to be afraid of the pastor.

"Perhaps we can talk about this at another time?"

"I want you to protect her."

His face grows grim for a second as he seems to slip to another place. But that's just for a second. Someone comes up and talks to him, and I just wait. I stand there and wait and don't even think about leaving. When the pastor is finished he stares at me again.

"I will do my best."

"No," I say. "No, I need to know that she is going to be okay. I'm sorry, but I don't think your best means anything."

"Some things are out of my control, Chris."

"Really? Even if I'm there to help?"

He laughs for a minute, as if I'm an idiotic teenage boy who doesn't quite get what he's talking about.

Which, in fact, I am.

"She will be fine."

"For real?" I ask.

"Yes. For real."

I'm ready to leave, but then Marsh calls my name. I turn around.

"Just remember. It's okay to play around. But don't make any serious commitments."

"What? With Kelsey?"

Marsh shakes his head, glances around, then grows scary serious again. "No. With God."

62. A Mess

"Want a smoke?"

Brick asks me this as we're standing at the top of the steps of Harrington High braving the cold and the on-and-off-again drizzle.

"Are you always going to ask me if I want a cigarette even though I've said no a hundred times?"

"Seems the right thing to do."

I laugh. "Well, thanks, but no. I need something stronger than a smoke."

"Seriously?"

I shake my head. "Just kidding."

"'Cause you know—"

"Yeah, yeah. I know."

Occasionally I'll hang around with skinhead here because he makes me laugh and because I don't feel the need to be anybody else for this guy. He doesn't have a set group of friends. Rather, Brick is a loner who everybody knows and pretty much likes.

I wonder what will happen to him when he's no longer at Harrington High.

"What are you going to do after graduation?" I ask.

"Didn't you hear? I'm deciding between Princeton and Yale."

"No, thanks," I say. "You know how hard it is to get a job after college."

"Yeah. And that's now. In another four years we'll be in a depression."

"Don't joke about it," I say.

"Who says I'm joking?" He takes a drag and looks out to the road below. "Nah, I'm staying around here. Figure someone will always need a mechanic, you know? Especially if everybody's broke and driving around broken-down cars."

"So you don't mind this place?"

He looks at me as if he's wondering why I'm asking. "Remember—people leave people like me alone."

"Yeah."

"Any more stuff going on with Staunch?" Brick asks. "I know you and the hot chick asked me all about the dirt on him not long ago."

"Nothing going on. Nothing now."

"You ever check out what I told you about?"

I think of the pit in the woods not far from the Staunch house. I think of the remains of the hand I found in the woods.

"Yeah. But they got rid of whatever you saw."

"A lot to get rid of," Brick says.

"They burned it."

Brick goes "Hmm."

"Hey—if I needed your help sometime, would that be cool?" I ask.

"What kind of help?"

"Just—actually, I don't know. Just help—maybe watching my back or something like that."

"Yeah. From who? Gus?"

"No—he's laid off. Ever since his father attacked him with a serving spoon in front of the town. Just from other people."

"Yeah, sure. You just tell me when."

How about Memorial Day weekend when something big is going to happen?

"Thanks," I tell Brick.

At least I know someone who is willing to help with no questions asked.

But Brick does surprise me with a question.

"You ever think of Lily?"

I'm not sure what to say at first. So I just tell him the truth. "Yeah. Pretty much every day."

"Man, she was fine, wasn't she?"

I nod.

She probably didn't realize how fine she was.

"It's just a mess, isn't it?" Brick says.

"What?"

"This world."

Maybe this is a chance for me to share some hope and inspiration with Brick. But I have no idea where to start without sounding lame.

"Yeah, it is" is all I can say.

The world is a mess. Doesn't mean it's God's fault.

But it does mean that He can save us from it. And from ourselves.

I'm heading back to class when I see a tall guy walking down a hallway all alone.

I stop for a second and feel a weird sense of déjà vu.

A tall kid walking in sweatpants and a sweatshirt.

He turns to look at me, and I see what I didn't want to see.

It's him. It's the guy again.

I saw him last summer at school. The same exact kid. He has a bloody neck and cheek, as if they've been eaten away by something.

Or shot.

I almost put my hand in front of my face, but I can't stop looking. The guy just turns and looks at me, then he keeps walking toward the end of the hallway.

I look around me, but nobody else saw him.

I bolt down the hallway just to make sure that there's not really some guy there who's shot and wandering.

I go into the room at the end of the hallway; it's dark and I quickly turn on the lights. It's cold in here, and I know that any second he's going to jump out and make me give him a big kiss on his missing cheek.

But no.

The room is empty and silent.

Like my head. Like my sanity.

I'm going to leave, but then I glance at the chalkboard. It's not empty.

The writing is large.

In big, thick letters, the message is pretty clear.

Marsh killed me and killed Jocelyn and will kill Kelsey too so be careful

I look around the room again and then sneak a peek back outside the hallway. Nobody is around.

Even after everything that's happened, I still feel like someone's playing a prank on me.

Surprise! This whole last year has just been one big reality television show trying to freak you out!

The kid I saw …

Was that Stuart Algiers?

I'm going to ask, but I have a feeling what the answer will be.

I go to the chalkboard to wipe the message away. I touch it, expecting the chalk not to be there, but it is. It's very real.

It takes me five minutes to erase it all.

As I'm heading out of the classroom, I see Miss Harking waiting for me in the hallway. Almost standing at attention, her narrow eyes and face judging me in an instant.

"Do you need help, Chris?"

The way she asks this isn't like someone asking another person if they need assistance. This is more like someone who thinks the person is trying to hide something.

"No, I'm good."

"Are you sure?"

I see her eyes staring at me with guilt and judgment.

"No. But thanks."

I smile and then walk away.

I have to hide the fact that I want to take off in a sprint. My back feels watched by the rigid lady.

When I'm finally seated in my next class, I can't get the message out of my head.

It's not so much that I question whether Marsh is bad or not.

But does this mean he was the one to physically kill Jocelyn and Stuart and others?

Is he planning to do the same to me maybe? Or is he using Kelsey as bait?

This is the reason I'm not doing particularly well in my classes. It's hard to concentrate when you're contemplating a message a ghost sent you about how he died.

63. THE SUN AND THE RAINFALL

Things must change.

This seventeen-year-old stuck in this cabin glancing at an image of a pretty blonde on the computer screen while *A Broken Frame* by Depeche Mode plays.

This cabin stuck on this road stuck in this town stuck in this nightmare.

He looks at the pictures and knows he has to save her.

If it wasn't for you don't know what I'd do.

He breathes in and wonders about the darkness. He wonders if the light can force the darkness to go away. He wonders what doors there are to open to let the light in.

Things must change.

He's supposed to be doing homework, but he can't.

He's just thinking how to save her.

What comes next?

He tries the Zippo lighter, but it refuses to ignite. He plays with the leather band he still doesn't want to wear around his wrist. His eyes wander to the picture of himself smiling in the sunlight. Then they find the image of the road in the woods with the handwritten quote from the poem underneath.

Random pieces of an unfinished picture. The real true broken frame is me.

The rain falls on the roof, and he longs for spring and sun and light and hope.

He prays.

And deep down, he believes.

We must rearrange them.

So the song says and so he believes.

Shuffle the deck and let them suffer.

What if he's able to open the door and bring light back into this town?

But how?

Things must change.

The Crag's Inn is gone.

But maybe there's another doorway. Another lock and key. Another bridge to go over or under.

Another way.

Iris isn't there to ask. So who else can he ask?

Mr. Meiners might know.

64. WHAT COMES AROUND
GOES AROUND

"Do you know of any places around Solitary that are, like, holy places?"

Mr. Meiners glances at the doorway to the empty class, then looks back at me. "Holy?"

"You know—something opposite of haunted?"

He raises his eyebrows as he starts collecting the tests on his desk. "There's nothing around here that seems to fit that description."

"Anything. Like an old church or maybe an old house. Somewhere that you know good was done."

He thinks for a minute, sticking the tests in his faded leather briefcase. "Well, they say Marsh Falls has a magical quality about it."

Yeah, I know that. Come on.

"Okay. But anywhere else?"

"You want more than one place?"

"Yeah, sure," I say.

I don't know what I want.

Yeah, you do. You want the opposite of that Indian Bridge. Or what's underneath it.

Even though he's wearing glasses, I can see the dark rings under Mr. Meiners's eyes. As if he hasn't been getting enough sleep.

He's got his bag ready, and for a second I think he's not even going to answer me.

Which is pretty typical of what he's done the last year or so.

"The Corner Nook."

I don't expect to hear this. I might have thought of many places, but the bookstore and café on the main strip of stores in downtown Solitary?

"Really? The bookstore?"

"Used to be an old general store. One of those you might see in a movie or a television show."

I shake my head. I don't get it.

"I know—sounds crazy, huh? But that place—the owners of that store helped more people out than probably the entire town of Solitary."

"Let me guess," I say, thinking I got this. "They were an elderly couple. Kind of like a Mr. and Mrs. Mother Teresa?"

"Um, no," Mr. Meiners replied. "They were actually a couple named Joe and Sara Evans."

Everything suddenly stops.

There's no way.

I blink and remember the field where Jocelyn showed me her parents' gravestones.

Joseph Charles Evans.

It can't be the same, can it?

"They came to this town and did some great things and really made that general store almost a safe haven. They were a godly couple."

I shake my head, and all of a sudden these things seem to pop up in my eyes, making my vision all blurry. I wipe them away quickly.

"Did Jocelyn ever tell you about them?" he asks.

And of course it's them.

Of course.

What comes around goes around. The circle of life. The gift that keeps on giving.

All the circular clichés my silly little mind can think of go off like fireworks.

Like the fireworks I was never able to see with Jocelyn.

"She didn't, did she?"

I shake my head. "Her parents owned that place, right?"

Mr. Meiners nods, again looking at the doorway. "The place was bought and sold—gutted, more like—after they died. About ten years ago."

"She never told me."

"I can understand. She didn't know how to grieve them when she was six. So she ended up spending the rest of her life trying to find a way."

I want to say more to him, tell him how I miss her and ask how he helped her. But as I go to say something, he shakes his head.

"Check it out sometime," Mr. Meiners says. "Let me know what you find."

He leads me out of the room, and I know our brief conversation is over.

For now.

65. A BRIEF LULL

I don't know how these things go, these guy-girl things. 'Cause honestly I haven't the best of luck with them.

But the apocalyptic snow doesn't come, at least not this year. Warmer weather comes to thaw the ground, and Kelsey is there to thaw my heart.

And she continues to make me believe.

Believe there is hope in today and tomorrow.

Not in anything grand she says, but in the small things she does.

Waiting at my locker in the morning as I come to this grave of a school. Kelsey can raise the dead, because I feel alive every time I see her.

Sometimes she'll hold my hand at the oddest and most wonderful times. For no reason except that I have a hand and she wants to take it.

This little girl that I considered a mouse in my art class is now a roaring tiger who leads me around on a leash.

March arrives, and with it comes something bigger and heavier and harder and more real.

Is this love? Is it strong enough?

I don't know. I think so, but I don't know and I'm not going to say it.

I don't want to ruin this.

I don't want to overshadow the times I make her laugh for stupid reasons. I'm not that funny, but she laughs easily and blushes even easier.

She comes to my track meets even though I tell her I'm not that into them.

But I'm into her.

And yeah, she's into me.

And sometimes when I think of it all, I think that we're going to make it out of here okay.

That's when I don't think of anything else.

The storms aren't always raging.

Yet when they come back you realize you've been lulled by the warmth and the softness and the smiles.

When they come back, they seem to hurt you even more.

66. BUMMER

I finally get an invitation the first week in March. It reminds me of the bad old days when I was first here and kept finding random thing after random thing in my locker. The notes. The gun. The clipping from the magazine that was once in Jocelyn's locker, with the Robert Frost poem underneath it.

Still don't know where that came from.

Maybe my long-lost son will show up saying he sent it to me from the future.

This time it's a yellow note with a day, time, and directions in handwriting:

Sunday 10 a.m.
North on Sable ten minutes. Look for logging trail on left by tree cut in half. Head down it until you reach the barn.

The last word gives me goose bumps.

Barn.

I think of the place Jocelyn led me to, where she was hiding Midnight.

Did she tell them about this place? Or is it commonly known?

I know—well, I'm about 99 percent sure—that this is from Mr. Meiners.

This is the group he's meeting with.

I crumple up the note. I know how to get to that barn without directions.

"I have some bad news," Kelsey tells me.

This is one of the rare days she's wearing her glasses. They're a different pair than when I first met her, a stylish pair, and I love them on her. She wears them when she doesn't have time to put in her contacts or the lenses are bothering her for some reason.

"You failed a test?"

I'm joking, because Kelsey is a straight-A student. She gives a mild laugh.

"We're going to see my brother next week."

Next week is spring break, and Kelsey had said that they might be visiting her brother at the University of South Carolina. Making a family trip out of it. She even asked if I wanted to come along, but I said no.

I mean, even if things are okay, there's the reality of everything. Like Mom. And, well, yeah, everything else.

"That's okay," I say. "I'm heading to Cancun, so I'll be busy."

"Could you take me?"

"I'd love to. I'm riding my bike there."

"Is that even possible?" she asks.

"Well, maybe technically, but I don't know. Either the bike or my butt would give out before we'd make it."

This gets a pretty big laugh out of her.

"The week will go by fast. I'm going to try and get my license. Can you believe it?"

"I can't believe you've been driving your motorcycle all this time without getting a ticket."

"Do they give tickets around here?"

She shrugs, and I know she's the last person around who'd ever get a ticket.

"I'm bummed."

I put an arm around her and squeeze her tight. Kelsey is tall and still growing, it seems, but she has such a slender waist. Sometimes she seems so easy to break, like a long, thin glass vase sitting at the edge of a kitchen counter.

"I'm really going to miss you," she says.

"I know. It will be tragic for everybody."

"You're in a weird mood today."

"No, this is the real me. I'm just not freaking out about anything."

"Any more word on college?"

The warning bell rings for class, so we start heading toward the classrooms. I usually walk Kelsey to her class after lunch.

"Not really," I say, giving her a soft nudge. "And you're not my mom."

"Well, you need someone responsible taking care of things for you."

"Is that a proposal?"

She smiles and says she'll see me later, then heads into her classroom.

The thought of spring break actually bums me out now too. I didn't want to tell her because I want her to have a fun time. But I wanted Kelsey around.

Now I'll just have—well—

Don't think about it.

Yeah. I don't want to break my mood.

I know something's going to do that for me any day now.

Any day now.

67. ACTION

Ever since Jocelyn showed me the group of people meeting in the woods under Marsh Falls that one day, I've been curious about them. I've thought they were some kind of weird cult that meets and passes around a bowl and mutters strange things to each other.

But that's when I let my imagination run wild. Because the group meeting is nothing like that. They're just people getting together to sing and share and listen to somebody give a message. Just like any other church.

Church isn't about the building, Chris.

Dad once told me that. I'm sure I heard it from someone else too.

I do my best that morning to make sure nobody is watching me when I'm in downtown Solitary. I park my bike and then go into the Corner Nook as I've been doing lately to see if there's anything different or weird that I can spot. Just like always, there's nothing strange about the bookstore and coffee shop. I order an iced tea, since I'm not a coffee fan, and then casually walk across the street.

Nobody sees me, and nobody follows.

I'm walking down the tracks, remembering that this is where I saw that haunted creepy boxcar. But it's not there.

Did I ever see it to begin with?

I don't know how this works. I really don't. Seeing something one minute and not seeing it the next.

What are the rules and logic to how this "gift" works?

Rules? Logic? Yeah right.

I get to the point where I stop and go into the woods, still checking behind me every few minutes to see if anybody is watching. The barn is there like always, an old and abandoned building at the end of a dirt road.

Just a few cars are parked there. Maybe the people carpool to this hidden church in the woods.

Mr. Meiners greets me when I enter the barn. It's light enough outside that there's no need for lights inside the barn. It's shadowy, but we can see decently enough.

Over the next ten or fifteen minutes, I'm introduced to half a dozen people.

There's an elderly couple with the last name of Franklin, who supposedly have lived here for years. I wonder what kind of stories they could tell. Then there's a woman named Tracy who's older and heavyset and very nervous-looking.

Then someone calls me by name.

"Hi, Chris."

The dark-haired guy looks familiar and says his name is Jim, but that doesn't mean anything.

"Mr. Charleton," he says, adding, "from summer school."

"Oh yeah," I say. "*Breakfast Club* guy."

He laughs. He seems the same—upbeat and friendly and totally positive.

Of course someone like that is going to show up here. Instead of, say, Mr. Taggart.

"Glad to see you here."

The last couple I meet turn out to be Oli's parents.

Oli, or as Sheriff Wells told me last summer, Oliver Mateja. His father is Hispanic and greets me with an accent, but his mother doesn't appear to be. She's dark-haired but looks more Italian. They both seem to know me and even seem to be expecting me. Mrs. Mateja gives me a hug and leaves me smelling like her perfume.

I suddenly wish I hadn't come.

I feel guilty being around Oli's parents. I know I didn't cause his death, but still I feel somehow like it had something to do with me.

We meet in the open area at the back of the barn. There are some folding chairs in a circle. Mr. Meiners starts off with a prayer, and then we sing some songs. It's very casual—a bit too much so. I feel stupid during the singing since I don't know any of the songs.

"I want to thank Chris for coming today," Mr. Meiners says after the singing is over. "Chris—this is usually the time we share what's going on with our lives and things we can be praying about."

"Okay," I say in a hushed voice.

They wait to hear what my prayer requests are.

It's odd to think that I can share concerns or whatever with complete strangers.

Will the prayers even be heard? Will they carry more weight? Are they going to make me pray for them?

"I guess just, uh, prayer for my mom. She's had a rough time since coming back here. And yeah—prayer for me. Just cause, uh, I can sure use it."

Understatement of the century.

During the prayer something happens. These strangers all share something that is going on in their lives. But when Mr. Mateja prays, in his thick accent where it's hard to make out the words, something inside me just snaps.

I feel tears coming to my eyes. But it's not because of the grief that he's sharing, about their sad days of missing their son.

No.

It's because Mr. Mateja is praising Jesus and thanking Him for life and for breath and for health. He's thankful.

He's not asking for anything; he's thanking God for all He's done.

And it makes me feel awful and joyous at the same time.

Awful because I'm so not that way, but joyous because someone is like that.

Someone who lost his son.

But doesn't God get that? Doesn't He understand that?

I wipe my tears and stare at the ground below me to try and comprehend what's happening inside of me.

I feel better. Safer.

I feel like I belong.

And for the first time since praying to God on that train and giving my life over to Him in the flawed way that I probably did, I feel like I get it.

These people around me seem to get it, and they're showing me.

After prayers, Mr. Meiners starts talking again.

He talks about the prodigal son. He reads a bit of the Bible and then talks about a father loving and wanting the best for his son, even when he does dumb things.

I'm listening, but then I seem to jerk when Mr. Meiners says my name.

"And, Chris, this is something that we know, but that I thought I'd share since you're here. I hope you don't mind."

I shake my head.

Is he going to use me as an example?

"I got to know Oli during his sophomore year. I was his guidance counselor, and that was the year when he was getting into a lot of trouble. His parents know all of this, but I wanted to share it with you. There were some run-ins with the law. He got busted for having drugs. He was involved in a fight and arrested after he beat up a kid."

Beat up a kid.

That kid could have been me.

"I started to get to know him, and God worked in his heart that year. He was much like that son we were just talking about. He gave his life to Christ and began to mend his ways. I was fortunate to help him, and to help the Matejas, too, in their faith."

I still remember Oli sticking up for Kelsey and me when Gus confronted us in the art room.

"He was trying to learn what to do with that faith and how to live by it," Mr. Meiners said. "It wasn't always easy for him. He still had his friends, and he couldn't figure out how to tell them. At least at first. But eventually he did."

I wait for more, but Mr. Meiners doesn't say anything more about Oli.

So is that why he died? He found faith, and Gus and his father didn't like it?

"Real, authentic faith isn't welcome around here, Chris. But it is alive. It is real. And Jesus said, 'For where two or three come together in my name, there am I with them.' God is with us, right here in this barn. It doesn't matter what point you're at in life. God wants you to serve Him no matter what. Oliver did this—he was starting to do it before he died. But as we all know—even though we have grieved his loss—he is in a better place right now."

I can't help thinking of Jocelyn.

Same could be said of her, too. Right?

"Faith isn't just believing in something, but it's putting that faith in action."

I nod and get what he's saying.

Never in a million years did I ever imagine myself nodding at something like this in a deserted barn in the middle of a creepy Southern town.

I guess God had to bring me here in order for me to finally believe.

Now I wonder how exactly I'm supposed to show that faith in action.

Maybe I can do so with a sword and a spear. A literal *sword and spear.*

Because something tells me that Marsh and the others aren't going to be happy knowing about this faith thing of mine. It's real and it's there and I can do something with it.

68. THE BALLOON

Oli's parents give me hugs before I leave.

I feel I know and trust them even though I've only been around them for an hour.

I thank Mr. Meiners, then head out of the barn and back toward the tracks. I feel lighter, like a balloon full of helium. Except instead of helium, it's hope.

The light almost seems to drip through the treetops in these woods. The leaves and the color are coming back now. It's nice to see and hear the life filling back in.

I almost walk right by him.

Almost.

But I stop and dart my head and eyes toward the thing that's out of place.

It's not the object but the color.

Something orange.

Then I see a figure move behind a tree.

"Hey," I call out.

That's when he runs.

Whoever it is, he starts heading to the tracks.

I hesitate for a second until I see the face look back at me.

Jared.

The guy who told me he was my cousin, only to take advantage of me. I take off after him.

He's running fast, but so am I. He looks back at me, and I see that he's got a faint beard and mustache, and for some reason that reminds me of something.

New Year's Eve.

Spying on the group of hooded men out to make a sacrifice. Hiding in the trees and then being found by one of them.

Fighting with him and taking off his hood.

It's the same guy.

The same guy I wrestled with and shot. The one with the boyish look and the attempt at a mustache and a beard.

But if I shot him, then how——

The Falls.

Maybe they made him better the same way they made me better. Maybe Kinner helped save him or heal him.

I keep running now, even more angry and intent on catching up with him.

He's fast, but I'm faster.

He's strong, but I'm stronger.

Jared breaks into daylight by the train.

Where's a train when you need it?

I'm only seconds behind him.

I've been waiting to see him. Waiting to let him know exactly what I think about his lies and about him burning down the Crag's Inn.

Soon I'm close enough to launch myself and tackle him. We both go tumbling down the embankment to the railroad tracks.

I hear his heavy breathing as I grab his arms, then his neck, and then see him cover his face as if I'm going to punch him.

"Why'd you do it?" I ask.

He launches an elbow that makes me curl up breathless. Then I feel another elbow crack over my cheek. Jared shoves me away and gets back on his feet.

From somewhere he produces a gun, pointing it directly at my forehead.

"Lay off, or I swear I'll put a bullet in you that counts."

I'm sucking in air and wincing from the blows. Jared spits, then curses.

"You're so stupid, you know that?" he says.

"What are you doing?"

"I'm spying on you. That's what I'm doing. Follow me anymore and I'll shoot you."

"Why are you spying on me?"

"You just don't learn, do you? You don't get it."

"You're a liar," I tell him.

Jared laughs. "And you're a sucker."

He looks around and then wipes his mouth. "It's so easy with you. I swear. I think they're wrong about you. You're not special." He slides the gun back in his belt. "You touch me again and I'll kill you."

Not if I kill you first.

He starts walking away slowly, without a care. It makes me wonder why he bothered to run in the first place.

When I'm finally back on my feet, I no longer feel like a balloon. Unless it's one of those that's come back down to earth and gotten tangled up and torn in tree branches.

Jared's time will come.

I know that.

69. STUCK

I sit on a bench on the sidewalk lining Sable Road and the buildings behind me, between Brennan's where Mom used to work and the sheriff's office.

If lava suddenly began to spill out onto the road, I wouldn't really be surprised.

Or if that giant boulder chasing down Indiana Jones in *Raiders of the Lost Ark* suddenly came zipping by, I wouldn't be surprised by that either.

At this point nothing surprises me.

Nothing.

I sip on a soda and think about what just happened.

I guess I hadn't really thought what would happen if I actually caught Jared. What was I going to do?

But I know what he will be doing. The same thing he's been doing ever since I got to town. Spying. Staying in the shadows. Seeing what I'm up to. And sharing all his little notes with Marsh and Staunch.

Since it's the start of spring break, there's no way to tell Mr. Meiners about being spotted. I'll figure out how to find him this week.

They'll have to come up with another place to meet.

Well, Chris, we ran out of places, so how about your cabin?

A few cars pass as I sit here. I don't bother looking to see if someone's glaring out of them. Maybe Aunt Alice is driving a tiny car, looking for another mannequin for her house.

I sigh and rub my cheek and jaw. They feel swollen.

It's spring break.

And this is where I'm stuck.

70. THE MEMORIES
YOU TRY TO BURY

Seeing Jared is a sign.

No, make that an omen.

Any minute now that little dark-haired boy is going to come around the corner and the screeching violins are going to start playing and things are going to get really bad.

They aren't already?

It's 1:24 a.m., and I'm wide awake.

I'm wide awake because someone is screaming outside our cabin.

It's been going on for ten minutes or so.

I'm waiting for Mom to hear it and come upstairs. But so far I haven't heard anything below.

Midnight is sitting up on my bed, looking at me every time another howl sounds.

I used to watch horror movies all the time on cable back at home. Mom and Dad didn't really pay much attention. Sometimes I'd watch them at Brady's house because his parents definitely didn't pay any attention.

Brady. There's a name from yesteryear.

That sound outside is from one of those movies. A werewolf movie.

Could this be the demon dog howling in the night?

I slip out of bed. Mom has got to be awake. There's no way to *not* hear those screams outside.

It's so black downstairs, I might as well have my eyes closed.

You have to hear those sounds, Mom. Don't you?

But her door never opens, and I never hear her feet shuffling on the floor.

I crawl back into bed.

Eventually the howling stops.

I can only imagine what's next.

Mom is waiting for me when I walk downstairs the next morning. "Can we talk?" she asks.

She looks like she's been up for a while; she's dressed and ready for the day. Though what that means I don't know.

"Sure."

"Want me to make you anything for breakfast?"

I shake my head and get my usual bowl of Raisin Nut Bran and then sit across from Mom at the round table. She's got a big mug of coffee in her hands.

"Did you hear that last night?" she asks.

Even made up and not drinking anymore (at least not that I know of), Mom's face still looks hard. Not just the lines, but the look. It's heavy.

Wonder if mine's starting to look that way too.

I let out a chuckle that says *Uh, yeah* and then nod. My mouth is full, so I don't say anything.

Mom sighs, takes a sip of her coffee.

Is this the moment she's going to tell me she's a vampire?

"I should have never brought us back to this evil place, Chris. I'm sorry. I'm sorry for everything I've put you through."

"You've already apologized," I say. "It's okay."

"Listen to me. It's too close to your graduation for us to leave. I can't do that to you."

No, Mom, you can. And should.

"But right after graduation we're going back to Illinois," she continues.

"For real?"

"Yes. What? Why does that surprise you?"

"I didn't think you ever wanted to go there again."

She swallows and gives me that heavy, hard look. "I learned something in rehab, Chris. Something about myself that's not so flattering. It's not about my drinking. But it's why I drink. The other day when you walked in on us arguing I was telling Robert this. Of course, he doesn't want to talk about it. He wants to keep it buried just like I have all these years."

"Keep what buried?"

"The facts about our parents. About my mom—your grand-mother. I told you she passed away when I was young, but I've never told you how."

I have a feeling the *how* isn't going to be so good.

"Louise—that was your grandmother's name. She was Aunt Alice's younger sister."

I really don't think I want to hear this. I finish my bowl of cereal and have a hard time looking Mom straight in her face.

"They killed her," Mom says. "I was ten years old and remember it like it was yesterday. It's strange the memories that you try to bury.

They never really go away. Not totally. I realized that while getting help these last few months."

I shift in the chair that I suddenly realize is really uncomfortable.

"Robert and I were at our house when Daddy came home and got his rifle. All he said is that something happened to Momma. He told Robert to take care of me. There were some neighbors at the time just a couple houses down, and Daddy told Robert to take me there. I remember walking to the house scared out of my mind—it was still light out 'cause it was summertime. I spent the night there, but Robert got out. I never knew this until the other night. He didn't spend the night at the Carsons' house."

I nod, waiting to hear. The cabin feels warm as morning sunlight splashes over the room.

"He went back home to wait and hear what happened, but he hid because he knew Daddy would beat him if he disobeyed an order. And he saw your grandfather come home covered in blood. No rifle, no Momma. And Robert told me he just—"

Mom tears up, and her voice suddenly begins to shake.

"Mom?"

"I'm okay—it's just—" She wipes her eyes and nose. "Robert heard our father weep. He didn't think anybody was home—he was too tough to cry in front of anybody else. Especially his children. But Robert had to hear that."

"What happened?"

"Daddy told us it was a driving accident, but Robert knew it wasn't true. All he ever got out of our father was that it had something to do with our mom's sister, Alice, and their father. But Chris—they killed her. The evil in this town killed her. I know that now. Just like they killed your grandfather."

And just like they killed Jocelyn.

I almost say this.

But I can't.

Mom is sitting across from me, weeping softly in her hands. I go over and sit beside her and then hug her.

I will tell her about Jocelyn. But not now.

I don't want to add fire to the flames.

"Chris—I—it just—" She can't talk for a while. I hold her and wait for the tears to stop.

When they do, Mom grabs a Kleenex and then sits back down with another sigh.

"My parents were God-fearing people, Chris. That was why my grandfather didn't want to have anything to do with them. And that's why—that's what happened."

"Why they got killed?" I ask.

"Yes. But also—that's what happened to Robert and me. Why we grew up—at least why I started to hate God. All this time I've been angry, Chris. I didn't even know it. Not really. But what happened with your father scared me, because it made me think of my own parents and their faith and the faith I once had. A faith I thought was real until my mother died and I was forced to live a completely new life. That's when my resentment began. So when your father showed up saying he had been born again, I didn't want to hear any of it. But deep down—deep down I was afraid."

"Of what?"

"That the same thing that happened to my parents might happen to your father. Or to you. And I just—"

She begins to cry again.

If only you knew the rest of the story, Mom.

"We're going to be fine," I tell her.

She nods, but I can tell she thinks this is her son trying to say anything just to make her feel better.

"No, Mom, listen. We are going to be fine. We are going to get out of here. God will take care of us."

For the first time in my life, I see Mom as someone else. Not an old, broken-down lady, and not the person trying to take care of me and raise me.

No. I see a girl just like Jocelyn and Lily and Kelsey and any other girl. Just a little rougher around the edges.

A girl with the same fears and frustrations that any of us might have.

"We gotta believe that, you know?" I ask. "It's either that or we let the howling wolves get to us."

She shakes her head and starts crying again. "I just don't—I don't know what those things are—they're chasing me. They've been chasing me my whole life. I thought … I really believed coming back here meant they'd stop coming after me. I didn't know all this time that that's what they wanted."

"What?"

Mom wipes her cheeks. "For me to come back here with the thing I love the most."

I feel an ache deep inside my gut. I give her another hug.

Maybe they've been chasing her all her life. But it's almost time to make a stand and fight back.

I know how much longer we have, and I know what they ultimately want.

When the moment comes, I'll be ready. For whatever happens.

71. UH HUH

"So do you know a lot of the urban myths and all that for Solitary?" I ask.

Mounds has a jumbo-sized thing of soda in his hand. "I hate that term, 'urban myths.' That's a way to cover up genuine ghost stories. And this town is full of them, my friend."

"Do any of them involve werewolves?"

We're sitting at a McDonald's after visiting a cemetery over by Hendersonville. We didn't find anything there, not like the stuff we've found in Solitary.

"Why?" Mounds asks through a mouth full of Big Mac and fries. "You seen some horror movies recently?"

"Just wondering."

"Yeah, but why werewolves?

"Am I right?"

He picks up six fries and slides them down across the glob of ketchup, then rams them into his mouth.

"I don't know anything about werewolves, like people turning into them. Not around here. But a lot of people say there's a pack of wolves that's haunted. Or cursed or possessed. One of those."

"Why?"

"You saw those wolves at the old burnt-down church, right? This place is full of wildlife roaming around. People say they've seen glowing wolves or black wolves standing at their door. Doesn't mean they're werewolves."

"Ever heard them howling in the night?"

Mounds shakes his head, and I notice his three chins. "You hear one?"

I nod.

"I'm telling you, Chris. You could make a fortune out of ghost hunting. Start a television show, become a brand. You've got the knack."

"A knack for finding ghosts?"

He chuckles. "No—it's more like they find you."

"You think I heard some kind of ghost?"

He nods. "I think it might have been a wolf that got killed years ago. Or one looking for the rest of its clan."

"Seriously?" I can't believe he's accepting my brief story as fact.

"We can check it out if you want to. Not today. I'm tired."

It's only two in the afternoon on a Wednesday.

"Sure," I say. "Anytime."

He slips the rest of his second Big Mac into his mouth, then wipes his hands. "I got something for you. Hold on."

His faded backpack where he carries everything important is sitting next to him. Mounds digs around in there and pulls out a camera.

"I bought that online," Mounds says. "It's supposed to take pictures of dead people. Like *The Sixth Sense* camera. Takes an idiot like me to fall for it. Got two packs of special 'sixth-sense film.' Nothing more than a Polaroid."

The camera is white and black and has a special star sticker on it. It's lightweight and snaps open and shut.

"It's yours," he says. "I'm hoping that perhaps with your abilities you'll be able to actually get some shots of ghosts. Who knows?"

"Why don't you get your money back?"

"I tried. The number's disconnected and the website is gone. Guess I can understand why."

He grabs the two rolls of film, square blocks that look like large candy bars.

"Knock yourself out," he tells me.

With my luck, I probably will.

Later that day, I load the camera and try to take a picture of Midnight. The camera makes some weird catching sound and then does nothing. I play around with it for thirty minutes until I decide that Mounds was sold a hunk of junk.

I'm in my room, listening to albums and playing around on the Internet. Facebook just overwhelms me when I go to it. I still don't like seeing what my old friends are up to, because if they only knew what I was up to …

Hey, Brady, I'm battling dark supernatural forces, but other than that things are fine.

Yeah. No thanks.

I like going on iTunes and discovering new groups or old albums or stuff I'd never in a million years discover without listening to a sample.

So yeah, this is my spring break.

Sometime around dinnertime Kelsey texts me.

How's it going?

I can't help smiling. It's nice hearing from someone. Especially her.

Sorry—can't text. Super busy.

I can't help teasing either.

Really? she asks.

Oh, sure.

I miss you.

Okay, when she goes and says stuff like that, I can't joke around anymore.

I text, I probably miss you more.

Any job prospects?

I already have one!

A real job.

Should I be looking? I ask.

What about college?

Should I be looking? ☺

We keep texting. I don't worry about the time or whether we have unlimited texting or about eating or about the wolves that might be howling at my door.

We talk about her time seeing her brother and her time with her parents. She loves them, but they drive her crazy sometimes. She says that they tend to put her brother on a pedestal while they baby her. I tell her I don't know what either feels like.

Then we lighten things up and talk music. I share bands I've discovered, and she shares stuff she likes. A lot of the music Kelsey enjoys is from Christian bands I've never heard of. She tells me to check them out, and I say I will. She says it's good to listen to some songs about hope.

I look at the time and see we've been texting for almost an hour.

I decide to call her. "You know how long we've been texting?"

"Not really," Kelsey says. "Hello."

"Hello."

"You okay?"

"Yeah. I just—figured I'd talk to someone live and in person."

"Okay."

She's suddenly less verbal.

"Wait, let me guess. Are your parents nearby?"

"Uh huh."

"Same room?"

"Uh huh."

"Now I get why you were texting me."

"Uh huh."

"Is that all you're going to say?"

"Uh huh."

We both laugh.

"You think that Chris Buckley is like the most amazing, cool guy you've ever known."

"Uh huh."

"And every day you wonder whether to steal your parents' car and drive to Mexico with him."

"Uh huh."

"You're searching for a really cool gift to buy Chris since he was left alone on spring break."

"Huh?"

We laugh again.

"Well, it's nice hearing your voice. Even if you're not saying much."

"You too," Kelsey says.

I hear Mom calling me downstairs. "I think we're having dinner. Or Mom is making me eat something."

"You need your carbs. You know what Coach Brinks says."

"Don't remind me," I say. "I'll text you later, okay? Will you be around?"

"Uh huh."

"Will you be thinking about me and how cool I am sitting in my little room in my cabin?"

She laughs. "Uh huh."

"You're just totally crazy for me, right?"

"Yeah, Chris. I am."

Nice.

I say good-bye and head downstairs.

Sometimes I think that the girls have all been pretty distractions from the ugliness around here. I focus on them and temporarily forget about the mess around me.

But the ugly mess always comes back.

The night arrives, and I find myself wondering when the mess is going to slip back into my room.

I know it's only a matter of time.

So I pray for God to keep the darkness and the ugliness away for a while. As long as possible. To bring a little light during this boring spring break.

72. WEIRD AND SURPRISING

The next day I go to the high school to practice at the track.

It's not like I'm so dedicated. I'm just bored. And I figure if I keep in shape, then when I get back to school the practices won't be as hard. They'll still be bad, because Coach Brinks will want to work off the flab and the laziness from spring break.

As I pull back into the driveway on my bike, I see Dad's SUV.

Something's gone bad.

I fly up the steps to the deck and fling the door open.

Dad and Mom are sitting in the family room on the couches.

I'm out of breath. "What's wrong?"

"Hi, Chris."

Dad smiles, and Mom doesn't look dead.

Okay, I guess that's a good sign.

"Everything is fine," Mom tells me.

"How was the workout?" Dad asks.

"Good," I say.

"I didn't tell you I was coming because I wasn't sure until the last minute whether I'd be able to. I wanted to surprise you."

I nod and sigh. "Yeah. You surprised me."

AKA freaked me out.

"I'm like you—no classes this week," he says. "Go clean up. We're going out for dinner."

"Okay."

I think of my prayer yesterday and wonder if this is the answer. A year ago I wouldn't have seen it that way. But I do now.

A lot can change in a year. Around you.

And inside your heart.

Dad looks different.

Then again, so does Mom.

I don't pick this up at first. Or when we sit down at the table at the Olive Garden. Or when we order drinks.

But then I seem to notice it.

Those lines on my father's forehead and the scowl that seemed to always be there aren't as noticeable. In fact, he smiles a lot.

And Mom doesn't look as hard anymore. Sure, not drinking every night and slogging through the day probably helps a person look a little healthier. But it's more than that. She's got makeup on, and she looks younger, brighter.

She's smiling a lot too.

This is an answer to prayer that I could not have dreamed of. Both my parents sitting at the table looking like—well, looking like friends.

Am I dreaming?

Soon enough Dad seems to get that I'm watching both of them with curiosity and questions.

"Chris, I wanted to be here—both of us wanted me to be here—to tell you something."

The last time Dad said something like this was when they told me they were getting a divorce. I saw that coming miles away.

I don't see this one coming.

"Your father and I have been talking a lot lately," Mom says.

That's news to me.

Then both of them start to say something, and then they both pause and look at each other in a weird way as if …

What is going on?

I blush because I feel utterly out of my body sitting here. I'm not used to them looking at each other unless they are glaring. Even years ago, when I was a kid, it was never like this. Not like this scene in front of me.

Who drugged my parents, and where can I find their supplier to get what they have?

"Go ahead," Mom tells Dad.

"We want to let you know—and I know this is going to surprise you—that we're trying to work things out."

A server comes to bring us breadsticks and salad. I want to just start stuffing my face to get away from the awkward feeling I have in my gut.

"I know I told you we would be going back to Chicago," Mom says. "We're going to be staying with your father."

I look at Mom, then at Dad. I'm not sure whether I should be angry or happy or confused. I mean, this was what I wanted once, until I decided it was exactly what I *didn't* want. Until—

"Okay," I say.

I know they're probably thinking and expecting more. But I don't know what to say.

Did You really do this, God?

Mom clears her throat. "Some of the feelings I've had, Chris—well, we're working through those. And we can't—we're not going to promise anything. But it's a start."

I want to laugh.

There was a time in my life when I wanted so badly to hear this. When my parents were still together but not really together. When they were married but not really living in any kind of marriage.

Then it changed when Dad found faith and Mom found anger. I took the side of Mom and her anger and moved away to Solitary.

Little did I know I'd go back home and find faith.

I know they both want to ask what I'm thinking and feeling. But I can't tell them that I halfway doubt I'll see the summer. I can't share with them that I'm a bit happy and a bit sad but mostly I'm totally terrified. They're back together or at least trying to be, but I won't be around to see it happen.

"That's cool," I say.

It is cool. It's just—unexpected.

Nothing in the last year and a half has been expected, has it?

"I knew you were on break, too," Dad says. "I figured I could come down and stay a couple of days. Is that—cool with you?"

I laugh. Dad is trying. I appreciate that.

"Yeah."

We focus on eating, and there's no more weird, surprising talk. Yet as we eat, I realize I'm not the only person who seems to be surprised here. Both Mom and Dad seem quieter than usual, more hesitant to say something, more—

Acting more like a couple teenagers might.

It's kind of amusing. At least for now. I just hope this doesn't last for long.

They're still my parents. And the last thing I want is to see them suddenly making out.

No thanks.

73. PRAYERS

I have to get it out there. I don't want to make a big deal, but I know I have to tell him.

He's going to be leaving pretty soon. The last couple of days have been good. Strange but good. Okay—really, really strange, but also pretty good.

And I just know I need to tell him.

It goes something like this.

"Hey, Dad."

"Yeah?" He's reading *USA Today* like he always did at home. But this time he moves the paper away so I have his full attention.

Mom's gone grocery shopping but will be coming back before he leaves. That's another reason why now's the right time.

"I just wanted to let you know something."

But I'm not sure how to let you know. It seems private and personal and nobody else's business.

But it's Dad's business because it's partly due to Dad.

"What is it?" he asks.

"I just—the stuff about you and being a Christian and all that. I'm—I mean it's okay. It's all right now."

He looks puzzled and smiles and nods. I'm babbling, and I know it.

"No, what I want to say is that I—that I believe. That I'm— things have changed. Between God and me. For the better."

Dad's face changes. He looks glad. Surprised but glad.

"I'm happy to hear that," he says.

I nod and shrug, and now I want to just get away. I could say more, but I don't really know what to say. I don't know how to say it because I'm not sure what to do and how to do it and how this whole thing—

"Chris?"

"Yeah."

"Just keep praying, asking for God's guidance. When I suddenly opened my eyes and saw the world in a whole new light, it was overwhelming. But don't let it be too overwhelming. Be happy. Be thankful. Know that there's more to this world than just the here and now. There's more than just this life."

"I think I tell myself that everyday. Mostly because I hate Solitary."

Dad laughs. He doesn't realize I'm serious. "Prayer works, Chris. I know. I've been praying for you guys ever since you left. I've been praying that God will bring both of you to Him. And back to me."

He doesn't finish by saying it's happened and that we're going to drive off into the sunset and live happily ever after. Even Dad knows better than to say that.

But I don't need him to say any more.

Dad prayed, and God heard those prayers.

Somehow, God brought Mom and me closer to Him.

Maybe not in the way I would have chosen, but it happened.

74. FREEZE

Maybe it would be good to freeze this moment in time.

The second week in March. A bright and warm morning where the birds wake up singing and somehow ignoring the fact that they're stuck in Solitary. A fun and relaxing ride to school on Uncle Robert's motorcycle. Seeing Kelsey for the first time since before spring break, noticing that she looks more beautiful than she did when she left as I hug her and then feel her give me a kiss on the cheek.

The classes seem lighter and quicker.

The food in the cafeteria seems to taste better.

The blue in Kelsey's eyes seems brighter.

Harris's stories seem funnier.

Even Newt seems taller.

I share the news about my parents with Kelsey. And doing this makes me realize that it really has had a big impact on me. Things seem to be better. My life seems to have a future. A better one.

All of this is wonderful.

All of this is temporary, because April is going to morph into May, and the joy is going to morph into some newfound pain.

The open skies are going to cloud up and start pouring down hurt and anguish into my life.

That's what the voice deep, deep down says.

That's why I drown it out with Kelsey and school and the wind and the skies and everything around me.

Chrisssssss.

The voice is always there. The memories and the beating heart of fear.

Chrissssss.

I want to lock this day down and never move on. Or fast forward to September or December.

Maybe you'll never see them.

This is the voice of fear, the voice of something evil, the voice of something empty.

Maybe this will be the last joyous day of your miserable little life.

When the sun sets and the darkness creeps in, the voices come.

Dad is back in Illinois, attending classes at a Bible college and dreaming of the future. Mom is back working at Brennan's, dreaming of the future. Midnight is next to me on the couch, dreaming of hot dogs.

And I'm here, not wanting the dreams to come.

I'm here, wanting the day not to fade away.

But the sun always sets, and the nightmares always arrive.

75. NOWHERE FAST

I'm already having a bad day when Pastor Marsh shows up.

Just call him Marsh because he's no pastor.

It's a gray, cool March morning, and I'm feeling groggy and totally incapable of being happy and thankful like Dad suggested. Watching the news reminds me that it's not just Solitary that's messed up, but it's this world. There are riots in the streets and wars in other countries, and a mother is suspected of killing her two-year-old daughter.

It's enough to make you not want to open your door and go outside.

Why go outside when you have the joys of Facebook at your fingertips right here in the house?

My classes suck, and the teachers are killing us with homework and exams, and college is laughing at me from afar. Even Kelsey seems different, because she's feeling the overload herself, and she's a straight-A student.

So when I see Marsh standing there looking all high and mighty I want to throw up on him.

Then I notice he's standing by Mr. Meiners, and I get a little worried.

"Chris, just the man I wanted to see."

It's lunchtime, and I was looking forward to a nice break with Kelsey. But nope—doesn't look like that's going to happen.

Mr. Meiners just says hi and returns to his classroom.

"Let's go grab a burger," Marsh says.

"I really can't."

He laughs, then quickly nods and says, "Yes, you can."

I don't have a choice.

I put my books in my locker and leave with the pastor. Several students greet him. Unfortunately I don't see Kelsey to tell her I'm going. I'll text her when I get outside.

I get in Marsh's car, and he heads to the closest fast-food place, a burger joint that I've only eaten at once because it's really bad. I order a burger and fries, but I don't feel like eating them. Marsh only orders an iced tea. We sit in a booth away from the other diners in the small eating area.

"You're starting to disappoint me, Chris."

Here we go.

Both of his hands hold the plastic cup, and I notice how girly his hands look. They're soft and thin.

Those same hands slit my wrist, didn't they?

"I hate being disappointed," Marsh says.

"What'd I do now?"

"Why don't you tell me?"

I want to tell him that I only have one father, thank you very much. But I know I can't.

"Your mother came home in one piece, didn't she?" he asks.

"Yes."

"So why then are you continuing to play with fire?"

"What do you mean?"

"Chris—"

"Is this about Jared?"

He slaps the table suddenly, and the crack it makes startles me. For a brief second I see a wild look on his face, an expression I can't remember seeing before. It's brief, but I know I saw it. He clears his throat and smiles at me.

"Don't blame others, Chris. This is about you. Just … you."

"Okay."

"Why would you go visit that group?"

"Which one?"

He curses and then moves his head so that he can whisper to me. "You know exactly which group I'm talking about. This is why people are getting very irritated by your actions, and why I won't be able to do anything about their response. Do you understand?"

"Yes."

"No," he snaps in a controlled whisper. "No, you don't understand. You're still out there trying to do it your way. When will you learn? Huh? Tell me that."

"I'm sorry."

Marsh laughs. "What a lie. You're not even mildly sorry. But these people, Chris—Staunch and others—they can make anybody sorry for anything. I've seen it. You've seen it, but you tend to forget. And I don't know if that's because you think you're untouchable or what."

"No."

"Because you're not," Marsh says. "You're very touchable, I promise you. Their patience is running out. Staunch will do whatever he has to—and believe me, he has when he's not restrained. He's a big bull, that one. But he does what Kinner tells him to. He's Kinner's hands and voice. I'm just trying to bide our time."

I notice the words he uses.

Our time.

"And what do you think you're doing with the girl?"

I'm about ready to say who, but decide that I shouldn't. "What about her?"

"What about her? Why is there a 'her' to begin with? Haven't you learned?"

"You said that she wouldn't be harmed."

Marsh curses, but this time it seems like it's to himself. He glances out the window and then around the restaurant. Nobody is paying us any attention, and even if they were, I doubt Marsh would care.

"I'm trying to figure you out, and I just don't seem able to. I mean—I first thought you just wanted the hottest girl around for one reason. That your so-called 'nobility' is more due to fear and hesitation. But then this comes along. Where do you see this thing going?"

"I don't know."

"Well, I can tell you where it's going," Marsh says. "Nowhere fast. You need to end things with her."

I begin to shake my head, and Marsh shakes his like he's frantically copying me.

"Do you want her to end up like Jocelyn or Lily? Do you?"

"But you said—"

"It doesn't matter what I say. You believe anything coming out of my mouth, and half the time I'm just making something up to shut you up or try to stop you from doing something even more stupid. This isn't a love story, Chris. Eventually you can find the things you need—and yes, down the road you can even convince yourself it's love, if that's what you need, though it will never last. But you can't have that now."

"Why?"

Marsh sits up and tightens his jaw. "Maybe for starters because I say so."

He looks like he could easily take those girly hands of his and strangle me without a bit of hesitation.

He sits back and sips his tea and seems to gain control of his anger. "You don't want anything to happen to her, right?"

I nod.

"Then you politely and calmly end it."

My heart starts beating, and my mind starts racing.

"You do it this week. Kinner is concerned for you, Chris. Kelsey and her family are all believers, and that worries him. That, along with you going to visit that group in the woods. I mean—what's going on with you, Chris?"

"Nothing."

"Is that girl having that much influence on you? Are you feeling guilt for late-night longings you have for her? Or for the things you've seen that you've kept from others? Things like what happened to Jocelyn. And Lily. What is it?"

"I don't know," I say.

"I think you know. Look—I've had my moments, and I can understand. But Kinner doesn't. So the solution is you break it off with Kelsey. You won't be trying to convince her to sleep with you, and you won't be having doubts and confusion and all that nonsense. I mean—don't you see it's just nonsense? Guilt and fear and frustration. The only thing that faith gives you is guilt. And that's what I've been telling you all this time. I can find a way for you to let go and be free."

Liar.

This man across from me doesn't look like he's ever let anything go. And he sure doesn't look free.

For a moment he waits for me to respond, but I don't.

"End things with Kelsey, or Staunch will end things his way. You understand? Look at me. In the eyes. Do you understand?"

I force myself to look at him.

I want to kill this man and end all the pain and suffering he's brought to this town and these people. And to me and my family.

"Yes," I say. "I understand."

I understand that one day I'm going to kill you, you sick freak.

"You have a little over two months to go. You don't need to be worrying about Kelsey and her broken little heart. You'll find you have to deal with enough on your own."

He smiles.

"What do you mean?"

"Come on. I gotta take you back to school. Don't want to break any rules, do we?"

76. MAGICAL

I'm tired. Tired of people telling me what to do, what not to do, what I have to feel, what I'm supposed to be.

I'm just tired.

It's late and I should be sleeping, but I'm staring at that picture of me that I once found, that happy carefree guy smiling in the sun.

Did someone give this to me to taunt me, to show me a snapshot of someone I'll never be able to become?

I look at the picture of the woods with the Robert Frost line on it.

Then I stare at the beaming and bright picture of Kelsey on her Facebook profile. She's happy and carefree.

I should never have gotten close. Should've known better. Should've been more careful.

For a long time that night, I stare at her.

Thinking what to do.

Thinking what to say.

The next day, I come to school with a plan.

I still don't know if they have spies planted everywhere. Or if I'm bugged in my boxers and my backpack and my lunch bag. I don't know.

Somehow in some way they have known my every step ever since I've come to Solitary.

They.

Staunch, Marsh, Great-grandfather Kinner.

Whoever else is part of *they.*

So I have to be careful.

But they got Jared to keep an eye on me. So they don't know everything.

That's right.

They got Lily to try and do the same. To try and control me.

That almost worked.

I know there's no way they can read my mind. Because if they could, they'd already know the truth: this faith I have is real even if it's just a spark. A spark that's started melting away the hard ice around my heart.

They don't know.

But there might be a time coming soon when they will ask and I will have to make a choice whether to admit the truth or not.

I'm not there yet. It's the end of March, and I'm going to tell Kelsey the truth. As much as I can.

It's a warm spring day, and after lunch as we're walking toward our lockers, I ask Kelsey the question.

"Have you ever skipped a class?"

She looks surprised. I know her answer before she says, "No. Why?"

"I want you—no, I need you to do something for me."

"What?"

We're walking slowly, like any other day. I whisper, "I need you to come somewhere with me."

"Where?" Kelsey looks a bit amused.

"Just somewhere. But it needs to be now."

"What? Right now?"

"Yes," I say.

"Chris—what's going on?"

"I need you to trust me."

"Okay."

"Then just keep walking to your locker. Then act like you normally do, except instead of going to your next class, go outside and meet me in the parking lot."

"But I have to—"

"Kelsey, please."

"What's wrong?"

"I'll explain."

"Explain what?" She looks nervous now. "Chris?"

"I can't. Not here."

She looks at me for a long time and then nods.

She means it when she says she trusts me. Which is good, because she's going to have to keep trusting me a lot.

I go to my locker and then walk to my trigonometry class but don't go inside. I keep walking, making sure nobody is following me.

I wait in the parking lot for a few minutes, then see Kelsey coming down the steps toward me. I can't help but smile. She seems to bounce.

If you only knew.

She climbs on the motorcycle behind me, and I drive off.

It takes about fifteen minutes to get to Marsh Falls.

We park at the edge of the woods and then head toward the base of the falls. I'm not pulling any sort of wild stunt like slashing my wrists and showing Kelsey how they heal or anything like that. But somehow, for some reason, this seems like a safe place to come. Or at least a mysterious middle ground.

It seems to make sense to tell Kelsey what I need to tell her here.

I walk with her hand in hand, and it takes us a while to get to the small creek flowing from the falls. Large rocks surround the area, and I find one that's flat to sit on. It's near the edge of the creek and provides a scenic view of the falling waters and the pool underneath.

"You're scaring me a little," Kelsey says.

"Don't be scared."

She smiles and looks around. "This is beautiful."

"You've never been here?"

Kelsey shakes her head. I tell her that it's Marsh Falls and that the waters are supposed to be magical.

Her bright blue eyes study me in the middle of these woods. "Why'd you bring me here?"

"Because it's the only place I can think where someone might not be watching me," I say. "I don't know why I think that. Maybe someone is behind the falls with a video camera and recording equipment. I don't know. But this place seems … safe."

"Safe for what?"

I sigh and sit up and face her and take her hands. "I have to break up with you."

Instant confusion fills her pretty face. "What?"

"No, listen. That's what it's supposed to look like. Kelsey—there are bad people around here. Bad men. I could try and go into detail and tell you every little thing I know about them, but I think that would just make things worse."

"Are you in trouble?"

I nod. "Yeah, you could say that. Not because of something I did. But just—these people—it has to do with who I am and who I'm related to. And it has to do with my family."

"But what's it have to do with me?"

I squeeze her hands and smile. "Nothing. That's the thing—they think that I shouldn't be with you. And these people—I have to do what they tell me to do."

They might be able to control what I do, but they can't control fate. They can't control the fact that one day a guy decides to talk to a girl in his art class and it turns into something more.

"I don't understand."

I nod.

Of course you don't.

"Kelsey—there are people in this town who are evil. I know— I know that you've heard stories and weird things—everybody has. But it's real. They don't want me with you. They don't like the fact that you and your family are Christians. They don't like that at all."

"But what—why do they care?"

"Because …"

I don't know exactly what to say because the more I say the more insane I'm going to sound.

"Because they feel they own me," I say. "And they don't want to have anything to do with God or Jesus or anything good. And that includes you."

I can see her mind trying to make sense of this, but I know it's not going to happen, not here, not now.

"I can't be seen with you anymore. We can't talk. Or email or text or anything."

She lets out an exasperated and bewildered chuckle.

"I know. It's crazy. Listen—I'm coming to Illinois with you. I'm going back there for college. Or at least to live. And this—you and me—we're not done. But we have a couple of months to go, and I don't want anything happening to you."

"This is about the stuff you've told me—about the bad people who have it out for you?"

I nod. "Yeah. These evil people—they want me for something, Kelsey. They think they own me because of who I'm related to. Because of my great-grandfather. And yeah, it's totally insane. All of it. But it took me a long time to finally stop saying it was insane and realize it's all true."

"What are you supposed to do for them?"

The steady pounding of the water falling into the pond keeps our words from being heard. Yet still I end up scanning the woods around us for a moment.

"I don't know what I'm supposed to do," I say. "It's like the family business or something. Like the mob. They're coming to tell me I'm a part of them and have to do what they say or else. Except this isn't the mob. This is some cult."

Kelsey doesn't laugh in my face. But that's because she lives around here and goes to Harrington, and anyone who does that has to know a little deep down. The rumors and the weird things and the disappearances and the overall vibe of Solitary. Anybody knows something.

Instead of looking confused, Kelsey looks scared.

"It's going to be okay," I tell her. "But we can't—this, you and me, can't be anymore. Not public."

"Chris?"

"Yeah."

"Did something happen to Jocelyn? Is that why she's gone?"

I nod and stare at her.

Then I see the tears forming in her eyes.

"It's okay," I tell her. "Nothing is going to happen to you."

She swallows and wipes her eyes.

"I swear, you're going to be okay," I tell her.

"But can't we tell someone? What about my parents?"

"No. I've tried that. Others have tried that. That's why—I swear, Kelsey, you have to trust me. You have to do this. Just stay quiet. And stay away from me."

She continues to cry, so I move over and hold her in my arms.

"Nothing is going to happen to you," I tell her as my mouth is gently pressed against her ear. "I'm going to take care of you."

Kelsey moves back so she can look at me. I see those vibrant eyes looking scared and hurt but also lovely. They stare up at me in a strange and magical way.

"I love you," Kelsey says. She's shaking as she holds my hands, and tears are in her eyes, but somehow she's also smiling. "I really do, Chris. I really love you."

I don't expect this and don't know what to say.

But Kelsey solves that for me when she moves over and kisses me. I move my arms around her waist, and I kiss her for a very long time.

I kiss her hard and kiss her knowing it might be our last kiss for some time.

77. MIDNIGHT

On Friday afternoon of the same week I tell Kelsey good-bye, a face from the past is waiting for me after school lets out.

Gus used to be an everyday menace, but he's left me alone this year. I'm sure it's because of the vicious beating with a spoon that he got in front of everybody at the Labor Day picnic at the Staunch house. A beating that his own father gave him. A beating I can relate to, since I've felt the brunt of his father's anger too.

I'm sure Staunch has told Gus to lay off me. But there have been other things too.

Oli dying over the summer. I don't know if Gus was involved in any way, but that seemed to take the high school bullying antics to a whole new level.

I figured Gus and I were never going to cross paths again, and that was fine by me.

Instead, he's standing there by my motorcycle in an Avenged Sevenhold T-shirt, looking the same as always. In fact, he looks even fatter and uglier than usual. As if the spoon beating just made him meaner and more miserable.

He greets me with an offensive and colorful word that I'm not surprised to hear from his mouth. "Thought you were done with me, didn't you?"

"What do you want?"

He's still just a dumb redneck. Yeah, he's got a monster for a father, but it doesn't excuse his being an idiot.

"I've been waiting and watching, Chris. You think I was just gonna let you go and not get you back for everything you done?"

He still has a hick accent and a mean, beefy face.

"Get out of my way, Gus."

"Or what? What're you gonna do?"

I just stand there. I'm in no mood to fight or to argue or even communicate with this big lug nut.

"I know what you're gonna do," he says. "I know exactly what you're gonna do."

"What's that?"

His eyes shrink as he glares at me. It's like looking at the hot coals of a fire. I can just feel the hatred coming from him.

"I don't care who you are," he says in a lower voice. "I don't care what you're supposed to do. I don't care when you're supposed to do it. Or why."

Gus curses and spits out something thick onto the pavement.

"I don't even care if I get in trouble, because I'm always in trouble. Don't matter. I just want to see you cry. I want to see you on your knees scared and begging for help."

He smiles in a way that makes me nervous.

"So I know exactly how that's gonna happen," he says.

"Gus, come on—I didn't do anything to you."

He barks out another curse. "Nothing? You did everything. Nothing's been the same since you moved here, and I'm tired of it. Tired of you. Tired of having to stay away from you. But I'm not laying a single finger on you. Not at all."

Gus lets out a sick and twisted laugh.

"What?" I ask.

"I promise, I won't hurt you. Maybe your dog, but not you."

I look at him for a second. He laughs again, and his face seems to glow in delight.

"What'd you say?"

"Woof woof," Gus says.

Midnight.

I don't say anything, because the chances are high he's lying. I just wait for a minute.

"What do you call that little black mop of a poochie you got there?" Gus asks.

"Midnight."

"Ah," Gus says, acting and gloating and doing a lame job at both. "Well, that's very fitting."

"Why's that?"

"You ever want to see that dog of yours again?"

My stomach drops, because I suddenly know Gus isn't lying.

He's smiling way too big to be bluffing.

"What'd you do?"

"Oh, she's fine. For now. But come *midnight*, I don't know."

"Gus, I swear, if you did anything—"

"What? What are you going to do?"

"Where is she?"

"You can find her around the stroke of twelve."

"Where?"

He shoves me back, since I'm in his face. "You do anything now or get me in any kind of trouble," Gus says, "and I'll squash her. I swear. I'll sit on her. I don't care."

"Where?" I ask again.

"Midnight is going to be down in the tunnels."

"What tunnels?"

Gus just laughs. "That's funny."

"Where in the tunnels?"

"That's the fun part, Chris. Mr. Golden Boy. Mr. Chosen One. You'll have to find your little doggie in the dark. And trust me, you're not gonna want to go down there, not after midnight. Not when *he's* roaming about."

Gus laughs and starts to walk away.

I grab him on his shoulder, and he whips around and almost pounds me in the face.

But he holds himself back.

"Ever wonder about the animals around here?" Gus says with a smirk. "How they're all just a bit weird? Why you find dead animals all around? Huh?"

"Is she okay?"

"What? Your dog? Yeah, sure, she's fine. For now. But the evil spirits don't like animals. They like to feed on them. And so does he."

He just glares at me, and I say nothing. I can't.

I think I'm a bit too shocked.

The mental images going through my mind won't leave.

"Good luck, Prince Buckley," Gus spits out as he walks away.

78. Heading In

That evening I realize just how attached I've grown to the dog Jocelyn named Midnight. My family never had an animal growing up, so this was my first dog. And while maybe I always imagined it would be nice to have a big one, maybe a golden retriever or a strong Lab or even a German shepherd like my uncle's, it didn't take me long to fall in love with the little black Shih Tzu.

Maybe because I fell in love with her owner.

Midnight isn't just a dog, however. She isn't just this little companion that has been a bright spot (even if she's pitch black) in a dark world. She stands for this wonderful thing I didn't know I was looking for when I first arrived at Harrington High.

This wonderful thing that Jocelyn found before I did.

Hope.

I don't really know what I'll do if something happens to Midnight. If I can't find her down below. If that creature ends up …

Stop it.

Mom knows something is wrong, but I don't tell her what. She just assumes it has to do with everything else going on. The overall blah of being here. Midnight is such an easy dog to take care of that Mom doesn't even know she's missing.

I get a backpack that belongs to Uncle Robert and load it with stuff I might need. I wish I still had that gun I once used on Wade, but it's long gone, just like he is. I have a knife that I'll carry in my pocket. My flashlight will be in my hand. I stuff a jacket, an extra set of batteries, and a digging tool that one would use in the garden into the backpack. I'm not really sure what I'll use that last thing for. I mean—if the ground caves in I don't exactly think I'll be digging myself out with a tiny shovel used for flowerpots.

I grab a bag of chips, then make myself a sandwich. Mom just assumes I'm still hungry from dinner. You know, like most seventeen-year-old boys tend to be. She doesn't see me slip the sandwich into a plastic baggie as if I'm going on a picnic or a school field trip.

She makes a little small talk as we're watching television, but I don't really talk back. It's an art to talk with someone but really not say anything. But I can't stop thinking of the dog that may or may not be lost somewhere in the tunnels.

Gus might be lying. He might have already done something to her.

"Where's Midnight?" Mom eventually asks.

She's usually lying right next to me on the couch like some guard dog that resembles a chocolate-covered donut.

I don't want to lie to Mom. I've lied—no, make that we've lied enough to each other.

"I don't know," I say.

And I don't.

I'm just not telling her that I have to go down to the tunnels and look for her.

Mom doesn't seem worried, since I'm not. We start watching one of those Friday night news shows about a man who murdered his family. Mom changes the channel, and on that show they're talking about a woman suspected of killing her baby.

"I'm going to bed," Mom eventually says, in a way that says *I'm so tired of this dark and dreary world.*

"Good night," I say.

She tells me good night back, and for once I really, truly hope that those words mean something.

I can't exactly head into Mom's bathroom and then disappear down the ladder into the tunnels. That entrance has been boarded up for a while, and it seems we haven't been visited recently. I'm not sure why, but I don't care.

The less I have to think about those tunnels, the better.

But now I head back to the creepy little cabin that in so many ways was the start of everything. The start of the realization that I had moved somewhere really bad, and that things were only going to get worse.

It's cool but not cold. I'm wearing a sweatshirt and jeans and can feel my steady breathing as I walk uphill. The cabin looks just like before—small and abandoned and left to rot in these woods. My flashlight scans the empty windows that remind me of empty eye sockets—

Stop it.

It doesn't look like anything has changed since I was last here. No remodeling by one of those television shows that brings in the semi and gets the town to make a dream home for a poor, helpless family.

"We made this into a special black well just for you, Chrissssssss!"

I'm already a bit freaked out, and my nerves are making me think crazy thoughts. And this is all before I'm even down in the tunnel.

I step inside the cabin and see the torn floor in the center, the hole looking just like it did the first time I stepped over decaying wood and fell through to hit a dirt bottom.

My flashlight finds the bed next to the wall, the one with the shackles next to it.

I think of what Pastor Marsh told me about the Solitaire family in France.

They weren't real vampires, of course. But they acted the part. They really were just monsters. They would slip inside people's home and rape the women and kill the men. Selectively, of course. To make sure they ruled with fear.

A bed with shackles in a tiny cabin in the middle of nowhere suddenly makes sense.

This wasn't some little place a family lived once. It was where someone was imprisoned.

I think of Mom screaming that something was coming into her room in the middle of the night.

Are demons physical beings? Or do they have to inhabit someone in order to get around?

I've tried reading up on demons in the Bible, but I haven't gotten a lot of information. It seems like most of my "knowledge" is from movies like *The Exorcist* and *Paranormal Activity*, and I don't think they should be regarded as the definitive truth.

Can demons rip people out of their beds?

I don't know.

I think there's a lot—a lot—that we don't know about the spiritual side of things. That maybe we'll never know.

That I don't ever really want to know.

I shiver and then remember the extra few things I packed away for this little late-night journey.

They're there for when I need them.

I find a little comfort in that.

I soon find the rungs of the ladder going down into the cold, gaping hole. I head down carefully, not wanting to fall again and knock myself out.

For a moment, I stand at the entrance of the round tunnel. Whoever carved these tunnels out did a lot of work. And I know they're all around the town.

I exhale, then clear my throat.

"Midnight?" I call out.

It's just a few minutes after twelve. I'm doing exactly what I was supposed to do.

A gasp of cool air seems to come from the mouth of the tunnel. As if it's daring me to enter. I wait for a few minutes to see if I hear anything. But there's nothing. Nothing but cold silence.

"Okay," I say out loud.

I don't know if it's okay to pray for missing dogs, but I know it's okay to pray. So I pray for Midnight. And myself.

And then I follow my narrow beam of light into the pitch black.

79. A Familiar Face

The dirt underneath my tennis shoes sometimes crunches as I step over a rock. Every now and then air blasts through the tunnel like someone is trying to blow out the candle on a birthday cake. My one wish is to find Midnight and get out of here. Of course, I'm not even sure if she's down here. This could all be one big setup by Gus.

Maybe he and his friends will jump me and beat me up and leave me for dead.

But I don't think that's the case.

I think Gus is terrified of his daddy and won't do something like that. He can touch my dog, but he still can't touch me.

Maybe that's what you think.

At times it seems like the top of the tunnel is dripping or leaking even though it hasn't rained for a while. I keep track of every turn I make on my iPhone by typing down the opposite of what I did. When I take a right-hand turn, I type *left* so that I'll do that on my way back.

Of course, if I'm being chased by a zombie or a demon dog, I don't think I'll be casually looking at the fine print on the note I made to myself.

Maybe I'll whip out my iPhone and try to beat someone's head with it just like Staunch did to me.

The air is stale down here. Maybe I'm breathing faster because of my nerves, but it seems like I just can't suck down a decent enough breath. The sounds echo. When I occasionally cough, it seems like something is erupting all around me.

I reach an intersection that connects with another tunnel. I can either keep going straight, turn right as I already have three times, or take a left.

You're lost and have no clue.

"Midnight."

Calling her makes me worry more. It makes me feel that even if the sleeping ghosts didn't know I was down here yet, they sure do now.

"Midnight, you around here?"

I'm growing more annoyed, which means I'm growing impatient and starting not to care if I'm heard.

I decide to head straight. I don't mark this down since I'm not turning. Maybe I'll remember, and maybe they'll never find me again.

Have people ever gotten permanently lost down here? Like the guy at the end of The Shining?

I really don't like that thought.

At least it's not snowing.

Yeah. That's really encouraging.

I'm not sure how long I've been down here or how far I've walked when my flashlight goes out.

"Oh, come on."

I think I shout this, because I'm seriously angry. I jostle the flashlight and turn it on and off and then undo the back and twist it back on to see if that does anything.

Nope.

Come on. I mean—really?

Then I remember my iPhone, which is sorta my generation's

answer to the Swiss Army knife. I go to turn it on, and it seems as dead as the flashlight.

Emphasis on the word dead.

I eventually stop trying. I shiver and bring my arms close to my body for the moment, and stop and listen.

Silence.

What was that?

It was nothing. I didn't hear anything.

Something shuffling on the ground.

I might be imagining things. I don't know.

I'm about ready to get the extra batteries from my pack when I definitely hear something ahead of me. A crackling sound.

Then I smell it and know what's making that sound.

Something's burning.

I stare ahead and suddenly see an orange and red glow. Up ahead the tunnel veers right, not allowing me to see the fire but to see the illuminating flickers of light coming from it.

Get out of here, Chris, run back.

I hold a hand up to my mouth, but think for a second.

Something tells me I need to see this.

It's a trap designed by Gus. He brought you down here to choke.

I cough and try not to breathe in. My eyes are burning and tearing up.

I decide I have to look. Now or never, so I decide now.

I sprint straight ahead with one hand still over my mouth and the other one holding the big metal flashlight. At some point I still need to crack somebody over the head with it. That's why I got it. That's why it's so perfect.

The tunnel is getting thicker with dark smoke and warmer as I get to where it turns.

Except when I look around now, I don't find myself in a tunnel anymore. Instead I'm standing in front of a burning house. Not a casual flame that a firefighter could put out, but hellish, scary flames that look more like an inferno. I duck back because they're so hot and I feel like my face is being burned, my hair getting singed.

Where am I?

It's still hard to breathe, still difficult to fully look ahead without squinting.

The two-story house could be anywhere. It's not in a neighborhood. It seems to be surrounded by woods, maybe at the end of the road or a long driveway.

Then I see a dark figure standing out from the flames.

A guy, not very tall, standing and staring at the flames. He almost looks like he's part of them, but he's not.

In one hand is what appears to be a gas can.

He did it, this guy did this.

I wonder if the tunnel ended, and that's how I suddenly came upon this scene. Yet another part of me knows that the tunnel didn't morph into this. I'm here, and yet I don't think I'm fully here right now.

Sure smells and tastes and feels like you are.

The man standing in front of me facing the fire turns, and I see that he's a kid just like me.

A kid who looks a lot like a young Pastor Marsh.

No, that is *Pastor Marsh. That's Jeremiah Marsh before he ever became a pastor.*

I see an awful expression on his face even as I see the tears streaming down both sides of his cheeks. It's awful, because the look is of pure and utter joy. Like a guy who has found his place in life.

He turns back around and keeps watching the house that he just burned down.

Is this what happened to you? Is this why you turned out the way you did?

I want to leave this place, this vision or nightmare that's full of raging fire and hot despair. I want to run back to the tunnel. Yet just as I turn to go, something brushes by me.

Someone.

And then he's next to the teenaged Marsh. The figure is a lot taller and skinny, and he puts an arm around Marsh.

He turns and faces the boy, and I see that it's Kinner. This is Walter Kinner, my great-grandfather, taking a weeping Jeremiah Marsh in his arms and holding him like he might do his own son.

I don't want to see any more. I begin to back up and I shut my eyes and I say no over and over again.

Then I remember what else I brought with me. Besides the batteries and the jacket. Something I'm not carrying in my pockets but rather in my memory.

I draw a blank. I know I should've written the Bible verses down. I can't remember them.

"The Lord is my rock," I say. "Reach down Your hand and deliver me."

Then another one.

"Have mercy on me. When I pray."

It's something like that.

"I come to You for protection, God—Lord. Help me. Save me."

The verses that I memorized—half a dozen—all blur and morph like the flames reaching out to the heavens and drifting to black.

"Be my rock and my fortress, God. Please protect me."

I open my eyes and find myself back in the tunnel. I'm still holding the flashlight in my hand, and it's still not working. Same with the iPhone.

Now I'm turned around and have no idea which way to go. The flames and smoke are gone, even though I can still taste them and smell them.

That fire was real.

I decide to just keeping heading straight.

And as I do, I keep whispering and saying fragments of the psalms that I thought I knew.

I guess God doesn't really care as long as you mean what you're saying. And I do. I really do.

80. PROTECTION

When I hear the tiny bark, more of a little yelp than anything else, I almost start to cry.

"Midnight! Midnight, where are you?"

I yell out and run in the direction of the barking. My iPhone turns back on and says that it's 2:25 a.m., which means I've been walking for over two hours. I might be in Chicago as far as I know.

Or maybe I'm going to encounter a big wheel, and once I turn it I'll end up in the desert, and the town of Solitary will disappear.

If that's the case, let me get a few people before it goes away.

My flashlight is working again, so it had to be the batteries. At least that's what I'm telling myself. But with the phone not working and the sudden visit to Infernoland, I get the feeling it had nothing to do with batteries or electronics.

I jog toward the sound because I don't want to trip and fall on the rocky floor. I stop and listen for Midnight. I know I heard her.

The bark comes again. "Midnight!" I stop and move my head, straining to hear. A woman's scream pierces the darkness.

What the—

It's an awful scream, and it just keeps going until I hear it stopped.

No, not stopped, but rather muffled. Like a hand going over a mouth.

I take a few steps, but suddenly I don't want to go any farther. I don't want to see anything else. I just want my dog and then I want to get out of here.

Something brushes by me—something or someone.

"Midnight!"

I flash the light ahead and see that the tunnel has ended in a door. An average door with an average handle. It doesn't look like something that belongs down here in an ancient tunnel.

Don't open it don't Chris.

I wonder how many times I've heard that voice in my head and how many times in my life I've refused to do what it tells me to do.

I know why. It's because I'm stubborn and don't like being told what to do. And because of that …

Jocelyn happened.

And because of that …

Jared happened. And Lily. And Kelsey. And not telling my parents. And trying to do it my own way.

It hasn't worked out well. Yet I still find myself turning the handle and

When are you going to learn little boy little stupid ignorant boy?

I open the door and see a grim light in the corner of a bedroom revealing a grim scene.

A woman sits on the edge of her bed, crying and shaking. For a second I think it's Heidi Marsh and the man standing over her is Jeremiah Marsh, but then I realize that the woman is dark-haired and I've never seen her before. At least not that I know of.

Even though she looks a bit familiar.

She's got a round face and swollen eyes and one of them looks really swollen, like a boxer's eye during a fight. There's blood at the edge of her mouth. Her makeup is a mess, just like her hair. She's wearing a jean jacket as if she's ready to go out. Then I see a suitcase on the bed.

The man standing over her is saying something to her, but I can't hear it. He's whispering.

She starts to cry, and the man lashes out and slaps her in the face like he …

Literally swatted a fly.

I think back to Newt being slapped like that in the hallway by Gus on one of my first days at Harrington.

The woman shrinks down and weeps and holds her hands over her mouth as if to try to keep quiet, but it's not working.

"I told you to shut up," a strong Southern voice says. "You hear me, girl?"

I'm standing in their bedroom, and I realize that this is another vision or dream.

I don't want to be here get me out please Lord.

I shut my eyes, but I still hear the voices.

I know.

I know who this is now.

It's not Gus swatting Newt; it's his father swatting his mother.

Whom I've never ever seen.

"I swear this is the last time you're gonna back talk me ever, and I mean ever," Staunch says to the woman. "No one in this house will ever—ever—disrespect me."

My eyes are still shut, and then I hear the screams again.

I'm squinting, begging God to deliver me from this. But the screams keep coming.

They become howls. Awful, hurting howls.

I open my eyes and see Staunch with his right hand on her throat and his left hand over her mouth. Pressing her down on the bed while her body flails. Pressing. Pressing.

He's suffocating her.

I look around and find a lamp, and I try to pick it up but I can't. I can feel it but I can't move it.

What are the rules of being in this nightmare? Tell me, God. Please.

For several minutes I hear the muffled sound of Mrs. Staunch trying to scream and then it stops. Just like her body stops. Just like her life stops.

Staunch doesn't stop, however.

He just keeps holding her down, as if he's trying to shove her through the mattress. He continues to mash her down, squeezing and squashing.

I start to cry, and I yell, "Stop it please stop it," but of course he doesn't.

Because of course this already happened.

Finally Staunch lets her go, but she's been gone long before he does this.

He sits on the edge of the bed, facing me. He's younger, but he looks the same.

He also looks possessed.

There is a blank look on his face. He doesn't show any remorse or fear or surprise. Just utter emptiness.

Then it grows cold again, and I know what's going to happen.

I see the figure walking next to me and then standing beside Staunch.

"It is done, my son," Walter Kinner tells Staunch.

Kinner puts his hand on Staunch's head the way a preacher might put his hand on a baby's head during a baptism.

"I will protect you from this day on," Kinner says.

I watch and wait.

The vision is going to go away. Surely it's going to go away. Right?

He delivered me from my powerful enemies from those who hated me and were too strong for me.

I stand and remember now.

They attacked me at a moment when I was weakest but the Lord upheld me.

I stand and watch and breathe slowly.

He led me to a place of safety, He rescued me because He delights in me.

The tears are no longer falling down my face, but I'm still scared and sad.

"Hold me up, God."

I say this over and over again.

"Lead me to a safe place."

And then a blink turns to darkness, and I find myself back in the tunnel.

Back in the tunnel with something at my foot.

I know it's going to be a hand now. It's going to be Kinner's decomposing body lying on the ground, grasping after me like one of the walking dead. I shine the light down, and instead of seeing anything scary, I see Midnight.

She wants me to pick her up. And you know—I don't blame her.

"Come here, little thing—are you okay?"

I check her out and let her give me kisses, and she turns out to be fine.

Thank You, God. Thank You.

I'm holding her and kissing her, and I wish that someone would do the same for me.

But they already have, Chris, and you know it. You know it deep down, and that's what makes you different from these monsters.

I feel a slight chill coming from in front of me. So I start walking, hoping that this is a good sign, hoping and praying for no more visions.

No more come on this night or early morning. Thank God.

The tunnel morphs into a mouth of a cave, the same one I stepped outside the first time I came down here.

The time Kelsey's father picked me up and brought me back home.

I wonder if that was a coincidence. At the time I didn't think anything of it. Kelsey's father happened to be driving at night in the distance of Solitary, and he picked me up.

No big deal.

But it was Kelsey's father.

Maybe God was controlling things back then, just like He's controlling things now.

Then I realize there's no maybe about it.

This is a comforting thought after the horrific scenes I just saw. It's comforting just like Midnight is in my hands.

I'm still holding her, and I'm not going to let her go. Not until I bring her back to a safe place where I can make sure she's okay.

81. SWEET DREAMS

Others aren't having this sort of life, so why are you?

Did God choose this for you? This path, this destination, this fate?

Did He pinpoint this place on the map to lead you to? To suffer and to shiver? To wonder deep in the night like now, listening to headphones and wondering why?

Will you break down and need Kinner to come and save you?

Will you unleash the gate under the bridge and let Aunt Alice roam with the wolves, or find yourself imprisoned in some little cell below?

Will the demon dog delight in your demise, or will Marsh take one too many trips to the falls?

Will this all feel like some brilliant, bewildering dream that you'll wake up from ten years later in Chicago?

The questions have answers, but they won't come now or tomorrow or maybe even the next day.

You want to believe God is in control, but if He is, then why? Why? And why you?

Maybe some don't get the sweet dreams after all. Maybe for some those are just in the pages of a story they read. Then they go to sleep and the nightmares come. And when they wake up, the nightmares are still there.

82. MONSTER STORY

A little while later, after pulling off my headphones and turning off the music, as I lie in bed in a house that's supposed to be safe and secure, I realize I need to talk to Kelsey. I need to see her. I miss her, but more than that I just need to see and feel and know she's right there. I want to kiss her and escape in a warm glow of light that crushes this darkness.

I try and think how I'm going to do this.

I'm not supposed to.

But they don't have to know, and they don't have to see.

These are monsters, Chris.

Yes. But every monster story has a hero who slays them.

And every hero has his heroine.

And if he needs to save her at the end, so be it.

But the hero needs to see the heroine.

There's no way of getting around that.

And yet, when the sun rises each morning, then sets each night ...

I don't do anything.

I don't sneak away and meet with Kelsey. Nor do I contact her in any way.

I just wait.

I guess I'm learning.

Maybe. Possibly.

I don't know.

83. PEACE

"I want to go to church on Sunday."

It's weird to hear these words spoken by Mom. She's been doing better, and not just with the whole not-drinking thing. It's like she's started to warm up and have more life in her, just like the spring outside. I don't know exactly where she is personally with God, but then again, I'm not exactly sure where I'm at. It's a little like putting your feet in the water but staring out at the vast ocean, knowing there's a million miles left to go.

"Okay, sure."

"I just thought—since Sunday is Easter. Maybe we should go."

I nod. "Yeah, sure."

"Do you still go to the New Beginnings Church?"

I laugh and shake my head. "No, not exactly."

"Oh."

"I've gone to Springhill Baptist a few times with Kelsey."

"Okay."

Mom tells me to plan it and make sure I look up the right times. It doesn't dawn on me until after I head for school that this might be against the rules, that the evil three might not like this. But I'll just tell them that it's part of my mom wanting something, and me going with the flow.

But deep down, if I'm to be honest, I really want to go.

I think it'll be good for Mom. And yeah, for me, too.

It's the second Sunday in April, and it's warm outside with clear skies and the promise of a wonderful day. Mom looks pretty in a blue and yellow dress that I've never seen her wear. She tells me that she bought it recently with the Ann Taylor gift card I gave her on her birthday. I actually wear one of Uncle Robert's ties along with khakis and a button-down shirt. It feels good to do this, to arrive at the small church and see a very surprised Kelsey along with her family before sitting down.

It feels good because it's normal. It's what other people do on Sundays.

But I think it also feels good because this is where we should be.

When the middle-aged balding preacher comes out and greets everybody, I find myself thankful that he doesn't have highlighted hair and funky glasses. He's got a nice Southern accent and a belly that looks like he enjoys Southern food.

"Jesus has risen!" he says in a way that doesn't sound phony and doesn't feel like he's going to ask for money in the next breath.

We sing some songs and we pray and there's a nice little portion of the service for kids. But it's not until the preacher is almost finished that I suddenly become aware of something.

This whole thing. Easter and what it means.

I've heard it before. Dad sure made it a point that I heard it again and again after he found faith. This whole thing of Jesus rising from the dead, of the tomb being empty and all His desperate followers suddenly seeing the light again.

I feel a chill going through me when I hear the preacher talk about those people. How terrified they were. How lonely and abandoned they felt. How isolated.

How very Solitary.

This man they had believed in had died. And He didn't die in some accidental way, but in an awful, brutal way in front of their very eyes.

Some of those closest to Him even denied they ever knew Him. Peter, the apostle Peter, cursed and swore he didn't know Jesus.

Evil had won, right? The darkness suffocated the light, right?

Yet this day arrives, and the tomb is empty.

An angel tells the two Marys one simple thing. A simple thing that gives me goose bumps and makes me almost get teary-eyed.

"Don't be afraid!"

Okay, maybe it does get me teary-eyed. The preacher says that the women were very frightened but filled with great joy.

He tells of Mary Magdalene crying and being asked who she's crying about. Mary just thinks that it's a gardener asking her, since she's full of doubt and questions.

But then she finally opens her eyes to see.

It makes me think and wonder.

Who have I talked to before without fully seeing?

All these things that have happened in Solitary. To me and to others.

I've spent so much time running around trying to figure things out, and then trying to handle things on my own, and then trying to run away from everything. All while I could have just slowed down and opened my eyes to see.

Opened my eyes and heard the words "Peace be with you."

That's a phrase I've heard a bunch, but man—when I think of it now, it really sounds like something.

Peace.

There's only one who can give you that.

I think of Uncle Robert and his anger.

Then I think of my father and his regret.

Both men have made their choices. But only one seems to have this peace that is talked about.

I believe this. I really honestly believe that the tomb was empty and these conversations happened. And that this peace is within my grasp.

As the preacher prays the final prayer and asks God to bless all of us, I pray my own little prayer silently.

Help me to see when You're there helping me out even if I'm just too stupid or scared not to know. And help me to find peace. However I can, Jesus.

84. LOVELY

What I really want to say is *I've missed you so incredibly much*, but instead I mutter a "Hi."

What Kelsey probably wants to ask is *Why haven't you spoken or contacted me these past few weeks and what's going on to make you avoid me?* but instead she says "Hi" back.

My mom talks with her parents. They know each other from Thanksgiving, which we spent at their house, and Kelsey's parents even invite us over, but Mom politely declines.

I want to say *Do you mind if I just borrow Kelsey for a week or two?* but instead I just listen to the parents talk.

Kelsey possibly wants to say *You're an idiot if you think I'm going to wait around much longer for a moron like you,* but instead she does the same thing I do.

I want to hug her and tell her it's okay, but I don't know how to do it in this context. I'm already a bit disoriented from sitting in the church pew, feeling overwhelmed and both happy and sad. Now I only feel sad. Now Kelsey just reminds me that not all prayers are answered in the way you hope they will be.

Then Kelsey and her parents are saying good-bye.

There's one moment.

Just one.

I go to say something, and then Kelsey looks at me and smiles and nods and says, "Bye."

What does that mean?

Is she saying good-bye to us? Is she through?

But the smile—it was a sweet smile.

Does she have any other kind?

Has she moved on without my knowing?

She'd still be her sweet, adorable Kelsey self, right?

I leave church a bit confused but knowing that I can't do anything to threaten her life. Well, to allow it to be any more threatened than it already is.

"She's a lovely girl, Chris," Mom says as we're in the car driving back home.

"Yeah."

Maybe Mom wants to say more about Kelsey, to ask where things are or make some suggestions, but she doesn't. Which I appreciate, because I couldn't even begin to try and explain where I'm standing with the pretty blonde.

Yeah, we're a couple, kind of, but then again, who knows what's going to happen these last few weeks of school and after graduation?

I just keep reminding myself of the pastor's message, and of the words of hope I heard.

I keep reminding myself because I know eventually the reminders will fade away like they always seem to do around this place.

85. THE THIRD PASSAGE

Now that it's warmer, I sometimes ride my bike around, trying to find the road that led to the Crag's Inn. I still haven't managed to find it; it's as if it's gone, just like those visions I used to have of Jocelyn.

One evening after trying to look for the road and coming up empty, I decide to look at something I haven't bothered to check out for a while.

The laptop that Iris gave me.

Something always seemed wrong about using it. Somehow I don't mind using the old motorcycle she gave me, since it had belonged to Uncle Robert, but this MacBook never really belonged to me. It was part of the project I did while working with Iris, the project about the history of the Crag's Inn.

I open the laptop and start it up. I'm nervous; I feel like something's going to happen, like Iris is going to be talking to me from the dead or wherever she might be. Or maybe a long-haired creepy girl will walk right out of the screen like she did in *The Ring*.

No no go back you're in the wrong story!

I'm on the computer for five minutes when I finally start to relax. Creepy witch girl must be sleeping in a nearby well. I go to open the document I was looking for when I discover other files on my computer. Ones that I know I didn't create.

One is called *A. Bridge*.

Adahy Bridge?

I open it up and find a page of information just like it might appear on Wikipedia.

THE THIRD PASSAGE

THE SOUTHERN UNITED STATES

VERIFIED 1787 BY CHIEF SHANNAKIAK

CONFIRMED 1804 CALVIN JEFFERSON WALKER

AUTHENTICATED 1882 BY HAROLD ELLIS MARTIN

UPDATED 2000 BY IRIS

The Adahy Bridge

The word Adahy *in Cherokee means "lives in the woods." The bridge that was built back in 1820 was part of a road from Asheville, North Carolina, to Greenville, South Carolina. It is a stone bridge with a gothic arch that stands over the Little Dogwood Creek.*

Activity at the bridge is high, steady, and somehow growing. Even with the stability of the inn nearby, the balance is still one-sided toward the darkness.

The resurgence began after the incident with Alice Kinner back in 1958. It has intensified with the arrival of Jeremiah Marsh in 1998.

By all accounts this could be one of the strongest passages in the country due to its secrecy and remote location.

I reread this just to make sure I understand everything. The whole "verified and confirmed" stuff seems formal and weird, like someone in the government wrote it. Then a simple *Updated by Iris.*

But the thing that really sticks out is the Alice Kinner "incident."

I think back to my visit to the bridge and the sound of the ...

Don't go there. Just forget about it.

Maybe I need to pay Aunt Alice another visit.

This makes it seem like there are more of these "passages" out there.

I look back at the file names and try to open them, but I can't. Along with A. Bridge, there are H. Caves, S. Quarry, and V. Ridge. The last two file names are identified simply with numbers, 6 and 7.

If there're seven files, why do I only see six?

Part of me wonders if Iris put this on my computer on purpose, knowing or at least hoping that I'd open it up one day. I wonder what the other files say and if there's more info on them.

I hear Mom calling for me, so I shut off my laptop and go downstairs.

I was hoping the days of discovering cryptic information were over, but I have to remember that I'm still in this crazy place called Solitary. I'm sure the weird info is going to keep coming until I'm finally (hopefully) leaving this place.

86. Driver's Test

"Okay—start it up."

I look at Mr. Taggart sitting in the old Subaru wagon that unfortunately is stick shift.

"You work here?" I ask.

"What? Disappointed to see me?"

Uh, yeah.

"I didn't know—"

"That I gotta get other jobs?" He curses and shrugs. "Yeah, that's what happens when you're no longer the coach."

My former summer school teacher—still looking like he just came back from a spring break gone bad—hunches over as he looks at me. "Come on, let's go."

"I'm not the best with a clutch."

"Whatever. It's my car, and it drives fine."

I start it up and back it out of the spot and realize the car and the clutch are a lot like its owner. Worn and broken and difficult.

This is my driving test. I'm finally getting my license. Or so I thought until Mr. Taggart got in the car.

I mean, come on.

Seriously.

It's a license.

I'm doomed to never get my license.

"Come on, we don't got all day," he yells, even though I'm driving through the town at the speed limit.

I do as he says and wonder if he's even going to care how I drive or what I do.

Mr. Taggart leads me through Solitary to do some parking and various exercises. I do fine. Then he tells me to go on the winding side streets outside of town.

Suddenly I spot it.

The road leading to the Crag's Inn. Or what's left of it.

Without even asking, I turn the car and head up the hill. He doesn't say anything. I don't think he even notices. Sometimes he just stares ahead as if he's on a beach, looking at the ocean, daydreaming, or sleeping.

We're almost up to the top—almost—when Mr. Taggart tells me to turn around.

"How about I just—"

"Turn around."

"Okay," I say. "There's a place where—"

"Here. Right here. Turn it around."

We're on a narrow stretch of the road where the hill juts upward on our right side and then drops almost straight down on the other side. Woods are on both sides, thick dense woods I remember from coming up here every weekend.

I slow the car down, drive it as far as it can go toward the ditch on our right side, then I turn. I don't want to get stuck in the ditch, of course, but I don't want to topple over on the other side. I turn, then back up, then turn a little more, then back up a little more.

I do an awful job. The stick shift keeps getting stuck, then grinding, then I'm nervous at wrecking his car, so I'm trying harder and sweating, and Mr. Taggart isn't saying anything but looking at me like I just got off the stupid boat.

I have the Subaru wagon directly facing the edge of the sharp dropoff when I accidentally press the gas and send us jerking forward. Mr. Taggart lets out a curse and whips up the emergency brake, but that doesn't really do anything except make him curse more. I jam on the brakes.

The front two tires of the car are nearly over. Nearly. Like inches or centimeters.

"Back it up."

I start to, but the car is facing downward and it starts to lean forward.

"Come on, Chris."

I try to control my breathing and my nervousness.

You can do this. Look at all you've gone through. You went soaring off a cliff and you survived while your driver didn't. Come on, man. Get a grip.

I let go of the brake pedal while pressing the gas. But the thing is so dang slow. It starts inching forward again.

Mr. Taggart looks at me.

"Come on," he says. "Just lay on the gas before letting go of the brake."

"The stick keeps—"

"Shut it. No excuses. Come on."

Okay, fine. This is it. Joke's over. It's time to grow up and be a man and stop being so afraid.

So I do as I'm told and am the man that I need to be. I give it gas as I gently take my foot off the brake. More gas. More. More.

"What the—brake! Put the—stop!"

I hear Mr. Taggart screaming as the Subaru slowly drives off the road and down the hill.

He's screaming faster than the car is going. Because really, there's a slight incline and then a bunch of thick bushes that look like they have blackberries on them. We land on top of them not with a crash or a boom but rather like someone trying to slide into home plate but instead slowing down to a rather anticlimactic stop.

I look at Mr. Taggart, who has ripped up the emergency brake in his car. It's literally been torn off. He just looks at me and then looks at the brake in his hand.

Then something miraculous happens. Something that I couldn't ever have seen coming.

Mr. Taggart, the miserable grump from the summer, starts to laugh. Not just laugh, but howl.

Soon I'm laughing too. Because laughter can be like that. A spontaneous, joyous sort of thing.

Especially after, you know, you survive death by stupidity in a car.

We're laughing, and then I see something fluttering by my car window. I glance over and watch it land on a bush by my window.

The bluebird is back.

Of course it is.

Maybe if I knew what it sounded like, I'd know if the bird was laughing too.

A couple hours later, I arrive back home.

"How'd it go?" Mom asks me.

"Well, I drove us off the side of a mountain." I chuckle again in complete disbelief.

"Yeah, right."

I smile and then reach into my pocket. "There you go. A license. Well—not the official license—it's just a temporary certificate for now. But I finally got it. Real one is coming in the mail."

"Congratulations," Mom says in an excited tone. "About time."

"Miracles do happen."

I think back to the tow truck and Mr. Taggart getting back to the town and still laughing at the whole driving off the side of the mountain.

"That car is a hunk of junk anyway," he said to me. "You want to know the first thing I thought as we were going over the side of the mountain? Huh? I was hoping that we'd just blow up in a big ball of flames like they do in the movies. But no. We just—we just kinda got … stuck."

He laughed again and then said he wouldn't say anything about it.

So, yeah, I got my license.

And yeah, I got to see Mr. Taggart find the whole thing hilarious.

The license wasn't the miracle.

It was that smile.

And it was finding that road again. Finally.

87. START OF THE BREAKDOWN

Man, my faith is weak.

That feeling I had sitting in the pew got washed away with this morning's rain.

The vast, open, endless blue seems to be forgotten underneath this ceiling of gray.

Something about today is different, and I don't know what.

Something about Kelsey is different.

Every day we pass and smile and say hi, but that's it. She's waiting but doesn't understand why. And I know that one day I'll be able to tell her more of the story, but I can't. Not just yet. So I wait, and the days and the nights morph and then suddenly I see her on this gloomy, wet morning as I'm trying to dry off from my wet morning ride.

I see her talking to some other guy and smiling.

I see her smiling and laughing.

I try not to let her see me, but maybe she does. Maybe she wants me to see her.

You don't understand, Kelsey.

But later when I pass her in the hall, she doesn't smile or say hi. She just looks away.

Is this how it starts?

When one morning is enough, and that day is the day to change. When the hurting has morphed into something more. When the temporary break turns into a full-fledged breakdown.

I look for her at lunch, but she's not in her normal place.

I look for her by her locker later, but that doesn't work either. She's deliberately avoiding me.

Don't give it away, Chris, don't let them see you still care for her.

And then later I see her walking with her bodyguard Georgia. I start toward her, but then I see the same tall guy come up to her. A younger guy, a junior I think, but a jock and good-looking and so freaking tall.

I don't understand you.

I let them go, and I let this day go.

This day in the middle of April when I'm trying to just be patient and wait.

But maybe she's no longer waiting on me.

88. THE WHEEL GOES ROUND AND ROUND

The note in my locker is supposed to comfort me. And I guess in some ways, yeah, it does.

It's a typed note without a name at the bottom. But I know it's from Mr. Meiners.

Chris:

It's not safe to come around. The group isn't meeting anymore. At least not for a while until things die down.

Remember this from Psalm 61:3—

"For you are my safe refuge, a fortress where my
enemies cannot reach me."

Keep this verse by your heart. Remember it when you
need it the most.

I fold up the note and look around to see if anybody is spying
on me. But I know that someone is probably always keeping tabs on
me, everywhere and all the time.

I want to believe that God is my refuge and fortress. But it feels
like I need to find that place first before I can be safe. Right now it
seems like my enemies are all around me. There's nothing I can do
but just walk amidst them and hope that one of them doesn't grab
me and slit my throat.

A nice thought before heading to English class.

A little while later, I'm beating myself up.

Wondering what happened to that take-charge, stubborn guy.

He left the moment that stubbornness got him nowhere.

What happened to the guy who refused to take no for an answer
and didn't like being told what to do?

Jocelyn happened. Then Poe happened. Then Lily happened.

They all either died or were forced away.

It's the middle of the night, and I'm counting the minutes
until tomorrow and the days away until May and the weeks until
Memorial Day.

Just counting and feeling the dread seep in and doing nothing about it.

I know I can pray, and I do pray. But I don't see any burning bush in the middle of Solitary or any parting seas on Marsh Falls. Nope. Just nice, raging silence.

There has to be something I can do.

There has to be a way to stop whatever's going to happen on Memorial Day before it arrives.

I try and think who I can ask for help. Somebody out of the norm, somebody not in this crazy story. Mom and Dad are out. Uncle Robert is useless. Aunt Alice—well, I've got some other questions to ask her, but she won't help me figure out how to solve this mess.

Kelsey is still avoiding me and talking to the basketball star.

Newt knows, right? Yeah, maybe he does know, but he's been avoiding me too. He wants me to keep fighting, but then he ends up hiding out while watching me do so.

But sometime in the circling wheel of my thoughts that keep spinning and changing, the wheel stops and lands on someone unexpected.

Yes.

I picture a guy nicknamed after a candy bar. A guy who pays me for doing—well, I'm not exactly sure what I'm doing, but he thinks I'm doing something.

Ask Mounds.

Of course I can't tell him everything. But he's one of the few people who won't wonder if I'm losing my mind when I ask about something to do with ghosts and demons and dark things.

89. What Is Imagined
and What Is Real

The soft and steady sound of the cicadas singing along with the crickets makes me almost believe this is a perfect night in April. Almost. Mounds and I are about an hour away from Solitary. We sit at the edge of the woods that open up onto a railroad bridge towering over a small river below. The bridge hasn't been used in a long time, of course, but Mounds says that sometimes late at night people can hear the sound of a train whistle or even feel the rumbling of a runaway ghost train.

We've been here for an hour … and nothing. Mounds knows we're probably not going to hear or see anything tonight.

I bring up the conversation I've been wanting to have with him all night.

"What would you do if you knew there was some kind of, like, real evil around you. Threatening you?"

Mounds doesn't laugh, because naturally he believes in this sort of thing. "Like *Paranormal Activity* style? Pulling you out of bed and stealing your children?"

"Yeah. Something like that."

"The first question would be what exactly are we talking about. A vampire? A demon? A ghost?"

"Someone who attacks at night. In the darkness. Draining bodies of blood."

"Well, then, that's a vampire you're talking about."

I don't think Staunch is a vampire. I don't think they really exist. *But demons do.*

"But couldn't like a demon do that sort of thing?"

"If it walks like a vampire and talks like a vampire and sucks blood like a vampire, then chances are high that it's a vampire."

"You really believe in them?"

Mounds takes out a candy bar, which I'm sad to see is a Milky Way. He offers me one, but I say no. So far I haven't ever seen him actually eat a Mounds bar. I'm tempted to joke and ask if he's really who he says he is, but I'm actually trying to get some info from him.

"I believe in anything that is unexplainable. These tracks, for instance. This one girl came here and for some reason walked to the middle of those tracks. People thought she was doped up, others thought she was trying to kill herself. She claims to have heard a train coming for her, and she ran and jumped off the end of the bridge. Broke both her legs but was fortunate she didn't die."

"You believe her?"

"Why not?" Mounds says as he chews his candy bar. "That's the thing with unexplained phenomena."

"So what would you do—about this evil—about this person who you think is a vampire?"

"You do what they've always done. The brave ones, of course. The heroes. You go and put a wooden stake through their heart."

"You think that would work?"

"If a hundred or a thousand stories share the same basic info with you on how to kill a vampire, then you might want to believe in them."

"Do you believe in the Bible?"

"Of course. But I believe there's also room for interpretation, since there's so much in the Bible that makes absolutely no sense."

"I don't think there are vampires in the Bible."

"Yeah, but there's other freaky stuff," Mounds says. "Who's to say that one of those demons or monsters isn't really a vampire? Maybe they just didn't call them that. Like Goliath. He was some giant. But what if he was like Frankenstein or something? Or maybe a god that had been thrown out of heaven?"

I think Mounds just managed to combine a gothic horror story with a Greek myth and a Sunday school tale.

That guy has a future in horror mash-ups.

"So you'd try to kill him?"

"What? A vampire?" Mounds chuckles. "Man, did you ever read *Salem's Lot?* By Stephen King? I read it and then saw the miniseries and was like totally freaked out. Forget *Twilight*. These vampires scared you. These were ones you didn't mess around with."

"So no?"

Mounds curses. "Absolutely no way."

"But you're a ghost hunter."

"Yeah, a ghost *hunter*. Not a ghost killer. I'm not Van Helsing or someone like that."

"Van who?"

"What? You didn't see the movie? Hugh Jackman?"

For a while Mounds gets off track talking about the movie and how it should've been an epic series like X-Men and other comic-book movies. He's a big geek who not only loves horror movies and comic books but makes them his life.

"Let's call it a night," he says eventually, picking up his big body off the forest floor and heading back to the minivan.

As I follow, he asks me a question. "Is there really some kind of evil vampirelike thing you know about?"

"I don't know," I say.

"That means yes."

"Like I said—referring to it like a vampire—I don't know."

"Think about it. Books and movies that twist and distort these things—like Casper the friendly ghost or vampires that glitter in the sun—I think they desensitize us to the original horror of the story. Like watching violence on YouTube. You know? Or porn. You watch enough of that—and believe me there's enough of it out there—and you become numb to it all. You play a video game where people's heads are being blown up around you, and suddenly you might not be so absolutely horrified if that actually happened."

"You sound like you're against that kind of stuff," I say.

"Me? No way. Dude, I'm a two-hundred-and-fifty-pound dork who eats all day and hunts for ghosts. I'm online all the time watching everything. No. Not against anything, to be honest. But I do long to know the difference between what is imagined and what is real. The stuff we've seen together—that stuff is real. I don't know what it is, but I know it's real. *Call of Duty* or *Van Helsing* or *Twilight*—that stuff isn't real. It's just faking it, like a kid on Halloween. I do all this because I'm tired of seeing the costumes and eating the candy, you know? I want the real thing."

I want to tell him that I don't need to do anything else to understand that the evil in this world is real and concrete. I don't say anything, however, because I can't.

But I keep thinking of Staunch and Kinner.

I wonder if there's anybody who would actually ever come with me to the Staunch house to see if he's really sleeping in a coffin in the dark basement.

Then I remember the guy who told me about some of the skeletons in Staunch's closet. Some of the *literal* skeletons that he found on Staunch's property.

Brick.

He'd come along for the ride. He's just crazy enough to not really care as long as it sounds kind of fun.

90. QUESTION MARKS OR BITE MARKS?

What story am I really in?

Could it really be a … ?

No.

I don't want to begin to believe it, because it can't be.

But if it walks like one and talks like one and bites like one …

I think of all the vampire movies I've seen. No, I haven't seen the *Twilight* movies even when Trish back in Libertyville wanted me to go see them with her when we were a couple. But there are others I've seen.

I saw *The Lost Boys* late night once and thought it was kinda corny. But maybe it's because it's ancient, from like the eighties.

I saw a foreign movie called *Let the Right One In* that freaked me out but also forced me to read subtitles, so I don't think I got the full freak-out intended. I never saw the American update.

I'm sure I've seen others. Once I watched a little of that vampire show on HBO called *True Blood*.

But I don't honestly know much about vampires except that I've seen a lot of clips of them in those teen love stories that keep getting released.

There's that guy who never wears his shirt and turns out to be a wolf.

You've seen wolves of your own.

There's a family of vampires who are like a clan.

Sorta like the group who hide under robes.

But I don't buy it.

No.

There's no way.

There's only one way to find out.

I wonder if it's true. Really true.

What if I could take a stake and kill off the bad guy?

What if Kinner is a real, true vampire?

You've never seen him in the light, right?

That's crazy.

You've seen the tunnels he lurks around in.

A hundred thoughts swirl around, and I wonder if it really was a good idea to ask Mounds those questions.

But I know I need to try and answer some of them. At least the one big one.

91. A NIGHT OF ROMANCE
AND MYSTERY

I still get weird looks from kids I don't know. Maybe I'm just used to it, because it doesn't bother me like it once did. But today, as I'm in a familiar place with Brick outside the glass doors in front of the cafeteria, I notice the stares. Maybe it's because they're looking at the skinhead next to me smoking a cigarette. Maybe they're wondering why Brick and I are even talking and if we're friends.

Or maybe some of them are paid to spy on you just like Jared and Lily were.

I have a little over a month left at this place. I can deal with it. The stares of strangers are no longer that big a deal.

Whoever—or whatever—is living inside the Staunch house … now that's a big deal.

"So what are you saying, Buckster?"

I've been talking around the issue and haven't really gotten to what I want to ask him.

"I need someone to help me break into the Staunch house."

Brick takes a drag from his cigarette as he nods and raises his eyebrows, looking intrigued. "Turning into a thief or something?"

"No."

No, I actually need you to help me find out if a Dracula is in the basement.

"Well, you gotta tell me why we're breaking in."

I glance around to see if anybody can hear us. Nobody is close enough. "Remember when you told me what you found on his property—in the woods?"

"How could I forget that? Still have nightmares of that pit with all those dead bodies in it."

"I want to see who's living in the basement."

"What do you mean 'who's living' there?"

"I think that—the person who did that—I don't think it was Staunch."

"Then who was it?"

"I don't know."

Brick laughs. "And you want to just break in and find out?"

No, I want to break in and put a wooden stake in the heart of the guy sleeping downstairs.

"I want to just find out—to see if I'm right."

"Uh uh," Brick says. "There's something you're not telling me. Give me a reason why you want to do something like this."

"There's an old man living in that house. I've seen him. Face-to-face. And I think he's a monster."

Brick doesn't flinch or laugh.

I guess people around here know better.

"What kind of monster?"

"I don't know."

"Who says he won't try to kill you?"

Because I'm his great-grandson? And because he wants me to become what he is.

"Because I'll have someone helping me out."

"And who's that?"

I smile. "You."

Brick lets out an amused chuckle and shakes his head. "You're crazy, man. But I kinda like it."

"Can you help?"

"Sure. But I'm bringing a shotgun."

"Okay with me."

I was hoping he would say something like that.

As I head back inside and then through the doors leading to the main hallways of Harrington High, I see a huge painted banner over the doorway. There are burning torches and what looks like a fountain and a balcony.

Written at the top is *O! she doth teach the torches to burn bright.*

Below is the reason for the banner:

Escape to a night of romance and mystery.

A Romeo and Juliet Prom

Brought to you by the senior class

The dates and times are written on it.

I think back to last year when I attended the prom and had no idea it was an eighties-themed event.

Guess they like their themed proms around here.

I keep walking down the hallway, and then I see Kelsey again. Standing and talking with the tall guy I now know is Lance. He plays basketball and is a junior, and it's obvious he likes her.

Kelsey sees me coming and tries to stifle her laugh.

I give her a smile and a nod.

She only looks back at me. Not an angry look or a confused look, just a waiting stare. A look on pause, a glance on hold.

I told you to wait, so why can't you just wait a little longer?

This is the time of year that couples suddenly pop up out of nowhere. It's because of stupid things like prom. Like idiotic Romeo and Juliet dances.

I'm trying to fight for my life and your life and maybe other lives, and you have no idea.

I keep walking.

Now isn't the time to talk to Kelsey.

I just hope there will be a time, and that I won't be too late.

92. TIGHTENING

It takes me a while, but thankfully the old mill where Uncle Robert was staying is still on the map. It's not like the Crag's Inn, which disappeared until finally reemerging on the day I hit the lottery and won my license. I've ridden out here to see if I can talk to Uncle Robert again. Or at least see how he's doing. But after checking out the house and the surrounding area, I realize that Uncle Robert is long gone.

It's a pretty little place even if it is an abandoned property. I hear birds chirping away and crickets buzzing and bees flying.

In another life, I might decide to settle down here.

I'd fix this place up and bring in animals and then do something. Like milking the cows and making cheese and baking fresh bread.

Who are you trying to fool? Farming? You're an idiot.

I walk across a field of grass, through weeds that come up to my shins. The sun beats down on me on this Saturday late morning.

I wonder if Uncle Robert is really gone for good. If he spoke his piece and couldn't do anything else and just left.

Like the coward that he is.

I don't want to hate Uncle Robert. Nor do I want to think that he is a coward. But I still don't get it. I don't understand how someone can just hide and wait.

What are you doing with Kelsey then? Aren't you hiding just a bit? Aren't you forcing her to wait?

Maybe.

It's April 28, and Memorial Day is a month away exactly.

I know because I've been looking. I know the date by heart.

I need to find Uncle Robert before then. If he's around to find.

I need to see Aunt Alice, too.

As I get on my bike, a list of other to-dos goes off in my head.

Time is beginning to tighten around me like a noose.

I just hope I can figure out what in the world I'm supposed to do before they open the trapdoor and I'm left to plunge to my death.

93. Return of the Beast

I'm skipping school with Brick.

Yes, I'm such a rebel.

It's ten in the morning, and we've made sure that Gus is at school and Staunch has left the house. Nobody else should be there. Nobody except Walter Kinner.

"Told you it'd be open," Brick says.

Brick worked with a landscaping team one summer and helped build the small waterfall behind us. That's how he came to find out about some of the creepy things happening on the Staunch property.

There's a wooden door in the side of the hill, well camouflaged but, as Brick predicted, easy to open. I shine my flashlight and see a tunnel just like all the others. The hole dug deep into the earth.

"That heads into the basement."

"You know this?" I ask.

"Yep. Tried it out myself."

"But you didn't see anything?"

"I didn't stay around for long. Thought I heard some stuff, but I don't know. Maybe I just psyched myself out."

"And you're cool with everything?"

Brick lights up a cigarette and nods. "Any sign of a car or anything, I call you. No problem."

"I have a text ready to send. If anything—anything—gets sent, you come after me."

He nods and then points at the ground. "That's why I brought my shotgun."

"Let's don't shoot anybody, okay?"

"Not unless I have to."

I think of what's inside my backpack.

A hammer and, yeah, a wooden stake that's sharp at the point.

I don't really want to use it.

But I will.

I know that if I spot Kinner sleeping in a coffin—well, I have to do what I have to do.

"You going?" Brick asks me.

"Yeah."

"Be careful."

Things start to go funky midway through the tunnel. I know this because my flashlight starts to go off and on. It's not the batteries, because I just put new ones in. But the temperature suddenly drops and my light starts to flicker, and I know that I'm getting close.

Maybe something doesn't want you closer.

When I arrive at another wooden door with a rusted handle, I pause for a minute.

It's not only cold, but I'm having a hard time breathing.

The light keeps going out, then going back on when I click the switch. I finally test the door handle and feel a bit disappointed that it actually turns. I really don't want to go in. I really don't want to look inside this basement and in that room that was pitch black when I first came here.

Chrissssss.

That's just my imagination. So shut up. Stop the hissing.

The first thing I notice is the musty smell. And the cold breeze blowing through the basement as if the air conditioner is set on maximum. The room is dark, and I scan with the flashlight, expecting to see the same surroundings as before.

The place looks familiar, but it doesn't belong to Staunch's basement.

What happened, and how did I end up here?

I see a small table with chairs around it. A small kitchen area. Then I move my light to the other side, and sure enough, I see a bed in the corner of the room.

The bed is no longer old and run-down and rusty. It actually looks new.

Someone is on it.

I've had this dream or vision or nightmare before.

"Daddy," a voice says.

The voice belongs to a boy. Just a kid. Maybe nine or ten years old. He's under blankets, and it sounds like he's shivering.

"Daddy?"

I can hear the wind outside this little cabin, the same cabin that's just above ours, the one that's run-down and contains the hole in its center. The floor here is intact from what I can see.

The boy is crying. Or more like whimpering.

Then I hear it. A deep moaning sound. At first I think it's the boy himself or the wind, but then I realize it's something else, something different.

At first it just goes "Waaaaaa" for a long time. Then I make out a "Walter." Like a low, grumbling moaning sound that's saying *Walter*.

The boy starts to cry again, but this time louder.

Figures begin to rise out of the floor.

I turn off my flashlight but can make out faint light coming from a candle in the kitchen.

Three figures emerge from the center of the cabin, the place where the hole was located. I can't tell if there's a hole or an entrance that's been opened or if they're coming through the floor itself.

Anything is possible at this point.

The tall, hulking figures remind me of the ones I saw at the bridge in the dark. Ominous, scary people bathed in shadows, but getting closer and closer with every second.

These three things don't walk; rather they seem to hover closer to the bed.

Then I hear the boy screaming.

Is this Walter Kinner? Is it a younger version of him?

"Make it stop make them go away Daddy Daddy make them stop please!"

The sound hurts me to even hear. I want to help, but I can't tell if my feet can't move or won't. I'm freaking out from fear, but I also want to help this boy.

Suddenly I see one of the shapes start to fade away. No, make that start to bend and lean over the bed.

The screams continue. I try to run, but I can't.

The boy is howling. Terrified and in pain and trying to get away. I hear the sound of chains grinding against each other.

Then the figure over the bed disappears.

My eyes have adjusted, and I see the kid—tall and skinny—lying on the bed. An arm and a leg shackled.

All of a sudden he begins convulsing. Shaking like a cartoon character. It's crazy ridiculous, and I try to shut my eyes but I can't.

Then suddenly everything stops.

The two figures continue to stand over him like the last ghost in *A Christmas Carol*. Standing as if they're watching and waiting.

No, not like the ghost in A Christmas Carol, *but like those dead creatures that attacked Frodo in* The Lord of the Rings.

I can't think of what they're called, but I also can't think of where I am. For a second I think I need to get out of this cabin and go home.

Then I hear a shotgun blast and remember where I am.

I blink, and the picture in front of me is gone. Boom, just like that.

I hear another gunshot go off, and I stand there, looking at an empty finished basement.

If I keep going down the hall, I'll spot him.

But Brick's shooting at something.

I breathe in and know I only have minutes. Seconds even.

Just look. Just peek.

I sprint down the hall and go to the last door, the one I was led to and then brought inside.

I open the door expecting to see darkness and feel cold, but instead the room is empty. No coffin. No Walker Kinner hanging upside down. Nothing.

A third shotgun blast goes off. I can't help but curse.

Where is he if he's not here?

Turning around, my legs move as fast as possible back to the door. I get through and close it and then haul down the tunnel without even bothering to turn on my flashlight. I can see a small circle of light that keeps getting bigger as I get closer.

Soon I'm outside and sucking in air and shutting the door. I call out Brick's name, but I don't see anything or hear anyone.

I climb up the hill, slipping a bit but managing to break my fall. When I get to the top of the hill I look out on the lawn of Staunch's property.

Brick is walking toward me, limping. He keeps looking back, again and again, his shotgun in his hand and a pained look on his face.

Then I see his legs. Both of them look muddy, like he was ankle-deep in sludge.

He stops at the edge of the woods and starts screaming profanities.

"What?"

Brick yells and says something about a rabid animal. He scowls in pain and sits down on the grass. "Take my shotgun," he says.

"What happened?"

"This dog came out of nowhere. I mean, I think it was a dog. I don't know. A wolf or something. I mean—it just ran up on me and starting biting—" He curses again as he looks at his legs. "Man, I got bit like a dozen times."

"Where is it?"

He shakes his head. "I don't know. I shot it three times, last time in the face. In the face. And then it just—it was chewing at my leg, and I shot it point-blank in the brain and then the thing just blew up like a balloon."

The demon dog.

"You find what you were looking for inside?"

I'm about to say no, but that's not entirely true. "Yes."

I say it more to make sure this doesn't feel like a complete waste of his time.

"Let's get out of here," he says, adding a few more colorful words.

94. WHAT'S YOUR DEAL?

"You know what that thing was?" Brick asks. We're on the deck of my cabin, and he's cleaning the blood off his ankles and feet.

"No."

I got some bandages from a first-aid kit inside. Thankfully Mom is working and the house is empty.

"But you've seen it before?"

"Yeah."

I'm a bit dizzy from the whole experience. I haven't had time to make sense of the vision I saw, and meanwhile I'm trying to keep Brick from completely freaking out.

"Man, I feel like I'm tripping, you know?" he says.

I can't really tell him anything.

All I know is that the person I went to see was missing.

While Brick was attacked by the wild beast that mysteriously vanishes into thick and stinky air, leaving behind a coating of goo.

"Man, you're into some weird stuff," Brick says. After he wraps up both of his ankles, he takes a cigarette out of the pack and lights it. "Sorry—my last one."

"And I might have said yes."

We sit there on the deck under the warm noon sun and stare at the trees below.

"Well, that pretty much tops the weird stuff I've seen around here," he says. "And I've seen my share."

"I think everybody has," I say.

"What's your deal, Buckley?"

"What do you mean?"

"You know what I mean. What's the scoop with you? Weird stuff has been happening around you ever since you came to town."

"I wouldn't even know where to begin."

"Just tell me you're a good guy."

"What's that even mean?"

"That you're not part of them. The ones who dress up and play Ku Klux Klan."

"You've seen them?"

He nods but doesn't act like it's some big information.

"I'm not a part of them."

"Good."

And that's all he says.

I've already gotten him involved enough. Neither of us wants any more.

"Thanks for looking out for me," I tell him.

"No problem, man. Anytime."

I wonder if he seriously means that.

Staring at him, I think he really does.

95. Sweet Dreams Part 2

Do they wait for when you're weakest?

Hovering in the dark, hidden in the shadows. Hiding and waiting to prey.

Do they see when you're confused and angry?

Do they hear when you're asking God why?

Do they laugh when you cry?

Do they strike when you start to wave the white flag?

What do you do?

Where do you go?

Where can you run?

You don't run, Chris. Not anymore.

Is fear like a pot of stew, something that can be stirred?

Is guilt like a shackle, tying you down and making you unable to move?

What if you could not only see them but do something about them?

But I can't.

In the silence of night I think about these visions and nightmares I've witnessed. Time after time I'm just a spectator.

I wonder what would happen if I could strike back.

If I could throw some light on the shadows. If I could stop these things in their tracks.

Are they really, truly real? And if so, what can be done against them?

Pray, Chris.

So I do.

Believe.

Okay.

Sooner or later, I think the time is going to come that those figures will stand in front of me and attack me.

But I'm not shackled down, and I'm not going to give in.

Those nightmares are going to turn into sweet dreams.

Maybe that will be my ability. I'll be the first and only one in this bloodline to do something about the darkness and madness and sickness that keeps building and growing.

It's going to come to an end.

I'm going to make it come to an end.

96. SOMETHING ELSE
FOR THE SCRAPBOOK

I'm persistent. I might not be a lot of things, but I am persistent.

More like stubborn and hardheaded like a mule.

I keep going to the Corner Nook even though nothing happens, but today for some reason it seems that my perseverance has paid off.

I'm doing what I always do, looking around at the books and buying an iced tea and sitting around waiting for something to happen. Waiting to see something that doesn't belong. But up until now, nothing has happened. I haven't seen a magical door open, letting in a bunch of bright and glowing angels.

Today, however, something does show up.

I'm near the back of the store where photographs and paintings by local artists are for sale. Some are leaning against the wall, stacked on top of each other. Others are framed and hanging up.

There's a black-and-white shot of what looks like Indian Bridge, and all I can say is that it looks intense. Like everything is heightened. The shadows and the white and the blacks all feel etched with chalk or in stone. It's a perfect photo because it fits the mood of this bridge.

Wonder if the photographer knew it's haunted.

As I study the picture, I notice a necklace dangling off the ledge the photo is resting on.

I lean in, wondering if it's part of the photo. When I see what's written on the heart locket, I quickly reach out and grab it. I stick it in my pocket and then take a few minutes to calm down. My heart is racing and I'm trying—hoping—to make sure nobody saw me snatch the piece of jewelry.

I have a good feeling the owners have no idea about this.

In fact, I'd bet my life on it.

Later on at home, I examine the locket. It's heavy. The thick round piece held up by the necklace may be gold, but it's dull and faded. It takes me a while of playing around with it before I manage to open the locket, revealing a picture of a baby on one side and a date etched on the other.

I hold it up close and look at the name on the outside again: *Indigo Jadan Kinner.*

And on the inside: *May 28, 1963.*

I try to remember anybody mentioning this name. I'm not even sure if it's a boy or a girl. This baby is older than Mom and Uncle Robert.

A sibling they might not know about?

I decide to ask Mom. I've spent enough time keeping secrets from her. Maybe everything would have been better from the start if I had told her about all that was happening.

Or maybe that would have made things even worse.

I sit on the couch as she's watching a cable show on cooking.

"What's up?" she asks.

"Does the name Indigo Kinner mean anything to you?"

She shakes her head and looks puzzled. "No. Where'd that come from?"

I show her the necklace. She asks me where I found it, and I tell her the Corner Nook. I don't say how it was just hanging there in plain daylight as if a ghost put it there.

Nor do I tell her about the picture it was hanging from.

"This looks real," Mom says.

"I know."

She says the name over and over. "I never heard of an Indigo Kinner. There weren't too many Kinners around."

"Maybe an older brother or sister you didn't know about?"

"I don't think so. Mom would have been—let's see." She does the numbers in her head. "She would have been eighteen when this baby was born."

"She left home and got knocked up."

Mom shakes her head and gives me a *Yeah right* look. "There's no way. We would have heard."

"Think Aunt Alice knows?" I ask.

"Last time I visited her, I don't think she knew what planet she was on."

I can't help but laugh as I recall the first time I met Aunt Alice. Mom and I are both laughing, which is pretty nice and pretty rare in this little cabin.

"Can I keep it?" I ask Mom.

"If you want. Why?"

"I have a little collection of random things I've found around Solitary. I'm going to create a scrapbook."

"No, you're not."

"Yeah, sure. It's going to be like red and have animal fur covering the outside and—"

"Stop." Mom hands me the piece of jewelry. "What a strange name," she says.

"Maybe it's some kind of Indian name."

I slip the piece into my pocket and decide to ask Aunt Alice myself. Sometime.

I have to be in the right mood to go visit the crazy house that belongs to my great-aunt.

Then again, maybe Walter Kinner knows this baby. Maybe it's his.

Maybe it's one that ran away but in the end is going to come out of the woods riding a white horse and save us all from something.

I doubt it. The white horse and saving part.

The something happening, however … I still know that's going to occur.

97. GETTING OUT

I see Poe standing and waiting for me by my locker, and I know that it's just a mirage. She doesn't look all Goth Girl anymore. In fact, she looks quite stunning without all the makeup and layers of clothing and black on.

I can still picture that kiss in the stands of the football stadium. That unexpected kiss after I set the track record.

I blink and still see her. Then I stop. But she's still there.

"Hi," I hear her say.

For a second I really think I'm dreaming. I take another step, and she starts to walk toward me.

Before I can say anything, Poe gives me a big hug.

"What are you—"

She won't let me go, so I just hold her there for a long time. When she does finally open her arms and look at me, I still can't believe it. Those blue eyes still sparkle like they always did, but they appear different. Stronger. Older, maybe.

"You look great," I say.

"You don't."

Same Poe, telling me like it is.

"What are you doing here?"

"Making sure you don't ignore another email or phone call."

I shake my head and start to say something, but she silences me with a *Shhh.*

"Listen, I'm in town visiting relatives." Her eyes widen to acknowledge the lie. I know she doesn't have any other relatives in town. "I'll only be here for a couple of days."

"You going to classes?" I ask, since it's Monday morning.

"No. You think I'd do that if I didn't have to?"

"Then what—"

She hands me a note and smiles. "Read it later. I wanted to make sure it actually reached your hands."

"Okay."

She glances at me with what appears to be a fond look. "I've been worried about you."

"Yeah, I've been worried about me too."

She laughs, not out of amusement but almost out of pity. "See you later."

Her eyes widen again as she says that. I'm sure the note will tell me where and when.

I hug Poe again and then look at her. "I was always right about you."

"What?"

"That underneath all that stuff there was a really gorgeous girl waiting to be found."

"Yeah? Well, tell me when you find her," Poe says. "Bye."

She walks back down the hallway, and I go to open my locker door. Then out of the corner of my eye I see someone watching me.

Kelsey.

Oh, come on.

"Hey," I say.

She turns and walks away.

Seriously?

Sometimes I really think I can't get a break.

"Why'd you want to meet here?"

We're at a Starbucks in Greer, South Carolina, not too far from the city of Greenville. It took about forty minutes to drive here.

"Did you want to meet in Solitary?" Poe asks. She appears to be very comfortable in her chair, sipping her drink. "I wanted to get far away from there."

"Sorry I'm a little late. Took a wrong turn. Can't do GPS on my phone while riding the bike."

"You look like you drove through a tornado."

I pat my hair down as I get something to drink. I come back and sit across from her.

"I can't believe you're here."

"Yeah, me neither."

"Did you drive from New York?" I ask her.

"We're not in New York. We're living in Harrisburg, Pennsylvania."

All this time I've assumed that her family went back to New York, where she said she was from. She moved right around the time Pastor Marsh popped up again, after I'd stabbed him in the stomach. So yeah, maybe I wasn't paying that much attention.

"It took about thirteen hours to get down here," she said.

I'm drinking a warm chocolate coffee drink just to give me some caffeine and to heat up my chilled body. Just as I'm about to ask her why she's here, Poe tells me.

"That FBI agent—the one who came down here—she's missing."

So I guess Sheriff Wells was right about the FBI agent being real.

"You spoke to her, right?" Poe asks.

I nod. "I didn't know she was real. I thought …" I sigh. "I thought she was lying. A lot of people have been lying to me."

"I think she's—I think something happened to her."

Poe doesn't want to come right out and say *dead*. I understand. I'd be the same way.

"How do you know?"

"Because I've tried contacting her. Someone who worked with her came to me. But I didn't really say much."

"If they did something to her, people are going to find out."

Poe nods. "That's what's kind of scary. If they did do something to her, then maybe it means something."

"Like what?"

"I don't know. I doubt they would do anything unless they knew they could get away with it. I wanted to make sure—I had to warn you."

For a moment I'm just studying her face, noticing her intensity.

"What?" she asks.

"It's just—kinda surreal to see you sitting across from me."

"Without all the makeup and the dark hair."

"Oh, yeah," I say. "It's lighter."

"Guys," she says. "Always clueless."

"Yep."

"Chris—what's going on? With you and Marsh?"

"I wouldn't know where to begin."

"Start with what's happened since I left. What do they want?"

That's a hard question, because I still don't know exactly what they want. Marsh seems to want control, while Kinner wants me to take over for him.

I stumble in trying to tell Poe some of the facts. I mention my great-grandfather having to do with it, that he's still alive and how he controls things, including Staunch.

"Wait a minute," Poe says with wide eyes. "Is he demon possessed?"

"This guy named Kinner? I don't know."

"That's real, you know. It really does happen."

"Yeah, I don't know."

"What? Are you serious? You stabbed someone and watched him die, and then he shows back up. But you don't believe in demons?"

"I didn't say that. It's just—the whole possession/exorcism thing. Seems a bit Hollywood to me."

"Maybe the body doesn't have to be spinning and vomiting pea soup in order to be possessed," Poe says. "Have you thought of that?"

I glance around to see if anybody can hear her. There's a guy in the corner, a college student, working on a laptop. Then there's a man in his thirties drinking a cup of coffee and studying his phone.

"I don't know what's happening. Or what they have planned."

TRAVIS THRASHER

"You have to get out."

I shake my head, thinking about Kelsey again. I have to explain to her about Poe. I have to tell her what's really happening.

"I can't just leave without other people."

There's my uncle Robert, I explain to her. Mom, who is doing better.

"The cute blonde—what's her name?"

I act surprised. "What do you mean?"

"Kelsey—that's her name. Right?"

I nod.

"You guys a thing?"

I shake my head.

"Yeah, you are," Poe says.

"No. It's not—we are, but we aren't. Because I don't want something …"

Poe grows serious and nods, understanding what I'm talking about.

We will forever be connected by the death of the girl who was a friend to both of us.

We will never be able to forget Jocelyn Evans.

"I don't want you to end up like her either," Poe says.

"I won't."

"How do you know that?"

"I just—I just know."

"If they can—" Poe stops in midsentence and lowers her voice. "If they can kill an FBI agent, that means they can do anything."

"But you don't know for sure."

"We still don't know about Stuart. Or those others. Right?"

I think of the tall figure in sweats that I saw walking the halls of Harrington.

"Poe—was Stuart—was he tall?"

The question seems to come from out of the blue, and her reaction says that. "Why?"

"I just—I saw a snapshot of someone who might have been him. Tall guy. Wearing sweats."

"He ran cross-country and was always in sweats. Yeah, he was tall."

Well, good, because I saw him, minus some brain and skin and tissue and all that.

"Something big is going to happen on Memorial Day," I tell her.

"What?"

"I don't know. But—I'm going to be involved. I'm like the star of the show or something."

"You have to get out before then," Poe says. "Graduation is before, right?"

"The nineteenth."

"Chris—what, are you going to spend the summer around Solitary? You need to leave."

"It's not that easy."

"Yes, it is. How easy was it to come here?"

"There are others."

"So you do whatever you can to get them out too. Buy a bus and drive it out of town. I don't know. Do anything."

They'll hunt me down, the same way they got me to come back after I left and went to Chicago over New Year's Eve. If not my mom or Kelsey, they'll find someone else or some other way.

TRAVIS THRASHER

I'm going to try and prove Poe wrong, but I'm reminded just sitting here how strong her personality can be.

Good ole Chris, always surrounded by strong-willed women.

"What are you thinking?" she asks.

"That obvious?"

"What?"

"That I'm thinking?"

She laughs. For a while we talk about lighter things, about things that don't involve life and death and midnight sacrifices. It takes about fifteen minutes for her to reveal the real reason for her outward transformation.

"You have a boyfriend," I say.

"No, not really. Not official."

"Oh come on," I say.

"Yeah, we like each other."

"And you let him tell you what to do, huh?"

"No," Poe says. "I did this myself. Weston was curious, that was all."

"Weston, huh?"

"What?"

"Sounds like a made-up name."

"What?" Poe thinks I'm being serious.

"I'm just kidding."

The humor is certainly welcome.

We talk for a long time about school and track and jobs and licenses. It's nice to talk about normal things.

We suddenly realize that it's ten o'clock.

"Tell me you're not driving home tonight," I say to her.

"No. I'm not. I'm staying with a girlfriend I knew at Harrington.

She was a senior when I was a sophomore. She goes to Furman University. I should probably get going."

There's so much more to say and do, but I nod and stand up.

When we go outside to the cool night, Poe looks anxious again. "You have to be careful."

"I will," I tell her. "You too."

"Chris—I mean it."

"I know. Thanks for—for coming all this way."

"I wanted to see you. Just to make sure."

"To make sure what?" I ask.

"That you were still really here. That it was you and not some random person emailing me. I wanted to see you face-to-face."

"I'm glad," I say.

And yes, I am glad.

I hug her again.

"Keep me in the loop," Poe says. "Okay?"

"I will. I promise."

"Get out of Solitary. Get out soon, Chris. Or you'll end up like Jocelyn. You know it too. I know you do."

98. THIS JERK

"You don't understand."

This is all I manage to get out in one conversation with Kelsey.

"Just wait, give me a minute" is another.

"I gotta talk with you" is the third one.

But no. Kelsey is done.

And for the moment, I resort back to seventeen senioritis.

If someone wants to complain, fine, fill my shoes and see what you'd do.

I told her to wait, and she waited.

I told her to trust me, and she was trusting me, right?

Even as she managed to slowly sink away, I didn't think it would really happen. I didn't think I was really going to lose her. We were both going with the flow and acting the part, but somehow I think the part grabbed her.

So did big and tall and handsome Lance. What a big dumb lug.

But Poe coming and then that moment and Kelsey seeing … it felt like it was all part of the grand plan. As if someone planned it so that Kelsey would see and finally say *enough*.

But then I decide to ask around. I come back to planet Harrington and I ask Harris if he knows what's up with Lance and prom, and Harris gets the scoop.

Yes, Kelsey is going with Lance.

I guess my drama—my life and death drama—isn't going to get in the way of a girl going to prom. Heaven—or hell—forbid.

When I hear this, it seems that something gets cracked and broken. All of a sudden I need to reach out and try to convince Kelsey of what's happening and what I'm doing. I'm not avoiding her because I want to or because I want Poe or because of anything other than the desire to save her life.

I mean—that's heroic, right?

Let's see Lance do that.

My attempts to reach out to her go unnoticed. Or unwanted. It's some kind of un-thing that's making me come undone. So eventually I go to Georgia and ask her what's the deal.

"What's your deal?" Georgia bites back.

"Is she really going to prom with Lance?"

"Uh, yeah."

"But I just—I don't get it."

"You know—I don't get it." Georgia looks like a pit bull ready to bite.

"What don't you get?"

"You? You—Mr. Chris Buckley ooh ahh."

The added bit on my name makes me laugh in disbelief. "Okay."

"No, I really don't get it," she says. "I don't get what these girls see. I mean—you come in and you have Jocelyn—Jocelyn—and her friend Poe all aflutter and gaga. And yes, of course, Kelsey too. Little old Kelsey who you keep ignoring and keep overlooking and keep breaking."

"Stop being dramatic."

"Oh, I haven't even started."

"Really?"

I've never wanted to strangle a girl, but suddenly I want to, here and now.

"I don't get it. I just don't. Guys like Lance, sure. But you, I don't get."

I stare at Georgia for a moment. I swear her nose has suddenly turned up and she's looking a bit like Miss Piggy.

"I don't get it either," I say. "I've never claimed to, okay? But there's a lot—no, pretty much everything between Kelsey and me is something you don't know about. You don't understand."

"You're a jerk."

"Yeah, maybe I am. But Kelsey likes this jerk and has for quite a while, and for some reason, she doesn't think I'm one. And the only thing—the only thing that matters now in this place is that girl. That she ends up being okay."

"Oh, she's going to be okay," Georgia says in a way I don't like. "She's going to be fine."

I've always found something to like about girls. But I've never found anything to like about their friends.

99. No Light, No Light

I hear gunshots going off in my gut, round after round ripping through me.

I see my stomach bleeding and my soul leaking out, and I realize this is all something I did myself.

I'm not sure I can do this without you, Kelsey.

It seems you've been here from the beginning.

In the darkest hour you were there, painting away the light. The grays I smeared on the screen were eclipsed by the blues in your eyes.

You made me feel again.

You chased after me.

You kept coming time after time. You never gave up even when you didn't know if I had any hope.

And now with the night coming to an end and the dark, deep jaws of the wolf starting to close around my throat I know this one thing.

I'll do anything to make you stay in my life.

I'll do anything to make you continue to love me.

I want to see the twentysomething version of you turn into the thirty and forty and fifty version.

I can't do this thing without you.

I don't want the grays to come back.

I don't want that dreary field. I want your light wheat swaying back and forth under a clear and steady sky.

I'm afraid the lights are going to go out.

I need a revelation to show me now tonight what to do and where to go and how to do it.

Don't give up on me.

Don't leave me.

Don't take your light and go somewhere else.

Not now and not tonight.

100. Sæglópur (Do You Understand?)

The next day I get past glaring Georgia and towering Lance to talk to Kelsey.

I take her hands in mine.

"Listen to me—Kelsey, please. Look at me."

Her wide eyes are already starting to tear up.

Yes you hurt her but not because you wanted to or because you messed up but because this place made it happen.

"I want you to come with me."

She shakes her head, looking confused. Lance is nearby and says something, and I look at him. And I don't know. I'm not an intimidating sort of guy, but I think I might have the tendency if moved enough to look absolutely bonkers—like I do now. Enough to make the guy just look at me with a bit of reluctance.

"Please, just—please."

I tug her and don't feel resistance.

I keep tugging and lead her down the hallway.

I see Mr. Meiners staring at us from the doorway of his room.

I see Miss Harking pass us by with her dull glance.

I see Brick outside smoking and nodding.

I lead Kelsey down to my bike, and then I hop on.

"Come on."

"Where are we going?"

"I don't know."

I start up the motorcycle, and I guess it works. There was no grand plan. No wanting to look all studly and manly on my bike.

I'm just wanting to escape.

I feel her arms wrap around my chest.

"Hang on," I shout out.

Then I drive. And I keep driving. And I lead us far away from this place just because it feels right and because I want to dream and want to hope that there is a place outside of this one that can belong to us.

I feel her rigid arms around me, but ten minutes in, Kelsey seems to relax.

Or maybe relent.

She gives in as she clutches me tighter.

Then she really holds on to me, not in a way someone riding passenger on a bike might but the way someone needing to hold another might.

"Don't give up on me, Kelsey."

We could be anywhere. It doesn't really matter.

A high school gym or library or bathroom or hallway. A park or a parking lot or a national park.

It doesn't matter.

The girl in front of me matters. The girl shaking her head and not saying anything.

"Go to prom with me."

"What?"

"I messed up when I didn't ask you last year. When I didn't walk you home after our dance. I told myself that wasn't going to happen again, and look what's happening."

She shakes her head, wiping away more tears.

"I'm sorry, Kelsey."

"What's going on with you?"

My mouth starts to move, but I don't say anything.

"See," Kelsey says. "That's what always happens."

"I don't want you dying," I blurt out in a frustrated, awkward way.

"What—what are you talking about?"

"They took Jocelyn away and they managed to take Lily away and I don't want them taking you away."

"Who? What?"

We're at a rest stop off the highway, and nobody is near the bench we're sitting on.

"Staunch and Pastor Marsh. These men are part of an evil cult, one that's run by my great-grandfather. They want me—and they're willing to kill anybody—*anybody*—in order to get me."

"But why?"

"Because they think I'm special and I have some crazy powers and I don't know …"

Kelsey stares at me.

"I know—ludicrous, right? I could keep going, but it would just keep getting more and more crazy. And I don't want you to give me goofy looks."

"I'm not giving you any kind of look."

"Go to prom with me," I say as I take her hands.

"I'm already—"

"Lance? Really? Kelsey—really?"

She looks down, almost ashamed.

"Do you really like him? I mean—if I thought you really wanted to go with him, then I wouldn't be here. But I get this feeling that deep down inside you really kinda want me to—"

She interrupts me with a kiss. I put both my hands on her slender, soft face and kiss her back.

After a few moments, Kelsey pushes me away.

"How does stupid prom have anything to do with what's going on with you?" she asks. "Is that why I'm in danger?"

"They don't want me to be with you."

"Why? I don't get it."

"Because they don't like your faith and your influence. They think that—they think that somehow you're going to ..."

"What?"

"This all sounds so ridiculous."

"What?" Kelsey asks. "Prom?"

"This whole discussion of—listen—I just want you to know that I think that I kinda love you, if that even makes sense."

Kelsey acts like she was just sideswiped by a train.

"I know it makes no sense to hear that, but I do. I mean, I think I do." I can tell I'm babbling, but I keep on. "And if I have to tell you that and take you to prom to prove it, then fine, but then you have to promise me—you have to understand that you have to stay away from me."

She looks up at me in a relieved, happy way.

"Do you understand?" I ask her.

"No." But then she kisses me in a way that says she maybe doesn't care.

And I kiss her back in that same sort of way.

Maybe all the evil-people-out-there stuff doesn't make sense, but this right here does make sense. And it feels like this can overcome anything and can destroy anyone trying to break it.

This love feels right even if everything else around us feels wrong.

"So am I going to have to beat up Lance or something to get you to be my prom date?" I ask her.

"No," Kelsey says. "All you had to do was ask. That's all you've ever had to do."

101. END THEME

The initial days after my conversation and prom proposal to Kelsey seem to tiptoe away like a thief leaving the scene of the crime. Soon I'm stepping with ease and not worried as much. I keep thinking about what she said.

How does stupid prom have anything to do with what's going on with you?

And she's right. It's stupid prom.

It's a stupid Romeo-and-Juliet-themed prom.

Nobody's going to care if I go with her.

I hear Marsh's smug, threatening voice.

Do you want her to end up like Jocelyn or Lily? Do you?

But I'm not doing anything; it's just a dance.

End things with Kelsey, or Staunch will end things his way. Staunch will find a way if he wants to make it happen.

And I'm fine, I'm really fine until the night before prom when I can't sleep and I Google *Romeo and Juliet* since I didn't really pay much attention when we studied it in class.

Tragedy is the first word I see.

Teenage lovers.

Balcony scene.

Vow to be married.

Executed.

Murder.

Deathlike coma.

Poison.

Stabs herself with a dagger.

Children's deaths.

Elegy.

And after reading this wonderful synopsis on Wikipedia I really miss the eighties theme of last year.

The school knows. They're just preparing me for the ultimate end.

One last dance will soon turn into one last day and one last breath.

102. THE MOST BEAUTIFUL
SONG ON YOUR PLAYLIST

The dark weather goes away for a while, leaving the skies clear and the wind calm for the big night.

Leaving the ocean ready to sweep into the hallway where I'm waiting and ready to blush when I see Kelsey.

She comes in wearing a strapless, flowing light blue dress that makes me nervous to examine too carefully. Her hair is up, her eyes bright and matching her dress, her smile all made up and adult.

"Ready?"

She seems calm, but I'm not calm.

Driving in my mom's car to Georgia's house, I'm not calm. Even when Kelsey holds my hand.

One might think I'm nervous because of what this might mean and about the warnings, but those have gone away. I'm nervous because Kelsey is no longer this cute girl I'm interested in.

She hasn't been that cute girl since last year.

This is taking it to a whole new level. She truly is a seventeen-year-old who looks like a twenty-four-year-old.

Made up and ready to take on the world.

"Your hand is sweaty," she says.

"Yeah."

"You're nervous."

"Yeah."

She leans over and gives me a kiss on the cheek. "Don't be."

"Okay."

But I stay nervous for a while.

The whole Romeo and Juliet thing doesn't make my anxiety go away. Everything seems to point toward one thing.

Death.

The decorations; the displays, including a whole balcony setup; the colors and the lighting ... they all seem to share the gloom and doom. The songs played are not typical prom songs. They all carry a theme as well. Themes of love and loss.

But through all this, there is Kelsey. Smiling, glowing, happy.

Happy.

Now there's a wonderful thing that I never want to see go away.

This light happiness that is as clear and pure as the color of her dress or her eyes.

We never leave each other that night except for brief bathroom breaks. We forget there are even others in the room. There's no drama, no teenage angst or spirit thing going on. There's just Kelsey and me.

When the final song begins to play, we slow dance again and for a brief moment look into each other's eyes.

Imagine the most beautiful song on your playlist. This is what is playing.

The lyrics, written by someone I will never meet in my life, don't mean a thing.

The melody, created by someone more talented than I will ever be, doesn't matter.

For the moment, this last song of the night doesn't matter. The girl in my arms does.

We hold each other, and I find myself thinking a prayer that I hope will forever be answered.

Don't let this girl leave my world, God. Don't let her go.

We sway to the sweet song, and I hope and pray that Kelsey will always be there. Regardless of what happens tonight and tomorrow and the thirty thousand days afterward.

103. Now We Are Free

You know that feeling you have when you think something's about to happen, but it hasn't happened just yet? That feeling you get, like a silent buzz going off all around you? If you were a superhero it would be your Spidey sense, but unfortunately you're not exactly a hero and you're really not super.

But you are ready.

Ready to take on the world, right?

That's what the guy speaking to all you graduates is talking about. You're thankful it's not Pastor Marsh. That's the absolute last thing you'd need right now: a motivational speech by that guy. Yet in your cap and gown, as you sit on a chair, not really paying attention to the Mr. Believe-in-Your-Dreams guy, you have a feeling that Marsh is somewhere behind you. You know Staunch is, because Gus is graduating. Staunch and Marsh are probably sitting together, playing hangman on the graduation brochure.

The letters spell out CHRISTOPHER BUCKLEY.

The man talking about following your dreams doesn't get that you want to get far, far *away* from your dreams. Because people die and get suffocated in your dreams. Nope, no dreams for you.

You glance back and see her, the lighthouse that never shuts off in this foggy sea. She catches you looking back and shines a smile your way.

It reminds you that so far, everything is good.

It's May 19, and so far, everything is fine.

You haven't decided what college to go to and you haven't sold your soul to the Devil.

So far so good.

Your mom is sitting behind you too, waiting to see you walk across the small stage in this gym, the same gym you had prom in a week earlier. Your name will be called, and you'll receive a piece of paper that tells you you're finally free. Dad couldn't be here, and it's okay because this isn't the important event he needs to be at.

Dad needs to be there when you and Mom get back home.

Back in Libertyville, you probably wouldn't have felt so joyous. You would have been joking with the guys and planning how to celebrate. But now you feel like the guy at the end of *Gladiator*. No, not the main hero whose corpse ends up being brought out of the stadium, but his friend who talks about finally being free.

The kids around you don't understand. Not even Kelsey.

Your parents have a slight understanding, but not really.

Marsh and Staunch—well, they might understand the most, but they don't care in the least.

No, you've been a prisoner here for long enough.

Today you're not just graduating.

Today you're being set free.

You take that slip of paper but know that you've learned far more around these classrooms than inside of them.

You celebrate with the rest of the students, but not really.

When it's finally time and you've said good-bye to high school, you do the thing that matters most.

You find Kelsey and hug her and stay at her side.

You're going to keep doing this until May turns to June and then maybe, hopefully, if God allows it to happen, you will truly be set free when you leave this solitary place forever.

104. MY SON

Aunt Alice seems permanently distracted, lost, always wondering where she happens to be. Mom picked her up and brought her over for dinner. This is the first time, and judging by how Aunt Alice is acting, it's probably the last. She doesn't eat much, barely responds to the things Mom says, and glances at me like I'm one of her mannequins.

After dinner, as Mom is cleaning up and I'm sitting on the couch across from Aunt Alice watching *Wheel of Fortune*, Mom makes a suggestion.

"Why don't you show Aunt Alice the locket you found?"

I nod and go upstairs to get it. It's in my little assortment of strange things I've found around Solitary. I bring it to her and then sit on the sofa next to her.

"I found this the other day. We were wondering if you know who this baby might be."

I show her the locket in my hand and see her slow eyes move toward it.

I expect more of the same—the distant glance, the half-deaf ears, the barely spoken words.

But it's like someone switched an *on* button. She blinks and then keeps blinking as if she's thawing out.

"Indigo," she says.

She hasn't even taken it from my hand.

Bingo for Indigo.

Mom walks into the room, surprised that Aunt Alice said the name so quickly.

"Aunt Alice—have you seen this before?" Mom nudges for me to open the piece.

I do, and then something crazy happens to Aunt Alice.

She looks … scared?

No, not scared. Mesmerized. Shocked.

"Aunt Alice?"

"Where did you find this?" she asks Mom.

"Chris found it. In the Corner Nook."

Bony, spotted fingers take the locket in their grip and bring it up to her eyes.

"Aunt Alice, do you—"

Mom stops talking because she sees the tears coming down Aunt Alice's face.

If I didn't see them myself I'd never in a million years believe in them. I thought that Aunt Alice didn't have enough of her left to feel whatever it is that she's feeling.

Mom glances at me, and I look as amazed as she does, and then it hits me.

Indigo. It's her baby.

"Alice?" Mom says.

I bet she's not going to say anymore. I bet that this is going to be one of those many Solitary back stories that we never end up hearing—

"Indigo was the son I gave birth to many years ago."

She's still looking at the picture inside the locket. Yet she also seems more awake, more *there* than she has since she walked through that door.

"You had a son?"

"A vile thing," she says, shaking her head and almost spitting out the words. The tears are gone now. "A wicked thing."

"Your ... son?"

Aunt Alice strokes the locket and shakes her head.

"What do you mean?" Mom asks.

"What happened?" I ask.

"He's old enough to know," she says, looking at me. "He's older than I was when it happened."

"When what happened?"

"When that monster of a man called my father took me outside in the shadows of the towering stone and took away my innocence. Took away whatever good I had left in me. Leaving me with nothing but a hole. A hole and this. This." Her shaking hand holds up the necklace.

Mom looks over at me in shock and surprise. She can't say anything. I don't have anything to say.

Kinner.

Something that Aunt Alice once said comes to mind. Something about Uncle Robert and me and hope. About putting an end to hope.

No.

I feel something deep inside. Not fear. It's fearful, but it's more like a sickening feel, a feeling of diving into something heavy and dark and wanting to go back up to the surface as fast as possible.

Aunt Alice starts rocking like a crazy person. She's holding the locket like she's rocking a child.

It's an awful sight.

"I replaced evil with evil," she says.

Mom looks pale as she says "It's okay, you don't have to—"

"I killed him."

Mom knew it was coming and didn't want it spoken out loud. Maybe she didn't want me to hear it.

It horrifies yet somehow doesn't surprise.

"I took him back to the place it happened. I took the baby back to that awful bridge, and I left him there. I let them have it. I let the baby go."

386

TRAVIS THRASHER

Mom puts a hand over her mouth, and I see her eyes full of tears. She shakes her head.

"You can't live with something like that," Aunt Alice says. "Don't matter if you didn't know any better or if you were young and dumb. Don't matter a bit. You take that with you the rest of your life. It eats away at you like a bird. Chipping away. Day. Night. Day. Night."

Her aged Southern drawl is slow and haunting.

I don't want to hear anymore.

"I thought it'd appease 'em, but it just got 'em more riled up."

"Who? Who are you talking about?" Mom asks.

"Chris knows." Aunt Alice looks at me and smiles to reveal her missing teeth.

Just like her missing mind.

I shake my head and act like I don't have a clue, but yeah, I think I know the "them" she's talking about.

"Heaven got no place for a baby killer," Aunt Alice says, shutting the locket and then, surprisingly, giving it back to me. "Maybe you can give this to Indigo one day. I'd take it all back now, everything I done. I know that now."

Mom wipes her eyes and then glances at me. There's nothing to say. Nothing to do. At least not with Aunt Alice.

"I'm so sorry," Mom eventually says, taking Aunt Alice's hand in her own.

"Y'all think I'm the crazy woman with the house full of mannequins," Aunt Alice says. "But I'd rather spend my days and nights around a family of fake faces than have to constantly see the face of the little one I let go."

For a moment, maybe a whole minute, maybe an hour, I just sit there frozen in place. Unable to move or speak or do anything. And I think Mom is the same.

A house with a phony family to avoid the ghost of the real one haunting her.

My heart aches. Really and truly. It burns, and I need something to douse the stinging flames.

I've come to realize there is only one who can do that. Over and over and over again.

105. HOW YOU CARRY ON

"Well, that was a real … bummer."

This might be the most understated thing I've ever said in my life.

Mom just got back after taking Aunt Alice home. I'm sitting in the same place on the couch as I was when she left.

"Have you started packing?"

"No."

I still don't really believe I'm going to be leaving this place. It still feels like a nice dream, a fantasy that looks great and sounds great but definitely won't happen.

"You have a week left," Mom says as she goes into the kitchen.

One might interpret that statement in a lot of ways.

One week left, buddy. Breathe in life, because in seven days it's going to be choked away from you.

Mom and Dad decided that we would move back to Illinois the day after Memorial Day. For a while I was hoping Dad was going to come down and spend the last week with us, but he still has some classes remaining. Plus he has a commitment at his church. Some kind of charity work.

"Any last words from Aunt Alice?"

Mom shakes her head. I know she's probably thinking she could use a good drink right about now. She's probably thinking that, because I'm thinking it. Anything to try and forget about the conversation we just had.

"I'm sorry you had to hear all of that," Mom says, sitting next to me and letting out a sigh.

"I'm just sorry that it happened."

Mom pats me on the leg and stares at the television in a far-off, distant way. "Such a crazy world."

"Yeah."

"I'm sorry for ever bringing you here, Chris."

"You've already said that."

"I know, but I'll say it again and keep saying it. This place—this is a wicked place. They just need to come in and bulldoze it over."

"How about *after* we leave?"

She laughs. "Yeah. Okay."

I turn down the volume on the program I wasn't really watching anyway. "Remember that first time we visited Aunt Alice? When we got in the car and couldn't stop laughing?"

Mom nods.

"Now I feel—well, like totally bad."

"I feel sorry for her," Mom says. "And for my mother."

"At least we know why Aunt Alice is—that way." I say this not trying to be mean, just stating the obvious.

"Everybody carries hurt in their heart. Some more than others. But all of us carry some. Part of growing older is realizing this. But, Chris—it's what we do with it that counts. It's how we move on in life with it. I don't believe it ever goes away, not fully. Even if we try and give it over to God. There are scars and remainders of pain that will always be there. But how you carry on—that's what defines your life."

"Wow."

Mom looks surprised by my comment. "What?"

"That was pretty powerful."

"There were a lot of good things that came out of going to rehab. It's one thing to stop drinking. It's another thing to start living."

"Yeah."

What I want to say is *Yeah, Mom, and way to go and I'm proud of you.*

What I want to tell her is *Yeah, Mom, you're finally living again and I love you for being brave enough to do it.*

But I just say "Yeah," which seems okay for Mom. She adds one last thing.

"Don't wait until you're forty to start really, truly living." She glances at me. "Nah—I don't have to worry about that happening with you."

106. Tick of the Clock

I get my first FedEx package at the cabin the Wednesday before Memorial Day. This actually excites me because I think it's from my father. It's a regular-sized box, not too heavy. The cabin is empty, since Mom is working her last few days at the tavern.

I open the package and pull out something that at first looks like a black blanket. Then I examine it and see that it's no blanket.

It's a robe.

A piece of cloth falls to the ground. It's a hood with openings for eyes.

Whoever sent this might as well have sent me a pumpkin with a knife stuck in it and the word *You* scrawled over its top.

I look back at the box to see who it was from, but there's just an address I don't recognize. Then I see a note tucked away inside the box.

Suddenly I can feel my heart pounding away.

> Chris:
>   Show up at the new building for
> New Beginnings Church at 8:30
> p.m. this Monday.
>   Take Heartland Trail past the
> old church, and you'll see where it used
> to dead-end. There's a newly built
> road that will take you to the church.

Bring this robe with you. I'll be there to meet you.

Further instructions will come when I see you.

Don't tell anybody. Don't bring anybody. Don't play any games.

Just do as I say, and nobody you love will get hurt.

JM

I haven't been to New Beginnings Church for a while, but it's still surprising to hear about the new road. I think of the last time I was there, the time Poe and I hiked through the woods. The church with the gravestone devoted to its founder, Solitaire, front and center. The one with the strange French saying.

Maybe Marsh will tell you what it means.

I pick up the robe again and then throw it to the ground.

All this time and all these secrets and all this buildup just to get back to the place I ended up stumbling across. Some ceremony with a bunch of crazy people in robes.

I recall the people in the robes when Jocelyn died. They were wearing red robes. Why do I get a black one? Were they running low on my color and size?

What if you're the sacrifice?

That's a nice thought. But I doubt it.

I read the note again.

Don't tell anybody. Don't bring anybody. Don't play any games.

If the old Chris had been told this, he wouldn't have listened. He

would have nodded and said fine and then proceeded to tell someone
and bring someone and definitely play some games.

*I might be totally different from the guy who ran and found Jocelyn
dead, but I'm still Chris Buckley.*

Seeing this robe and thinking that they actually expect me to
wear it … it really does something to me.

It angers me.

I put it back in the box and hide it under my bed, then I get on
my bike and head out.

To find someone I trust.

It isn't Kelsey I've come to see.

Nope, there's no way I'm telling her what's about to happen.
Kelsey is leaving on Friday to go to Columbia, South Carolina, for
the weekend, and I'm delighted.

No, the first person I go to see is one of the first people I got to
know at Harrington High.

He hands me a tray that holds a hot dog, fries, and a drink.

"That's six thirty," Newt says.

I remember Gus swatting him like a bug and how outraged that
made me feel.

Even if that incident had not happened, I know I would have
had run-ins with Gus. But who knows if I ever would have gotten
to know Newt.

Maybe he would have been one of those people giving me messages without my knowing about it.

I hand Newt money. He sorts the bills and then sees the folded piece of paper in the middle of them. Like a 00-agent or a member of a *Mission Impossible* team, Newt simply puts all the bills in the register while casually placing the note aside. I make small talk but deliberately act like someone is watching me.

I eat the hot dog and fries and then leave.

Two hours later, Newt shows up in the place I marked on the note. I figured he would be working through lunch, so it's two thirty when we meet. I chose the slope of seats facing the football field at Harrington High. It's empty of course, but the gates are always open to go practice on the track or field. From here it's easy to see if anybody is around watching you. It's a random place that probably isn't monitored, especially for secret covert meetings like this.

Our conversation is brief. I tell Newt everything he needs to know and then I ask him if he can help me.

I have a plan, but I'm still not totally sure about it.

The plan or really anything, to be honest.

"Yeah, sure."

I nod and thank him.

I scan the stairs descending to the stadium below. For a moment, it reminds me of a scene in one of my favorite television programs, one that Newt loves as well.

"See you in another life, brotha," I say in a horrible attempt at a Scottish accent.

Newt instantly gets it and laughs. "I sure hope not."

It's nice to see the serious-looking guy ease up a bit.

When I leave Newt, I have two more people to contact.

I meet up with Brick at a graduation party where the smell of pot is thick and almost makes it difficult to breathe.

I ask him, and he nods and says yes.

I ask if he'll remember me asking, and he says yes.

I'm not really sure I believe him, but it's enough.

If he shows up, he shows up.

The last person is someone I simply write.

DEAR MR. MEINERS:

IF YOU DON'T SEE ME THE DAY AFTER MEMORIAL DAY, THEN GO CHECK OUT MY FORMER LOCKER AT HARRINGTON. EVERYTHING I KNOW ABOUT WHAT IS HAPPENING IS WRITTEN DOWN AND WAITING IN AN ENVELOPE.

GIVE IT TO SOMEONE WHO CAN HELP.

IF THERE IS ANYONE WHO CAN HELP.

CHRIS

The notes would never make a set of books but they might at least provide some answers.

I just hope Mr. Meiners won't need them.

I hope I'll have all the answers and that I'll still be carrying them. Alive and ready to leave this place.

But I don't know.

I'm getting the feeling that I'm really on my own here.

107. ONE FINAL POSTCARD

I've received a handful of postcards from my father with Bible verses on them. Some were psalms that were cheery and hopeful. Others made me think. I have the stack of them bound by a rubber band.

The latest one shows a sculpture of a lion in front of the Art Institute of Chicago. I've seen the lions before while visiting the museum with a class.

On the back is a simple note.

CHRIS—I KNOW YOU TOLD ME ON THE
PHONE THAT GRADUATION WASN'T
IMPORTANT. I STILL WISH I'D BEEN
THERE. YOUR GIFT IS WAITING BACK HOME.
  I CAN'T WAIT TO SEE YOU BOTH.
  REMEMBER LUKE 12:8-9. I TAKE THIS AS
ENCOURAGEMENT TO SPEAK UP FOR WHAT I
BELIEVE. TO BE A LIGHT.
                                    LOVE YOU.
                                        DAD

I find my Bible and look up the verses.

> I tell you the truth, everyone who acknowledges me
> publicly here on earth, the Son of Man will also
> acknowledge in the presence of God's angels. But

anyone who denies me here on earth will be denied
before God's angels.

I read it, then read it again.

Somehow I don't take it as encouragement.

Somehow it feels more like a warning or a threat.

I guess I think this way because I know myself. Because I don't know exactly what I'd do if forced to reveal what I believe.

Especially if it would hurt the people I love the most in this world.

108. GOING AWAY FOR GOOD

"What's wrong?"

"Nothing."

I want to convince Kelsey that nothing is wrong, but everything in life that is wrong weighs me down. I wonder if this will be the last time I'll sit with her in her family room on this couch. Or if I'll ever be in this house again.

Or if I'll ever sit next to her again.

The clouds that are normally blown away by Kelsey's brightness are immovable this evening. She knows it too.

"I told you that I'm coming back late on Monday night," she says. "I'll be here before you leave."

I nod, already knowing that.

"Chris?"

"Yeah."

"Talk to me. Are you still worried—about everything?"

"Yeah."

"You're going to be fine. Everything's going to be fine. I know it is. I know you, Chris. You'll figure it out."

I can only laugh about that. I'll figure it out. Yeah, right. I've been trying to figure out things since I first set foot in this awful place.

"That's funny," I say.

"Why?"

I think for a minute. "You know—when I came here, I didn't really know who I was. I didn't have much of a personality. But being on my own and dealing with this—this craziness—helped me. It's like I've had several different personalities. But I think that's the only way I could have found me. You know?"

She nods. And yeah, I think Kelsey does know.

But she doesn't know this blanket of burden thrown over my head. All this shaking worry buried deep inside of me.

"I just wish that this feeling—all this stuff I worry about—all this hurt—I just wish it would go away once and for all."

Kelsey leans into me and holds my hands. "We all hurt in our own way. You know I—I've been around these people most of my life. And most of them don't have a clue who I am. That's why—when I saw you and met you—I thought that I had a chance."

"A chance for what?"

"To be someone different. And that's why—that's why I've been the one who's chased after you."

"You really have, haven't you?" I say.

"That's not me. At all. But I just thought—I didn't want to wake up the same Kelsey as I had been every other day in my life."

"I like that Kelsey."

"I always thought—if someone took the time—if someone just actually took the time and I wasn't so stinking quiet and shy—that they could like this person, this—me."

"I'm glad nobody else knows. That makes it even more special."

"Does it?" Kelsey asks.

I nod. "You're special. And you're not like the others. That's a good thing."

"You're not like the others either," Kelsey says. "That's why you're going to be okay. Why things are going to work out just fine. I know they will."

I breathe a little lighter sitting next to her.

I worry a little less.

The hurt inside seems to go away. Just for a short while.

I move and kiss her and try to bury everything even further.

Maybe with enough time and enough kisses, the hurt will go away for good.

109. RABBIT HOLE

Maybe this is what my story is all about. A guy being the hero. A guy finding his fate. A kid suddenly growing up and finding out something about life.

Something awful.

I want to run away, but I'm forced to be here.

Inside this hole.

I don't want to go there.

I don't want to go underground.

I don't want to see the black or the grays or the haze or the blurry mess.

I can feel my heart beating and waiting and wondering.

Wondering what will happen and who will make it out alive and who will die. I know death is inevitable, and I can feel its breath against the back of my neck like some horror movie. Like the horror movie that's been playing out for the past twenty months.

Twenty months of this nonsense.

Twenty months of insanity.

I will finally figure it out, won't I? To see if the girl stays with me or ends up as another sacrifice. To see if my family stays intact or splinters into ashes.

I'm tired.

I still want answers.

I just wonder if the world will listen and if it will even care what's happening in this sweet little tranquil town called Solitary. Where the blood flows and the water pours and the endless madness never ever stops.

I want to run away, but I can't.

I have to stay here and fight.

There's the hole I need to go down.

Right now.

Right this instant.

This boy is about to turn into a man, and this might be the first and last glimpse of what he finally could and should be.

110. SOMETHING I SHOULD'VE DONE

It's the middle of the day on Friday when I receive a text from Kelsey.

TAKING OFF. WILL CALL OR TEXT LATER TONIGHT IF I CAN.

This makes me feel a little less worried. Now, if only Mom makes it home on her last day of work. Then I'll scratch that off the good old "To Do and To Keep Alive" list.

This little bout of ease remains short-lived, however, because someone comes barging in the door, causing me to jump up off the couch.

It's Uncle Robert. A messy and hungover Uncle Robert.

"Where's your mom?"

"She's at work," I say.

He just looks around for a moment. He's breathing heavily like he's been running, and I see his hands moving, balling into fists as if he's squeezing something.

"When's she getting back?"

"Tonight. She said maybe nine."

Uncle Robert curses, looking around as if someone else might be in here, then he takes a note out of his back pocket and unfolds it. He tosses it on the coffee table.

"Make sure she gets that, okay?"

I nod as he bolts up the stairs and heads to my room. In a few minutes, he comes back down carrying a handgun. It's a short, stubby black gun that I think is a Glock. I've seen enough of those on television to recognize it.

"Did you get that upstairs?" I ask.

I remember the gun I found but ultimately lost.

That gun could've come in handy.

"I had a hiding spot in the bedroom. No way you could have found it."

"Was it in the closet?"

He only shakes his head. He stuffs the gun in the back of his pants. For a minute, he just scans the place.

"What's going on?"

Uncle Robert sees the key belonging to the bike parked outside. His old motorcycle. He picks it up.

"Wanna know why I got that bike?" he asks, holding the keychain. "Ever see the movie *The Great Escape*?"

I shake my head.

"See it one day. It's a classic. About a bunch of prisoners in World

War II trying to escape a Nazi camp. It's got Steve McQueen in it. The role was legendary."

I suddenly remember Brick wanting to buy the bike from me and mentioning Steve McQueen.

"I got that bike when everything—when I was busy being a hero. I was trying to be like the Cooler King."

"The what?"

He chuckles, lost in his thoughts. "Captain Virgil Hilts. Nicknamed the Cooler King. That's the role Steve McQueen played. I wanted to be cool and reckless like him. Brave and fearless and always with a funny quip. And for a while I was. But now I know that all of that—the stuff of trying to save Heidi—it was all just one big role. I was just acting the part. Because in the end I wasn't Hilts. I was just Robert Kinner. A man doomed because of his last name. A man who wants to escape everything in his life."

I want to do something for this man who's twice as old but even more terrified than I am. "Do you want me to—"

"No," he says. "I'm fine. Everything is just—just right where it belongs."

He laughs as if he just made a joke, and I shake my head, not understanding.

"What if all the world you used to know is an elaborate dream? Good question, huh? That's the only Bible I've been reading. The only verses that make sense to me. The King Reznor Bible. Full of hopelessness and despair."

Uncle Robert tosses the key on the table next to the note. Then he looks at me with a serious, heavy glance. "You're a good kid, Chris. Don't let that part of you go away. Protect it. Okay?"

He goes to the door and opens it.

"Uncle Robert?"

"Yeah."

"Where are you going?"

He looks at me, smiles and nods, then shuts the door behind him.

It takes me about ten minutes to decide to open the letter.

Maybe it should've taken less time. Or maybe I shouldn't be opening it at all. But I'm worried that Uncle Robert is going to do something stupid. Or that he's truly running away once and for all.

I open up the letter and see his messy handwriting. It's actually worse than mine.

DEAR TARA,

I'M SORRY FOR NOT BEING THERE. WHEN WE WERE YOUNGER AND NOW. IT'S MESSED WITH ME MORE THAN YOU CAN POSSIBLY KNOW.

I'M SORRY I DIDN'T DO MORE.

BUT I'M FINALLY GOING TO DO SOMETHING I SHOULD'VE DONE A LONG TIME AGO.

ROBERT

He's finally going to do something. But what?

I think of his gun and his comments about escaping. About playing the part. About trying to rescue Heidi.

Suddenly I realize that's what he's going to do.

He's going to try and save Heidi.

No.

I swipe the key to the motorcycle in my hand and then tear open the door to get out.

Maybe I can still help.

Maybe I can make sure Uncle Robert doesn't do something really stupid.

III. FIXED

I'm heading to the only place that Uncle Robert could have gone. Wondering why he didn't go there a week or a month or a year ago.

I wonder why he no longer drives the motorcycle he got in order to escape. Or why he left his cabin with all his music and T-shirts behind.

He wanted to escape, but the wind whipping around makes me think that maybe it's not Solitary he's wanting to escape.

Maybe it's the guy he used to be.

A hundred songs that I never would have discovered play in my head as I wonder if the track list for Uncle Robert has changed. What happened, and why?

A girl.

Maybe.

I turn a corner.

Maybe it's because of her.

I turn another corner.

Maybe it's because of Heidi.

Maybe it's because he turned a corner one day somewhere and came across someone who changed his life.

I can understand.

And now he's trying to finally deal with the situation in his own way.

Like you did, right?

Like I tried.

I head down the street to Pastor Marsh's, thinking of Jocelyn.

Waiting too long.

I race down, thinking of Lily.

Not knowing enough.

I hold my breath as I approach and see the silver Nissan Xterra and know I'm right, and I can't help thinking of Kelsey.

Holding on to hope that she's far away.

My head is spinning and I'm feeling heavy and I don't want to go in there. 'Cause the thing is that I've arrived in time and I know enough and I still carry hope in my back pocket.

But will it matter?

Uncle Robert, what are you going to do?

If he kills Marsh, will I be punished in some awful way?

I open the door and hear shouting and cursing.

Uncle Robert is saying stuff that doesn't quite fit or make sense.

He's using a name I've never heard. Not Marsh, but something else. I don't get it.

Jerry Turner? Who is Jerry Turner?

Then I see them: Uncle Robert with his gun aimed at Marsh. The pastor looks composed and silent standing there by the table.

"Hello, Chris," he says with a grin.

Robert turns around and doesn't seem to believe that I'm standing there.

"Stay out of this," he tells me.

"Don't," I tell him.

"Don't what? Aim a gun at this monster? I know what you've done." He hurls more curses at Marsh.

Marsh moves a little closer, and Robert tells him to stop. Bringing his hands up, Marsh seems to find all of this … amusing.

Yet even as he smiles, I see his eyes seem to have grown dimmer. Thinner.

Why am I nervous, when Uncle Robert is the one holding the gun?

"You disappoint me," Marsh says.

"You're a sick freak, that's what you are."

"The Bible says marriage should be honored by all, and the marriage bed kept pure, for God will judge the adulterer and all the sexually immoral."

"Shut up." Uncle Robert's hand shakes as he holds the gun.

"I have given her time to repent of her immorality, but she is unwilling. So I will cast her on a bed of suffering, and I will make those who commit adultery with her suffer intensely, unless they repent of their ways."

"Told you to shut your mouth."

"What?" Marsh asks. "Don't want little nephew to hear about the uncle's indiscretions?"

"Where is she?"

"Secrets and lies. That's the only thing that goes on in this town. *Secrets. And lies.*"

The way he says those last few words makes my skin crawl.

"Heidi!"

"She's somewhere meeting you," Marsh says. "She doesn't know that her supposed one true love—this loser stuck in the past, stuck in the memory of his long-lost parents—she doesn't know that the man she thinks she should be with is really a dead man."

"Where is she?" Uncle Robert moves closer, pointing the gun at Marsh's head.

"Meeting you to run away. That's what your note said, right? Only, well, she thinks you're meeting her by the old barn. But no. Not today. She'll come back home and find out what happened to you, and then once I pick her up off the ground I'll have my way with her like I always have."

Marsh laughs, and I hear a click. Then another click and another and another.

The gun is a toy gun.

No. Not a toy gun. There are just no bullets.

Or something's not right.

Marsh keeps laughing.

"What'd you do?" Robert says.

"I fixed it. Just like I fix things. Like my parents. Like your silly stupid cabin. And like that silly stupid wife you're in love with."

Uncle Robert starts to rush at the pastor, but Marsh moves like a snake over to a drawer and opens it. Now the pastor is holding a gun too

no not again not now

and he's smiling and forcing Uncle Robert to back up.

"Do you remember when you first met Heidi?" Marsh asks. "When you wanted her more than anything in this life? Or the next?"

Uncle Robert curses and glares at Pastor Marsh. I can tell he's unafraid.

"So tell me, *Robert*. Tell me something. Tell me before I wipe the floor with the messy bloody body that is yours. Will you stand by her now? Will you walk through the fire?"

Marsh grits his teeth and looks like some deranged animal. The gun goes off once and twice and again.

I close my eyes and scream. Because I know I'm next.

I'm still screaming when my eyes open.

I'm holding my hands over my head, and I'm kneeling on the floor only feet away from Uncle Robert.

Marsh looks at me.

Uncle Robert is dead.

I'm trying not to look at him, but I can't help it. I'm crying and screaming, and Marsh comes over to me and sticks the gun to my temple.

"You ignorant little mouse. What are you trying to do? Huh?"

He rams the hot barrel into my forehead.

"All of you Kinners are the same. Stupid. Just dumb. Dumb dumb. And I'd get rid of you all, every one, if I didn't know better. But I do know better, Chris. I know well."

He shoves me back and then tells me to get up.

"You're going to go back home, and you're going to do nothing. You're going to say nothing. You're just going to wait until the clock strikes the right time, and you'll show up to your great-grandfather's ceremony, where you'll renounce God and be given the gift. The magic, the key—whatever it might be. You're going to play the part, you got that?"

Marsh wipes away spit from his lips.

"I'll tell you why you should get it. Because of sweet and darling little sunflower. Your little friend. Nobody is going to know that she didn't arrive in Columbia this weekend. Until, of course, it's too late. Until, of course, you make sure that she's fine. Right?"

"What'd you do ..." is all I can come up with.

I feel like someone trying to talk at the end of a marathon.

"You do what I tell you to do and you'll be fine. Do you understand? I killed your fool of an uncle just because I felt like it, and your little Kelsey can be next."

I wipe my eyes and cheeks. I'm terrified.

"Go on, little boy. Look at you. So young and so scared. After all this ... you're still just a little boy. It's pathetic."

I start to say something but a haunting, raging "Go!" sends me on my way.

I get on my bike and take off down the road as tears stream sideways off my face.

That's when I see the Mercedes SUV drive past with the movie star hidden behind shades at the wheel.

I know one more thing.

I won't be the only one here bleeding with tears.

112. COME ALIVE

One more time.

I click on the track again and listen to it for the fourth time.

Each time I feel the rage burning inside of me.

I'm listening to my iPod while lying in bed, and I have a vague memory of listening to this Foo Fighters song while exploring in the woods. Back when I was naive. Back when I didn't worry about things like what I did or didn't believe in. Back when I walked without scars and without baggage.

But now it's all different.

Now I feel the soft fur of Midnight next to me, a sweet reminder of a girl long gone.

This song says everything I feel right now.

I want to believe in it, but I'm not sure.

I really want to believe, Lord, but I'm not sure.

Did You really die, and did You really rise?

That sweet little story is as precious as this dog, but is it really true? It sounds nice and heroic and utterly unbelievable, but I want to believe it's true. I do, but I have doubts because I'm here in this rotten and rotting world.

Come alive.

I want to see Your face.

Come alive.

I want to feel You here next to me.

Come alive.

I need You to be next to me.

I don't know what to do and I feel alone and I have nothing and nobody to turn to and these prayers these prayers just keep going up like bubbles blown and popped for nothing.

Did You really save me on that train in Chicago? And if You did, then why and what for?

I want to see You.

I want to know You're there.

I need to know that all of this is for a reason.

Please, God, tell me.

Show me.

I'm not an Abraham and I'm not a Moses and I'm not a David but I'm a somebody and I need You, God.

Please help me.

Please open my eyes.

I don't want to keep doubting.

But I don't know, because all I feel is utter and overwhelming anger.

Anger.

Anger at everything, including You.

113. ALONE

Kelsey doesn't return my voice mails or my texts, and I know I should have left her alone. Now I find myself waiting and wondering.

I have this odd déjà vu from right after Jocelyn died. Going through the motions in front of Mom. I don't want to lie to her, but I can't tell her the truth. I can't say anything to anybody else. I wonder if they know about Brick and Newt and the note to Mr. Meiners.

Saturday hovers like a piñata above me. I want to strike it down and get rid of it, but I'm blindfolded and can't do a thing. Blindfolded and muzzled.

I want to grieve over Uncle Robert's death, but I'm too numb. Maybe all of this has been a lost cause. There's no point in trying to fight. Right?

I curse at myself and say that I have to fight.

I have to fight for Kelsey. I have to fight for all of these people who have been infected with this sickness and darkness for so long. Some are already gone, but there are good people here. I know that.

Like Newt, who originally stuck his nose into things only to have his body become scarred for trying to be a hero.

Like the group that meets on Sundays at hidden locations, not to plan and scheme but to worship.

Like the families who are still trying to do what they should. Poe's family. Kelsey's family. Oli's family.

Like people like Mounds and Iris and Harris.

There are still decent people around this place. Somehow, in some way, I have to not only fight for Kelsey and my family and myself, but I have to fight for these people.

Otherwise the evil will spread.

The darkness underneath the bridge will continue to feed into the night.

The monster in the tunnels below will continue to strike during the day.

The savages in robes will continue their strange and sick rituals.

The demons inside Staunch and Marsh and Kinner will continue to plague this town.

Do I believe in these demons? Yes. I don't understand them, but I know they're there. One or a dozen. I don't know. But they're there.

An imprisoned Saturday turns over to Sunday. I go to sleep and have nightmares, unspeakable ones where I find myself strangling my mother and then running away with blood on my hands. I can't tell if this is a sign of things to come or just my messed-up imagination.

All I know is that Sunday comes, and I have one last day to do nothing.

Of course, I've never been able to listen to those telling me what to do.

And I've never been able to simply do nothing.

114. PROMISE (1)

You don't need to sit in a pew to pray.

And you don't need a preacher to show you how to worship.

You don't need a designated time and specific songs and a request for cash to feel like you're in a church.

You kneel on the edge of a mountaintop looking out at the rolling valley below. You can see the clear blue sky between the tops of the trees. You can hear the wildlife around here. You can feel the soft breath of air.

You feel right praying.

Asking God to help.

Asking for strength.

Asking for things you don't even know you need.

Your heart feels like a heavy, rusted-out muffler that's barely hanging on. Yet your eyes can see what's around you. This beautiful place that God created. These hills and forests and animals.

God made all of this.

And even after it all went to hell, God never abandoned all of this. He made a promise. One to Noah after destroying the world and saving his family with a big boat. You know that the Bible is full of promises.

About never abandoning you as a father might. About never letting you down as a mother might. About never failing you as a friend might. About always loving you.

You look up in the sky and ask for help. For more help a little longer. So you can get through today and tomorrow and then leave.

You don't need answers. You just want the hope that God promises.

It sounds easy, but the way you're feeling, you know it's not.

Maybe one day you'll be like Iris. But today you're just Chris. You have a long way to go. And you still don't really know how to get there.

115. PROMISE (2)

Much later, after the sun sets and the night settles in, you find this in the stack of postcards from your dad. Even though he's far away, these postcards make him seem like he's just around the corner.

"FOR I KNOW THE PLANS I HAVE FOR YOU," SAYS THE LORD. "THEY ARE PLANS FOR GOOD AND NOT FOR DISASTER, TO GIVE YOU A FUTURE AND A HOPE."

116. THE THINNER THE AIR

Is it possible to have a dream without sleeping? To be lost in a night-mare without actually ever slipping into slumberland?

I'm not sure, but it seems I've stepped over into that other place, the place of visions and horror shows. It's suddenly very, very cold. And pitch black. Not the darkness in my room, where I can still see my alarm clock glowing in the corner. No, I can't see a thing.

But I can feel something. Something out there in the black. Something watching me.

The night is nearly over.

The voice, speaking as clearly as if she was right in front of me, belongs to Iris. I try to call out, but I can't.

The day is almost here.

I start running toward the voice, but it sounds all around me. I see a spot of light that seems a million miles away, slowly but surely growing larger.

Do you fear the Lord?

Again I try to call out to her, but I can't. The light in front of me is growing, and I keep heading for it.

Do you obey His words?

I nod and say yes, but I'm silent. Silent and running.

Let those who walk in the dark, who have no light, trust in the name of the Lord and rely on their God.

The light is growing so bright that it burns. Suddenly I have to stop because I can't breathe. The air is getting thinner as if I'm somewhere high up on a mountain.

Let your light shine before others, that they may see your good deeds.

The light is suddenly slipping away, and I can't breathe.

I try to scream out to Iris to help, regardless of where I am, in a dream or a vision or my imagination.

See to it that the light within you is not darkness.

117. NEW SURROUNDINGS

The gray cotton-ball-filled sky seems to get darker earlier than normal. I haven't done anything today except worry and pray and try calling or texting Kelsey. By the time I get on my bike and slip the backpack over my shoulder, I pretty much realize what's about to happen.

I'm either going to save the girl and be a hero or I'm going to die alongside her.

Riding down these narrow, winding roads, I'd love to say that I'm filled with peace. But I'm not. Maybe I'm doing something wrong with this faith and these prayers. I don't know. I just know that I'm half adrenaline and another half petrified terror.

The first sign of anything—life, impending death, doom and gloom—is the figure I see at the place where the Heartland Trail used to end. By the time I get here, the sun behind the clouds is almost gone. Yet I can see there's a man standing by the area in the woods that's been cleared for the road.

He's holding a torch.

Thankfully he's not wearing a robe.

I slow down as I approach. I'm far enough away in case I need to bolt.

Then I see his face.

It's Jared. Or the person who called himself Jared.

He doesn't react to seeing me. Instead, he just motions for me to keep going.

Like he's a guard on duty. Or a gatekeeper, only allowing certain people access.

I don't say anything. I simply keep going.

It only takes a few minutes to reach the church. It looks just like I remember it from when I came here with Poe. Two stories, a combination of wood and stone, a steeple at its top.

But all the old run-down buildings are gone. The weeds and overgrowth are all gone too. The road I'm on connects with the road I remember seeing heading the opposite direction. It's paved in both sections, with only the church connecting it. Dozens of small trees and bushes have been planted alongside the road. But there's no reminder of the burnt-down town.

I see a few cars in the parking lot. I'm not exactly sure how any of this should go. Do I wear the creepy robe into the church? Should I be wearing it now?

This is all completely crazy.

I'd laugh like this was a *Saturday Night Live* skit except there's nothing funny about it. Especially the part about being in the middle of nowhere and not knowing where Kelsey is.

When I get off my bike, I feel I'm being watched. Not like that's anything new, but I feel it especially now in the muted light. There's no welcoming light on the outside of the church. No lights on inside either.

Other than the three cars parked outside, there's no sign that anybody is around.

I slowly walk to the front of the church and then try the door handle. It's unlocked.

For a second I hesitate.

Then I push forward the door. The inside is pitch black. I have a flashlight in my backpack that I'll need to get out in just a second if—

Something clamps onto my face.

A hand presses against my mouth and nose, and I suddenly know what's happening by that familiar awful smell even as I try to scream and jerk them off me.

It's no use.

I breathe in and cough and then—

118. FACING THE GRAVE

Rumbling. Around me. Inside my head. Outside my head. Something like the bass at a concert, or no … an organ.

An organ is playing.

And drums.

Really?

Maybe not an organ, but it's something that sounds like a bunch of chords playing. Not a song, but more like a droning.

Something nudges at my side, but I can't stand up because something else is pressing against me. I'm either strapped in to something or weighed down.

"Stand."

I feel pulled up at each side. I wobble, but I'm propped up by people holding me.

My eyes open, and the shaking light is distorted. Slivers. Streaks.

I've got a hood over me.

"Move."

The voice is barely audible because of the organ or synth-gone-to-hell sound. But I take a step forward and almost fall. Then I'm held up again.

"Move."

I look down and just see black. My robe has been put over me. I can feel my warm breath against the sheet covering my mouth. The eyeholes are round and clean, allowing me to see out.

Something shuffles to my side. I try to turn but can't. I'm still wobbly.

"Put your hand on the shoulder of the person in front of you and walk slowly forward."

There are lit candles circling me. Or I should say circling us. Because there's another circle of dark-robed freaks, which I'm now a part of.

Superman can't come out because they stuffed his face with Kryptonite.

I can barely stand, barely take in my surroundings.

Help me, God.

The wailing organ keeps going.

I'm part of a circle surrounding that gravestone—which is in the shape of an upside-down cross. I know Kelsey is here, but from where I'm standing I can't see her.

A figure in white moves to the base of the gravestone.

Then my vision starts to go blurry as I see him pick up something that looks like—yeah, it's definitely dead, whatever it is. Some kind of animal. He puts it on a hook and then pulls on a chain hanging from the roof.

That's so not a sheep, no it can't be.

I hear someone—no, I know for sure it's Marsh—talking. He's talking, but I can't understand what he's saying.

It's Pig Latin and that's a pig he's pulling up and soon all of us will be frying bacon.

My mind is a mess. I can barely stand, I can barely see. My mind is going in and out, and I'm fighting for every breath.

Come on, Chris, come on.

The words keep coming, and I finally realize that he's speaking French.

I don't know why except for the fact that Solitaire was French.

Guess that French class would've come in handy right about now.

Soon the words morph into English, like a confusing movie ending its subtitles for no reason. It's definitely Marsh talking. Maybe he's speaking to me.

"The severed dark of the heart will answer the call," he says. "The blood of the sacrifice will bleed over the Chosen One. The angel's servant will be summoned, and the casting will begin."

After he stops talking, the music seems to get louder again. The others are chanting, and I feel it. I feel something heavy and real and …

I know this feeling.

It's like the time when I felt the cold dread coming out of the mouth of the tunnel underground. Or the moment I was in Staunch's cabin, that time when I felt something brushing against me. Or that time I was under the bridge. I could feel this same awful pressure against my whole body, especially against my heart and soul.

I try to remember the Scripture from my dream where Iris spoke. My mind is twirling, but I remember bits and pieces and I try to replay them over and over.

Marsh is chanting, and the group answers. We're walking now. I don't feel awkward or stupid; I just feel numb.

Lord help me protect me.

I don't know how long this lasts, but it seems a while. Eventually the music stops—thankfully—and the group stops moving, which I'm even more thankful for. My head is spinning.

I see a figure in white walking toward me.

"The blood is spared for one, and he who is blemished will be given the power to heal the blemished."

He's trying to talk like the Bible ... or The Godfather.

He stands before me. "Figure of night, escape the shadows, and take off your blinds."

A hand extends, and I see the white robe beckoning me. He raises his hands as if he wants me to take off my hood.

I pull it off and finally manage to breathe a little better. But the air is also full of the same cold despair that I feel in my heart. I hear a few voices and murmurs and even a high-pitched gasp of surprise when I take off my hood.

There are maybe twenty or twenty-five people in black robes. No—strike that, they're blood-red robes. All facing me.

I want to take off each hood and demand to know why they're here and if they know exactly what they're doing.

"Bow, my son," Marsh says as he puts a hand on my head.

I get on my knees, still wobbly and still worried that I won't be able to recover from being knocked out. I kneel and then see a bloody hand reach over and wipe my cheek. Both cheeks. Then my forehead.

Something tells me the blood he's wiping on me isn't fake.

I shake my head and blink to get a better look at everything. Slowly but surely my mind is waking up.

I wonder if they're here.

I think of Newt and Brick. I wonder if they were able to do what I wanted them to do or if they're like Kelsey—missing after being contacted.

Marsh opens up his hands and starts praying, and the words are awful. No, awful isn't the right word. They're vile. They're sick. I try to not hear them.

I scan the room for Kelsey, but I still see no sign of her. Nor can I see any sign of Kinner.

I thought he was going to give me a key or something. Is that like passing a baton?

After the prayer, the robed figures move to the pews facing the grave. Marsh tells me to stay so I do as I'm told. I'm dizzy and tired, and probably the fear factor in my veins is bubbling over.

"The blood has proven that this is the chosen one," Marsh says.

We've been walking under the bleeding animal. I guess it rained blood on top of me.

Maybe that can be a song you write one day when you're singing along with all of Uncle Robert's greatest hits.

"Come to the throne, Chris. Cast your doubts aside and surrender. The night opens its mouth, and the enemy knows. The enemy is far from here."

Then I look up and see him.

Kinner.

Great-grandfather Walter Kinner standing there in the kind of suit a man might wear while lying on his back in a coffin.

He looks at me and smiles.

119. The Pretty Picture
in Front of You

The shaking motion of light moves around me like a shivering animal. I'm still on my knees by the time the old man steps in front of me. He doesn't look well. I'm surprised that he can still walk and stand.

It's suddenly gotten very quiet. Creepy quiet.

"Where is that brave young man I've heard so many things about?" Kinner speaks in a hoarse Southern drawl. "The boy so desperate to be a hero?"

I look around. Figures in red robes. Seated. Watching. Like inhuman, unsympathetic monsters.

"Tell me, Chrisss. Tell me the truth."

I look at him, then at Marsh, who stands at his side. Marsh has a delirious look on his face and in his eyes.

"What—" I begin to say.

"Tell me what is in your heart. Do you believe in God, or do you reject Him? Confess before this group. Confess before me."

I shake my head, my heart beating, not quite knowing what to do. *Can't I just lie?*

I don't say anything. Marsh curses, then walks up to me and pulls back my hair. I feel his mouth against my ear.

"This is the moment, right here and now, Chris. They're just words. That's all. It's just part of the ceremony."

Kinner's eyes say otherwise. He's staring like a frustrated father. Waiting. Watching and waiting.

"Go ahead," Marsh says.

"I can't."

"You can't? Or you won't?" Kinner asks.

Marsh slaps me in the face, and I jerk back, tasting blood in my mouth.

"You do it now. Right here and now, Chris."

"Please," Kinner says as he brushes Marsh aside. "I'd rather spare the violence for someone else. Chris doesn't deserve hostility, do you? No. Please—will someone please find our guest for tonight?"

It takes a moment for one of the figures in red to disappear and then come back in with another figure in white. A big man guiding a cowering girl at his side.

I knew this moment was coming. It was just a question of when.

Suddenly I want to throw up.

Kelsey's hands are bound, and her mouth is taped over. Her eyes look swollen and tired. Her hair is messy. She looks at me and tries to scream under the tape, but the figure in white cups her mouth and nose and curses at her to be quiet.

I stand, but Marsh forces me back to the ground.

When I look up, I see Kinner.

He looks amused. The ancient lines on his face seem to get darker and deeper in this crazy mad light.

"Remember when this was all just some silly story that a little girl told you?" Kinner says. "It couldn't be real. It couldn't really happen. Until—yessss."

"Let her go." I stare at the figure standing next to Kelsey. "You don't need to hide behind a mask. I know who you are, Staunch."

"Shut up, boy."

Again I try to get up, and this time Staunch reaches out and punches me in the gut. I go to the ground, curl up, and begin coughing.

"Chris. It's very simple. Do you or do you not believe in God the Father, the so-called Maker of this universe?"

A hundred thoughts fill me. I hear distant songs and remember random Bible verses. I hear Newt telling me secrets and Mounds telling me stories.

"No," my mouth says without even thinking. "I don't. Okay?"

I can't think of what else to do. I'm lying and that's wrong and so is saying I don't believe in God, but I'm not going to let her die. I can't let her die.

Kinner's eyes grow larger. Kelsey is still squealing through her tape. Marsh looks like he's about ready to open the most amazing Christmas present ever seen.

"Are you a true believer, or do you reject the notion that Jesus came to die for you on a cross?"

I want to lie again, but I feel something deep down that says I can't.

I'm shaking.

I think of Peter, the disciple who denied Jesus three times.

Three times.

"Answer the man," Marsh says.

I look at Kinner and Marsh and then Kelsey, and once again I deny that I believe anything. This gets a low chuckle from the man.

"Your eyes and your heart give you away, Chrisss. I know what's in your heart. You're lying, aren't you? You thought you actually found hope in Christ, didn't you? The amazing grace that everybody sings about. You thought you found it, didn't you, Chrisss? Didn't you?"

"I don't know what you're talking about. No! Leave Kelsey alone. Take me. Do whatever you want to me."

For a moment there's just complete and utter silence. Even Kelsey is quiet. Then a sickening, throaty laugh begins and gets louder and louder. I'm not sure if Kinner is doing this for effect or if he's really, truly amused.

"The hero," he says softly. "There he is. I see it in your eyes. Put a pretty picture in front of you and look what happens. Just like they said. You will learn, Chrisss. You will learn."

"Leave her be. Just—just give me the key and be done with it."

Kinner laughs again. I'm feeling both hot flashes and cold sweats. I feel like I'm falling, and at the same time I feel like I'm cemented on this platform.

"Do you know what the words on that plaque mean? Below our great ancestor's name? Do you, Chrisss?"

"No."

"The literal translation is 'when you talk about the wolf, you see its tail.' Or as we say, 'speak of the Devil.' Except here, when we speak of the Devil, he appears. Just like it says. That's what this sanctuary is built for, Chris. To see the face of the Great Destroyer. To see the face of darkness burn through the night."

I look at Kelsey and see tears streaming down her face.

I'm so sorry, Kelsey. I'm sorry for ever talking to you after that art class.

"You will see the face of the Devil tonight, Chris. You just need to do one more thing. You see, the key you talk about—it's not a literal key. It is not something that I can give you."

Marsh looks at him as if he's confused.

At least I'm not the only one.

"*You* are the key," Kinner says. "That is our power. We unlock the gates and control who goes in and out. When my last breath is taken, this power will go into you."

"Let her go."

"Shut up," Marsh says. "Is it time, sir?"

Kinner nods. Marsh goes over and babbles some instructions to the group behind us.

"All you have to do is one more thing, Chrisss."

Kinner nods, and the figure in white, who I know is Staunch, retrieves something from the back of the room. It's a long sword.

Come on.

It's handed to me. Not to Marsh or Kinner.

Maybe I can kill them all and get Kelsey out of here.

The sword is lighter than I thought it would be, but it's still real. I hold it in one hand, not sure what I'm supposed to do with it.

"Take it and kill me, Chris. My time is now. Stab me in the heart, and you will succeed me. You will see the things I've seen. You will learn to take whatever you want whenever you want it. Chris, thrust the sword right here, in my chest."

Kelsey tries to scream. I'm holding the sword only inches away from this man. I turn and see the figures behind me holding cups of some sort. As if this is some weird kind of communion.

"No."

"Do it. Take the hate I see all over you and dip it into my flesh. Tear it open, son. Do it and do it now."

"No," I say again.

"I watched that pretty little girl you were running for in the woods die. Do you know that? I tasted her blood."

"Shut up."

"And this one—what are you going to do about her, Chrisss? Tell me. Do you want her to bleed and die too?"

"Stay away from her."

"One act," the old man softly says. "One act of pure hatred. You did it once so easily. You killed without hesitation. Except this will do the job and end it right here and now. Then the Devil will be summoned, and you will see and you will feel it, Chrisss."

I want to shut my eyes and my ears. There is a ringing that seems to be going off all around me.

I shake my head and look around and hear Kelsey's muffled cries, and then I look at Kinner and force myself to say it one more time.

"No."

I drop the sword.

I'm no hero, and I never will be. My faith is weak, if it's even there in the first place.

For a second it's deathly silent again. But then all hell breaks loose. And I do truly mean hell swooping in and emptying out in this room.

Kinner is in front of me, standing at the base of the upside-down cross that's the tomb of the sick freak who started all this craziness. I'm standing in front of him. Staunch in the white robe and hood is to my right with Kelsey by his side.

The twenty-some people in robes and hoods are behind us. So is Marsh.

I hear a scream. At first I think it's Marsh going crazy, but no.

One of the figures in red is coming toward us. I have an idea who it is, but it can't be. The figure is too fast to be who I think it is.

But the howling. It's worse than the wolves outside my house that night. It's terrifying. It's a high-pitched wailing and it gets right in my ear as the figure swoops in and picks up the sword.

With two bony, shaking hands, the figure picks up the sword plunges it into Kinner's heart, just as he asked. But I'm not the one doing it.

"No!"

That's Marsh's voice behind me. He's screaming and hurling curses, but meanwhile the figure in red stabs Kinner again. And again. And when Kinner crumples to the floor, the surprise on his face growing, the figure keeps howling and stabbing.

I don't do a thing. I don't know what to do.

After maybe six plunges of the sword, the figure stops and takes off the hood.

"That's for the two lives you took, you monster," Aunt Alice shouts in an awful, raging voice. "Mine and my son's."

Marsh is pulling her away, but it's too late.

Kinner is dead. He's not groaning as if he's about to die. No—he's dead. His eyes are huge and mouth open, and it looks like he's staring into the face of death, knowing he got this one all wrong.

Marsh wrestles Aunt Alice for a moment and then slams her to the ground.

I stand for a second, unable to move.

Staunch puts an arm around Kelsey, who's suddenly jerking and fighting to get away.

The figures in red behind us are starting to disperse and sprinting to the door. Marsh runs to stop them, shouting.

I look for the sword and see that it's underneath Aunt Alice.

I'm about to go to Kelsey, but just then a big ball of flame ignites in the front of the church right around the doors.

The closed doors.

There are screams as the fire spreads, and we're surrounded by flames.

120. AGAIN

Kelsey.

I rush to her and kneel at her side, trying to prop up her head, but then something hits me. No, make that kicks me.

I slam to the floor.

Marsh stands there, without his robe, an insane look on his face. He curses at me, and then he kicks me again. It feels as if one of my ribs has cracked.

He's breathing in and out like he just ran a marathon. Behind him I can see the flames spreading on the walls.

This is no accident. This was planned.

"You ruined everything, you—" he says, and proceeds to tell me exactly what he thinks I am.

Kelsey is on the ground next to me, shaking and trying to undo the black tape around her wrists. People are screaming, and it's getting harder to breathe.

Marsh yanks Kelsey up by her hair and holds a blade, short like a hunting knife, to the side of her face.

I'm about to lunge at him, but he juts the blade toward me. "Don't. Don't move, or I'll kill her."

I get on my knees, still coughing, and see the fire really burning now. There had to be gas in this sanctuary for it to be spreading this fast. Aunt Alice has crawled in a daze toward the side of the platform, away from Kinner. She doesn't seem a bit fazed by the fire.

Marsh drags a squealing Kelsey over to Kinner and then examines the old man. He looks at me and curses again. "You stupid boy. What were you thinking?"

"Let her go!"

"What? What!" He clenches his teeth and jerks Kelsey back with his left arm. His right hand is shaking, holding the knife. "I've waited for my chance, and I didn't get it. I waited to see if I was chosen, and I wasn't. I waited and waited, and then you come along, and now this."

The pastor suddenly sounds like a bratty kid. A bratty, messed-up kid. He curses again and looks at Kinner.

Some woman comes up to him, screaming, and I see that it's Principal Harking. I'm not surprised.

"Get out of my face," Marsh screams at her as he bats her away.

People are going crazy. I hear the sound of glass breaking. More screams. The ripple of fire.

I see another familiar face, then recognize it as the weird mannequin maker. Of course Alfred Graff is here. Unfortunately, these are all real people who are about to be burned alive.

"It was going to be just you and me," Marsh says, facing me. I'm on my knees, trying to get closer so I can grab the knife. "All these fools—I was going to get rid of them. The world is going to burn, and you're going to burn with it, because you're of no use anymore. You stupid, silly little boy."

"Please—let her go."

Marsh looks at me, and suddenly there is no expression on his face. It's like any kind of emotion—hate or love or fear or anger—went away. It's just blank.

Then he slits Kelsey's throat.

She falls back, and he grabs her wrist and yanks her up with it. He cuts her there, too.

I tackle him, and we both fall backward. I can't get back on my feet. Marsh ends up over me and is about to lunge at me with the knife when he jerks in surprise at the sound of gunshots.

There are four shots, one that chips the upside-down cross behind us. Marsh ducks and runs to the back of the church.

It takes me a moment to pull the tape from Kelsey's mouth and undo her hands. I have blood all over my hands and arms as I hold her and tell her she's going to be okay. She's crying and she's probably in shock and I know that she's dying.

no no no NO!

This is what happens when you reject your faith. This is what happens when you abandon the God who's supposed to save you.

The fire is burning, and I don't hear the voice calling my name at first. Then I feel something tugging at the back of my neck. I whip around, ready to strike out, when I see the buzzed head belonging to Brick. He pulls me up and says, "I'll get her, come on."

I look around at the chaos. People are trying to climb out a broken window that has flames blazing around it. Another figure is running in a robe that's in flames. A group is banging at the front door.

Another tug gets my attention. "Not that way."

I follow Brick to the back of the church.

I cough, and my eyes are watery from both the smoke and the tears. I follow him through a dark hallway, touching his shoulder and feeling the strap of his shotgun. He's carrying Kelsey in his arms. He kicks a door open and leads us outside to the fresh air.

"Come on," he tells me.

I follow him to the edge of the woods. I can hear the crackling of wood behind us.

"That building's going up like a meth lab," Brick says.

I lean over and see Kelsey. I breathe out and for a moment I don't know what to do.

"Chris, come on," he says. "We gotta get her to the hospital."

I'm frozen, and I stare at Kelsey and know that it can't end like this.

It can't.

God wouldn't do that, would He?

Would He do this to me again?

A terrible thought fills me.

If I rejected God, He has every right to reject me.

TRAVIS THRASHER

121. THE END

Reach out and touch faith, Chris.

I watch fingers of fire waving at me through the cool black night. For the moment, I'm not really here. I'm somewhere far away from this burning structure. From this cursed town. From this wretched life.

You know what you have to do.

But I can't move and I can't breathe and I can't think. I just want to run.

I've tried everything else, and I can't do any more.

You don't have to.

But I have to do something.

I think of Jocelyn. And I think of Lily. And now …

There's only one thing you can do.

A part of me thinks I should play it safe just in case. Just in case the magic doesn't work. Or more like just in case I get it wrong and God above doesn't come down and deliver.

You have to go there.

Another part of me says that it's already over, she's already dead, everything has built up to this outcome.

It's called foreshadowing, idiot, and it's as clear as day, as clear as this fire blazing in the night.

The flames prove that everything is going up in smoke. My faith and my fears and my future.

Soon everything will be ashes, and I'll be left alone.

Move, Chris. Move now. Reach out and take a leap and put every-
thing on the line for this thing deep down that you believe in.

Another voice reminds me of my rejections. Of my denials. Or
my failure.

How's God gonna help me if I just declared I don't believe in
Him?

But I can't lose somebody else. Not again. Not this way.

I have to try.

I have to believe.

122. ALL THE DIFFERENCE

Suddenly I know what to do.

No voice tells me. It's just a gut thing. Or maybe a spirit thing.
I just … know.

I dig into my pocket and pull out the trinkets I brought just in
case I needed them. Not knowing how I'd use them or why.

I take the leather band that Jocelyn gave me. The one that disappeared with the bag I tossed over the falls, only to reappear in the
field where her parents were buried. I wrap it around Kelsey's bleeding wrist and tie it as tight as I can.

This isn't some medical procedure that I think will work. You
can toss science out of here at this point.

Then I get the necklace that once belonged to Aunt Alice, with the picture of the child she abandoned and basically murdered. I tie this around Kelsey's neck.

There's just—so—much—blood …

She's still conscious, but woozy. I whisper to her to try and keep her from leaving.

Both of these items I tie on her have some kind of supernatural thing about them. Maybe … hopefully … I don't know.

Enough with the self-doubt: act do move now.

"I have to get to Marsh Falls."

"What?" Brick looks confused. "Why?"

"I can't explain. You know how to get there from here."

"Man, Buckley, that chick needs the hospital."

"How do I get there from here?" I spit out, angry now that I've wasted a few minutes while my brain needed CPR.

"You gotta go back out to where—well, no, actually, there's an old road heading into the woods. Nobody uses it, and it might not really be in any sort of condition to get there. But it's a straight shot."

"What? A real road?"

"Yeah, off the main road here, right behind the church, through the woods. I used to take a three-wheeler around here. It's rough. Real rough. Nobody's traveled on it for a long time."

That word does something.

Traveled.

I pick up Kelsey and rush toward my bike.

Two roads …

In a wood …

I took the one less traveled by.

And that has made all the difference.

"Come on, Kelsey, it's going to be okay," I tell her as I jog toward my bike.

The flames are reaching for the heavens right next to us. Brick follows, though he doesn't know what I'm doing.

Has the message been clear for me for this long?

Has this moment been predetermined, the question already answered long ago?

Jocelyn's locker and the picture and the poem ...

"Stay with me, come on," I tell a fading Kelsey.

She's so light in my arms.

I didn't have a chance to carry Jocelyn to safety. Nor Lily.

But now I have a chance.

I believe. I have faith, Lord. I trust in You.

"Help me," I cry out.

I position Kelsey on the seat, then pull one leg over the bike. She begins to fall, and I pull her up, talking to her and trying to get her to stay awake.

"Brick—you got a belt on?"

"Yeah."

He takes it off while I undo mine with one hand and hand it to him. I ask him to tie them around Kelsey and me. "I don't want her falling off while I'm driving."

Brick is fast, and he doesn't give me any attitude or freaking-out mentality. I sit behind Kelsey, and a memory of the night I rode behind Lily after the party where I was drugged flashes through my mind. It seems like a million years ago.

Brick ties us together. I lean forward and can feel Kelsey snug against me.

It takes me a few tries to start up the motorcycle.

"So the road just takes me straight there."

Brick nods. "Yeah, basically. You may have to walk a little bit, but not far."

"Thank you."

I take off without hearing a response. I get on the road behind the church, and sure enough, there's a cleared-off dirt road heading into the woods. My headlight beams down it. The forest is thick and creepy-looking, and who knows what's inside it.

I turn around and look at the furious blaze behind me. It's now heading into the surrounding woods like some wild brush fire.

Marsh must have planned to burn this whole place down.

But why?

I jam on the gas to head off into the woods. A Bible verse comes to mind.

The terrible flames will not be quenched.

Now I know that even that wasn't just a random verse.

There's nothing random around this place. Nothing whatsoever.

I ride down the road as fast as I can.

Still praying that Kelsey's going to make it.

Still praying that this is going to work.

123. LIFE AND DEATH

The road just ends.

There were points where I literally had to stop and walk the bike over ruts or around a dead tree. But I managed to drive for fifteen terrible minutes until the road just stopped.

It's a dead end, surrounded by trees.

I shout out loud and for a second wonder if Brick fooled me.

He didn't come in and risk his life to rescue you both only to lead you into the middle of nowhere.

I turn off the motorcycle and hear Kelsey groan.

"I'm right here. I'm going to take you somewhere and get you some help."

I kiss Kelsey's cold cheek, and then I look up at the sky. It's still thick with clouds, leaving me in pitch black. I listen but can't hear the sound of the falls. Then I realize something else not-so-great.

My backpack—containing my flashlight—is somewhere back at the church.

I undo the belt and get off the bike and then scoop Kelsey into my arms. I'll be able to carry her for a while, but if I have to walk a long ways we won't make it.

I have no idea where I'm supposed to go, but I just start walking straight ahead.

There has to be a path or something. Right.

"Come on," I yell out.

Maybe at myself or maybe at God or maybe at Brick.

Maybe all three.

I'm sweating and tired, and I suddenly picture Mr. Page's face looking across at me at Kelsey's funeral.

That's when I have to put her down. I put her down, and then I walk a few steps away and throw up.

Some hero you are.

It's just nerves, like the kind I might have on the day of a race. Or the kind I have when someone I love is about to die. I've been there before, so I know.

I wipe my mouth and stare at the wall of black all around me.

All this for nothing, you loser.

I dry off my messy hand on my jeans and suddenly feel something in my pocket. I quickly take it out.

The Zippo lighter my mom gave me. The one I haven't been able to fix.

My hand is really shaking when I try it. I know it doesn't work, but the very first time I try it, a spark ignites, and then a flame suddenly glows.

And suddenly everything in these woods looks … different.

Like I'm in a fairy tale or something.

It's like the glow-in-the-dark stars Dad put on my ceiling when I was little. That's how the woods look. The Zippo lights up the area around me, but it also seems to reflect pieces of silver that are embedded in the trees.

I hold the lighter up, and the glowing around me gets brighter.

Then I see it.

A two-foot-wide path a stone's throw away from me. A trail that might as well be called the yellow brick road. It has pebbles that seem to be lit up like gold, and they go as far as my eyes can see.

I try to keep the lighter on and pick up Kelsey, but that doesn't work. I don't want to set her hair on fire. I prop the lighter on the ground, and it falls over and goes out.

But the glowing lights around me don't.

I laugh and suddenly realize that I'm crying. Not out of fear and not out of joy, but out of pure amazement.

Maybe heaven looks a little like this.

I put the lighter back in my pocket, then pick up Kelsey and go over to the lit-up trail. When I step on it, I wonder if it's going to burn. Or maybe the glittering rocks will pulse. But no. It doesn't do anything except keep shining.

I start to walk and then find the path heading downhill.

Five minutes later, I see a splotchy patch of black across the path ahead of me.

I blink a few times, but it doesn't go away.

Kinner might have died, but the evil around here hasn't. I know this because of the dog that's blocking the path in front of me. It's all black except for awful slivers of white in its eyes. And teeth that look like fangs.

That's no ordinary dog.

It looks more like a sickly and bloated leopard. It doesn't quite have thick fur but does have something shaggy hanging off it, like dried leaves or clumps of mud. It's snarling and growling.

That's the same dog that attacked me on the Staunch property that one time.

I stop, unsure what to do. Keep walking and just ignore it? Put

Kelsey down and try to fight it with … with a Zippo lighter? I'm all out of supernatural stuff in my pockets.

Why couldn't I have found a magical dagger or something?

There's a howling from behind me that sounds like a dying wolf.

No. No, don't let there be more.

The demon dog starts walking toward me. Its open mouth is dripping gray spit. Its eyes are glowing, a disturbing kind of glow, not a majestic kind. I smell a rotten odor.

I back up. One step. Two.

I have to get to those woods.

The dog is coming faster, and I know I have only seconds.

Suddenly I hear the wild wolf sound again, but this time it's ahead of me.

Then I see something coming out of the woods, rushing toward the demon dog.

It's a wolf.

No, it's not a wolf. It's *the* wolf, the one I've seen before. The gray wolf that I saw at the creek and also near the barn after Jocelyn died.

I hear its teeth ripping something apart and then hear the high-pitched wailing of the dog. It's awful and makes me close my eyes.

Another wolf comes out of the woods and attacks from the other side. And I realize—not all animals around here are possessed or evil.

Especially not these wolves.

I hear gnawing and biting and growling and wailing, and then it seems like the air around us gets sucked in and the lights go out for the moment and I feel a chilling breeze

death

blow past Kelsey and me and then it's done.

The dog and the smell are gone.

The wolves are sniffing the ground where it was standing and seem as puzzled as I am about the disappearance.

They turn and face me, and I look at them. I want to say thanks or toss them a hamburger or something. I'm not sure what to do.

The gray wolf bolts into the trees and is followed by the darker one. The path ahead is empty now. Empty and safe.

I just hope that it's not too late for Kelsey.

Five minutes later, I hear the sound of the falls. I don't know which direction I'm coming from, but since this trail in the woods is heading downhill, I know I'll wind up at the base of the falls.

Maybe thirty or forty yards from the falls, I see the sparkling water, lit up and a deep blue. Like something out of a Lord of the Rings movie. It's like a fairy tale.

No. Fairy tales aren't like this.

Staring at Kelsey in my arms, the deep wound around her throat caked with blood but no longer bleeding, I know this isn't a fairy tale.

I swallow and rush to the bottom of Marsh Falls, to the same place where Marsh slashed my wrist and then watched as the wounds went away.

"Lord please help her please God."

I don't know how this goes.

I just know that there's nothing I can do to make it happen. Marsh said it had something to do with me, but I don't believe that.

I think God makes everything and anything happen, and I have to believe He will take care of Kelsey.

My feet go into the glimmering water. I can see the bottom as I continue out toward the deeper part. Soon I'm in water knee deep, then close to my waist.

I look up at the falls. They seem taller tonight, and wilder. Even though I'm standing far away from where the water drops onto the pond below, I'm getting soaked from the splashing.

I don't know what I'm supposed to do.

I look at Kelsey. Her precious, sweet face resembles an angel. Her eyes are closed, her hair streaked back and wet. I kiss her forehead.

"Forgive me, God, for denying You. Please don't deny me. Please save her. Please God, I beg You. Please, in Your Son's name, I'm begging You."

I lower Kelsey into the water until she goes fully under.

I wait a second, then I lift her back up.

She's not coughing or gagging or anything.

I try again.

And I keep praying. Begging God to hear me.

I try again.

Then I hear her beautiful, glorious cough. A sweet, wonderful choking sound.

My teeth are chattering as I kiss her forehead again and then try to prop her up so she can catch her breath.

"It's going to be okay," I say.

I'm crying now and holding her and watching her cough and open her eyes and wonder what's happening.

"Chris?"

"You're okay."

Kelsey coughs and spits. I hold her and then examine her neck. She's still wearing the locket, but the bloody gash is no longer there.

"Chris?"

I wrap my wet arms around her and hold her.

"Where are we?" she asks.

"It's a miracle," I tell her as I look into her eyes.

"What? What's a miracle?"

"You. You, Kelsey."

And just like that, the glowing lights around us fade away, leaving us in the dark.

But the darkness has no power here. And instead of being scared, I'm filled with love.

124. IS YOUR LOVE STRONG ENOUGH?

I will never leave you. Not again. Not ever.

I tell Kelsey this as I lead her out of the big, bad woods. I was a kid when I first entered these woods, but I'm no kid anymore. I recall Iris telling me about that fire deep inside and how I was stronger than I thought.

But I also know now what the big, bad world is capable of.

I've lost track of the trail I came on and simply wander, hoping
to reach a road.

I hold Kelsey and promise I won't let her go.

But you'll eventually have to let go.

I'll keep protecting her.

But you can't protect her all the time.

Maybe it won't be the darkness. There will be other things to battle.

Time.

Indifference.

Forgetting.

Life.

Look at your parents. At your uncle. At the whole rest of the world,
Chris.

I'll stay by her side.

But what will be the point, when in the end you'll surely fail?

I tell her I'll always be there.

But is your love strong enough?

It can be.

Will it be strong enough?

125. MAKER AND JUDGE

We found a side road leading to Sable Road. Kelsey can barely keep
going. Not because she's bleeding to death, but simply because she's

so tired. She doesn't remember anything from the last few days. I just keep encouraging her to keep going.

Headlights coming toward us give me hope. Until I see the car swaying back and forth. Thirty yards before getting to us, the vehicle runs off the road and crashes into the bank.

I stand still with Kelsey, watching to see what happens.

A door opens, and the interior light comes on. It's an SUV.

I think I know that SUV.

Then someone gets out—no, make that *falls* out of the car.

Someone who is groaning and calling out my name.

"Chris. Help me, Chris."

Of all the people to come to our rescue tonight, and all the people for me to hear those words from …

Jeremiah Marsh is not the one who would come to mind.

"Chris, please," he shouts in agony.

"Stay here for a minute," I say to Kelsey.

I look around and don't see anybody else.

This could be a setup, Chris.

Then I change my mind and take Kelsey's hand. "No, come with me."

We walk over to the figure sprawled out in the road. Marsh is wincing in pain, holding his gut and midsection.

"Heidi did this to me. She finally decided to fight back. Because she was in love. Because I killed her one true love."

I look inside the SUV.

"Get in the car, Kelsey," I tell her. I lead her around the body just in case he suddenly gets a surge of energy.

She climbs in, then I look over at Marsh.

"Save me," Marsh says. "I know you saved her, didn't you? She wouldn't still be standing if you hadn't gone to the falls? Right?"

"I didn't save anybody. God did."

Marsh spits and laughs. "You stupid fool. The only thing I wanted to do was free you. You have no idea. She'll bring you down, Chris. She'll be a noose to your life."

"What happened to you?"

"I'm bleeding like a stuck pig." He coughs uncontrollably and curses again. "I tried, Chris. I tried everything in my power to make you believe. But the only thing I couldn't have ever foreseen was you falling in love with that stupid girl. Then going on a mission to find out why she died."

"You're the reason she died."

"She would have ruined you, just like this girl will ruin you. That's what happens. This is what happens." He holds out a bloody hand.

"Jocelyn helped save me."

"You say that now, Chris. But when a gun or a knife is aimed at your head, or at someone you love, you'll say something different. Just like back there at the church."

I don't say anything, because this time he's right. I failed. I got scared and said whatever I could to save Kelsey.

He moans and tries to hold his gut as if it's leaking and falling out. He mumbles something I don't understand.

"Please, Chris, please," he says. "I'll do anything. I'll be a better man. I'll go away. Just, please … have mercy."

I've heard enough of this man's lies. I shake my head as he crawls over to my feet and grabs the leg of my jeans. Then he starts crying.

"I wanted us—I wanted to live as long as I could—I wanted to just take—I just wanted to make all this awful stuff inside go away. You gotta understand—please, Chris, have mercy. Please. Forgive me like your God would forgive me."

I shake my head. "I'm not your maker. And I'm not your judge."

I jerk my leg out of his grip and head to the SUV. Marsh begins to scream and cry out, but I shut the door and back up the car. Then I head back the other way toward Solitary and away from this dying man.

126. Coming Out Party

So we drive off and never see anybody ever and I mean ever again.

Wonderful thought. But nope.

I drive a woozy but very much alive Kelsey back to my cabin. I'm heading there because I'm afraid for Mom and wondering what's going to happen next.

Next, it seems, has already knocked on our door and come inside.

Next seems to have woken up the entire town.

It starts with the five cop cars lining our street and driveway. It looks like more are ahead, blocking the street.

I know that Solitary doesn't even have five cop cars.

Then our doors open and people greet us, and I see Mr. Page rush to hug his daughter. Mom is standing on the deck and calls out my name. Then I see Poe, of all people. Then Newt. And I have this great thought that this would be a really cool surprise party, except that it's not my birthday.

Mom comes down to hug me and tell me that it's finally okay. She tells me that these people are with the FBI and it links back to Poe and the agent she spoke with and the missing body and Newt backing up her story and my head hurts from hearing all this.

Then she says, "They arrested Staunch."

Staunch is still alive.

But Kinner and Marsh are dead.

I go over to Kelsey while Mr. Page thanks me. I guess now everybody knows that they were living next to the boogeyman.

And it took ME to finally show all of you?

I'd kinda like to say that, but I'm too tired.

There's a doctor looking over Kelsey.

I stay next to her and hold her hand.

Mom tells me she knows what happened to Uncle Robert. I mention the bleeding body of Marsh that I left behind, and a little later someone tells us that he was found dead.

A million questions, and now all the answers feel like …

Empty.

It's after midnight, and this coming-out party for Solitary is still raging.

"Are you sure you're okay?"

"Tell us again what happened."

"And who else was there?"

I tell them I'm okay and tell them again what happened and who else was there.

"Has anybody seen Brick?" I ask.

Nobody has.

I tell them everything.

Well, almost everything.

I leave out the part about Kelsey being sliced and almost bleeding to death. And the whole part about getting to Marsh Falls. I just said that we ran for the hills.

A crazy cult can be explained. But other things—there's no explanation.

There's only faith.

All this time and all these questions and finally, as Memorial Day becomes a new day, the world knows. And the world is doing something about it too.

For a moment I shut my eyes. Yeah, I'm tired, but I'm also thankful. I never thought I'd be sitting by the fireplace in this cabin surrounded by so many people and feeling so completely and totally thankful.

I open my eyes and see Kelsey. She smiles at me.

127. WELL, IT'S ABOUT TIME

The last person I expect to see around here is Sheriff Wells. He's no longer the sheriff, and as far as I knew he'd taken off. His place in the story of Solitary was no longer important or necessary, so off he went.

Turns out I was wrong about him.

After heading to the hospital with Kelsey and her father just to make sure she's okay, I'm questioned again by several officials, including someone from the FBI. Wells is a part of this group, and it turns out he's working with them now. I say everything I know without adding any details that might not be believed. Like pretty much everything to do with Marsh Falls.

After an exhausting hour of talking, Wells says he'll take me home. My bike is still somewhere between the torched church building and the falls. It's five in the morning, and the sheriff asks me if I'm hungry. The very mention of food makes my stomach rumble, so I say yes, and we go to the hospital cafeteria.

I sip some coffee just to wake up and go to work on a huge omelet. While I eat, Wells tells me how heroic I was to stand up to Marsh and the others.

"Thanks," I say, not feeling very heroic at the moment.

"Do you know what did it for me, what finally made me believe that you weren't making all of this up?" Wells asks.

I can only shake my head.

"It was when you saw that man in the alley. Remember? The one who looked like his face had been torn off?"

For a second I wonder if this is part of the questioning.

"It's okay," Wells says. "This is unofficial. Nobody would believe me. Or you. But that man you said you saw—I know who that was. His name was Roger Epal. He worked with Staunch and did some of his dirty work for him until he decided to try and blackmail Staunch for not sharing his secrets. Staunch did that to him."

"So that man—he was real? I really saw that?"

Sheriff Wells nods, then shakes his head. "Confusing, huh?"

"Yeah," I say.

"That happened five years ago. Epal died. Staunch literally beat the life out of the man. That's what he looked like when I found him. How you described him."

"So then—what—"

"I covered it up. Said nothing. Epal was a sleaze, so I didn't have any guilt about that. But that was when I realized what Staunch was capable of."

"Will he be able to get out of this?"

"No," Wells says. "We have too much on him. What they found on his property alone—and that's not including his house. The testimony from you and others. There's no way. He's not going to just get bail and go back to his nice little life. He's done, Chris. Thanks to you."

Wells looks as tired as I feel. He sips his coffee while watching me eat.

I don't want to explain the vision to him. Or ask what he thinks of it. I don't want to talk about it at all.

"What's going to happen next?" I ask.

Wells sighs. "I suggest that you keep a low profile. Because the world is going to hear soon about all this craziness. People are going to ask you for interviews."

"Mom and I are leaving. At least, soon enough."

"Yeah, that's probably a good idea. I'll do anything I can to help you, Chris."

"With what?"

"Anything."

128. THE ROAD NEVER TRAVELED

There are still unexplained mysteries, of course.

Starting with where my motorcycle went.

It's midday, and I'm standing near the burnt remains of the church Pastor Marsh built. The upside-down stone cross is still upright, surrounded by the scorched woods. I think that Kinner ordered this church built. But Marsh wanted to get rid of Kinner and the rest of his followers with a mass murder, offering up everyone as sacrifices.

Everyone but me.

At least that's the idea that's been talked about. Five other people died in the fire, including Principal Harking.

What Marsh intended to do with me, had I accepted Kinner's proposal and killed him myself ... who knows?

It makes as much sense as the path I took to get to Marsh Falls. In the daylight, I can see that there really is no such path. It's grown over with bushes and small trees. There's no way in the world I could have ridden my bike through it. It's as if the path suddenly disappeared.

Like the road to the Crag's Inn.

Regardless of what happened to it, I head down the path into the woods on foot. Brick is waiting for me back at the burned-down church; he drove me out here because he wanted to see the wreckage himself.

I walk for a couple of miles before realizing that there's no motorcycle to find. This isn't the road less traveled by—this is the road long forgotten.

But I know I came down here, and I know that it took me to Marsh Falls.

When I get back to Brick, who's leaning against his car and smoking a cigarette, he waits for a verdict on the bike. I just shake my head in disbelief.

"I saw you head straight ahead through those woods," Brick says.

"So I'm not crazy?"

He takes a drag and shakes his head. "Nope."

We look at the dense woods that surely hold many secrets.

"You don't look surprised," I say.

"I just rescued you from a pastor who torched his church and tried to burn off his congregation. So yeah, nothing much is probably ever gonna surprise me again. Like ever."

I want to laugh, but everything is still too raw. People died in this fire right next to us. It could have been us. It could have been Kelsey.

"That's just a shame," Brick says to me.

"The church?"

"What, that? No. I'm talking about the bike. That thing was priceless."

"If I still owned it, I'd give it to you. In a heartbeat."

"You wouldn't have to do that."

"I owe you my life. And Kelsey's life."

"You don't owe me. Think it's the big guy in heaven that helped you out."

"You believe in God?"

Brick rubs his buzzed head and then chuckles. "After this ... yeah, definitely. But I think it's going to take me a while before I want to hear another preacher preachin' behind the pulpit. You know what I mean?"

"Yeah. I do. Unfortunately."

Brick is the only one who knows that I took a bleeding and dying Kelsey into the woods to get to Marsh Falls. He's only ever asked me how she's doing—not how she survived.

Most people would want to know and then want it explained over and over again. But people around Solitary, people like Brick, don't seem to need long explanations. I think they just get it.

I take a look at the upside-down cross still standing amidst the charred wood. I look at it for a long time, a symbol of something twisted and evil, surrounded by soot and ashes. Abandoned in the middle of nowhere.

"Let's get out of here," I say.

129. WAITING TO EXHALE

I assume we're just going to pack up our things and leave Solitary as planned. But life is never that simple.

Things are put on hold because of the whole pastor-trying-to-kill-us situation, which has left not just Solitary but the country mesmerized. I see reports on the evening news where reporters are talking in front of the burnt church or in downtown Solitary. People keep trying to interview Mom and me, but Mom thankfully keeps them away. I have to get rid of my Facebook page because of all the requests and comments.

All of this happens while Mom plans Uncle Robert's funeral. Dad is driving down and will be here soon. I ask her if she really needs to have a funeral, considering everything, and she answers a big-time yes by ignoring my question.

Kelsey is back home, dealing with the same thing—a world knocking on her door after hearing that she was involved with Marsh and Staunch. The good thing is that she and I are both seventeen, so there are certain laws protecting our privacy.

So we keep going, and we start to …

You know what?

Enough.

All of that stuff, that outside stuff, that noise in the background—none of it matters.

I could go on and on about it, but it doesn't matter a bit.

I unplug the headphones so I don't hear any of it.

I turn down the volume and focus on Mom and Kelsey.

My mother just lost her brother and almost lost her son.

This girl who's crazy about me finally discovered why I was a little worried about her hanging around with me. Yet she still doesn't remember anything about her abduction.

The news makes for exciting headlines, but the reality is that I don't want to be a story. I don't want to be the face of a victim or the figure in the middle of it all.

I just count the seconds until I'm away from this place. Part of me keeps waiting for Staunch to break out of jail and come knocking on my door with some random object in his hand ready to strike out and kill.

The outside still seems to be hostile and threatening. It's like a wild animal waiting for its moment, holding its breath in the darkness.

I won't exhale until I'm finally gone.

130. TRUE FAITH

All these deaths, yet this is the first funeral I've been to.

We're at a small church just outside of North Carolina, about half an hour away from Solitary. Mom said that her parents attended this church years ago, but really, I think she just wanted a church far away from this town. A church specifically out of North Carolina.

There's only a handful of people here. There's not much to say. Even Mom doesn't want to say anything about her brother. I guess when things end up the way they did, there's nothing to say. But there is a body to lay to rest.

Kelsey and her parents are by my side. Dad is here as well.

As we stand around the grave site, I stare at a tall figure in black who looks like a widow grieving her husband. Heidi Marsh is in fact grieving, but the tears on her face are for the wrong guy. At least, the wrong guy technically.

I can't help but think of Jocelyn and the makeshift gravestone I made for her. She deserved so much more.

There are others I think of too. Lily, of course. Wild Lily who proved to be yet another sad surprise in this scary town. She didn't deserve to die like that. Nobody does.

When the pastor prays his final prayer, I feel tears falling down my face. They're not just for my uncle; they're for all those who died. For what? For what purpose?

I remember Iris's words: *There has been a great war going on. Over you, Chris. Not just with those you've been able to see. But with those whom you've just started to see.*

When the last amen is uttered, I grip Kelsey's hand.

I continue to thank God for her, for saving her life and sparing mine.

I never want to stop thanking Him, either.

"Chris?"

I stop and turn to see Heidi Marsh looking at me from behind large black sunglasses and a wide black hat. I know enough to know that no matter how big a hat or shades might be, they can't keep out the hurt.

Heidi has got to be torn in pieces. Yet she still looks like the movie star she did when I first met her.

"I'm sorry for your loss," she says.

My loss?

I shake my head. "I don't—I'm not—"

But my teenage tongue gets the best of me. After all this, some pretty lady still makes my mouth get all gooey.

"He spoke very highly of you and always did," Heidi says. "You surprised him by being the man he was afraid to be."

"I didn't do anything."

Heidi takes off her shades to show bloodshot, swollen eyes.

"You made the night finally go away," she tells me, her long hands holding onto my wrists. "You stood up for something good. You stood strong. You kept your faith."

I fight tears.

No, not in front of her. I'm a man, I can take it, I can be strong.

"Don't ever lose that part of you," Heidi continues. "Your uncle … I think he was a lot like you, at least when he was younger. But he let it slip away. He let it get away, and he knew it. Because when he looked at you it was like looking in a mirror."

The tears are falling again. I wipe them away but know I can't hide them.

"Robert always wanted—always hoped—that one day I'd be able to leave this place. He's finally getting his wish, thanks to you."

I nod, feeling sad and full and unsure what to say.

Heidi gives me a hug, and I smell her flowery perfume. Then she walks away.

I catch up to Mom and Kelsey and the others. I peek at the figure in black walking back to her car.

I wonder how soon I'll be following her out of this place.

131. TRIUMPH

Mounds stops the minivan, which now smells like McDonald's, right underneath dripping branches by a familiar path that leads into the woods.

He stopped by my house to talk about everything that had happened and then said he wanted to show me something. I explained how I really, truly didn't want any more surprises.

"But this one's kinda cool," Mounds says in his twelve-year-old-boy kind of way.

Mom and Dad have gone to take Aunt Alice to the nut house. I can't say that out loud because I already said it twice and angered Mom. But it's true, that's really where they're taking her. She's turned into a zombie since the whole church thing.

Guess that's what happens when you stab your father to death.

These thoughts are borderline ridiculous, but they're true. I'm not trying to be mean. Aunt Alice was the mean old lady.

I guess now groundhogs everywhere can breathe a sigh of relief.

"What's so funny?" Mounds asks.

"I'm just being stupid," I say.

I think I'm nervous because I know where we are.

At the bridge.

The bridge. The Indian Bridge, the one with the strange name I've already forgotten.

It's a murky day and perfect to go see the creatures that live underneath. But it takes me just a few seconds to see what Mounds wanted to show me.

The bridge has collapsed.

It's cracked at the middle and now looks like a giant V. There are stones and rubble all around the base. The archway at the bottom is gone.

"Can you believe this?" Mounds asks. "It's like there was an earthquake here, you know? But there wasn't any kind of earthquake."

"I'm surprised you don't have your equipment."

"Oh, I already checked it out. Twice, actually. But nothing."

"When did this happen?"

"I heard about it yesterday. But I think at least a couple of days ago."

It's been four days since everything happened at the church.

I step toward the edge of the caved-in bridge. It's like a knife cut the bridge in half.

I feel a chill as drops of rain fall down from the towering trees above.

"Crazy," I say.

"Yeah, no joke. This bridge has been here for a long time. There's some insane stuff going on around here."

For a second I stare down below and think I see something. No, not a doll or anything to do with a baby, thankfully.

No, it's something silver. Almost like the engine on my motorcycle.

Suddenly I want to go down and check it out.

I see something else. A tire in the rubble. One that looks exactly like the kind that might have gone on my bike.

I keep looking below, squinting, to study it.

"Do you see that?" I ask Mounds.

"What?"

"The tire."

"Yeah. I found this not far from the edge the other day."

Mounds hands me the silver Triumph emblem that was on the gas tank of my bike. I shake my head and then peer back over at the mess below.

"Unless somebody else has the exact same kind of bike you had ..." Mounds says, his voice trailing off.

"What happened to it?"

He just shrugs. "I figured you knew and were just playing around with me."

"My bike's been missing since everything happened the other night."

"Maybe one of them crazy loony-tune cult guys decided to trash your bike because they didn't like you."

"Yeah."

But I don't believe that.

This bridge was an entryway to some other place. And the wonderful, magical "key" that Kinner had spoken about wasn't one you could hold in your hand, but was someone.

Me.

I wonder if riding my bike through the woods had anything to do with my bike being down there below.

Could I have possibly traveled over this bridge on my way to Marsh Falls?

"What are you thinking?" Mounds asks.

I just shake my head. "Just more questions. Lots of them."

"That's what makes life interesting. It'd be boring if every single question we had got answered. You know?"

"Yeah."

But I'm not sure.

I think it would make me feel a lot better if all of my questions were answered.

I toss the Triumph badge down below into the valley of stone and brick. It seems like one last heroic thing I can do.

Maybe just to prove one last point.

132. ASLEEP

This could be the last night Kelsey and I ever hang out together. Of course, leave it to me to think this. She's cuddled up with me on the couch in her family room, acting like the last week and month and year haven't been that big a deal. She's content, watching television while I hold her.

There's a lot to say. Tomorrow I'm leaving with Mom to head back to Illinois.

I had all these grand plans of stuff I wanted to say, stuff I wanted her to know. But leave it to me to not say them.

I want to believe she knows, and that holding her in my arms is enough.

But who knows.

Who knows if we'll make it past midnight.

Who knows if she'll be there to say good-bye.

Who knows.

Maybe I'll blink and find her by my side, older but still beautiful, acting like the last few decades haven't been that big a deal.

You're a big deal to me, Kelsey. You always will be.

I wonder what would have happened if this quiet, shy blonde hadn't chased me down.

I wonder where I'd be right now.

I'm glad I'm here. Right here.

One more night.

She peeks up at me staring at her. She doesn't ask *What?* and doesn't go back to watching television. She just smiles.

I kiss her.

I finally feel like I belong somewhere.

I just want to fall asleep and then wake up and see her next to me.

What will happen after I leave Solitary? What about later, when Kelsey comes up to Chicago to college? What about a year from now? Or when we get out of college?

I don't want to wake up on my own anymore.

Yeah.

I hear a song playing in my head and in my heart. I guess there's always some soundtrack playing somewhere.

And there's always somebody who inspires it.

133. JUST LIKE HEAVEN

I hear the sound of rocks crunching as the tires of Mom's car roll over them. I can't believe that I was able to find this place again, not to mention being able to make my way up the hill without sending the car over the edge. I get to the last turn in the road before it levels out and dead-ends into the place where the Crag's Inn used to be hidden amidst the trees.

But when I turn the car and finally see it for the first time since it burned down, I have to stop since I'm out of breath with surprise.

I wonder if I took the wrong road and wound up somewhere else.

The open sky is the first thing I see. It's like a light blue tablecloth stretched out over everything.

But that's impossible, because there used to be trees here blocking most of the sky.

Everything else looks the same, so I know I'm at the right place. I coast the car past the point where the road ends, then I see something else strange. The ground I stop the car on is grass. Thick green grass, green like the kind the pros play golf on.

Then I see the flowers.

A thousand—no, a million flowers. Of all kinds and colors. A massive bed of flowers.

It's like someone came in here and leveled off the top of the mountain, getting rid of the charred remains of the Crag's Inn along with all the trees, then replaced it with flowers.

They're all mixed together like some gigantic bouquet.

I hear birds, just like the first time I came here. There are still some trees on the edges surrounding this field of gold and pink and red and purple. But where I'm standing, right at the edge of these thick, lush flowers, the sky is immense and the sun is bright.

I stare around, seriously wondering if this is the same place Iris's inn used to be.

Then I see it. The wooden sign with the emblem on it that I first passed. Except it looks like the emblem has been freshly cut and stained in the wood itself.

The image is of a pair of wings.

Maybe I would have noticed it the first time, but that bluebird was sitting on top of this sign. Like a watchdog. Watching me and biting at my finger.

So this is really the place.

I'm here not to get one last look at this hilltop, but to say good-bye. To leave some things behind.

I walk carefully to the middle of the field. The sweet scent is so strong my eyes start to water. There are flowers that have names I'm sure I've never even heard of. It's impossible not to step on some as I walk into the center: a hundred different kinds of lilies.

I shake my head and laugh out loud because really, this is just as insane as everything else I've seen here. Except this is in a good and beautiful way. The lilies vary in color. Some are pink, white, yellow, bright gold. Some even have sides that are brown and purple.

The lilies seem to be staring at me, hands outstretched and waiting.

This is the perfect place.

I pull out the items I had carefully placed in my jean pocket. This time I'm grabbing them not out of desperation but out of thanks to God above. The first thing I find is the leather band that had to be cut off Kelsey's wrist because it was tied too tight. A medic did this, and thankfully I had enough sense to ask for it back. I'm sure he thought I was crazy, but that's fine. I am a little crazy.

I'm intending to dig a little hole and put the bracelet inside, but someone calling my name makes me stop.

I turn and see Jocelyn walking toward me.

I blink, then wipe my eyes, then look again. She's still there, that dark hair still falling to her shoulders, those beautiful eyes still hypnotic in their glance. She smiles as she strolls over through the flowers.

She's wearing a T-shirt and a light brown corduroy jacket with jeans. She's not as dressed up as she used to be when I pictured her or had these kinds of visions, but she's still older. In her twenties or thirties.

You stink when it comes to judging age, so don't even try.

I stand there wondering if this is all some rosy-colored dream.

"No," Jocelyn says with a smile. "I'm really here. And so are you."

I nod as she stops just a few feet away from me.

I don't know what to say.

"You don't have to," she answers again in that weird way. "You've said enough, Chris. You've done enough."

"What are you—"

"Doing here?"

I nod.

"I came to see you one last time."

"Why one last time?"

"Because you have a life to lead. That doesn't mean forgetting me, but it means moving on. Like you're doing this afternoon. Leaving Solitary. When you leave this place, you leave me, too."

I'm not sure how to answer. There's nothing more I want than to leave Solitary. But that doesn't mean I want to never see her again.

"It wouldn't be fair to you or to those around you," Jocelyn says. "I just came here to see you."

"To say good-bye," I say, trying to do what she's been doing and finishing her thought.

"No. To take that back."

She opens up her hand, and for a second I'm not sure what she's asking for. Then I realize it like a fool, and I give her the leather band. It still has bloodstains on it.

"I gave this to you because I knew it fit," Jocelyn says. "Because I knew you fit me. And you did. You always will, Chris."

"Maybe I should keep it then."

Jocelyn shakes her head. "No. Your heart is only so big. I can no longer keep any of it."

I want to tell her she has no choice. There's always going to be a part of my heart that belongs to her.

"I know," she says. "But what you don't know is this, Chris. This world—this life is just a flicker of light. It's just the tiny flutter of a bird's wings. It's so tiny compared to the vastness of … everything else."

"That doesn't change anything—"

"I say that because there are going to be days and nights when that same heart is troubled and burdened. When it feels broken and in need of mending. And you might long for others to help and heal.

You might sometimes even long for me to come back in your dreams or memory or places like this. But no one—not me and not anybody else—will ever be able to fill that emptiness inside except God. The love you've felt inside that heart is but a drop in an endless ocean. The love you have is nothing compared to His love—it's not even like one single petal in this entire field."

I think I understand even though my heart is suddenly hurting. I want to say or do more.

"Remember the love that saved you, Chris. Keep it there as a reminder, the way you've kept this bracelet."

"Okay."

I think of all the things I want to say and thank her for, and then she says, "Give me your hand."

I hesitate for a moment and then hold out my right hand. Jocelyn smiles as she touches my hand and then slightly bends over to kiss it.

Just as her lips touch my hand, she's gone.

Just like that.

My hand is still held out, and I can still feel her soft touch. I can feel those lips against my skin.

Jocelyn …

I look around the field, but she's gone.

I stare up at the clear sky.

A drop in an endless ocean.

"Thank You," I tell God.

I think that sometimes that's the only thing to say. Questions don't have to be answered and wishes don't have to be fulfilled. All you can do is thank God and move on.

I head back to my car, my head in a daze and my heart in a sling.

I'm a bit breathless and probably will be until I've been in Illinois for a few days.

No, make that years.

I pass the sign again and then remember something else I was going to leave up here.

The necklace is still in my pocket. The one that used to belong to Aunt Alice, the one with the picture of her baby.

I look at it again and read the name out loud.

"Indigo Jadan Kinner."

Some things in this world are too awful to even consider. Too wretched to think about.

I place the locket at the base of the sign, then glance at the wings etched into wood.

Yes, some things in this world are awful and wretched.

But some things are amazing and beautiful.

Like the stunning bluebird that flies out of nowhere and lands on the sign.

It's the same one that I first saw here, the one that's followed me around since. A brilliant coat of blue with a lighter shade on its belly. Black eyes and a black beak.

It moves its head like it's wanting to say something.

If the bird starts talking, I might just pass out.

Then it moves as if it's going to fly away.

"I'm not going to hurt you," I say.

It gets to the edge of the sign, then flutters down to the ground where I just laid the locket.

Then I see a bolt of blue streak back up, carrying the locket in its beak. I watch the bird soar up to the sky and then fly away.

I shake my head and laugh.

It's only moments later when I start the car that something dawns on me.

Maybe it should have been obvious the first time I read that name.

Indigo Jadan Kinner.

Indigo. Jadan.

Blue. Jay.

Bluebird.

A chill washes over me, and I laugh again, shaking my head, not believing in what I think I'm believing in.

But another voice says *why not?*

And yeah, I have no answer to that.

It's a nice thought, the more I think of it.

That little bird.

That little bluebird following me around.

134. THE LIVING PROOF

I wonder what would have happened if I hadn't met Jocelyn.

Would I have come to this point in my life? Would I be riding off into the sunset of my future?

I don't know. I don't think I would be.

But I know this now.

There's more to this life than the road below me and the motion around me. There's more than just the sky above and the setting sun.

Maybe she'll always be watching over me, already knowing this, already discovering a sun that burns brighter than we ever dreamed.

Maybe.

But I don't need a maybe to know that I will always love Jocelyn in the flawed, boyish way I loved her.

So brief like a day compared to eternity.

Or like that drop in the endless ocean.

I'm about to leave knowing who I am.

Maybe Jocelyn knew all along.

She believed in me before I ever believed myself.

135. CRYSTAL CLEAR

Maybe I'll take Jocelyn's cue and not say good-bye to Kelsey.

We're going to see each other sooner than we think. Her parents are bringing her up to Illinois in August. And they might visit even earlier than that.

We have texting and email and Facebook and Skype and all those other ways to keep in touch. Plus, Kelsey's family is moving too. They're going to Columbia, where her father got a new job.

So no good-byes are necessary. Right?

Yet I can feel that melancholy, romantic, don't-leave-me-now Chris Buckley starting to emerge.

It starts when I'm packing and trying to make sure I have everything. Mom has said to take whatever I need, and movers will take the rest. All of Uncle Robert's things now belong to us, so I pack away some of the T-shirts, making sure that the one I wore that first day of school is on top: the cover of The Smiths' last album, *Strangeways, Here We Come.*

Yep, and now here we go.

Of all the things I've stuck in my backpack and suitcase, the one thing missing is that picture. The one that magically appeared and proceeded to fade in and out ever since.

I haven't been able to find it since Memorial Day. Not that I remember when I last looked at it, but it's gone.

There are other things that I'm tossing. We have a garbage can outside on the driveway, full of stuff we don't want and won't need the movers to take. Some items from the kitchen and the fridge, some of Mom's toiletries. I tossed some notebooks and books from school that I know I'll never look at again.

I bring the last of the luggage down the narrow steps that I frankly hope I'll never have to climb again. Kelsey is waiting by my car.

"Parting is such sweet sorrow," she says.

"Reminds me of a prom I once went to."

"What are we going to do without another prom?"

"A lot," I say with a laugh.

After getting the last suitcase and bag to fit in the trunk, I close it and wait for Mom.

Kelsey and I have talked a lot about this moment. We're both trying to downplay it. It won't be long. It really won't be long.

"So how does the epic love story end?"

I lean against the car. The sun is shining bright, and it's a beautiful and warm day.

"Riding off into the sunset," I say. "Naturally."

"Don't you usually ride a horse?"

"A car will have to do."

"And doesn't the hero usually ride off into the sunset *with* the girl?"

"Are you saying you want to ride off into the sunset with the hero?"

"Of course I do," Kelsey says with those beaming blue eyes looking up at me.

"Well, first I'll have to find a hero."

"You were mine even before you saved me."

I want to say something witty or clever, but I can't. Her words make me want to hug her and not let her go.

"Well, if I can't go with the hero, at least I can have something to remember him by."

"And what's that?"

Kelsey goes over to the garbage and picks up the Polaroid camera that Mounds gave me.

I can't help laughing. "That thing is broken. It can't be fixed. I hope you won't keep that as a reminder of me."

"It sounds just like you," Kelsey says.

I break out into a laugh, and then I hear her snap a picture.

You gotta be kidding me.

The square photo slides out, and Kelsey just laughs.

"I tried fixing that sucker three times," I tell her. "Is that really the one I tossed?"

She holds the picture like a kid holding a stolen cookie. She waves it and waits to see the picture.

She looks at it and grins.

"Let me see."

As I take the photo in my hand, I stare at the picture that I've seen many times before. The one that was sorta blurry and then started to fade out again and then slowly began to fill back in.

My heart beats and my head spins and I don't say anything.

The picture is crystal clear.

"It actually takes decent photos," I say.

"It's perfect." Kelsey takes the photo. "I'll take this for safekeeping. Until I can return it safely back to its owner."

"Make sure you do it as soon as possible."

"I will," Kelsey says. "I promise."

136. SOLITARY

I'm standing outside leaning against my mom's car and waiting while she gets her final paycheck from the grill. I scan the main strip of Solitary for what I hope is the very last time.

I can't say what I'm going to think about this place and these days when I'm older.

I'm still too bruised and too numb to make sense of it all.

But I know this: a guy my age should not have to try and make sense of everything.

A guy my age should be given a little time to grow up and figure things out.

A guy my age shouldn't have to see a spiritual battle waging on his front lawn.

Kids have enough nonsense to think about without all that going on.

We have burning desires inside of us that we don't understand. We have burning questions that are never answered because grown-ups are too frightened of giving the wrong answer. We have burning goals that still seem real even if we're only seventeen or eighteen and life is just beyond the horizon.

We are burning all the time because that's what we do.

We ache and we long and we worry and we fear and we laugh and we soar and we fall and get up again.

We all hurt.

It's what we do with it that counts. It's how we move on in life with it.

I want to take the silent nights when I looked up at the stars and do something with them.

I want to take the pitch black where I doubted hope would ever come and do something with it.

I want to take all these colors and make something out of them, the way a rainbow came after God wiped out 99.9 percent of humanity.

I came here a kid on my own. But I leave here knowing I'm not alone. I'm not isolated. I'm not solitary.

Not anymore.

I look over the town and know that this snapshot will be the one I always remember. Even if I never, ever come back.

137. ALL FLOWERS IN TIME

Kelsey leaves me with a card and a playlist. Mom, Midnight, and I are already ten minutes away from Solitary on the highway by the time I open the card.

The front has a rainbow-colored iris on it underneath a half sun. Inside is one printed word.

Good-bye!

Underneath are Kelsey's words.

> Good-bye, but not for long!
> I made you a playlist to enjoy on the way home. The first song is the one that I found last summer while Googling your name. I never told you how I discovered it. I meant it then, and I mean it now.
> Remember this, Chris:
> "I am leaving you with a gift—peace of mind and heart. And the peace I give is a gift the world cannot give. So don't be troubled or afraid."—John 14:27
> I take hope in those words and want you to do the same.

Good things are ahead. For both of us.
I love you.
Kelsey

I try to not show any emotion as Mom drives in silence. She looks heavy with thoughts the same way I am.

"Can I put this on?" I ask her.

"Sure."

I slip in the disc, and a song begins to play. I've never heard it before, so that's surprising. The guitar starts playing, and I hear a woman's voice laugh in the background. Then she starts singing.

I recognize the singer from somewhere. From one of those many albums that I heard in Uncle Robert's cabin.

Then a male voice begins singing.

"All flowers in time bend toward the sun. I know you say that there's no one for you, but here is one."

I can't help laughing.

"What is it?"

I'm about to say "nothing" like I normally would, but I don't.

I tell my mom exactly what's up.

"Kelsey."

"What about her?"

"She wrote me a note last summer. I got it in the mail when I was basically ignoring her. It was a lyric from this song. The guy singing is named Jeff Buckley."

Mom smiles. "You better keep her close to you. She's good for you."

"Yeah I know."

The two singers keep singing the main chorus and reinforce what I've always thought.

That somehow Kelsey knew she was there for me.

She knew it when I didn't know. When I was running away.

But she was right. All flowers do indeed bend toward the sun.

138. TORNADO

You will have questions for the rest of your life.

But you're not alone.

You will question yourself and your actions all the days you breathe air.

But you're not abandoned.

You are only one and nobody else is like you.

But your life is not solitary and never will be.

You will keep hurting until your last breath.

But believe the hurt can be taken away.

Reach out for more because more is there. Reach out and believe with a heart as soft as the air flowing through your open fingers. Reach out and know that I'm there.

Reach out and touch faith, Chris.

Stare up in the eye of the storm. Don't let the tornadoes blow you down.

Don't ever stop.

Grow and question and wonder and cry and laugh and try and fail.

But don't ever stop.

Continue on.

As many days and weeks and months and years as you have.

Blinks, all of them, in light of the good grace you're given.

Keep going.

Look back not with fear and bitterness but with love.

Look ahead with the same love.

139. SOMEBODY

The mountains and the hills disappear. Suddenly I'm back on flatlands looking at the country.

Miles and miles of farmland just passing by.

I don't sleep. Instead I just stare out and wonder.

I wonder about tomorrow. And the next day. And the next.

Part of me feels like I can do anything.

Part of me is afraid.

Part of me knows I'll always be this way.

Maybe I'll find myself thinking back to these times as some middle-aged guy sitting there in his family room in a sunken chair with a beer belly and bags under his eyes.

Will I remember this guy, the one sitting in this car seat, thankful for every breath he takes?

Will I forget?

Help me, God, never to forget. Anything.

"You okay?" Mom asks.

I nod. And smile.

I wonder how old Mom feels. I know I feel old, and I'm not even eighteen.

The world is bright and open and endless, and I know something.

I know that somewhere out there, somebody loves me dearly.

Not just the woman driving this car, or the pretty blonde back in the Carolinas, or the man waiting for us in Illinois.

No.

This Somebody created the sun and the moon and the stars, and for some reason He created me too. And loved me.

I had to go all the way to a little town called Solitary, North Carolina to find that Somebody.

Actually, I think He found me.

... a little more ...

When a delightful concert comes to an end,

the orchestra might offer an encore.

When a fine meal comes to an end,

it's always nice to savor a bit of dessert.

When a great story comes to an end,

we think you may want to linger.

And so, we offer ...

AfterWords—just a little something more after you

have finished a David C Cook novel.

We invite you to stay awhile in the story.

Thanks for reading!

Turn the page for ...

- **Three Recommended Playlists**
- **Behind the Book: Say Anything**
- **A Snapshot**

THREE RECOMMENDED PLAYLISTS

HURT PLAYLIST
#1 FOR THE WALKMAN

1. "Black Celebration" by Depeche Mode
2. "Love Will Tear Us Apart" by Joy Division
3. "Cities in Dust" by Siouxsie & the Banshees
4. "Head Over Heels/Broken (Live)" by Tears for Fears
5. "The Sun & The Rainfall" by Depeche Mode
6. "Nowhere Fast" by The Smiths
7. "Sweet Dreams (Are Made of This)" by Eurythmics
8. "Start of the Breakdown" by Tears For Fears
9. "The Thinner the Air" by Cocteau Twins
10. "Is Your Love Strong Enough?" by Bryan Ferry
11. "True Faith" by New Order
12. "Asleep" by The Smiths
13. "Just Like Heaven" by The Cure
14. "Late Night, Maudlin Street" by Morrissey
15. "Somebody" by Depeche Mode

HURT PLAYLIST

#2 FOR THE iPOD

1. "Personal Jesus (The Stargate Mix)" by Depeche Mode

2. "A Real Hero" by College

3. "A Drowning" by How to Destroy Angels

4. "Nightcall" by Kavinsky (feat. Lovefoxxx)

5. "Know Who You Are at Every Age" by Cocteau Twins

6. "Need You Now" by Cut Copy

7. "Soon, My Friend" by M83

8. "Eternal Life" by Jeff Buckley

9. "Kingdom" by Dave Gahan

10. "No Light, No Light" by Florence + The Machine

11. "Sæglópur" by Sigur Rós

12. "Enemy" by Melanie C

13. "Wait" by M83

14. "Right Where It Belongs" by Nine Inch Nails

15. "Come Alive" by Foo Fighters

16. "Alone" by Moby

17. "Is Your Love Strong Enough?" by How to Destroy Angels

18. "All Flowers in Time Bend Towards the Sun" by Jeff Buckley (feat. Elizabeth Fraser)

19. "Tornado" by Jónsi

20. "Heartlines" by Florence + The Machine

HURT PLAYLIST

#3 For the Movie

1. "Personal Jesus (Pump Mix)" by Depeche Mode

2. "Rubber Head" by Cliff Martinez (from *Drive* soundtrack)

3. "When You Smile" by College

4. "Lighthouse" by Helios

5. "My Name on a Car" by Cliff Martinez (from *Drive* soundtrack)

6. "Sacrifice" by Patrick O'Hearn

7. "Constantine" by Thomas Newman (from *The Help* soundtrack)

8. "I Drive" by Cliff Martinez (from *Drive* soundtrack)

9. "Courage" by Patrick O'Hearn

10. "Wrong Floor" by Cliff Martinez (from *Drive* soundtrack)

11. "Sweet Dreams" by Moby

12. "Freeze" by Recoil

13. "End Theme" by College

14. "My Son" by Thomas Newman (from *The Help* soundtrack)

15. "Tick of the Clock" by Chromatics

16. "Hammer" by Cliff Martinez (from *Drive* soundtrack)

17. "Promise" by David Helpling

18. "Sandstorm" by Peter Gabriel (from *Passion*)

19. "It Is Accomplished" by Peter Gabriel (from *Passion*)

20. "This Was My Intention" by Thomas Newman (from *Welcome Home, Roxy Carmichael* soundtrack)

21. "A Strangely Isolated Place" by Ulrich Schnauss

22. "Eternal" by Above & Beyond

23. "Ain't You Tired" by Thomas Newman (from *The Help* soundtrack)

BEHIND THE BOOK:
SAY ANYTHING

So there you have it. My teen series starring Chris Buckley as the wide-eyed new kid in school who ends up discovering an evil town while also discovering hope. If I could, I'd love to hear each and every reader's thoughts about this series and its ending. Regardless of what you think—whether you loved it or hated it—I wouldn't change a thing.

That's the same thing I'd say about my high school experience.

I went to four different high schools. If you want to know their names, look at the dedication in each Solitary Tales book. At each school I attended I was a different character in a different tale. They say don't judge a book by its cover, but every time I changed schools, that's exactly what happened. I understand—people can't help themselves, whether they're sixteen or sixty. It's human nature.

When I came up with this idea for "*Pretty in Pink* meets *The Exorcist*," I knew the story I wanted to write. But what I didn't realize was why I wanted to write it. Now that the series is finished, I can look back and see that what I wrote was my swan song to my high school years, a summing up of my own experiences as a teenager.

I could show all the similarities, but that's not too terribly interesting. Why, for instance, does Chris have these love interests showing up in each book? Well, that's just the story that came into my head. But looking at it now, it makes sense, because every time I ended up changing schools, my old friends would suddenly be gone. Whether it was a close relationship that suddenly died or a friend who suddenly disappeared, the end was always the same. Leaving, moving on, sometimes not even getting to say good-bye, sometimes saying good-bye because of a mistake of mine.

There were many times when I felt isolated and abandoned. Hmmmm. What's a word to describe that feeling? Solitary. Of course, there were no tunnels or great-grandfathers who hissed or demon dogs, right? But sometimes the ordinary craziness of the high school experience seems to be full of things just like that. Things that are out of our control. Things that are stranger than fiction. Things that cannot be explained.

God was very real to me when I was a teen living on top of a mountain in North Carolina. When I moved, a part of that closeness and innocence left. I decided to change personalities to fit in, and in doing so I got a bit lost as well. At least for a while.

To say that I am Chris Buckley or that he is me is too simplistic. Chris is more like the brother I never had. In some ways, yes, we're very much alike. But after four books with this likable kid, I can honestly say he's a character that's come to life. I'd like to hang out with him and talk about music for a while.

What will become of Chris Buckley? Well, I have some ideas. Anybody who knows me knows I have some ideas. So we'll see. That's all I'll say. For now.

That's the beauty of this white open space. It's just waiting to be filled. It's waiting for those words. And the thing I've come to love about The Solitary Tales and remembering what it was like to be sixteen is that you can truly say anything in the confines of this space.

Thank you for taking this journey with Chris and me. It's been quite the ride.

after words

ACKNOWLEDGMENTS

Thank you …

Sharon, for asking me to be your partner in a high school play and never turning back.

Kylie, Mackenzie, and Brianna, for making every day shine brighter than the last.

Don Pape, for believing in me and in this series.

L. B. Norton, for being a wonderful editor and encourager.

Claudia Cross, for continuing to partner with me as we pursue writing dreams.

Amy Konyndyk, for producing four amazing covers.

Alex Field, Karen Stoller, Ginia Hairston, Caitlyn Carlson, and the rest of the fine folks at David C Cook.

Anne Goldsmith, who liked this idea enough to ask for a proposal years ago.

Jake Chism, Josh Olds, and Lori Twichell, for your enthusiastic support of this series from the very beginning.

My parents, Bill and Mary Thrasher, who moved my sister and me to the top of a mountain in North Carolina where an imagination could roam free.

My in-laws, Warren and Willamae Noorlag, for helping me continue to remain in this writing canoe of mine.

My family and friends, who continue to encourage and support me as I see which doors continue to open.

And last but definitely not least, thank you to my fans and

readers, who continue to remind me all these hours of solitary confinement are worth it.

Without all of these people, The Solitary Tales would never have seen light of day. So thank you.

This twelfth grader knew what he wanted to do and where he wanted to go. Little did he know he'd still have a long and a rocky road ahead of him in college. Maybe someday some of those stories will be reworked in another series....